THE GHOST OF KHE SANH

Rock DePerno

ISBN-13: 9780615902630
ISBN-10: 0615902634

Acknowledgment

My most sincere thanks to my wonderful wife, Linda for her extreme patience, unfaltering love and remarkable candor as my most dedicated critic.

Thanks to my terrific readers and editorial assistants, Marilyn Ickes, Maria Kroninger and Linda Wolowicz.

Cover Design
Heidi Sutherlin – My Creative Pursuits

Prologue

First Marine Aircraft Wing (1st MAW)
Khe Sanh, Vietnam — early February 1968

Over twenty thousand North Vietnamese Army troops besieged the air base at Khe Sanh. Six thousand US Marines fought them off with extensive and constant bombing barrages. President Johnson had demanded a victory "signed in blood" from the Joint Chiefs of Staff resulting in the NVA being hit every 90 minutes around the clock, but this month of February left that plan in dire danger. The Marines found themselves buried under hard weather with negative visibility. The bombers couldn't fly low enough to find their targets, which severely limited their bombing capability. Now, the NVA had moved within the 3 kilometer no bombing safety zone established by the Marine command to prevent the US bombers from dumping on their own troops. The area inside the zone became a literal free kill zone for both sides. The NVA were pushing closer and during the night often got within 300 meters of the base perimeter. The Marine ground troops dug deep into bunkers, often as deep as eighteen feet, in conditions beyond filthy, sometimes with rats as their only companions. They were living on half day supplies of c-rations, limited amounts of potable water and fighting around the clock just to hold positions. Marine snipers were sent into the area to keep the NVA in as much disarray as possible. Without the snipers the base position would be untenable.

CHAPTER ONE
Detroit 1960

Cinzano's on the corner of French Road and Gratiot Avenue on Detroit's east side was an earthy old country poultry market. A person didn't have to go inside to realize what was in there. The stink hit you ten feet beyond the door, forcing passersby to hurry on their way. The smell even sucked through the open windows of passing cars compelling occupants to quickly roll them shut.

Inside the dilapidated clapboard store, stacked to the ceiling, were cages of cramped birds smeared in their own feces, soaked in urine and cackling with an unknown fear.

The thin, frail boy slipped into the space next to the front door and watched from within his own fear. He came here often, trying to understand but always unable to comprehend.

A woman dressed in a black wool coat and a red babushka speckled with snowflakes crammed through the door inadvertently pushing the boy back into the upright crates. He stumbled backwards grabbed a crate and immediately pulled his hand back as the large rooster inside pecked sharply at his middle finger, leaving a small drop of blood between the first two knuckles.

Unaware the woman pushed forward and with every footstep raised small clouds of sawdust mixed with seeds and a pungent, feathery down. She coughed and held a handkerchief over her mouth. The boy instinctively pinched his nose as the air with a palatable taste of blood burned the back of his throat. He held his hand over his mouth.

Inside the shadow of the dust-filled screen door, he watched the women at the rickety counter. They were the pickers and choosers. "I want that one," someone would remark loudly and the chicken or duck would die. "No, no not that one," and it would live a little longer. It was done simply and without remorse. Strange, he thought, how people picked what would live and what would die. He was eleven years old and the thought of making something die was both interesting and oddly confusing.

"I'll take that one! The one on the left. Yes, yes, that's the one," the woman in the babushka demanded.

The bird was pulled squawking from the cage and the counter woman, her apron covered with blood, unceremoniously stretched the bird out and slit its throat, splattering lines of crimson amongst the white feathers. Then she shoved it head first into one of a dozen galvanized funnels suspended over a long sink attached to the wall behind the counter. Brilliant gobs of blood dripped from the funnel, coursing rivulets of red across the black iron sink. There the bird convulsing in an unknown panic, its feet driving it deeper into the tapered trap, was left to drain into the sink before it was held beneath a grinder motor fixed with a wire plucking wheel and the feathers removed. Lastly, the entrails drawn, the liver, heart and gizzard separately packaged, the warm bird was wrapped and given to the waiting customer, all in less than two minutes.

The sight of the bird thrashing forward into the funnel, pulled the boy from the door. Standing at the counters edge, peering into the sink, the water running crimson swirls like the popsicles painted on the side of *The Good Humor* truck, he caught the counter woman's eye.

"What can I'a do'a for'a you, il mio regazzo?" she questioned, her accent strongly suggestive of Palermo and the hills of Sicily. It sounded perfectly normal to the boy.

"Why do you do that," he asked, pointing toward the funnels and then added, "let them die so slow?"

"They tasta much a'better when'a you letta them bleed," was her quick response as she turned away and reached for the next bird. She hesitated a moment, her bright blue eyes suggesting a much younger age than her pasty grey skin laced with bluish surface veins offered. A Sicilian nose hooked downward over a silver cross suspended from a shiny chain and her wrinkled lips curved at a confusing angle leaving the boy with the vivid image of the wicked witch from Snow White and the Seven Dwarfs.

He wondered if anyone who killed as many things as she did, could ever go to heaven. His thought seemed to strike her mind and she paused and looked back, a small knowing smile on her twisted crone face, and as she bent toward him, slowly, a wisp of gray hair brushed his cheek.

She cackled in his ear, "Inna thes world, you neve' wanna be a chicken," and gave a small clucking laugh. "Haa, cluck, ha, cluck. Cluck, cluck, cluck." She brought the blade quickly across the throat of the next bird and continued to cluck as the frightened boy ran from the market.

The clouds coming from the west dropped large, pure white snowflakes into a sky filled with chimney spew from the auto plants. The snowflakes reached the ground as gobs of ice-encrusted mucky brown sludge that coated everything visible.

He made his way home, southeast on French Road, over the cracked and twisted rents in the sidewalks. He wore hand-me-down rubber galoshes, three metal snaps missing on the right and two on the left where there was a small hole in the toe but still managed to jump into every puddle that got in his way. He crossed over Harper Avenue and the rusted trolley tracks that ran down Montclair. A half-mile farther, he crossed Shoemaker and walked the tree lined street another half block to the upstairs flat.

The entranceway to his home was in the back at the end of a long narrow sidewalk that ran between the asbestos sided flat and the neighbor's fenced yard. The fence posts were painted green and the tops were crowned with round white balls but the paint had peeled and the balls were cracked and rotted and there were post beetles crawling inside the wood. He could hear them. Their scratching reminded him of the mice that scampered inside the storage room upstairs and ran beneath his bed at night.

Oscar, the landlady's Boston Bulldog, was stretched out in the dark shadows beside the garage at the back of the small lot. Black and white, the dog always picked the spot where the shadows crossed and confused the eye. He was watching the open garbage containers near the back fence for rats. Oscar loved to hunt the garbage for rats.

Nicholas knew he was there. He didn't have to see Oscar. It was like lying in the dark at night and moving the fingers of one of his hands toward the other, a game that he played when sleep wouldn't come. He didn't have to see his hands to know when his fingers would touch.

Tonight Oscar turned his head and watched the small boy approaching. Their eyes momentarily met, the black opaque eyes of the bulldog and the ivory and golden streaked eyes of the boy and for a brief moment, Oscar thought about the chicken coup in Mr. Barelli's yard down the street. He got up and quickly dashed around the edge of the garage and left the yard.

His mother hated the bulldog and she hated their home. She would tell his father they never had any rats where she grew up. His father would always tell her to 'shut up' then they'd have a big argument and he'd leave, going down to the corner bar at Shoemaker and Montclair.

His mother would end up in the living room crying on their tattered couch. It was a coarse couch covered with imitation maroon velvet. It probably should have fallen apart already but the edges, where the fabric met the wood, were held together with brass button-head French nails.

His father would leave and she would sit on the old couch and cry for hours and when her tears fell, they soaked in real fast and you couldn't see them for very long. How many times had he seen her retreat to the couch in their shabby living room? How many times had he watched her cry? They told him at school that God knew when you sinned. HE counted your sins. But did anyone keep track of the tears his mother had cried? Did GOD count her tears? The couch would probably last forever and no one would ever know how many tears it held.

The boy went up the backstairs. The pot was on the stove. He had smelt the sauce, thick with plum tomatoes and fresh basil from the backyard. His stomach grumbled and saliva started to flow around his back teeth. His mother was sitting on a yellow, vinyl dinette chair smoking a cigarette. She'd been crying again. Her eyes were swollen and red. The veins in them looked like the small wiggly worms that were on the sidewalk right after a storm. They looked like that a lot lately.

"Why are you crying Ma," he asked?

"Sit down with your brother and I'll get you something to eat," she got up and stood next to him for the time it took to give him a quick hug. Anthony, the oldest, was already at the table. The boy took off his jacket and cap, hung them in the hallway above his torn galoshes and sat across the table from his brother.

The small table was set very neat with a pastel flowered tablecloth and a vase filled with the field daisies that grew alongside the house. The dishes were Mel Mac and the utensils were stainless steel hand-me-downs that were old and worn. She fixed them both a plate of spaghetti and placed them in front of her two sons. She used to make meatballs but she didn't anymore. He would have liked a meatball.

Dominic DiCicci slipped from the barstool and Teresa caught him. Holding him up, she pressed into him and gave him a wet kiss.

"Don't go Domi. Stay with me," she cooed.

"Hey Sal, give Teresa another drink, eh," he slurred down the bar to Salvatore Terico, the bar owner.

"You haven't paid for the last one yet. In fact, you still owe for last week," Sal answered.

"Hey, you know I'm good for it, Sal. I'll get you next week, eh. Just give her a drink, capisce?"

"Sure, sure," Sal answered, wondering just how valuable some lifelong friendships really were.

"Look baby, I'll be back in a while. Just going to go home for a few minutes. See the kids, make sure the bitch is doing her job. Then, I'll be back. Alright?"

"How long Domi? Don't leave me for long."

"Look baby, you just put your pretty, little ass on the stool and have a couple of beers. I'll be back real soon. Okay?"

"Okay Domi, but not long, okay," she pleaded as he turned and stumbled out the door onto Shoemaker Ave.

Dominic DiCicci was born in America and raised by immigrant parents. Traditionally, the sons of immigrant Italians are raised like little princes and the daughters guarded like the national treasure. Within the family, the princes could do no wrong.

Teresa, his girlfriend, was Italian and she was hot. He probably should have married her in the first place. When they were together, he didn't have to think about everything that his wife, Rita, wanted. He didn't think about money and things for the house and paying the bills or what the fucking kids needed for school. When he was with Teresa, it was good times and Dominic deserved good times.

Rita Blanchette was eighteen and going to go to college when she met Dominic. When she graduated an arraigned marriage to an older French gentleman was planned. He was, as her parents explained to her, very well set and in the same business as her father. Rita's life was planned. These were the plans that had been arraigned three years ago when she was fifteen. It would have been a joining of business and financial power but Rita was possessed with the dreams of a wistful, young girl and a prince charming. Happily ever after filled her head to the point that sensibilities and logic were left no room.

Her parents didn't approve. A marriage was already planned. And it wasn't that they didn't like Italians, they just didn't like him. Her father told her, he was "a slacker, a loafer and a ne'er do well". Her mother told her, something that was incomprehensible, to the young Rita, "Dominic wasn't capable of loving anybody but himself." Rita refused and fought them constantly.

Then, against the wishes of her parents, against the customs and traditions of her family, against the better judgment of all her family, she married him.

Her father gave him a job in his factory, a laborer's job. He told Dominic he had to start at the bottom. Dominic thought that was stupid. He told them that he was their son-in-law, a member of the family and a family member doesn't start at the bottom. Dominic wanted to wear a suit and have an office of his own. He wasn't working on a greasy machine turning out parts for some stupid thing he didn't even know about. Rita agreed but her father wouldn't relent. He ran the business not his nineteen years old child. Dominic quit and got a job as a car salesman.

Within two months, Rita's parents were demanding a divorce. She should see the truth by now. Rita refused hoping that they'd give him more time. Then she got pregnant and thought the child might change her father's mind. The turmoil lasted through the pregnancy. With the birth of her first child, she finally decided she had no choice but to stay. Her parents finally cut her off and said that her refusal had left them no choice.

For Dominic it was different. He married Rita because he thought that it would be cool to do something different and her family had money. He married a French chick with money! But none of his friends understood it. Italians should marry Italians. Everyone knew that!

It turned out to be a fuck up!

Nicholas hears his father coming up the stairs. Anthony makes the button-up motion in front of his mouth signaling, '*be quiet*', hoping it wouldn't happen again. They hate it when he comes home.

Stumbling up the dark staircase and clinging to the banister, Domi manages the incline, cussing the entire distance. Nobody wants him there. His hollering and cussing always makes their mother cry.

"Rita get me something to eat," Dominic demands as he reaches the top of the stairs.

"Barely through the door and already giving orders," Rita says aloud.

"Watch your mouth woman... and hurry it up, ...I got places to go," his words are slurred and his walk wobbly and his shiny, new shoes leave wet spots across the kitchen floor.

"Where are you going?" she asks.

"What the hell's it to you? I'm the man in this house. You just stay home and mind your family." Shakily, he sits at the table with his sons on each side.

"How are my boys today?" he asks as he leans over and pats them both on the head. The smell in the room has changed. The aroma of the tomato sauce is gone replaced with the stink of sweat and stale beer.

The boy wants to hold his nose. He has lost his appetite.

She places a plate of spaghetti in front of Dominic and sits across from him. Nicholas can see her eyes are wet again. He doesn't like seeing her cry and knows it makes his father feel strong. He can feel his father's chest swell up and it hurts him.

"You're going to see that woman again aren't you?" she asks, hoping for a negative reply but knows it won't be forthcoming.

Dominic revels in her misery and part of the pleasure drawn from his infidelity is her inability to prevent it.

"Are you Domi? Are you going to see her again?"

"I told you before, it's none of your business," he snaps. "If you don't like it, go home to your family. Leave the boys and go back to your rich stuck-up family."

"You've got a family, Domi. Don't you care about them?" She said softly, hoping not to anger him but her eyes fill with tears again and the boy starts to cry.

"Shut up. And you," he stares the small boy down, "stop the damn crying." Turning back to Rita, his voice rises harshly, "You just take care of the kids. I make the money, I pay the bills, and I see who I want. Lei capisce? Now, shut the fuck up."

Nicholas is shaking. His mother is mad and when she gets mad, she gets quiet inside. He can feel it. Deep inside of her everything comes together into a little hard ball. It sticks in her heart and she holds it there.

"I told you to stop swearing in front of the children," she says softly as if she isn't angry but the boy can feel the ball inside her and it's on fire. "You sound like a pig," she continues. Even the word 'pig' is said with a gentle reverence.

"Shut up," he screams it at her. "I can't stand your quiet preachy shit. Shut up and let me eat my dinner! Then wash the dishes, pack your bags and get out."

"You, get out of my house," she echoes! The tears are streaming down her cheeks and she is half out of her seat. "You leave me and my children alone. We don't want you around here. Just get out. Go see your Italian whore." The words are spoken so low that the boy strains to hear them.

Dominic lurches shakily to his feet, lifts his plate, staggers sideways and throws the plate of spaghetti across the table.

It misses Rita's face by inches and crashes against the white, metal cupboards above the sink. It hangs there for a moment before slowly sliding downward, falling to the counter and then to the floor in disgusting streaks of red and white. She glances momentarily at her second son, and then she turns and walks to the kitchen sink, her cheap shoes splattering in red sauce and slipping on long thin strands of spaghetti. She kicks off the shoes and stands staring out the window, out at the garage where Oscar lays in the shadows and out over the alley infested with rats, her shoulders slump and wearily she hangs her head.

Rita is worn out. She has made a great mistake in her life. Her family has wealth, position and connections but she refused those advantages. Instead, she married a very coarse, self-centered man and had been too infatuated to see his faults. The weight of her years with him has sunk in. The depression that followed rose up and stabbed like a barbed thorn into her heart. She knows that her children will suffer and that is unbearable. And now she feels the weight of every decision she has ever made crushing inside her skull.

Her head hurts. The pain runs from the base of her skull over the top of her head and rips through her frontal lobe. It shrieks in the center of her brain demanding payment.

Dominic takes her silence as a sign of submission. To Dominic that is how a household should run; a wife should listen to her husband. His decisions are always correct. She takes care of the kids, cleans the house and cooks the meals.

His second son knows she had just become still, as if she had withdrawn into some secret place. He can see it. The look is in her eyes. He sees it because he has his own secret place and when he is there, nobody can make him be afraid. Her shoulders were slumped but he saw her eyes. They shined with an unusual sparkle and like his are flecked with gold.

Dominic stumbles across the room and grabs her violently from behind. His left arm goes around her throat while his right wraps around her waist. She resists and tries to break free, pushing back from the sink and flailing with her hands and feet. But Dominic is too strong for her. He lifts her off the floor and slams her hard into the counter, knocking the wind from her and banging her head into the splattered cabinets.

Her family had cut her loose and gave her to him and today she would pay for how they treated him.

"I ought'a break your fucking neck, you bitch," he barks.

"Dad don't hurt her," Anthony screams and runs to his mother's side. He grabs his father's leg and tries to pull him away.

Dominic's right hand comes loose and smashes into the face of his oldest son. Anthony's face explodes as he is catapulted across the room and slams against the old ice box.

Rita twists free, turning against the arm chocking her throat. The younger boy has just a moment before Anthony could get to his feet. In that moment he sees her eyes again and the *fork* in her right hand. It streaks up Dominic's left arm and sends him staggering backward.

Stunned and drunk, he holds his arm out toward her as if to show her what she has done. A train track of six four-hole puncture wounds appear in his left forearm and blood spurts from them in a pulsating rhythm. Rita turns and now the fork is replaced with a butcher's knife.

She raises the knife and Dominic quickly knocks the knife hand aside and punches her in the face just as Anthony slams into both of them. The knife clatters to the floor as the trio stumbles downward onto the soiled floor. Dominic rolls over and manages to straddle Rita's chest. She tries to reach the knife lying alongside but another blow snaps her head hard against the floor. Nicholas not knowing what to do rushes forward and grabs at his father's arm and in an uncontrolled rage the youngest son is hurled across the room.

The boy doesn't know how long he has laid there. Would that ever occur to a young boy? His eyes are blurred but he sees his father lying in an ever widening pool of blood, the blood encased butcher knife protruding from his throat.

Anthony, filled with a released hatred, has rushed into the flowing blood and is kicking his dying father in the head, splashing blood everywhere.

Barefooted, Rita is standing still while the blood flows around her toes and gently warms her feet. Finally, Dominic was giving her some comfort. She walks slowly toward her youngest and kneels down, gently wrapping her arms around the shaking boy. She looks at him through tear filled eyes that, he wouldn't understand until years later, have an upward turn of happiness in them. There is red spaghetti sauce on her forehead where she had banged the cabinet and blood splatters on her cheeks and her nose. There is blood on her blouse, on her arms and across her throat. There is blood everywhere. She reaches down and touches his cheek, a clean bloodless touch. "It's all right now, Nicky," she says. "Everything's better now."

The room becomes a permanent mosaic of brilliant snapshots, his mother's white and red spotted dress, the crimson blood flowing smoothly across the floor, the streaked white metal cabinets with the red pasta sauce sliding downward into a puddle of blood, a collage of stark contrasts, a world in red and white. And Anthony kicking and kicking and kicking.

The sirens from the police cars fade and Nicholas remains as he was when he had received his mother's final embrace. He can't move; his feet are stuck. The blood is like glue on his shoes, forever stuck in that place, in that room forever.

There is a shaking going on in the middle of his brain, strange voices screaming in his head and his body vibrating, twitching; his teeth chattering and rivulets of blood running from both nostrils.

This is how the police found them. The mother bathed in red, kneeling in blood while holding her youngest son to her breast and whispering in his ear. The oldest still standing in his father's blood.

A police officer carries the youngest boy out. He is unable to walk.

When a police officer takes Anthony's hand to lead him from the house he lashes out and tries to run back to his father's body. Dominic's face is indiscernible, pulverized by small feet.

Later at the hospital in the child psychiatric care unit, when the doctors asked Nicholas what happened, all he could remember was an old Sicilian woman, her apron streaked with blood and a chicken flopping inside a small funnel.

CHAPTER TWO

T he Williamsburg Clinic was established in 1935 as an institution for homeless and wayward children. In 1943 with state funding and an appropriate medical staff it also became an administrative care facility for mentally disturbed youths. But the people there were more inmates than patients, many of whom were kept in individually restricted areas. Initially, Nicholas thought that he would get to stay with Anthony but they were separated immediately upon admission. Nicholas' problem was uniquely different than Anthony's.

The clock on the wall said one o'clock. It was covered with a heavy metal grate and had a plastic face with skinny, wet, red hands that dripped. Another hour and they would come get him. They always came at 2:00 pm. And then they would pretend again. Pretend there wasn't any blood on the floor. It was there. They saw it. All of them saw it. It stuck to their shoes and splashed the wall when they stepped in it. How could they not see it?

He told the doctor, he wanted a different room, a white one. The doctor told him everything was getting better. His mother was someplace happy and Anthony's feet had stopped kicking. They said soon the bad thoughts would go away and soon his room would be white.

When Dr. Jefferies asked about his father, Nicholas couldn't talk very good. It was like a knot in his throat that wouldn't let the words out. He had tried but they just wouldn't come out. The knot was always there. The doctor said it was really stuck someplace in his brain and when it was ready it would come out.

Several months passed before they told him that Anthony had gone back to school, and soon he would go also, but he had to stay a little longer.

His only visitor during his two years at the hospital was Sister Mary Elizabeth, his sixth grade teacher. She would come to see him every week on her free day. She would bring a picnic lunch and they would sit in the grass and she would help him with his studies. She didn't want him falling behind. She would tell him all about how God wanted him well, too.

They'd play checkers and take long slow walks around the hospital. There was a foot trail that went into the woods and there were squirrels and a few raccoons and different kinds of birds. Once they even saw a fox and Sister Mary Elizabeth told him how lucky they were. People almost never got to see a fox. Foxes were magical. If they didn't want you to see them, you never would. That fox must have liked them because he let them see him a lot. Nicholas really liked the woods. He imagined, if could somehow get there by himself, he could be like that fox and no one would ever see him. She would always stay the whole day, saying goodbye only after visiting hours were over.

His grandparents didn't have a car, so he only saw them every two or three months, whenever they could find a ride. It took some time but after two years, they allowed him to go live with his grandparents, his father's parents.

They wouldn't speak of his mother at all.

CHAPTER THREE
Two years later

St. Joseph's was located on Mack Ave on Detroit's lower east side. The school was in its death throes, as were many of the Catholic schools. Poor neighborhoods and smaller donations from an ever increasing older population, coupled with too much money going to the archdiocese, had precipitated their eventual failure.

Nicholas didn't know many of his classmates. He had just returned to St. Joseph's this semester. He was the new kid and everyone tried to ignore him, as if some air of indifference accompanied his newness, some intangible quality that dictated the need to make him inaccessible. It didn't bother him much because sometimes he thought there *really* was something wrong with him. All the time in the hospital spent alone, the isolation, became natural to him and the aloneness was what he expected for himself and from others around him.

Today the wind blew down the alley that separated the high school from the grade school, rattling cans, raising toxic dirt and shoving the foul odor of rotting garbage into the school corridors. It was the kind of wind that sucked into your lungs and crept down your spine making you feel as putrid as the alley you sat in.

Nicholas was thirteen years old and today he sat at the end of the schoolyard near the back door of the rectory. He spent most of his recesses there, leaning against the old wall, shielded from the direct wind that blew down the alley and partially hidden from the student's playground.

Inside the school, the wooden floors creaked and the hallways were unusually cold but the old exterior wall where he sat was warm and filled with vibrations and strange lyrical music.

When the other kids were playing tag or dodge ball, when they were laughing and having fun, he would sit with his back pressed hard against the wall, until the bricks pinched and creased patterns into his skin. If he concentrated, let the vibrations take him, he would hear, scratching through the masonry, old voices in the music. The murmurings were deep and the sounds distorted but there were words hidden in the music. When it played, he would close his eyes and almost fall asleep. It would give him a powerful feeling and help clear his mind of the terror from his past. Then his mother's dress was pure white and the kitchen floor was polished and sparkling and Anthony was smiling.

But today, it was different. Today all he felt were hard vibrations.

Several yards away, across the alley, at the edge of the schoolyard, were two cement garbage receptacles chipped and decayed with rusted iron hinged lids. The lids were held open by a three-week supply of delayed pickups. The smell was foul. On the fence next to the containers, ten feet up, a basketball hoop hung on bent and rusted screws. Shreds of a net, reminiscent of better times, were barely evident.

Three high schoolers were playing a shooting game and the tallest, a blond, was obviously enjoying his height advantage. Nicholas watched the shooters from behind the fence.

"Hey, it's my turn. C'mon John, spread it around."

"OK, just one more shot," the tall shooter answered. He was smiling a big toothy grin. "That's three in a row for me. You guys aren't doing too good," he said as he snapped a pass to the smallest shooter.

"It's not over yet. Losers pay up at the end of the week. We'll have you by then," Bill, the small shooter, answered, obviously not smart enough or lost in his own exuberance to realize that when you're five-foot-six you don't win basketball games.

"Sure, we'll see," the blond laughed again showing that big grin. He came from four miles east of the school, from a more affluent neighborhood. He was use to winning.

Other groups of students from the high school were starting to gather outside the fence, waiting in the alley for the recess bell to draw them reluctantly back to class.

Two greasers swaggered around the corner, making the others in the alley draw together into small protective groups. Greasers occasionally came around from the public high school, two blocks away. They enjoyed giving the religious creeps a little scare. These two had a bad reputation.

The greaser's collars were spread up in the back against hair that was slicked with Dixie Peach pomade. Both wore black leather jackets, tight pegged jeans and needle-toed shoes. They strutted up to the shooters.

There were a lot of gangs in the neighborhood, blacks, whites, Hispanics, jocks and greasers. Everyone could find something to join. It wasn't smart to be a loner. Nobody liked anyone too different.

"Hey punks, break out with some smokes, now!" the largest one snapped. He stepped between the basketball shooters, stopping the game and flicked the index and middle finger on his left hand outward, impatiently. The crowd moved away.

Only the small boy on the other side, pulling off his wall and sliding down the fence, moved closer, close enough to see their eyes. The basketball shooters stepped back until their backs were touching the fence. Their throats clogged up and they didn't answer. There was no place to go.

Nicholas was ten feet away, his finger skimming the chain-linked fence, feeling the vibrations coming from the shooters. He could see the shooters eyes. They flicked in every direction, looking for some way out. Nicholas could feel their fear. He felt it pulsing under the cement and coiling through the fence. No flecks of gold there – these shooters were scared.

He knew what was about to happen. He could see it clearly in his head, sense it sliding through the ground and into his feet. He could feel the hate within the largest greaser. The soft rhythm from the wall had changed tempo and it stayed with him as he walked toward the shooters until it became a growing crescendo of cymbals and blaring horns from some deep unknown space. A place filled with dank corners and dark slippery shadows, a place he could reach but as of yet didn't understand.

"Eh, Primo, don't these chumps hear me. I mean, what am I talking for if they're all deaf? Eh."

"Yeah, Lou, maybe they're deaf." Primo was short and wide, and with his impression of the shooters' growing fear, he moved closer to the group. The grin on his face twisted weirdly. His eyes were too close together with one obviously lower than the other, like he had caught his head in a vise and someone gave it a good hard twist.

"Hey punks, L.S.M.F.T. Don't you hear good? Lucky Strikes Means Free Tobacco," Louie laughed.

"We don't have any. We don't smoke," the tall boy found his voice. He looked to be about seventeen, probably the same age as Louie, the greaser.

"What's your name punk," Louie barked, the look on his face had turned mean.

"John, John Dixon," the blond answered. His voice quaked and he could barely hear his own words.

Next to the fence, only a few feet away, Nicholas's eyes had narrowed strangely and the voice in his head was saying, *NOW! NOW!* But the blond couldn't hear the silent warning. The music in his head was pounding some unknown tune that ran to the edge of hysteria.

"Well John Dixon," Louie said, his voice dropping one octave, "fuck you."

Louie's right fist crashed into the face of young, innocent and too scared to run, John Dixon. Dixon was out cold before the following left hook hit. His head snapped against the fence and his knees locked. He bounced off the fence and, just like a high diver the moment before he went into his jackknife, fell forward into Louie's waiting fists. For a second time, his head snapped against the fence and pearls of white tumbled from his mouth as Louie hit him with another deadly combination. After the second bounce, Louie stepped aside and John Dixon fell forward, his knees still locked, crashing down to where the pitted cement of the dirty alley finished off what once had the chance of becoming a pretty good looking face.

There were others in the alley but everyone seemed frozen. Nobody moved as Louie and Primo turned and casually strutted down the alley toward the open street twenty yards ahead.

The kids around them scattered, everyone refusing to become the next victim. Only the eighth grader walking next to them on the other side of the fence seemed undaunted. From behind the fence, he could see his older brother, Anthony, standing down the alley next to the garbage containers. Anthony's face was drawn and darkly intense and Nicholas was reminded of Oscar the moment before he rushed from his hiding spot within the shadows of the garage.

Louie and Primo strutted toward Anthony like Broadway stars making a grand exit and hearing the applause. Anthony was only fifteen years old, but he had seen things much worse than what just happened to the hapless John Dixon. He waited, almost casually, leaning against the putrid garbage container, thinking about his father, always thinking about his father, his right arm hidden from view, like Oscar waiting for the rat.

Louie paid almost no attention to the kid standing next to the garbage container. He was enjoying the attention, loving the fear he had invoked in these gutless Catholic school bastards. When he came to pass Anthony, he bent in the boy's direction and gave him a growling smirk. Nicholas was amazed at the speed of the bat but he had once seen a fork that was even faster.

Anthony moved with incredible sureness and the bat took Louie's head the way Joe DiMaggio took a fastball. The force snapped the head a full one hundred and eighty degrees and crushed the left side of Louie's face, destroying the jawbone and leaving what would eventually become a perpetual twisted smirk on his face. Primo backed up but not fast enough to avoid the second strike, which caught him high on the shoulder and ended with a soft crunching thud against his temple. He dropped like a gut bag at the slaughterhouse and lay motionless.

Louie struggled to get to his feet while blood gushed from his broken face and flooded into his eyes. His world became a disconnected blur with a red figure circling him. He got his feet under him and stood wobbling, holding his hands in front of his face, like a punchy boxer. The figure moved quickly and Louie's left knee snapped in an excruciating crush. His left foot disappeared from his brain as he dropped onto the broken knee. A foot caught his face and Louie collapsed forward much like John Dixon had only moments before but unlike Dixon, his nemesis didn't leave him. With the pain failing to numb his senses, Louie twisted on the rutted cement and looked up. His dimming vision allowed him one last glimpse of the red figure circling and the bat swinging again.

CHAPTER FOUR

Another two years

The inner cities of most large urban areas of America are divided both economically and culturally, with the cultural differences being based more on continental ancestry and race rather than any political agenda. In these cities, the youth gangs divide the streets into their own turf, and if they let the average, tax paying citizen alone, the police do their best to ignore them in the hope they just beat the shit out of each other.

If you were just another kid on the street and did anything to piss off a gang member, you were wise to stay in hiding for a few weeks. They might not find you, but at least everyone knows they're looking and you were hiding. The gangs kept their respect and you look like a chicken shit, which is what you really are. At least nobody makes you bite the curb before they kicked in the back of your head.

That was the way it was for most people. The average guy had two choices. Join a gang, stay in your area and you were not only cool but you were considered tough or you could be independent and risk getting your ass kicked on a regular basis.

Nicholas DiCicci didn't have that problem, he didn't belong to a gang but still nobody bothered him, - anywhere. He walked the neighborhoods with impunity. White, black, Little Italy, Hamtramck, Mick Town, it didn't matter. They would even call his name. "How's it going Nicky, eh?" People on the street, in the stores, in the soda shops, it didn't matter where. Everywhere. Nobody on the east side of Detroit wanted Nicky's big brother, Anthony pissed at them. It was much better to just give the kid free rein. Nicky, at fifteen, didn't even question why.

Actually, a little quirk permeated the entire Italian community, with a footnote that was well marked on the police route patrol sheet. This neighborhood had no problems! No opposing gangs tried to infiltrate the area because the Italian gang was so large; every family with a son had a member. Consequently, the older generation was never bothered and the police knew the reason. This was where Anthony DiCicci lived.

Joseph Palazola, a young Italian boy, was riding his Moped home from the soda fountain on Warren and Garland and decided to cut south of Mack Avenue before he passed St. Jean. The neighborhood was in transition, mostly black with every other group moving out. For Joey, it was a terrible mistake; he had crossed a territorial line. Some blacks down on Kercheval knocked him off his scooter with a brick. He bit the curb and bled to death two hours later, still lying on the street.

A small race riot, covering the lower east side, broke out. It usually happened a couple times a year. This one lasted six weeks and the streets appeared deserted with the exception of shadows moving outside the light. It took that long for the police to get some kind of a handle on it.

Anthony and his boys, all one hundred fifty of them, were out, cruising and hunting. Nobody wanted to get caught. Anthony wanted an answer and after two weeks of beating the shit out of every black who dared to come out at night, he got it. Two days later, a young black was found hanging from a tree on Kercheval and Bewick. His shirt was ripped off. His hands were tied behind his back and a rope lashed under his arms held him suspended six feet off the ground. A bullet hole entered his throat and exited the top of his head. He had a large 'J' carved on his chest.

After that, no one was on the streets for 3 or 4 weeks. It was a bad time. People everywhere were getting the shit kicked out of them. The small gangs stayed down and now the black gangs were looking for any stray white. The papers didn't want to call it a race riot. They preferred the term 'gang war' but for anyone who had to be on the streets the answer was perfectly clear.

When it ended there had been over 100 assaults, 30 of which involved knifings and more than 20 victims were beaten with pipes or chained half to death. Two more people died. One white kid name Brian Bresko got caught coming out of a beer store on Warren. His skull was cracked in three placed by a gas pipe. The second was an old black woman, who was unfortunate enough to be crossing the street during a car chase involving a group of Italians and Puerto Ricans. Nobody was ever arrested but the old woman got ran over by both cars.

A couple of detectives from the Conner Precinct picked up Anthony DiCicci at 2 am on a Friday night. They knew this punk kid was responsible for most of the recent gang problems and finding him out alone was comparable to a divine gift. They couldn't refuse the opportunity. They wanted to know about the black kid who had been found playing hangman's noose by himself. They took a handcuffed Anthony to an interrogation room where they held a phone book against his head and beat it with a nightstick. They also got a mop bucket from the janitor's room, stuck the bucket over his head and wailed on it with their clubs. While these two sweethearts of justice were massaging the punk, a third was trying to find out as much info as they could on the kid. What he eventfully discovered was the kid was still a kid and only seventeen years old.

Sergeant's Graham and Murphy both agreed he was the meanest seventeen-year-old bastard in town but they still didn't want to get caught working him over. If anybody complained, it could end their careers.

It was 4:30 am, late December, clouds were stacked six deep and the falling snow, large with thick flakes, covered everything in minutes. The city was blanketed, driving was hazardous, the north side of the Detroit River was frozen to several inches thick and all the approaching streets were deserted.

Graham and Murphy dumped the kid at the Seven Sisters incinerator plant at the foot of St. Jean next to the Detroit River. If he froze to death, well that wasn't their problem and besides, the whole damn city would be better off.

When Anthony came to, he was covered with three inches of snow and colder than a snowman's cock. He was lying on a rock pile looking at the sun starting to show itself over the Windsor skyline. His head was pounding and every spot on his body was aching with internal bruises. He spent the next ten minutes checking himself and looking for something broken. They had worked him over and never left a visible mark but every muscle in his body felt like it was a poor cut of meat from Tutti's meat market. Something old man Tutti had tenderized with his wooden mallet.

Kasta's Drive-In was located on Conner and Mack Avenue across from the Mack Avenue baseball field. The two cops stopped in every night at around 9:00 pm. It was late January and the ball field was covered with a sooty gray snow that smelled of iron dust, smoke stacks and dirty train yards. A cold artic wind swept the ball field freezing the fenced dugouts and leaving an icy glaze on the infield that wouldn't leave until the end of March.

"Hey Maxey, you sweet hunk of groove, how about a couple cups of coffee for two of Detroit's finest?" The inside of the drive-in was empty except for the two detectives.

"Sure Graham, just give me a moment." Maxine walked around the counter past George Andropolis, the owner of Kasta's Drive-In.

Kasta's was small, with only enough parking for about ten cars. The cement lot was broken and heaved with winter ice. The resulting cracks were two inches wide and filled with black tar. Four years ago it was in need of immediate repair. It was still waiting. The building inside was just as dismal. The majority of Kasta's business came from the auto plants. The breakfast and lunch crowd provided the most business and afternoon shift workers would stop in after having a drink at one of the local watering holes on their way home.

Sometime the workers could get pretty rowdy and Georgy liked having the police hang around. They kept the unruly people from stirring up too much shit, but most of the time, especially with this pair, because of the way they talked to the waitresses and Maxine in particularly, he couldn't stand the pigs.

Maxine lifted two cups off the shelves and proceeded to fill them. She leaned tightly against Georgy and whispered, "They're asking about the kid again. They want to know if anyone has seen him. Probably hoped they'd killed him," she said under her breath.

"You don't know anything Max. We don't know anything. Remember that. Stick with it," he whispered back.

"I wish someone would kill these bastards," she finished before moving up the counter.

"Two coffees, anything else?" She asked placing the cups in front of the two detectives.

"Well that depends on what's on the menu," Graham shot back with a large grin.

"Only what you can find on this," she grabbed a menu from one of the chrome-plated clips equally spaced along the counter and dropped it on the counter behind the coffee.

"That doesn't go for me does it Maxey girl," Murphy answered. "We both know you can't stand Graham but I thought we had something special. Like maybe later tonight."

"Murph, I don't even know why you come here. The local gossip has you spending all your spare time down at the Hub," Maxine snapped back. She knew instantly that it was a mistake.

Murphy exploded off his stool and hanging half way over the counter, the chrome menu holder bending under his weight, made a grab at Maxine. His face was twisted in a vicious snarl. Graham leaped across his stool and caught him by the shoulders.

"Where'd you hear that shit you fucking bitch," Murphy screamed just missing her with his extended hand.

"Hey," Georgy complained, hurrying to get in-between Murphy and Maxine, "you can't swear like that in here." He didn't want to get these guys pissed but he wasn't having them talk to Maxine like that.

Graham hollered while dragging his partner off the counter, "You shut up, Georgy or your old lady's going to find out you're balling the help. And you keep your fuckin' mouth shut or I'm gonna shove my cock down it," he shouted at Maxine. He shoved Murph back down on his stool and kept his hands on his partner's shoulders.

"You know what we're looking for and don't give me any shit asshole! That wop filed a complaint against us with the Chief and we want to see him real bad. Have you seen that fuckin' punk?"

"No," Georgy answered. He was scared. Maxine had hit Murphy's hot button when she mentioned the gay bar downtown and Murphy looked ready to kill. "He hasn't been around in months. Nobody's seen him," he answered, trying to calm them down.

"If you see that bastard, you or your little slut better call me," he paused to make sure the little Greek got the message, "you understand asshole?"

"I understand," Georgy answered, his voice barely audible.

Graham pushed Murphy toward the door and two of the city's finest reluctantly walked outside and got into the large, black cruiser. They sat for a few moments without talking, just letting their anger cool down.

Murphy finally spoke. "Bastards. They're all bastards."

"Forget it. Murph. It doesn't mean shit. You did the little fag a favor and now he shit-mouths you all over town. We'll find him and when we do, you can have him."

"You're goddamn right. I'm going kill that little fag." He paused, still visibly shaking. Perspiration beads we're forming on his forehead.

At that moment, a '49 Mercury swerved across the center lane on Conner, rolled over the curb and stopped just short of smashing the cement pillar that divided the parking area from the front windows of the drive-in. The driver's door flew open and a tall blond kid almost fell out. He appeared to be no more than eighteen and staggered around in a couple of circles before he seemed to get his directions. He held onto the door of the old torpedo-back coupe for a couple of moments, trying to stay upright and then, noticing the two cops, smiled crookedly and staggered toward them.

Murphy looked at his partner, "Hell of an informant. Shit, he can hardly stand up by himself," and started to open the door.

"Yeah, I know but he's one of them. Hell, don't get out. He's coming to us," Graham laughed, "and don't let him breathe on you."

The tall skinny blond was dressed in a black, studded motor-cycle jacket, tight jeans and black boots. His hair, long and thin like white corn silk, hung over his eyes. He moved toward the police car, more in a sideways motion than anything that could be construed as going forward.

Hillbilly Gene Radnor was nineteen years old. He was born in a holler in eastern Kentucky, the second of fifteen children in a family that couldn't afford to feed even one. He left home at thirteen, kicked around doing odd farm jobs for simple meals until he ended up in Louisville at sixteen. Once there, he found himself a gang that became his family. If you had a family, you could survive.

Uneducated, illiterate and lacking any marketable skills Gene lived by mugging the local citizenry and robbing small mom and pop shops in the poor parts of town, areas that even the police avoided. Like most of the kids, he was always look-ing for a big score, something big time but nothing ever came his way. Times were always tough and when the cops started looking for some blond kid who put the sharp end of a knife into a security guard during the burglary of a pawn shop, Gene decided to move north.

Now, Hillbilly Gene, cold sober with a .38 Colt in the right pocket of his jacket, stumbled sideways toward the two cops sitting in their shiny, black, new Ford. Gene thought he'd like to take the car for a ride, see how fast it was, you know, and listen to the police channel. But first, before the ride, there was the fun!

In the back of the Mercury, scrunched down so that only his eyes looked over the back of the front seat, Little Jackie Rohrer smoked a joint of the purest Colombian Gold. The grass was supposed to keep him settled but he was shaking uncontrollably. Jackie was a pusher and sold the best grass in the city. He supposedly worked for the Greeks down in Greektown who in turn worked for the Italians and Jackie liked that. He liked to tell everyone that he worked for the Italians. When you told someone that, they left you the fuck alone.

Jackie really didn't work for anybody. He simply bought the weed from the Greeks and sold it. Occasionally he sold some weed to some of Anthony's boys. And anything that Anthony wanted he got for free because Jackie worked for the …. well, the Italians.

Jackie had a good thing going with all the gays in the city. He had the Hub Grille on his route. He stopped by at least twice a week and never had any trouble. The homos always treated him fine. They always paid up front and he liked that. He didn't extend credit and they didn't ask for it.

He made a drop at the Hub on a Friday, almost a full pound. Those fags were getting ready for one hell of a party and Jackie left with a fat roll of money.

Everything was fine until the two pigs, Graham and Murphy, pulled him over on Monroe Street and dragged him behind the trash containers at the entrance to the alley. The fat pig, Murphy beat the shit out of him and kicked him down the filthy alley. They told him he was going to serve some time if they didn't get their cut. They took the money. Not some of it, all of it. Then the fat pig, laughing and dropping his pants told Jackie he had something else to do.

Now he was sitting in the back of the Mercury, shaking with the joint pressed close to his mouth. He watched as the tall raw-boned hillbilly stumbled up to the car and leaned on the door. On the other side of the lot, Jackie could see a shadow standing silently next to the building. At that moment Little Jackie Rohrer developed a case of incontinence and pissed his pants.

At the same moment, the drunken hillbilly kid almost fell as he reached for the car door.

"Get up on your fucking feet, you fuckin' stupid drunk," Murphy snapped.

Gene pulled himself, indignantly, upright and leaned toward the open window. He looked through the car at Graham, "Hey Sergeant, I don't like the way he's talking to me. I ain't no stupid nothing and, you know, like since I know what you want, I think he should apologize." He laughed in Murphy's face. "Eh, what do you think? Eh Sarge?"

"You got something to tell us, let's hear it." Graham said, leaning his head forward.

"Yeah, well I know where he is right now," the blond boy slurred.

"Where the hell is he and stop shitting around? Right now," Graham ordered.

Gene leaned his left side against the car while his right hand moved unnoticed from his jacket. He stuck his face into the window opening,

"Well, I guess you ought to know since you want him so damn bad. The scoop has it that he was going to leave town after you guys beat the shit out of him but he wanted to see you first."

"What the fuck does that mean?" Graham asked.

Gene's left hand, in an almost sobering slow movement, snatched a handful of Murphy hair and jerked his head backward while the right hand snapped the muzzle of the .38 revolver against the side of Murphy's nose.

"How would you like it if I blew a hole through this fag cocksuckers nose and right between your fucking eyes," he snapped at Graham. Both cops froze. "Now don't even think of moving. Don't even breath." He paused a moment as if he needed to think. "It means 'HE'S HERE'," he laughed.

The driver's side door flew open and as Graham turned, Anthony's right fist hit him, a mind-stunning blow, crushing the cop's left jaw and expelling four teeth in a rocket-like gush that splattered the windshield. Graham tumbled from the car his face smashing the inside door handle and tearing a gash across his cheek, while the back of his head was split with several additional hard blows. A crushing kick to his right side broke two ribs and pierced a lung. By the time he hit the ground, blood was already frothing between his lips and he was no longer conscious.

Hillbilly Gene pushed the Colt tighter against Murphy's already swollen nose.

"Relax," he chuckled, "you're next. And you know what, fag boy? Then I'm going for a ride in this pretty car."

CHAPTER FIVE

The intensive care unit at Detroit's Receiving Hospital was cold, white, shiny stainless and just as bleak as the winter outside. Graham didn't notice any of this, the beating had removed that possibility. He was in a coma and although Murphy, in intensive care, occasionally regained consciousness his level of sedation kept him well beyond any acceptable level of awareness.

That wasn't the case for the rest of Detroit's police force. They were hunting a vicious seventeen year old wanted for assault with intent to do great bodily harm, resisting arrest, assaulting two police officers and stealing a police vehicle. Anthony DiCicci was looking at a long time locked away if the police that caught him didn't kill him first. So, like fog hit by the morning sun, he evaporated and along with him went Nicholas' protection.

The Detroit Police tracked Anthony to New York where he had known relatives. The airlines records showed an Anthony DiCicci landing in New York on Friday. The police interviewed the cab driver that drove the young man to the residence of Pietro Conti in Manhattan.

The Police files listed Pietro Conti, Anthony's uncle, as a lieutenant in the New York mob. When questioned about his nephew, Pietro Conti didn't know what anyone was talking about because he'd never seen Anthony in the first place. Hell, he didn't even know his nephew was coming to New York. The cabbie was a known police informant and that made him a liar. Go figure!

The questions they asked twisted back upon themselves and ended where they had started, at the New York International Airport. The airline records for the following day showed an Anthony DiCicci caught an 8:00 am flight to Chicago's Midway. At 10:00 am he had a ticket to Dulles International. At 1:00 pm he apparently flew to L.A. International. At 4:30 pm to Dallas and at 6:00 pm to Minneapolis-St. Paul. All the boarding passes were stamped and utilized. Someone sat in every seat.

Anthony disappeared within the company. For Pietro, it was perfect. He considered the kid God-sent. His wife's brother, Dominic, was killed by his own wife. She cut his fucking throat right in front of the kid and in the process created a perfect monster. The kid could beat the living shit out of anybody and feel nothing. He could push the proverbial old lady in a wheel-chair down a flight of stairs and be waiting at the bottom to stomp what was left of her into the spinning, bloody wheels. No different than swatting an irritating fly. What a kid!

Pietro had heard that some of the old guys from Palermo were like that but he'd never met one until Anthony showed up.

"Eh He'sa justa a like from Palermo. And big - six foota two, one hundred eighty-five pounds and bam-bam. No one knows it'sa coming. Bam. Bam. Justa like a jackhammer breaka da cement. He'sa perfect and I gotta him a no name."

Pietro changed Anthony's name and living quarters at least four times a year. If the police showed up looking for a Louie Petrelli or Frank Colombo, he no longer lived there. He'd moved three weeks ago. A transient, who didn't make friends - unemployed - paid in cash and left at night. No forwarding address. Perfect!

The rumors of Anthony's efficiency spread and within a few years, he was doing work for other organizations. None of which were listed with Dunn and Bradstreet.

For Nicholas things changed traumatically. One year earlier, Anthony had been thrown out of St. Joseph's. After that, he went to Southeastern High School where he lasted one week. He hit a kid named, Jackson Deward in the cafeteria and broke his jaw. Anthony never came back but Jackson, a Cassius Clay wannabee who changed his name to Ali Deward, did.

When it was obvious that Anthony was really gone, when every patrol car in the city was looking for the 'Italian' and he couldn't be found, Nicholas's protective screen melted like thin ice on a hot windshield. Then Ali Deward let it be known that he would love to have Nicholas wander onto his turf one evening or simply bump into him after school.

The gangs lined up. White Boy Floyd from Harper and Van Dyke, Little Willie Sampson from Jefferson and Dickerson and two black gangs, one he didn't really know and one run by Ali Deward that split the area on Van Dyke between Jefferson and East Warren. Each of them would have loved to have some fun with him.

Anthony was gone and everything Nicholas believed in changed.

He was working at the Harper McClellan Market. They paid thirty-five cents an hour for packers and had a sign posted over each register. "No tipping allowed. The packers are sufficiently paid." He was trying to save some money for a car and because of that, worked as much as possible.

It was late Friday night and he was the last packer for an 8:00 pm closing on a cold night. Nicholas DiCicci was standing at a lonely bus stop waiting for the 8:15 which was always late. A four door Hudson made a quick u-turn on a snowy base and three guys jumped out and ran up to him.

"Hey kid are you Nick DiCicci?" the driver demanded.

He had seen this guy before around school but didn't know who he was. Now the voices were in his head, the same ones he had heard when John Dixon waited too long, and he knew he had made the same mistake. The guy doing the talking was right in front of him the other two were on both sides. They had him trapped.

"Yeah. I'm Nick DiCicci'" he answered. It was too late for running but maybe he could talk them out of this.

"Where's your brother Nicky boy. Everyone says he's blown town. Too many cops want his punk ass."

"My brothers around, just staying down," Nick lied.

"Your brother is gone punk and you see this lump on my forehead? Your brother gave it to me and now I'm giving it back."

The guy hit him with two hard rights before he could cover up. His head exploded in excruciating pain. He heard his jaw crack as he hit the ground, the subsequent kicks forced the air from his lungs and collapsed his left lung. He covered up us best he could but the guy was in a rage.

He had lain perfectly still during the beating. Hoping that they would leave but they didn't. The guy continued to kick him until the other two guys jumped in and pulled him off. He had no idea how long it lasted. At least, he thought later, he wasn't conscious enough to bite the curb.

A young woman who ran a shop across from the market had seen the assault and called the police. She was with him when the ambulance took him to the hospital.

Floating in a morphine induced cloud interspersed with moments of racking pain and gagging mouthfuls of saliva and blood, Nicolas fought an unknown battle for survival. The red was back glaring just behind his forehead, covering every picture that his brain painted within his mind.

They had broken his nose and two ribs. Blackened both of his eyes and fractured his jaw. Ligaments were badly stretched; the jawbone severely bruised. It took over a week before he came out of it. A week before a coherent thought became his own and that thought was *fear*. Several times while sleeping in the hospital he had awakened sweating profusely driven by the fear they might come into the hospital to finish what they had started.

Nature forces the human body toward its own survival and a struggle for some awareness of thought. Nicholas reached for the voices and when he needed them the most, when his wavering consciousness pleaded for them, they came.

For days they never left him, speaking constantly. He had separated them years ago. When he faltered, they pulled him back. When his mind went blank, they filled it with ideas. When his ideas went the wrong way, they sent him the straight path.

The realization that he had lived under a safety net provided by his older brother, something he was completely unaware of prior to Anthony's leaving now became shockingly evident. When he awoke his only true friend was there, putting a cold compress on his forehead and holding his hand.

Whenever times were bad she appeared, as if his need materialized her. Sister Mary Elizabeth sat at the foot of his bed, her bright blue eyes sparkling and a smile that never faded etched upon her face. She was quite beautiful, like the porcelain statue of the Virgin Mary that stood in the church entrance. Covered from head to toe in her black and white, his young man's mind conjured up the beautiful woman hidden within. Nicholas would wonder why she decided to become a nun, maybe it was the limp or maybe it was because he would need her help someday.

She was there every evening, arriving after his grandparents went home and because of the severity of his injuries and the fact that she was a nun, no one asked her to leave. She stayed most of the nights, always gently patting his hand and reassuring him that God was watching over him, and leaving only in time to catch a bus and get back to the church for morning services. His grandmother told him that she was his guardian angel.

The voices continued to come and go without warning, usually waking him when he finally found a comfortable position in which he could lay without causing the pain to wrack his body. His eyes would snap open and the ears inside his head would strain to hear the words, but then the background noise would wash the words and he would drift off again to sleep.

He could recognize differences in their tone and their direction. He was giving them names. Some he had to think up, others he already knew. They were *Righteous, Gabriel, Caution, Wisdom, Ezekiel, Redemption, Danger, Patience* and many more.

The beating he had taken and the fear it created melted into paranoia and finally became an obsession, which consumed Nicholas. When Anthony disappeared everyone became Nicholas' enemy. Everyone was his pursuer and everyone wanted 'The Italian's' little brother. Revenge manifests itself in perverse ways. Nicholas became the outlet for years of fear that Anthony had created.

The television was on in the hospital room and *The Shadow*, his favorite show was playing. What young boy's imagination wouldn't wander and conjure dreams of a comic book super hero? And then the voices were back and they spoke of things he could do, things he never dreamed of and it seemed so simple. *The Shadow*. No one could catch him because no one could see anything but his shadow. He was like the fox in the woods around the hospital. He was invisible.

CHAPTER SIX

I t was 9:00 pm and Scarro's Theatrical had just closed. The
iron fire escape, bolted to the red brick back wall, zigzagged
up to the third floor. It was that brittle cold, when a wet hand or
finger touching frozen iron would stick and have to be peeled
off, leaving the skin behind. The ladder eventually ended on
the snow covered roof of the Rialto Theater where each of his
steps left a vivid footprint.

This was his first night out of the hospital and it was perfect. The night they had wanted; the night they spoke of while
he was in the hospital. Now looking out across the skyline, he
wondered if they could make the night just happen. He stopped
for a moment to gaze out over Gratiot Avenue. Thick clouds
blotted the moon and ran in foamy, dark waves into the distant
horizon. In the blackness left behind, large crusty snowflakes
descended in heavy sheets, sticking to everything they touched.
A few cars were moving slowly down the road and slush was
accumulating between the lanes. His feet were already cold and
the wind cutting his ears with a vicious sting made him wish for
a pair of earmuffs.

The roof of the Rialto butted up against Scarro's. He went down the drainpipe to the second floor porch. He didn't have any gloves and his fingers wanted to stick to the pipe. He paused and push his hands deep into his pockets for a moment of warmth before he broke the window and entered Scarro's. Fifteen minutes later with two burlap sacks filled with theatrical supplies hung over his back, he was seated on a brand new Schwinn Roadmaster bicycle with hard, glistening chrome trim and multi-colored handgrip streamers. He had borrowed it from a yard near Cadillac Street and the freeway. He would leave it where he had found it.

He rode up Gratiot to McClellan then north to Harper. He went as fast as he could peddle and just being out of the hospital felt good. He stopped for a brief moment across from the market. This is where they had caught him, a place that left an imprint on his psyche, a place he must never forget.

A dark, ominous sky hung just above the rooftops and thickened everything at street level like wet corn starch. Nicholas hobbled down the dark street staying within the storefront shade. With each grueling step his feet were taking on more of the characteristics of ice blocks. The shoulders of his thin coat were covered with snow and his collar was pulled up as high as possible to protect his neck from the finger of ice that rubbed his spine. He was tall and spindly and appeared in the evening mist to be quite frail. He walked with an odd sideways gait enabling him to watch behind him more than in front. He was cold and afraid. He had already decided that the fear was good. It kept his awareness very sharp. Something the voices told him he needed.

The torpedo shape Hudson slowly turned the corner from Montclair onto Shoemaker, its tires searching through the slush and finally finding their way into the ice-packed ruts that would guide them like a toboggan down the deserted street. The Hudson's headlights glared across the small storefronts, while its spotlight searched the shadowed door wells.

The moon, haloed with silver stilettos of ragged ice, tried to cut an opening through the gray sky, possibly to help the occupants of the vehicle find what they were searching for, but the boy, who only moments before, was the solitary victim of the winter storm, was nowhere to be seen.

"Where is that fucking punk?" Deiter Hagen spoke low; the question posed more to himself than anyone else in the vehicle. "He's never where he's supposed to be."

"Yeah, he's a sneaky little bastard. Besides how many times you want to beat his punk ass, anyway?" Bull Breinig laughed from the shotgun seat.

"Every time I can get my hands on the bastard and ten times more for every time that son-of-a-bitch brother of his gave me a hard time." Deiter inadvertently reached up and touched a hardened lump on his forehead, a permanent reminder of his last encounter with the older brother, the Italian.

The car's heater bearings were shot and the irritating noise coupled with the lack of heat was getting on everyone's nerves. Ping .. ping ..pinngg. Pii..pinng. The wobbling fan sounded like silverware rattling off crystal during a wedding toast.

"Next time we catch him, let me have him. That way we won't ever have to waste our time looking for him again," Bull smirked.

They called him "Bull" because he was only five-six and just about as wide as he was tall. At twenty-two he was completely bald with a Neanderthal forehead, thick bushy eyebrows and hair growing in sheets from the neck of his ever-present t-shirt to the top of his low slung pants. "Ape" would have been more appropriate.

Bull was a consummate pool shark and he was, at least to hear him tell it, one shot away from the big game in Las Vegas. He lived above the White Tower hamburger joint next to the pool hall on the corner of St. Jean and Warren where he was almost a legend. He was also a closet fag and although no one was supposed to know it, everyone did. Fact was Al Scioto, the owner of the Billiards House had seen him on more than one occasion lead some new "Minnesota Fats" wannabee up the back stairwell for some personal instructions.

Bull carried a leather-covered sap in his back pocket with which he was pretty adept. He was really too old to be hanging with Hagen and his crowd but he liked playing the shooter with the younger kids and occasionally he would get the chance to break in some young ass. He would get some young hopeful pool shark out behind the pool hall and use the sap on him until he was within an eye flicker away from being unconscious. Then he'd carry him upstairs where he'd bend him over the back of his couch and give him a good ass fucking.

Later Bull would explain how it shouldn't have happened but he wasn't going to tell anyone about it. It would be too damn embarrassing. Besides, it was going to be all right because he was going to look after the new pool shark and teach him how to shoot 'real' pool.

"Hey Deits, you already fucked him up pretty bad. Besides, he's just a squirt punk and this car is colder than a dead man's dick. Let's get the hell out of here," Billy Ray spoke up from the darkness of the back seat.

Billy Ray had been one of the Italian's boys before he disappeared after that night at Kasta's and Billy really didn't like going after the kid, especially since nobody had seen the Hillbilly since that night. If Radnor was still around it could be bad news to be with Deits.

Nicholas slid silently out from between two parked cars and grabbed the moving Hudson's bumper. He inched away from the exhaust until he was centered in the middle of the car and dug his heels, ski-style, into the snow. The Hudson, prowling like a lone wolf, continued its slow crawl through the swirling and gusting snow with Nicholas riding piggyback behind. When it reached St. Jean, the car turned right and headed south. Nicholas rolled off, came back to his feet behind a telephone pole and stood still for a moment before continuing around the corner and up Shoemaker. He stopped long enough to take off his shoes and remove the snow that had been forced through the holes in the bottom of each sole. Then he rearranged the cardboard strips he'd torn from a spaghetti box, which he used to fill the holes. When he was satisfied, he put the shoes back on and ran down the railroad tracks south toward the old Fruehauf plant. A quarter mile later, he left the tracks and cut through a broken fence into the back of the deserted, war era, Quonset hut town. Two minutes later, he exited onto Conner Avenue. Once across Conner, he slid back into the safety of Parkside Projects.

Nicholas was living with his grandparents in the Parkside Projects. It was called Parkside because it bordered Chandler Park on Detroit's east side, making the uninformed think of a peaceful park like setting, but only God could explain the name to anybody who lived there. It was like calling Guam 'Paradise' to the soldiers during World War II.

The Monday after his trip to Scarro's, Nicholas broke into the R.O.T.C. supply office in the high school basement. He helped himself to a complete uniform, waistcoat, pants, two shirts, two ties and a peak cap. He hid the clothes in the gym locker room.

At the end of every school day, he would sneak into the gymnasium to one of his lockers, then up the back service stairs, out the second story window, across the short roof and down the fire escape into the back alley, from there he had the choices of exiting either from the east or west side of the alley.

A blond boy in a R.O.T.C. uniform would be waiting at the bus stop on Vernor heading east into the Pointe, or a dark haired boy wearing a Detroit Tiger baseball cap, large horn-rimmed glasses and carrying a trumpet case would be going west on Kercheval. An old man with a hump like Quasimoto would struggle north on Lillibridge, his head bent, too intent with the task of simply moving forward to pay the least attention to any passerby, or a middle-aged woman with straggly, brown hair protruding randomly from a red-striped babushka and wearing a long, black coat with flat black shoes would be hurrying quickly towards the bus stop on Mack Avenue.

Every day the image would change and the change would become not only Nicholas's challenge but also his joy. It was the one thing that he planned and looked forward to throughout the school day.

Or on some days he simply would hitch a ride.

He quickly realized some of the teachers who arrived before the main doors opened, instead of parking in the teacher's lot, would park in the back alley and enter through the custodian's entrance.

Mr. Willard, his chemistry teacher, was one of them. He was old, well passed retirement age. He enjoyed what he was doing plus his wife had died several years earlier and he didn't wish to be home alone. Consequently, he arrived before most of the other teachers, parked at the custodial entrance and was even the first to turn on the lights in the back section of the school. He lived in Grosse Pointe Park, east of Detroit.

All of this Nicolas found out while researching who owned the older model Willy's station wagon parked in the alley every day, the one whose tailgate lock was easy to pick. It was two-toned, white on the roof and lower level and light blue in the middle. There was a space between the back seat and the rear doors big enough to lie down in if he pulled his knees up, and the doors were easy to pull together.

Mr. Willard would drive home, east on Mack Ave. He would park in his driveway and enter his house from a side door on the driver's side. Moments after the side door of his house would shut the back doors of the Willy's would cautiously open. Nicholas would exit, quietly closing the back doors and walk up the street to Mack Ave. He'd hitch hike west on Mack and north on one of several roads, a different road every time, and always expressing a silent thank you to Mr. Willard.

But Nicholas' joy had become a cancerous sore to both Deiter and Deward. It had become something that they couldn't understand. Everyone at school knew about it. It was the talk of recess. Forget about how well the school team did in last night's basketball game.

What about DiCicci? Did he get his ass kicked yet?

Walking through the hallways the remarks were constant.

"That crazy fuck is really gonna kick your ass when he catches you."

"Hell, Nick I wouldn't even come to school, if I were you."

"Eh, man how you staying away from that nut?"

It wasn't just Diets problem anymore. Everyone at school was asking the same questions. "Where the hell is DiCicci?" "Everyone saw him in school today, He is here somewhere."

Eventually Deits had someone at every exit but still it continued. "Which door did he go out?" "How come we can't find this punk?" No one ever saw DiCicci leave school.

He just disappeared.

For Nicholas, the ultimate reward occurred when Deiter, Deward, White Boy or Sampson cruised the school at the final bell and drove right past him. Beneath the costume and behind the make-up, he would be laughing.

But it was during those moments when the boy who was Nicholas was fading, crossing over a line from clear to obscure and something else was emerging, something no longer opaque, but something transparent.

The few friends he had acquired, constantly harassed by the cruising gangs, had disappeared. Any association with him was too dangerous. At seventeen, his life had taken another dramatic change. The original loner sitting behind the rectory speaking to himself was back, but now he was hidden from the recognizable scrutiny of others and now he answered only to the voices in his head.

Anthony was gone and in a completely different way, Nicholas was also disappearing.

CHAPTER SEVEN

The attacks of acute diarrhea were coming daily and his stomach was in a constant churning turmoil. His grandmother tried coke syrup and chamomile tea and some pink stuff that made him even sicker.

Afraid to go out and reaching a point where he was almost as scared of her as he was of Deits, he would lock himself into the bathroom while she pounded on the door, "Nicholas, whatsa matta wit yu. Coma out. I fix yu somathin good. Yu canna stay inna there, Coma out. I giva yu soma chicken zuppa."

"I'm okay, Grandma. I'll be out in a minute," he would answer while wondering if he was going to crap himself to death before Deits had the pleasure of killing him.

Deits had made a hook up with Little Jackie Rohrer and was peddling small bags of Colombian to the student body. It was proving to be a lot of money. Smoking it made you feel like your cock was two feet long and if a guy gave a couple of hits to a chick, she was easy to drop. So, almost every guy in the school was lining up and Deits asked whatever he wanted.

The most amazing effect the stuff had was on the old Hudson. The car had taken on the look of a glitzed out, glorified pimpmobile. What every black, pink-suit hustler on Beaubien would have given his right nut to own. The wheels were chrome plated, the front end raked and the rear raised so that the whole damn thing looked like a pregnant frog. Deits added a new flamed-out paint job, chromed exhaust pipes and pink and black foo-foo balls hanging from the front and rear glass panels. And the fucking dice - how Nicholas hated the fucking dice! They bounced below the mirror like elephant nuts tied to a pogo stick.

To Nicholas, the Hudson had become a symbol of Deits' success. Since Anthony's disappearance, Deits had become the big man in school and sooner than later someone would see Nicholas coming down the fire escape. That information would be worth an easy bag or two. Then Nicholas would drop down from the second story fire escape and they'd be there waiting for him.

HOW LONG WILL YOU BE IN THE HOSPITAL NEXT TIME NICHOLAS? His name was *Wisdom* and Nicholas was beginning to understand.

How long? That is if he was lucky enough to be taken there.

For Deits the whole thing had become some kind of a game and he enjoyed the feeling of being a celebrity. He had the grass - he kicked the ass. That was his new motto!

Nicholas was staying in and trying to get it right in his head. Somewhere in his mind were the answers and those answers had music and if he concentrated, if he thought real hard, the music became words.

Today sitting in the bathroom it changed. The words became a voice and this one he knew well. He had named him *Caution* and today he made a statement as clear as anything Nickolas he had ever heard.

IF THIS IS THEIR GAME NICHOLS THEN, "IT SHOULD BE YOUR GAME." AND IN YOUR GAME "YOU MUST MAKE THEM WORRY."

He saw it at the Parkside Theater on Warren and Dickerson. Twenty-five cents to get in and don't lean your head back on the cushion. If you do, Grandma says you'll get the ringworm. The mob was after some innocent dude and he was scared shitless. He had no choice but to pay or run. An old ex-con told him the only thing that would work was playing topsy-turvy. But he had to be real good and he could never quit even if the people he was playing against wanted to call a truce. No, especially if they wanted to call a truce! He'd thought about it for a while and, this time, the harder he thought, the clearer it became. The words were soft. *Caution* meant there was time.

Nicholas realized his recent success wasn't going to last forever. The feeling that accompanied outwitting his pursuers was only a temporary high. Deiter Hagen didn't know how Nicholas got in or out of school but he was nosing around, asking questions.

But now Deits had something to lose and he parked the Hudson out in the open where anybody could get at it.

It was the end of May and while other kids were planning on their final exams, Nicholas was planning a grand finale. The clock above the counter inside the White Tower Hamburger Haven read 11:45 pm. The moon was hidden behind dark clouds giving the street the look of black coal tar. Several people were waiting at the bus stop near the corner. They had been there for a while. The bus service slowed down late at night and waiting was normal. A few customers sat at the counter under glaring fluorescent lights, finishing their late cup of coffee and cigarette before continuing home.

He stood pressed against the soot and mold covered wall that shaped the entrance to the alley on the north side of St. Jean Ave. Filthy and secluded, it wasn't a place anyone would want to travel through. He leaned against the drain trough five feet from the alley entrance and melted into the darkness that made the alley. The garbage cans were strung in a never-ending line behind the rear of the buildings. The line headed east and was covered with rushing dark little creatures with eyes that reflected piercing red even in the abysmal alley. Years of water running off the roof and falling straight down from four stories had formed a hole in the alley floor that ran under the wall. Nicholas' foot was blocking the hole. A family of four rats was busy rifling through the nearest container. The largest scurried the three smaller rodents toward the living thing that was blocking the drain entrance to their wall. She turned and with the arrogance, that possibly only a rat could muster waddled toward the bottom of the drain. She stopped no more than a foot from him. Her lifeless beady eyes met his, the pink tip of her nose twitched. Nicholas cautiously moved his foot. Then fearlessly the rat led her brood past him and down into the black hole.

The rat had no fear of him and the question poked inside his brain. *What did she sense?* For it had to be a sense, some innate knowledge. She had looked in his eyes and had seen something. Then she became the aggressor. If he had been Oscar, the rat would have instantly fled in terror. Deits ran from Anthony and yet pursued Nicholas the way a beagle chases a hapless rabbit.

Am I the Rabbit? He questioned himself. *Was I born to be a rabbit or have I let myself become one?* Questions of free and frail, aggressor and victim rubbed against the inside of his forehead and the voices, once again, started their deep chatter.

He pushed it back and realized that the rat had shown him something else. He wasn't Oscar and in order to be free he would have to become Oscar. The voices were back and the discussion elevated. This one was *Reason*.

"LAWS DON'T REALLY PROTECT PEOPLE. THEY SEEK SOME MEDIUM OF JUSTICE AFTER A CRIME HAS BEEN COMMITTED OR AT BEST THREATEN SUCH PUNISHMENT AS TO DETER A CRIME FROM HAPPENING. YOU HAVE BEEN SEVERELY BEATEN AND YOUR ASSAILANT HAS BEEN UNTOUCHED. THERE HAS BEEN NO JUSTICE FOR YOU AND NO DETERRENT FOR HIM. IF YOU DON'T LEAD THE CHARGE THEN YOU ARE WAITING TO BE TRAMPLED IN THE RUSH. THE CHOICE IS YOUR OWN."

He stepped from the dingy alley and lit a Lucky Strike. He looked across the street at the pool hall with the gaudy Hudson parked in front. It all seemed to come together and he knew the answer. In his mind the pool hall vanished and was replaced with something self-explanatory.

A vision of a winged warrior, mounted on a world engulfed in flames and brandishing a burnished sword with a tip of gleaming crimson, appeared at the opening of the Billiards House and exploded before his eyes. It was an angel with ice blue eyes holding the sword of righteousness, tipped with lightning and filled with anger. With a flick of its powerful wings, it overflowed into the center of the street, and arose into the night sky. The warrior's wings encompassed the entire world and contained the fire to a smoldering ember. When it swept back its wings of pure ivory, the unrestricted flames exploded above the horizon. And with that explosion came Nicholas' revelation that what he needed was not a mere spark but an explosion. His plan had to be powerful. The rat should show fear and know that wherever he turned, Oscar could be waiting.

The second week in June had arrived and school was over. It was time for summer vacation, going to the beach at Belle Isle and just hanging out. That was what Nicholas now planned for the summer, not hiding in his grandmother's bathroom, not being a fearful creature that stepped tentatively from the path of a rodent and not someone who lived under the protection of his older brother.

It was 11:30 pm and the pool hall closed at midnight. A light rain fell, coating the street with a sugary glaze. The incandescent streetlights, spaced two to a block, reflected off the gleaming brown hood of the Hudson parked in its official spot out in front of The Billiards House.

Above the Hudson, on the roof of the pool hall, Nicholas stood surrounded with the gas cans that he had spent two weeks accumulating and hiding on the roof. A steady rain ran off Nicholas' head and soaked the back of his neck, chilling him and enhancing an already prominent case of the shakes. He grabbed three cans and walked across the roof to the rear of the building. He carefully opened the containers and poured the gasoline gently over the back stairwell that covered the entrance to Bull's apartment and the back doorway to the Billiard House. He emptied two more across the roof surface. The gasoline was soaking into his cardboard shoe liners; he had to hurry. Next to his feet were eight gasoline filled balloons, four with self-made wicks. Two additional balloons were already placed near a newly cut opening in The Department of Public Works fence across Warren Ave. They were his safeguards. He was trying to cover everything and prevent a mistake.

He placed three of the filled balloons with wicks in a knapsack and hung them loosely over his shoulder, the fourth he held gently in his left hand. The significance of that balloon was overwhelming. It was time to stand up, time to become the aggressor, time to show the rat something in Nicholas' eyes that would cause it to run in fear. It was time to play *Topsy*.

He had spent weeks running this through his head. It was easy in his head. He dreamed of the warrior and the spiraling sword. He saw his enemies running from him and felt himself being fearless. But now moments before he had to finally act, he was shaking, knowing if they caught him, after what he planned, they would surely kill him. The shakes intensified and a premonition of standing alongside his grave seemed inexplicitly real. The thought of being fearless disappeared, replaced by a strong foreboding of terror.

The moments ticked by in which he was at once ready and then he wasn't. He could change his mind but he would have to keep doing what he was doing. Every time he went out, he'd have to make sure they weren't waiting down the street or right around the corner. That wasn't what he wanted. You either stood still or you moved forward, there was no going back in life. He wanted them to worry about going out, or better yet, worry they were going to be inside a car when it exploded.

The wick on the large balloon, held in his hand, made a perfunctory decision. It was starting to get wet. It wouldn't work much longer. He stood as if in a trance wondering if he had the guts to go through with it, while asking himself if he wanted to continue the way he was, and finally thinking that maybe next time they would take him someplace besides the hospital.

It was 11:45 Saturday night when Bull stepped out of the pool hall for a cigarette. The noise and the smoke inside, even though he probably contributed to more than half of the hanging cloud, aggravated the hell out of him. Besides, he'd been in the place most of the day and needed a breather. The rain drizzled off the overhang like a thin sheet of cellophane that refused to be broken. He stayed inside the drip line and watched the lazy stream of cars with their noisy sporadic wiper blades thumping a moody, rhythmic tune into the drenched night.

Bull knew he was very cool because he heard music everywhere. The rain beating on the pavement, the cymbals of water vibrating off the spinning tires on the passing cars, the wiper blades – swish - swish – swoosh, the cherry balls, pinging like c-notes from a piano on the break. Everything man! Cool! Even his shoes clicked along with their own beat. They were new, wing-tipped diarrhea brown, needle-toed points bought at Cancellations down on Randolph Street. If you wanted badass shoes in Detroit, you went to Cancellations. He lit up and, staying close to the building, walked away from the light coming from the White Tower Hamburger Haven next door. Raindrops had beaded on his new kicks and the spots were glistening like ice crystals on rich leather.

The thumps turned him. They were like hand strikes on a conga drum. Bull was in the process of taking one step forward and paused halfway through the movement. When he thought about it later it became difficult to remember, probably because the glare did something to him.

Four large gasoline filled balloons hurled down onto the Hudson, bursting open on contact and covering the car with gasoline. With his Zippo, Nicholas lit the wick on the one in his left hand, dropped it onto the car's hood and ran frantically toward the rear of the roof. His feet hit the balcony deck and he slid down the stairway. He paused behind the building long enough to watch the second wicked balloon hit Bull's stairwell and the back of the building explode in a wall of flame. The third arched high over the burning balcony and landed within two feet of the open gas cans on the roof.

Nicholas ran.

First the four conga strikes, thump - thump – thump and then the Hudson, six feet in front of him, exploded. Bull's new shoes became two flaming fuckin' fireballs, glowing fuckin' red-orange on the end of his fuckin' screaming legs. A huge air-sucking WHOOSH reverberated across the street and flames shot up above the second story roofline like cannons going off on V-Day. He stumbled backwards and hit the front wall, franticly pounding at the fire running up his legs as the occupants from the pool hall poured out into the street.

The Hudson was covered in flames while fire licked the tires like a big dog cleaning a gravy bowl. The cement under the Hudson's gas tank, dry only moments before was now burning like a high schooler on prom night in the back seat of papa's borrowed Lincoln.

Deiter Hagen was the last one out of the pool hall. He instinctively backed away, a constant diatribe of profanities spewing from his mouth. Across the street, he saw the DiCicci kid leaning against a fence, watching the fire. He was flipping what appeared to be a large melon-size ball in his hand. He paused for a moment and nonchalantly extended his left arm, slowly rolled his hand upward and with a snappy movement gave Deits the finger.

The gesture both infuriated and motivated Deiter Hagen. He charged past the Hudson and darted recklessly across the street.

Nicholas spread the opening in the fence apart and pushed through. He had been afraid it would be a problem, afraid he might get hung up. He had made the cut the night before and bent all the edges back to prevent snagging his clothing. He had practiced moving through the gate and it had been fine but practice and reality exist on different planes. Once through the fence he knew how to get out of the lot. It was used as a parking lot for city buses. The last bus in the northwest corner concealed another flap in the fence.

The fact that it was Deits running across the street was at the same time both more than he'd hope for and also more terrifying. Nicholas got through the cut fence and ran back ten feet. He flipped open the Zippo and held it poised. He wanted the balloon to ignite in the opening. The fire would deter anyone from following him. His plan was to arrogantly walk away, get across the lot and behind the last bus. From there, he would be gone long before anyone had a chance to catch him.

Deits was half way across the street running like a thoroughbred sprung from the starting gate. Nicholas thumbed the striker and the wick fizzled, he thumbed it again. Wet! Hit by a raindrop! His thumb frantically worked the round wheel, repeatedly raking it across the flint. Deits dodged a car and was at the curb. He was eight feet from the opening. The lighter finally flared and the wick caught the flame. Deits grabbed the fence and spread the sides apart as Nicholas hurled the balloon.

It struck the fence two feet above the opening and burst. The gasoline ignited and dropped fire upon Deits head and shoulders. He jerked violently upward and caught his neck between the vertical cut of the fencing just as the two balloons lying at the base of the opening exploded like flaming orange cantaloupes. Within moments, his entire body was engulfed in flames.

As Nicholas turned and walked toward the back gate, the image visible to the world, that of a very wet, bony seventeen year old, walking alone in the rain, started to shimmer and then flicker and finally it disappeared.

Turvy!

Three days later and two weeks before Nicholas's eighteenth birthday, a young Police Sergeant, Ben Armstrong, arrived at Nicholas's grandparent's house in Parkside and took him into custody.

Nobody knew who caused the fires. There wasn't any evidence. Both the Billiard House and the Hamburger Haven had burned to the ground. One man, Deiter Hagen, had died and another, Earl Breinig, had been seriously burned, his legs so damaged he might never walk again. Nicholas, because of the threats that Deiter Hagen had made against him, was a prime suspect. According to the witnesses, most of whom were distracted trying to escape the fire, nobody had any idea where Deits was going when he ran across the street.

Sergeant Armstrong seemed to think certain things provoked other things and there wasn't too much, without further proof, they could do about it. Besides Armstrong had more than his share of problems with the young thugs that hung around the Billiard House and he was glad to see the place gone.

The prosecutor's office felt otherwise. The talks went on for several weeks. It took that long to finally settle the matter and cut a deal the prosecutor could live with.

One week after Nicholas' eighteenth birthday, Sergeant Armstrong marched him through the bus depot in Detroit and placed him on an out-of-town bus destined for the Marine Corps base in Georgia.

CHAPTER EIGHT
Khe Sanh
1968

I t was raining. A rain you thought could go on forever, as if the clouds were a hundred feet deep and thick as dense cotton. It was the natural condition of this country. If it stopped, you might wonder *What's wrong?*

It dripped off your helmet, ran over your shoulders, seeped through your shirt, sucked into the skin, ran down your spine and discouraged your entire body.

His knapsack was flattened as if he left everything back where he came from or else he didn't have much to begin with. It was slung low over his left bony shoulder and bounced with a staggered rhythm each time one of his feet sucked out of the ubiquitous bog.

The bunker was approximately fifteen feet long and ten feet wide erected in what could only be described as a pothole of mud. It was constructed of stacked sandbags with a door hung in front for an entrance. Over the door was a makeshift sign with a single word painted haphazardly, "HeadQtrs". He knocked and waited. This is where they sent him. He had not requested a transfer. It just happened. He had no idea. There was a long unwelcome pause before a hollow reply reverberated in the sticky, wet, hot morning air, "Come in."

As opposed to walking, he slid through the door, as if the mud had somehow lubricated his way, removed his helmet and stopped in front of a desk made of empty ammo crates, topped with a sheet of warped plywood and piled shoulder high with military mumbo jumbo. A walnut plaque with a tarnished brass plate embossed with the name *Lieutenant Andrew S. Carlton'* sat in front of the clutter and looked like it had been carried across continents and suffered in the bowels of the earth.

The man seated behind it all was of medium build with a worn, unshaven, creviced face and tired eyes that spoke of too many answerless days. They lingered momentarily on the desk as if they didn't want to look up and see the reality.

"Private Nicholas DiCicci reporting for duty, sir."

Another pause, the Lieutenant looked up slowly at the skinny kid and shook his head knowingly. His look carried volumes, the deep fissures in his face said even more. He could write a library. The kid before him listed as nineteen years old but looked more like sixteen. His papers listed him as one hundred and fifty pounds. Carlton guessed closer to one forty. His helmet dangled loosely from his left hand, the face had mud spots interspersed with a juvenile attempt at a beard. His eyes looked at the Lieutenant's face but refused to focus, wandering away and taking in the room in a quick and sporadic manner. For a brief fleeting moment, an emptiness filled the room and Carleton felt like, moments before, he was still alone.

"Do you have any idea why they sent you here, private?" he asked.

"No sir."

"For some obscure reason that possibly only God can answer, and I doubt even that, your CO thought you'd be a service to your country. He also thought, for an equally inexplicable reason, you'd be good at this."

"Yes sir."

"Hmmm." He seemed to be weighing his words. "I can't begin to imagine what he was thinking."

"No sir."

"I know someone must have explained this to you already but I'll do it again." A deep, tired breath, "This is a sniper unit and being a sniper is the toughest job in this man's army," he paused a moment again, thinking of rows of dead waiting to start the journey home to waiting relatives and loved ones. "Do you know what your job is going to be out there private," he said, emphasized with a slow sweep of his arm.

"To fight the enemy, sir?"

"No, private, that's an answer for the heroically inspired and we ship them home weekly in body bags. Your job is to *just* stay alive. If more of us stay alive then they do, we win." Another staggered paused. "Remember *that* and you might stand a small chance. Forget it and you'll be in a body bag within the week."

"Yes sir."

"Report to First Sergeant Mallory and give this to him," he said as he handed the kid his replacement orders while looking back down at his desk. "You'll find him to the left in what is the mess shack. Now, get out of here."

"Yes sir."

"And good luck, private."

But it was too late, somewhere between the "sir" and the "And" the private had disappeared.

He turned left toward the mess shack, another sandbag bunker, five high and six deep, covered with the standard marine issue torn and mildewed camouflage netting. It was going to be a job just getting there. The mud was deep enough to be considered a long way below sea level. Every step threatened to bridge his boot tops. He pulled his foot out of another deep foothold. It sounded like a huge "slurp". He thought he could hide in that.

The rain continued. The sky hung heavy with low clouds that reminded him of balls of gray cotton candy impaled on the tops of splintered, burnt trees. The landscape was like something he would imagine on another planet. Heavy mortar holes filled with debris and shrapnel from direct hits on heavy artillery were everywhere. Garbage filled everything else.

Really, not much different than where he came from.

According to the helicopter pilot that dropped him twenty minutes ago, if he got to the next shack, without stepping into a mud hole and being sucked into the earth's core then he would most likely be rewarded with the unlucky distinction of being shot by a NVA later that night.

The private had arrived at Khe Sanh, and immediately and correctly labeled a FNG 'Fucking New Guy'. He was a replacement for an already depleted platoon of Marine snipers and became the newest addition of the 'Bushmasters', a group of highly skilled jungle soldiers, or "Carlton's Crazy Men," as they were called throughout the encampment. The 'kid' as he was instantly tagged, because of his youth and questionable experience, immediately made the seasoned squad members nervous. One look at him and the thought, *I don't want that watching my back*, became an *I'm not going home* idea.

If command was sending them in this young, then maybe they were losing this fucking war. The kid was jokingly told by some of the 'crazies', with a definite hint of reality, that he'd never get old enough to be called a 'man'. The Lieutenant wasn't wrong. Being a Bushmaster was the toughest assignment in the division. Regulars rarely volunteered. It was generally accepted that any marine who signed on, definitely deserved a free psychiatric evaluation. Someone with the hero mentality who thought he was going to win the war single-handedly, or possibly, one of the rare few who actually signed on to die. They were quickly wrapped in neat body bags and shipped out on the next C-130.

Consequently, replacement soldiers the top brass felt could handle the job, were transferred in. They were sought out from the very beginning. Enlisted men whose situation was akin to the shanghai surprise tactics of the early merchant marines and navies in distress. They were the men who had caused enough trouble back home that local judges were urged to offer them the choice of incarceration or serving their country. Most opted out of the incarceration, thinking they were smart or tough enough to survive anything, usually they weren't, but occasionally one would arrive who was unwittingly gifted.

As a group, the Bushmasters were proud of their position. There was an additional swagger in their walk and more bravado in their talk. They were given a little more space amongst the regulars, probably because most of the regulars considered them on borrowed time. And with the siege from the NVA, the increased bombing sorties and the nightly squad assignments, most of the incoming mail to Carlton's Crazy's was piling up in the 'undelivered' box waiting to be returned home with a telegram from Main Division Headquarters. If a 'Crazy' wound up in a military hospital in salvageable pieces, he could consider himself lucky.

It was uncertain to everyone, especially Lieutenant Carlton, why such a young soldier would be sent into the thick of the Marine Snipers Corp. The top command said the kid would be 'good' and that was all that Carlton had to go on. Maybe they knew something that wasn't evident to Carlton. He certainly hoped so.

His plans were to send the private out with 1st Sergeant Mallory on the first two excursions. It wasn't special treatment; he did it with all the FNG's but because this kid was so young he felt more of an obligation. What kind of a letter would he write home to the parents of a Marine who looked like he should still be in high school? He told Mallory to keep a watch over the FNG and see if he could keep him alive for a while.

The squads were going out every three days and reporting in whenever they were fortunate enough to arrive back. Radio contact was only allowed under extreme circumstances and rarely was anyone sent out to find the missing. Missing in a sniper squad meant something different than missing in another company and waiting for the whole team to report was agonizing, but expected. There was a detached form of solitary within a sniper company. Everyone worried about the next guy. Everyone agonized over anyone who was missing and everyone knew that outside the wire they were totally alone.

According to the manual, a sniper's job was to disrupt and destroy, to infiltrate behind lines. In this case, behind the NVA machine guns and small mortar bunkers, and make them non-functional for the next day. The object for the Bushmasters was to locate a bunker of NVA, wait for the precise moment when the men in the bunker were looking away in the same direction, and put a bullet through one of their heads. The two or three left would dig for the earth's core and that bunker would, for fear of lifting their heads, become non-functional.

That was the 'Dream Scene', what was preached in the squad meetings by Carlton. It rarely worked. What would often happen, because of the darkness and extreme distance, was the shot would miss and the NVA would attempt to put a 'spot' on you. Then the NVA would move onto your 'spot'. If you realized soon enough that you were a 'spot', you usually had time to relocate and by doing so gained an advantage. If you didn't, - well, you weren't going to receive any more letters from home.

The advantage was even if a kill wasn't recorded by the first shot, the NVA regulars would be out hunting the sniper and the bunker rats would be forced to keep their heads down and not operate as normal. At that time, when the NVA or Bo Doi, as the South Vietnamese called them, were trying to get into the area, neither side moved freely because other Marine snipers would be picking off any moving targets. This was the 'Nightmare Scene'. The classic no show, stay low and move slow situation. At least, if you hoped to walk out of this forest.

CHAPTER NINE

The First Shirt was a large unshaven, swarthy man. He reminded Nicholas of Wallace Berry from the westerns. His every movement echoed through the forest. 'Clumsy' came to mind, like the proverbial bull in a china shop.

"We're going to stick close together tonight. You got that DiCicci?"

"Yes sir, Sergeant."

"I don't want to lose my new replacement the first night. It wouldn't look good on my report," Mallory commented while wiping sweat from his face with an overused yellow handkerchief.

The remark seemed to get the kid's attention. His head did a little twitch and then he blinked while looking off into the distance, like he was listening to something, making the sergeant question why this nervous kid had been sent out with him to die. Most of the time Mallory found himself saying things twice because the kid didn't seem to be listening. And besides that, his weapon looked almost as big as he was, making Mallory wonder what the kid could do with a weapon he was going to have a hard time lifting.

The sky was covered with dense, foamy clouds the color of charcoal dust. The moon and stars had decided to evacuate the area. It was pitch black but the Weather Boys said it was clearing and the bombers would be stacked heavy at zero-dark. The scouting reports said the NVA were moving heavily into the no-bombing zone and setting up mortar bunkers behind a berm line six to seven hundred yards from the base The NVA had been in this close before but not when the sky provided any bombing light to keep them back. Apparently, the NVA had a different weather report.

They slipped through the Marine lines along with ten other snipers and disappeared into a gully, thick with undergrowth, spongy moss and a dampness that soaked through everything.

"Til you get use to this country, I want you to play it very tight. Take no chances. Stay down, always stay down, crawl, kiss the ground until you've got moss in your teeth and dirt in your nose, that way you'll have a chance. Don't try anything funny."

"If they don't see me, I'm okay. Right?"

"Yeah kid. Just don't let them see you. And remember keep your head down so you don't catch a stray."

"Hell, that's no big deal. Especially since they don't even know that I'm here."

"Seems that easy to you, eh kid? Well, let me tell you something. They do know that you're here. Get that through your head real quick or you won't make it through your first night. Another bad report."

"They won't see me. I promise."

"Just keep your head down, DiCicci."

They followed a small creek behind the base and slowly worked their way around the berm line before splitting into groups of three. The kid followed Mallory and Staff Sergeant

Hunwick in silence for another hour. The movement was slow, five or ten yards at a time and then a stop for several minutes before the next advance. Finally, Mallory left the kid on a small rise with instruction to bury himself under the shrubbery and he would pick him up on his way back. Staff Sergeant Hunwick, who had yet to say a word, fanned out to the north while Mallory, sweat and all, moved away toward the east.

The shot missed, coming within inches of the NVA's head and they spotted the muzzle flash. Sergeant Mallory knew that it had been a mistake to take to the trees but he figured, with the exceptionally dark night, he could get away with it and make them pay a little. It hadn't worked. He twisted behind the main trunk and slid quickly down the tree. Gunfire strafed the upper branches just as he hit the ground. Three NVA regulars had already left their guard positions around the bunker and were moving through the thick mahogany and teak tree line, their eyes and muzzles trained on the upper branches of the triple canopy cover. They were armed with Kalishnikovs; Russian made AK 47s. Every ten seconds one of the regulars would strafe the thick foliage Mallory had just vacated, while the other two moved forward. The cycle was quick and efficient and designed to cover a lot of ground in a very short time. Within minutes, they were within two hundred yards. They knew that he was either dead or already on the ground and moving.

Mallory rolled away from the tree base. The undergrowth was thick and moist. The strong smell of mold and wet fungus forced his nostrils to close. *God, I hate this fucking country!*

A farm boy from eastern Kansas, he was used to big spaces. Driving tractors in the bright morning light and seeing a sun that would go on forever. Now, he was crawling beneath the vegetation wondering about a schoolboy he left hidden approximately four hundred yards away.

He found a narrow gully heading in the right direction, which at that point was simply anywhere east and did the four-legged lizard walk for fifty yards. He rested a minute then kept going until he was exhausted.

Two miles to the north the clouds were thinning and the bombers were beginning their initial pass while NVA anti-aircraft tried to contain them. Balloons of white dust and orange fire started to splatter the sky. Between the bombs blowing trees a hundred yards into the sky and anti-aircraft shells exploding, the night sky had become a lovely spotted rainbow of death.

Mallory was moving as quickly as he dared. The forest was hot and thick with moisture. Sweat poured out of him like water draining from a fresh cut willow. He was tired, breathing heavily and well aware that he was thirty pounds overweight. He never could figure out how he gained weight on c-rations. He hated them. At moments like this, he hated everything. The three Vietnamese were probably within a hundred and fifty yards and closing fast. They had spread out and triangulated his position. They were going to flush him out like a rabbit.

He couldn't help but think about the kid. The Bo Doi had come from the west right through the area DiCicci was in, meaning the kid had dug a hole so deep only the maggots could find him or he was already dead and Mallory knew he had brought the NVA right to where the kid was. It was Mallory's fault because an inexperienced kid didn't have enough sense to know when to clear out.

Mallory had to stop thinking about the kid. It was done and he couldn't fix it now. He had to worry about himself. He had several choices, all of which were bad. In the end he decided to stay put. They had him pinned and any movement would betray his position. He decided to let them come to him. Maybe he could change the odds.

An hour passed and nothing. Now he was sure they weren't moving and his instinct told him their plan was to wait him out; kill him when the sun came up if need be. He laid on his back stacking vegetation into the webbing on his helmet while thinking and talking silently to himself. Eventually, he'd have to get his head up to get a fix on his own position and maybe that of the three NVA regulars. He was going to have to take the chance, and that chance would give them a crack at him. Another bad idea!

He stayed down, listening to the leaves, the breeze, anything that made a noise. It was impossible to move through the thick undergrowth without making any sound. He would hear them first. He decided to wait, sit tight and let the night pass. Eventually, they would have to come and get him.

Another hour and he still hadn't seen or heard anything except anti-aircraft shells cracking against his eardrums every time they lit the night sky. That was when he wanted to look but that would be the exact moment they would be looking and three pair of eyes could see three times as much as one pair. He knew they'd be willing to wait him out for days, if necessary. They had unbelievable patience.

He had seen South Vietnamese troops sit in foxholes like statues for days without moving and there were an estimated 10,000 NVA regulars surrounding the base. *God! Ten thousand of these fucked up bastards.* He had to get out of this goddamn country.

A third hour passed and the bombing intensified. Mallory was sure the explosions were killing his brain cells. He had to start moving soon. It would be daylight in three hours and he couldn't afford to be pinned down then or his dog tag would end up as a souvenir hanging around some Vietnamese kid's neck in Hanoi.

He could see it. They'd be standing around doing the circle jerk and laughing. "Hey, looki looki. Some dumb assshoolee Mariney got hids brain full of good Viet Cong bullets. Hah hah ahhhahhh. Stupid assshoolee Mariney!!!" Then they'd throw the tag on the ground and everyone would piss on it.

He thought about the countless patrols he'd been on. This one had gone wrong from the beginning. Experience had always forced him to rely on his senses. When things felt right, he instinctively knew it and tonight nothing felt right. He had felt it from the first moment they had entered the forest. It was different, maybe because he had a rawboned young kid beside him or maybe it was God's way of letting him know tonight was his last. A morose feeling settled on him, intuitively warning him his next mistake would be his last.

The forest had changed, its texture had thickened. Something hung above it, something Mallory had never felt. Dark and sinister as if death was sitting on his shoulders and soon it would climb down and get him. He knew about death. He had seen more than any man should. There was a pervasive smell that accompanied it, not only after it had arrived but even when it was coming. It was here tonight, all around and he was starting to shake.

Mallory's solitude was broken as a small crunch to his left shoved needles through his nerve endings. He gasped and stomach acid burned the back of his throat like a hot iron. He rolled to his left and started to raise his rifle just as the kid dropped through the underbrush and flopped down alongside him.

Mallory was dumbfounded. He stared at the kid speechless. The kid didn't say anything. He didn't even look at Mallory. His head twitched as he looked off the same way he had earlier, like he was listening to something special.

"What the hell! How'd you get in here? I thought you'd be dead by now?" Mallory tried to whisper but his voice had acquired a high falsetto pitch.

"Yeah, it's pretty scary out there."

By now Mallory was wound like a clock, his eyeballs bouncing like they were on mainsprings.

"There are three regulars out there right now and you came right through 'em." Mallory couldn't believe the kid was alive. He not only hadn't heard the kid but DiCicci had found him, walked right in and sat down. How in the hell did he know where Mallory was? He was stunned.

"Yeah, I know. They were hunting you. Almost picked your ass out of that tree," he did something with his mouth that was almost a laugh and it made Mallory pause, "lucky you got this far. It took me a while to find you," DiCicci finished.

"What," he stammered, "how in the hell could you find me? And the three Bo Doi, the NVA regulars?" Mallory gasped.

"They're gone," the private answered. He rolled over on his back, as the night sky exploded in another burst of brilliant orange and red, cupped his hands and lit a smoke, then took a deep drag and passed it to Mallory. "A lot of angels dancing around up there tonight," he added.

"What? What? Who's gone? The NVA?" Mallory stammered again, shaking his head in amazement as he gagged on the smoke and passed it back.

"Yeah, they're gone. No one else around. Not anymore."

"Well, how in the hell? Wait a second, they don't just get up and leave. That's not in their book."

"They were looking for you Sergeant. They couldn't find you. They're gone."

Mallory tried to look out but the vegetation was so thick and he refused to rise up too high. He looked back at the kid with something different in his eyes.

"What angels? I don't see no angels, eh? All I can see are fucking Cong devils," Mallory said, not believing what had just happened.

"No, I don't see 'em either but if you listen you can always hear 'em."

"Well, what the hell are they saying?" Mallory answered not knowing what else to say.

"That maybe we should get out of here, Sergeant."

"Yeah, yeah," Mallory stammered, "Let's get the fuck out of here."

For some reason the kid now led the way and Mallory followed. The private seemed to flow through the vegetation, like a soft breeze. Nothing moved as he moved. Mallory stayed low and tried not to disturb the thick vegetation but the branches beneath his feet cracked, small hidden birds left their nest and clouds of insects exploded as bursts of disturbances when he passed.

Fifteen yards behind where he had remained hidden, he caught a glimpse of the body of a NVA regular. The same as the three that were hunting him. It was in the thick undergrowth and if Mallory hadn't been so tightly wound, if his head wasn't rotating like a spinning top, he would have missed it completely. Mallory paused behind the kid long enough to see the small caliber puncture wound in NVA's left temple with very little blood leak. He had died instantly and Mallory realized he had never heard the gunshot.

And the smell of death was still with him!

If anyone said the new recruit was strange, well – that would get an affirmative nod, normalcy would raise eyebrows.

Private DiCicci spent the following day cutting pieces of khaki and brown strips of material from shipping bags. He also found discarded potato sacks at the base dump and blood stained green scrubs from the infirmary. He cut pieces into three-inch long nondescript shapes and loosely stitched them on his utilities. He ended up looking like a walking tree with multi-colored leaves flapping in the breeze.

It must have worked because, except for Mallory on that first trip, no one ever saw the kid once he entered the forest. The private had become invisible. After two weeks most of the Bushmasters were scrounging for material and sewing patches during their free time. Everyone agreed the regular camos worked fine but the new version was unbelievable. The kill rate was going up and the fatality rate going down.

The kid was not only strange; nothing about him fell in the range of predictability. He was unique. He always stayed alone and ate alone. He refused the c-rations. He said the pork tasted like fish, the chicken tasted like fish, the potatoes tasted like fish and even the fruit had a salty taste. He tried the c-ration spaghetti but declared that it wasn't Italian enough for him.

Every night his routine was the same. He passed on everything and eventually would whip himself up a large bowl of hot cereal. There were two choices, oatmeal and what he seemed to prefer most, plain hot Ralston. He'd sit huddled in the darkest reaches of the mess like a freshman in a room full of seniors, or in some filthy foxhole in the company of the ever present rats, quietly eating cereal and talking to himself, always talking to himself. The cereal created the nickname 'Ralston' and within the platoon it stuck.

The strangest thing about the kid was the relationship he had developed with the South Vietnamese that were attached to the base as scouts and advisors. He would sit with them during his free time and listen to their stories, picking their brains on Vietnamese customs and working on the language. He also made a study of individual mannerisms. It was mentioned that the private had even started to walk like a Vietnamese.

Within weeks Mallory reported to Carlton that the kid's eyes must have been narrowing because he acted more Viet than American. He also told Carlton about the 'Ghost' that, according to the Viet scouts, was scaring the hell out of the NVA.

CHAPTER TEN

There was a time, minutes past, years gone by and centuries forgotten buried in the lore of South Vietnam when a great War Lord from the north would ride with his mighty army into this small valley of Khe Sanh and exact tribute from the farmers that made their lives harvesting the terraces on the fertile slopes. Times were good, the harvest baskets full and the War Lord would always leave rich in tribute, while the peasants would struggle with having enough food to see them through the winter months.

The legend spoke of a farmer, a man of ample land, blessed with three strong sons and an exceptionally beautiful daughter who had caught the attention of the War Lord. The Great Lord had, on several occasions, generously offered to take the young girl into his household as one of his many wives. This would greatly help the family. There would no longer be an expected tribute. The family would be greatly favored and endowed with exceptional wealth. But, alas, to her father's great relief, she had repeatedly refused.

The War Lord over the years became increasingly angry at the refusals and continued to raise the tribute demanded from the family until they bordered on abject poverty and starvation.

Finally, unable to reason with the unyielding farmer and in a fit of rage, the War Lord overran the farm and took the daughter to be his own. Still she refused and the father and brothers fought valiantly until in a violent act of terror, the evil Lord had them strung up in the village square. Their hands were lashed behind their back and their feet tied tightly together. Then their nostrils were skewered with bamboo splinters, tied to a strong rope and stretched to a large tree branch running horizontally above their heads. They were pulled erect until they were suspended on their toes. When they could no longer move without ripping their faces apart, their wives and daughters were repeatedly raped before their eyes. The sons viciously fought against their restraints until their noses were torn off and their faces ripped apart.

Then the evil Lord slaughtered the entire family, leaving the death of the beautiful daughter until last so the village people would see what denial of his wishes would cost them.

The father, with his last breath, cursed the evil lord with death and promised eternal revenge on him and his army. He vowed to come back from his grave and kill all from the north that came into this valley.

Nguyen Phren came from a small mountain village, in North Vietnam, steeped in tradition and folk lore and he remembered the story well as he crouched beside the 60mm mortar and tried to present as small a target as possible. The mortar bunker was hidden in dense cover at the edge of a small glade. A thick canopy and crowded undergrowth supported the camouflage netting over the bunker. Four man teams operated the fast moving mortar squads. Nyugen carried the mortar, while Truong, his dear friend, carried the mortar shells. Two regulars, Bao and Ngo, armed with Kalishnikovs, provided small arm protection against US Marine patrols and snipers. They also helped carry supplies and assisted in locating targets.

Nguyen was a scholar and a teacher at the school in his small village. He had not wanted this war and had only joined because Truong had coaxed him. They would return heroes. Truong promised that all the young girls in their village would want to be the wives of such famous men.

The war was supposed to be brief and he should have been home a long time ago but he had learned that as life goes, so goes a man's plans for the future. There would be no young girl from the village because he was now growing old.

He had been at war for many years and had seen much in this long battle against the south and the capitalist Americans. Nyugen had come to know the emptiness of this war, from the deaths of many to very small moments of one, all brave hearts that ceased to exist with no benefit to the world or to those that loved and depended upon them.

Now it had come for him. Bright explosions filled the sky and he could see the moments of death within the bunker. He shivered in terror and prayed that it would be quick. He thought of his mother and small brothers and his sister back home. He had been a good son. He had sent home all the money that he could spare, keeping only that which he needed to sustain himself. He hoped they would remember him well and that his status as a soldier would bring respect to the family. And he hoped the 'Ghost' would be merciful as he had been to his fallen comrades.

Truong was sitting with his back against the wet earth and it appeared that he had needed to stop and rest during the heavy shelling. There was blood flowing slowly from a hole in the side of his temple. Bao had died behind a stack of old shells, while he was franticly dropping shells down the hot mortar tube and Ngo had died immediately after him.

It was truly "The Ghost of Khe Sanh". Nguyen was an educated man and had not believed such an exaggerated myth but now he knew it was true. The Ghost walked unseen throughout the forest of Khe Sanh and in his search for eternal revenge, killed the soldiers of the north.

Now, somewhere close, the Ghost waited before he continued his deadly traverse of the black Vietnamese night. The forest around him had become a cemetery where thousands had died. It was believed that the Ghost relished the smell of the rotting corpses so vigorously that he was obsessed with adding to their growing number. The forest floor was covered with the rotting dead and their overbearing stench filled the air and made each breath an act of nauseating survival.

Four nights ago the Ghost had killed seven soldiers. Their noses had been cut and their faces removed. This was yet another night to fulfill the legend, another night to seek revenge for the daughter of a good man, another night for the soldiers of the north to die.

Now the Ghost waited for Nyugen Phren to give up his soul. He would soon come to cut the noses of his companions. Invisible, he would move through the trees. No matter how hard one looked, you could not see him. Silently he struck and ghastly was his mutilation. Nguyen trembled and softly cried. He cried for his friends and for himself and for the people of the north. How could they ever hope to win this terrible war? How could they ever hope to defeat the round eyes with their constant bombs and the 'Ghost of Khe Sanh'?

Ralston, less than ten yards away, lay amongst a thicket of bramble and berry bushes. His improvised camo outfit ruffled slightly in the night breeze. The sky above appeared to be layered with black soot and, where an occasional star would glimpse through, the reflection was that of a red ruby blinking in the center like the eye of God.

He had waited patiently for the bombing raid to begin. Each new victim, always the soldier at the farthest point from the front of the bunker, was held above his gun sight until a fierce explosion would tear a gap in the blackness and, for a split second, light the ground below and shatter the silence with an ear piercing explosion. At that moment the small caliber gun with a muzzle suppressor would buck slightly in his hand, the victim would drop and the blackness would once again descend. It was done with such precision that the remaining soldiers rarely knew that one of their own was down.

Contrary to what the snipers were taught, there was never a long shot. What they were waiting for never came. The sniper rifle was rarely fired. The Ghost lived within the contradiction: be where you cannot be, fill the unknown space, kill at the most unsuspecting time.

But even more so, the Ghost wanted to be amongst them, he wanted to see their faces. He himself was not sure why. It was something that, in later years, would plague his consciousness because he had always known even without being aware of the why, that he wanted to touch their fear.

There was something that they could give him, something at the moment of their greatest fear that he desperately needed. That something took him back to a small kitchen in an upstairs flat with a floor covered in blood. Once, he had even reached out and laid his hand on the cheek of a Bo Doi. It was a gentle touch like a mosquito lightly landing just before the needlelike proboscis plunged in. The Bo Doi had reached up to swat the pest away and as he turned his head, looked right into the muzzle of a silenced pistol. That moment, just before the man died, Ralston needed.

He had learned on his first night, the Bo Doi regulars were not good at very close distances. They were trained to look out, to see dangers at the longest of bullet ranges. They would hide within the perimeter of the bunker with binoculars scanning the tree line and hill outcroppings between two to four hundred yards away. The grasses rustling at their feet, the leaves shaking lightly near their cheek did not concern them. The .22 caliber Ruger pistol mounted with a sound suppressor setting one-half inch from their temple was not even conceivable.

Tonight, the last NVA soldier was hunkered alongside his small mortar. He was terrified and the thought of killing him gnawed at Ralston. He momentarily paused but the feeling was short lived. Positions reversed, he knew what the outcome would have been. This enemy placed a low value on life. If Ralston set a standard higher than that of the North Vietnamese, he would no doubt be their next victim. Besides the 'Ghost' must be allowed to grow if he was to be able to move more confidently within the bomb-free zone.

The center post on the pistol nestled between the notched rear site and settled on the man's forehead. Ralston started the slow squeeze. He could feel the man's fear; the tears had formed at the corners of his narrow eyes. Again, Ralston held back.

The man stood slowly, his hands held above his head, rising from a squat position, to one of being half bent over, like a submissive wolf approaching the pack leader. He knew the 'Ghost' was watching and he was begging for his life.

The post never left his forehead.

He waddled toward the edge, his ass dragging in the dirt and his heels digging into the rich black loam that formed the bottom of the bunker.

"No shooty, no shooty. I solly," he said in pidgin English. "I solly." He had reached the bunker's edge and hesitantly looked around. Then, with his foot placed on the top edge of the bunker, in one motion he shoved himself upward and bolted out of the bunker. One, two, he counted them, three long strides and a rush toward freedom. He was out and he could see the cut to the pathway they had used to enter the bunker. Only two more strides and he would be into the path between the tall trees. And then he was there. Nguyen had reached the pathway. It was brighter there, much brighter. Like the gateway to a temple, it shone with brilliance. In the middle of the night, it was so bright, so white and so red.

Ralston ran the tip of his K-Bar just above the lip of the last soldier and placing his index and middle fingers into the nostrils pulled sharply upward, tearing the nose up into the eyelids. Within several days, they would be found. The legend would continue to spread and the NVA night patrols would hide more and hunt less.

It was April and the Ghost had raged throughout the hills of Khe Sanh for the seventy-seven days the American base had been under siege. Operation Pegasus and the tremendous battle which ensued had reopened the route to Khe Sanh and the Marines were freed. Once again private DiCicci had been given his orders and tomorrow he would be gone. This was his last night out.

The NVA were rapidly vacating the valley. Small squads were covering their retreat. The Bo Doi were still there but in far fewer numbers. The marines pursued them constantly during the day, relentlessly forcing them to fight a retreating battle. But there was no rest for the retreating Bo Doi because something else hunted them at night, something that no soldier had ever seen. At night the forest became deadly still and infinitely more terrifying. Now the dead with their mutilated faces were found miles north, right up to the edge of the North Vietnamese staging areas.

Those who eventually made it back home would carry with them the horrific story of a living ghost who single handedly had terrified the machine gun and artillery battalions of the NVA. They had lost thousands in the vicious onslaught from the Americans but the Ghost had killed more. The count could not be totaled but the legend had grown exponentially. The Ghost had exacted unbelievable vengeance on the soldiers from the north, a deadly payment for the rape and murder of the beautiful young virgin a thousand years ago. No death had ever cost the North more.

Ralston draped the sling over his right shoulder. The Cong lay dead in the thick brush at his feet. The bullet had entered at the rear center of the skull, soft-nosed expanding, it didn't exit, exploding the brain, — jelly. He bent down, slipped his knife from the sheath and precisely, with the expertise of a surgeon who had done this many times removed the head. Then he quickly sharpened a stake and jammed the head down upon it. He listened again, the second time in the last minute. They were nearer.

The noises came from the ridge above. The dead one had two others in his squad. They had heard the report of the rifle. He had used it to draw them in. They were coming, but slowly. Orders forced them forward but self-preservation made their steps hesitant. They wanted to leave, to finally go home.

He thought about them for a moment. He was leaving. This was his last night out and tomorrow he'd be gone. This senseless war would not be his anymore. He would be leaving this beautiful, horrifically scarred and maimed country, pocked marked with bomb craters, mortared flattened forest and a defoliated blasphemed landscape. It belonged to the unfortunate Vietnamese people and the bureaucrats in Washington who would never see it. He paused with that thought. Another tribute to man's protective investment in the planet.

The Cong were closer. He placed the impaled head upright next to the body where they would see it. Then ran his fingers over into the blood soaked head, down into nostrils and with one slit tore the face upwards. A warning, that no place in this forest could the Cong walk, without raging the Ghost. They would leave the area immediately when they found the head. The Ghost would watch them and this time he would let them go.

Finally for the last time, as silently as he came almost three months ago, the private disappeared into the thick, war blackened forest of Khe Sanh.

On April 8, 1968, the bloody siege of Khe Sanh ended and Carlton's Bushmasters headed south along the Ho Chi Minh Trail. The young private did not go with them. It had been only eleven weeks, but in that short time the legend of the 'Ghost of Khe Sanh' had spread across the front lines and upwards to high command.

The Head of Special Ops in Saigon made a request that the private, nickname "Ralston", be transferred to a forward unit of the Green Beret for additional training and Private Nicholas DiCicci left as quickly and as silently as he had come.

CHAPTER ELEVEN
Detroit 1985

I t was 5 am and Sister Mary Elizabeth hurried down the narrow third floor corridor toward the stairwell, her left foot, supported by a decrepit white oak cane, dragging painfully. It only took a couple of minutes to get to the church, down to the first floor landing, out the side door and across the narrow oak lined street, but as usual she was last. One of the younger nuns would always wait to accompany her. She never liked walking the hallways in the convent alone in the dark. Today it was her dear friend, Sister Mary Francis who escorted her. They hurried along as briskly as her body allowed and although Mother Superior understood her disability, she didn't approve of slackers.

The older and smaller of the two she trailed slightly behind, straining to keep up. The cane gave support to a shortened left leg, the lasting result of a childhood bout with polio, an illness which helped define her life's vocation. Her father with a definite smell of the old jack on his breath to mingle with the sweat and stink of an Appalachia coal mine always told her, "No man is ever going to marry a gimp." Not that she would have forsaken God's calling had the opportunity presented itself, but then the chance never did.

Her father wasn't right about much but he was right about that. Some thoughts never leave your mind, especially those given to a child. Like a blood stain that seeps under your skin and taints the bone beneath, they stay forever.

There had never been a boy that presented even the vaguest opportunity to question her choice. The blood that she might have hoped for was the small drip from her hymen, that could have given the promise of a different future, that might have shown hope for a child of her own. That blood was still there, encased in its unprecious shrine.

The polio struck at the age of five and its lasting effect left her sitting on the curb watching other kids playing kick the can, cheering from the upper rafters as the high school swim team vied for the regional championship and sitting on the porch watching a limousine filled with classmates arrive across the street for the neighbor girl to cart her away to the senior prom.

Today, the first light of morning found the lone window on the back wall of the convent, painting a ragged checkerboard on the drab opposing wall. The window and the wall were inward reflections of the convent, spotlessly clean but showing years of hard wear and inadequate maintenance.

The two sisters of the Dominican order had been at the church for many years and this morning's walk was a routine of forgetful repetitiveness. The sameness was broken as they paused by the solitary window, their combined weight forced the ancient oak boards to squeak like a mouse caught in a spring trap. It was a strange eerie sound, one they knew instinctively to ignore. For years the convent had been the source of "strange sounds, shuffling, rumblings and night time vibrations," at times filling sleepless nights with an eerie dread and at other times sounding as if music was playing in the deep furnace cellar, two levels below the ground.

Years ago the Monsignor had requested that the archdiocese have the premises inspected, always to be denied because of the prohibitive cost but even more so because the thought itself was a frivolity that was a reflection of ancient superstitions totally unacceptable with the beliefs of the church hierarchy and the Catholic faith. It was simply deemed that "The House of God is not subjected to strange sounds and shuffling."

Together, they peered out across the thin gravel playground that faded into a string of old rundown bungalows. Their attention was drawn to a large limousine parked beneath the dilapidated lamp post that stood at the corner of the graveled baseball diamond and the alley that ran behind the convent community.

The playground itself was no longer used. Saint Joseph's was an old parish, most of the parishioners were aging, their children grown and moved away and the sight of the long, black car gave them pause, if only that it was starkly out of place in the retiring shadows of the bluish dawn.

Two bulky men got out of the car, opened the trunk and dumped a large bag resembling a potato sack onto the coarse cement. Across the vacant lot damp with the morning air, they could be heard talking quietly to each other as they dragged the bag between two large cement trash containers. Something inside the bag moved and the nuns, with thoughts of their immediate urgency forgotten, stopped.

The aroma of oily cement, moist green mold and maggot infested garbage, stuck to the wet morning air and the larger of the two men covered his nose as he opened the sack and pulled the corded top down.

A man, his hands bound behind his back; his feet tied together and something shiny covering his mouth, knelt in the lamp's reflection. His faced was pock marked as aged cheese and his eyes rolled like dice bouncing off the backboard of a craps table. At that moment, a small, darkish man, dressed in a jogging outfit, slid from the back seat of the limousine.

Sister Mary Elizabeth grabbed the latch above her head and tried to push the old double hung window up. It moved up three inches and then stuck, allowing her little room to bend down and holler through but sufficient enough for the voices from below to find the narrow opening and echo down the empty hallway.

"What in the world is going on? What are they doing to that poor man?" she remarked to her younger companion, but Sister Mary Francis didn't hear her. She was already in a rush down the stairwell.

Sister Mary Elizabeth leaned her cane against the wall and without taking her eyes off the site below, she grabbed at the window again and this time she gave it a harder push.

"How do you like my outfit Bobby? Pretty nifty, eh?" the words rolled across the still playground. His hair was slick with gel. His head craned forward, his nose hooked downward and his eyes had a nervous, piercing intensity. Something about his presence ran a shiver up Sister Mary Elizabeth's shortened left leg and twisted backbone. She suddenly felt nauseous.

His face paid tribute to the gargoyle of doom carved at the highest peak on the temple of death. He resembled the beaked raptor that courses on spiked wings above the villages of man to feed off defenseless prey and rotting carrion.

"It's waterproof." He strutted arrogantly around the kneeling man. "You see Bobby, I don't want you crying all over my suit, and so I bought this outfit. Nothing gets through this stuff. Rain, snow, piss, whatever — you know, hah, hah, hah, ha — not even blood." The short laugh chortled in the base of his throat; a raucous chuckle and his eyes glistened with something akin to perverted sexual expectation. Sister Mary Elizabeth shuddered as she listened. "They call it Gore-Tex, use it on the space shuttle and that kinda shit. Real good stuff."

White surgical gloves, the cuffs pulled over the Gore-Tex jacket, covered his hands. He even wore a pair of surgical scrub shoe covers.

"You ever cut a man's throat, eh? Probably not. You never had big enough cojones." Like a peregrine looking down from several hundred feet, he circled the kneeling man, completely detached but enjoying the anticipation.

"You see, you were always a pussy, Bobby, a small time pussy that sucked off me. And now you're a prick that steals from my family. You shoulda known I wouldn't like that." He paused and looked around for a moment. Dawn was breaking over the eastern sky. He had to hurry. This was not the best place.

"Look where you're at, Bobby. It's your old house. I brought you back to the old place. I think people should stay with their own kind, in their own neighborhoods. Eh, you know what I mean? That way everybody is family."

His eyes flicked in every direction at once. "You remember when we were kids? How we use to play here, in the alley and on the playground, kick the can and stickball. Remember your mama's pizza. Aah, she made the best pizza."

Magically, a large, lock blade knife appeared in his right hand and snapped open like the talon of a hawk. Bobby Falhone's eyes stretched open so wide it appeared they would tear at the corners. Tears streamed down his cheeks and his body shook uncontrollably. A wet spot grew in the center of his pants.

The raptor stepped up to the shaking man, grabbed a handful of hair, stretched his head back and exposed his throat. The blade hand drew back high in an arc.

"Hell," he said, "what you did was stupid, man. You did a bad thing," and the blade hand plunged downward.

Bobby's eyes appeared to explode, his body convulsed and snapped and his unheard screams echoed across the schoolyard and into the walls of the convent. He rolled face forward crashing into the waiting cement. Blood gushed from the four inch long slash, his legs tied together pumped in unison like a child on a pogo stick.

Simultaneously, the window popped up and the side door flew open.

"Oh my God, what are you doing? My God, my God." Sister Mary Francis was running across the schoolyard. Her shouting mingled with screams that somehow fit within the raptor's concept of what it should sound like.

"Stop, stop, my God, please, please" her black and white habit shook with an unknown rhythm, a long wooden rosary clattered at her side like a hickory wind chime and her silver crucifix thumped like a cymbal against her winded breast.

At twenty-five yards, the killer had stripped the jogging suit off. He bent down removed the shoe covers and shook his head in disgust. His eyes flicked everywhere at once. "Where did she come from?" he said aloud, more to himself than his two companions. "This is some bad shit."

Twenty yards ... she was puffing ... large and overweight and out of breath and slowing quickly.

The surgical gloves dropped alongside the twitching body of Bobby Falhone, the blood still pulsing from his jugular like thick red oil.

Sister Mary Francis stopped five yards away. Her mouth was agape, sobbing as she tried to catch her breath, and all the while looking from the quivering body back to the faces of the three assailants.

The small man looked apprehensively at the nun and a moment of confusion spread across his face before he nodded slightly to his two bodyguards. Then he slid into the back seat of the long Lincoln and closed the door.

Sister Mary Elizabeth remained at the top of the stairwell looking out the open window. She was unable to react. Her body shook uncontrollably. It was as if an unknown presence looked down at the two bodies that now laid in the morning stillness. She screamed as Sister Mary Francis raced toward the men but the gunshots silenced her. She tried to yell again but something welled up inside and choked off her words. A voice in her mind kept repeating, "NO, NO".

It stopped her long enough to feel the shaking start in the heart of the convent. It was a slight movement from beneath the ground, but it quickly became a ripple, coursing within the foundation and escalating until it rumbled through the entire structure. It vibrated between the floorboards and through the soles of her shoes. The landing quivered; the building shook.

It breathed.

The air rushed in, as if some huge creature inhaled. It sucked against her habit. Her hemline flapped like being hit by a strong wind and for a moment all the air in the world disappeared.

Then a haunting exhale that hissed through the masonry and wheezed between the cracks in the bricks. It rushed down the dark corridors and howled from the same door that only moments before Sister Mary Francis had so gallantly ran. Gravel filled the air. Dirt and dust swirled in twisted funnels. The two gunmen stood transfixed as a great gust of air pulsed across the playground and pounded against the Lincoln. The car bucked up on two wheels and teetered precariously before crashing back to the ground.

The impact hurled the gunmen against the garbage containers and slammed them to the ground. Horror etched on their faces, they stumbled back to their feet and limped hurriedly to the car. A moment later, the engine started and the Lincoln careened across the alley, colliding with the lamppost in a mad rush to safety.

A cry of anguish, a desperate, mournful sound that ached from some unknown soul poured from the building, pushed the Lincoln down the alley, and like something alive, filled the space between the door and the dead. A dense dust covered the schoolyard and swirling rocks and gravel, from a height of ten to twenty feet dropped rapidly to the ground sounding with a thousand muted clicks.

A minute passed, and still Sister Mary Elizabeth clung to the windowsill, her knuckles bone white, sweat stinging her eyes and tears washing her cheeks. The air subsided, the morning became still again and the light from the damaged lamppost flickered once — twice — and went out.

The voice whispered again, *'TODAY ANGELS CRIED.'*

The face staring dully out the back window of the Lincoln was that of a man about to be executed, walking up the wooden steps of a freshly built scaffold, staring blankly at the swinging noose, before its tightened around his neck, the hood slapped in place and tied, waiting patiently for him to drop into hell. It spoke of eternity and unending pain, nuclear fire and corrosive hot coals that never stopped eating though your flesh.

"A nun," he screamed at no one. The two men in the front seat squeezed their shoulders and sunk a little lower in their seats, their minds blank chambers of a blackened muck. "We just killed a nun! God! What the fuck are we gonna do? A fucking nun, we killed a nun," his fist hammered the top of the seat as the Lincoln made a hard turn onto Mack Avenue.

"What the fuck was that? Did you see that?" The passenger was losing it. He resembled a man locked in solitary for months and scratching to get out.

"Shut up Santee!" said Jimmy.

"Yeah, yeah. But what was that?"

"How the hell would I know?"

"You saw it! You were there! What the hell was that?"

"Shut up, both of you shut up!" said the man in the back. "Oh shit, we killed a nun. Everyone knows you kill a nun, you go straight to hell. You don't even get to see the archangel Michael. Straight down, Oh my God! Shit we're fucked."

"What should we do Boss?" Jimmy asked.

"Just keep driving. Nobody knows. Just drive." And then again, "Shit we killed a nun!"

Santee again, shaking uncontrollably, "What was that, what was that?"

CHAPTER TWELVE
Wednesday

Thick clouds covered the Detroit skyline, thunder rumbled in the western counties and sheets of wet vertical lines, driven by a strong westerly wind pushed toward the city. Another summer storm was rolling in. The weather had been bad for so long anything but a deluge was downright pleasant.

Ben moved brusquely under the ragged awning, pushing past the panhandlers that crowded the doorway. The weather put him in a bad mood and the continuous haranguing from freeloaders didn't help any. They rushed to get out of his way. He knew many of them. Some had better homes than many tax paying citizens. They symbolized the city, a city of graft, crooked politicians, syndicated crime and well-heeled freeloaders. A city being restored around a small hub, financed by outside money, while for miles in all directions everything is rotting with urban cancer. A city in a nosedive pumped up by local newspapers thriving on sports, racism and unrealistic political double-talk and politicians that talk more about building casinos instead of creating jobs. And when jobs are available, they are so low paying that most of the citizens don't think they are worth their effort. Welfare or illegal enterprises always paid better.

Across the street a burnt out warehouse shadowed the neighborhood, piles of debris filled the empty door wells and several stray dogs sat inside watching the crowd. A few dark children played beyond the dogs and an occasional wanting face peered down from the broken windows above. Afraid to look out. Worried that the hell on the outside was worse than the one they lived in.

Another generation in the making, he thought, *another generation to wonder what the hell they did to deserve this, another generation that will do whatever it takes to survive, another generation to think he was the bad guy.*

Shit, he had to work on forming a more positive attitude.

Manuel Perez, his white apron smeared with chili and mustard, stood behind the counter inside the front window putting on his show. Manuel, probably the best Coney builder in the world, had eight styrofoam coney containers filled with dogs laid on his left arm while spooning chili, onions and mustard with the other, somewhere in between he was wrapping and shoving Coney dogs into brown paper carry-out bags. Manuel, his wife and three children had lived in a small two bedroom home east of Grand Boulevard for ten years. He was in his spot behind the counter seven days a week without fail. Cecelia said he had never missed a day. Manuel was an illegal. *Never missed a day! What would the business do without him? The country needed more like him.*

Manuel watched the large detective walk in giving him his standard nod and timid smile. The counter, facing the grill top, was filled with customers finishing their lunch. Lieutenant Ben Armstrong shuffled behind the stools and sat down hard in the third booth from the back. The seat released a large gush of air and collapsed to one third of its normal thickness. Ben let out a great exhausted breath. He glanced at his watch. It read 1:20 pm.

At one-thirty, Harry 'The Weasel' Teasel cautiously stepped into Trendy's stopping just inside the door and looking around.

When it comes to getting free money, Armstrong thought, *the Weasel never misses his time either.*

Glazed and red, the Weasel's beady ferret-like eyes, nervously twitched from side to side. They sunk into his skull and shouted cocaine to anyone who could hear the image. *He looks like he might turn and make a hysterical run at any moment.*

The Weasel tucked a soiled, oversized yellow golf shirt into his baggy jeans while surveying the faces above the stools. A Detroit Tiger's baseball cap perched crookedly on his head, disgust mapped his face and his mouth formed silent predictable words.

Trendy's walls hadn't felt the loving touch of a paint roller in at least two decades. Strips of greasy, yellow transparent packaging tape sealed a long diagonal crack that ran the length of the front window and there was enough bubble gum stuck under the main counter to coat Gratiot Avenue from downtown to 8 Mile Road. The countertop at one time was a yellow flowered formica. Now the surface was indiscernible, worn through the gloss to the hard brown underlayment. The décor was somewhere between Decadent Detroit and Nouveau Depression. It obviously wasn't a priority to Cecelia Bhatti, the Lebanese woman who owned Trendy's or to her customers but it made the Weasel nervous, as did most things.

Several moments passed before he appeared relaxed enough to walk toward the rear of the building. The split red vinyl seat scraped Harry's jeans as he slipped into the booth. He sat down carefully, like he was afraid of squashing something.

"Man, I don't know why you come here. What a craphole! This place is a roach dump."

"I like it. They treat me real nice," Armstrong answered.

The ceiling mounted air-conditioning unit made a strange gurgling sound followed by a couple of ominous clunks. Armstrong pulled down his tie and unbuttoned his collar. He bit into a Coney dog smothered in chili, mustard and onions; his second since he'd sat down.

"Yeah, probably 'cause they give you everything free; 'fraid you'll kick their ass for running their little book, and working their illegal's asses to the bone," Harry twitched nervously, looking away, avoiding Armstrong's eyes. They were dark, strong eyes with thick shaggy brows set in a face chiseled from human concrete that spoke of over thirty years on the streets.

"Well a little book isn't shit compared to some goon leaving his stooge sliced up on a school playground and pumping four shots into a nun, is it?"

Harry shook visibly, "I don't know nothing," he replied, "shit happens every day in this city."

Armstrong talked through his food, while looking over Harry's head and watching Cecelia and the front of the restaurant. Onions smattered with mustard slipped from the corner of his mouth and fell on the table.

"What's coming from the Old Man? How's he feeling about his boy?" Armstrong asked, while picking up the onions and flipping them back into his mouth.

"You shouldn't eat anything that falls on that table. Man you don't know what you gonna catch in this filthy joint," Harry shivered. "Hepatitis is, like everywhere."

"Hasn't got me yet. What's he say?" Armstrong repeated.

"Rumors says he isn't too happy. Actually, Rumors says he's really pissed. The Old Man doesn't want his nephew going down, doesn't want him doing any time but then he'd probably kick Willie's ass if he could get his hands on him. Wasting a nun was stupid. The Old Man's pretty religious. He's a good Catholic."

The old man picked up his cane, leaving the large window overlooking the wide expanse of Lake St. Clair, and walked slowly back to his desk. He liked being behind the desk when he talked business and today, this was definitely business. Bad Business, the kind he'd rather not have. His sister's boy, an uncontrollable little psychopath, a problem since she first squeezed him out, seemed to live his life to test everything around him. Always seeing just how far he could go and to what extent does society have to be pushed before it will push back. And now he was forced to reach outside. An effort totally against his way of doing business but, because of his sister, he was willing to engage but only, as he had told her, this one last time.

He reached for the water pitcher and poured the glass half full. Raising it to his lips, the right hand started to quiver, lately a more frequent reaction. He changed hands. The left hand never shook. Fuck doctors. He put the glass down and pushed the buzzer located on the desk next to his leg.

"Are they here yet Florence?" he rasped.

"Yes Mr. Castobelli. They've been here for ten minutes."

The right hand started a slight quiver, threatening to lose the cane. He quickly placed his left hand on top to control the tremor. Then paused a moment until it subsided. Palsy.

"Then let them in, Florence."

"Yes Sir."

Ten seconds later, Florence opened the door and stepped aside as two very well dressed men entered the room. As the door closed quietly behind them, the two men stopped five feet in front of the desk and stood motionless.

He scowled. It was obvious that he disliked them immensely.

"It seems to be getting easier for you to tell why you constantly fail to achieve my expectations, Mr. Cartolli. I give you a simple job. You, supposedly the best attorney in the whole damn state and my nephew is still in jail. Why is he still there Mr. Cartolli?"

"We're very sorry Mr. Castobelli. Initially it was an easy release, but now the police are saying they've got a witness, another nun. They say she saw everything."

"A nun. Another nun. What nun?"

"An old nun. They say she was with the one that was found dead," he made sure he avoided the other word. "She was still in the building."

"What kind of a lawyer are you? It was pitch black. How could she see anything? An old nun can't see anything in the dark."

"We've told them that. The distance was too far, it wasn't possible but they're hanging tough on this one. The cop Armstrong, he…"

"I don't want to hear about that cop. I've had enough of him." He was on his feet and the veins on his forehead looked like an aneurism about to erupt. His voice was controlled but his anger vivid.

"You go get my nephew out of jail. My sister is very sad about her son being in jail and when she is sad, I am not happy. Get him OUT! And call me as soon as he's out and get him here. No place else. I want him here. Now go."

He turned as they were leaving and looked back out over the lake, using its smoothness to quell his anger. He loved the lake.

He loved the blue flatness and the constant movement. It was dependable and he liked that too.

He didn't understand the youth today. They didn't listen to anyone; parents, grandparents, teachers. Nobody. How many times had he told Willie? Still, he did whatever he wanted and when he got in trouble his mother would come and ask for help. No brains. No respect. He felt the day coming when he would not respond to that cry for help.

As a youth, he remembered running down the brick paved streets of Potenza, the morning chill from the surrounding mountains always biting through his thin jacket. He held the warm bread close. It was his duty, every day, to deliver the bread that his mother had just taken from their oven to his grandfather. And for Giatano, it was always at a full run.

"Hey, Giatano. You going to your grandfathers?" Pietro, his friend, came from one of many narrow streets funneling like wheel spokes into the piazza, running hard to catch up.

"Yes, I'm taking the morning bread to my grandfather."

"Can I come?"

"Yes, but you must wait outside.'

"Why can't I come in?"

"Because my mother says he likes to be alone. He doesn't want to see many people. He doesn't even want to see me every morning."

"Then why are you going. If someone didn't want to see me, I wouldn't go to see them."

"My mother says that it is good for me to go. It shows him respect and he will like that. He will remember it."

"I don't understand why he needs to remember you. You're right there and he can see you anytime."

"I know but my mother says it."

He always remembered respect. He sat back down, thinking someday he'll let the little head case rot in jail. The morning sun reflected blue diamonds like a thousand rosaries across the lake. He turned away muttering to himself, "Armstrong, always Armstrong."

Armstrong stopped eating long enough to show his irritation with Harry's remark. He shook his head in disgust. The Castobelli Family owned the largest commercial real estate company in Southeast Michigan. They specialized in buying, selling and leasing restaurants and small to mid-size manufacturing companies. The company was involved in so many two and three man shops, the IRS couldn't tell which were legit and which were there simply to launder money from Castobelli's statewide drug operations. The thought of everything the Old Man had done over the years was plastered on the face of Armstrong's frontal lobe. It forced him to pause every time he heard the Castobelli name. He shook his head again, trying to clear the images.

Thunder cracked directly above and rain drops marked the broken window with wet shiny spots. *Even God is trying to wash this city clean.*

"Sure Harry, Giatano Castobelli, he's a real religious guy. He's filled a whole damn cemetery by himself. His favorite nephew leaves people sliced up whenever he gets an itch and you think he's the next thing to a priest."

"Hey, what the hell you want from me? Half the cops and every goddamn politician in this town are on his payroll. They probably pray to him. At least they pray to his money. I'm just tryin' to live with it," he paused for a moment. Then added, "and make a few bucks."

The Weasel ran small numbers for Castobelli's organization which gave him access to some of their low-end coke dealers. He occasionally got a freebie but even that didn't help. The coke kept him cash strapped and dirt poor. Consequently, the Weasel sidelined as an informant, something nobody knew except Armstrong, otherwise the Weasel would probably be laying someplace next to a new Gore-Tex jogging outfit.

They were both quiet for a minute, Armstrong, looking toward the front door while working on his third dog. Harry fidgeted. It always took a little time. The Weasel couldn't just spit it out. Like every informant, he had a psychological aversion when talking to cops.

Ben reached into his left breast pocket and slid a C-note across the table. The Weasel pocketed the bill, slipping it into his shirt pocket alongside a duplicate he had received earlier, and immediately relaxed. Tonight just got a lot easier.

"Rumors says, 'The Old Man wants the other nun'."

No one knew who 'Rumors' was, except if anyone needed to know what was happening anywhere in the Detroit, Rumors knew. And Harry had the string to Rumors.

"Well, I guess they had their chance, didn't they," Armstrong replied.

The day after they cleaned up the schoolyard, Armstrong arrested William "The Blade" Morolli, Santee Callucci and James Bedord. The Old Man's attorneys were close behind. It was supposed to be an easy in and out. The Blade should have walked, until the second nun was revealed. It was surprising to everybody that she lived. Even the lawyers looked confused. 'The Blade' and his two bodyguards screwed up. They thought all the noise came from just the one nun. Apparently, no one realized there was a second nun screaming her lungs out from the third floor or God knows what damage they would have done in the convent. Armstrong booked them on one count of first-degree, one count of second degree murder and multiple gun violations. It felt good.

Rumors says, "the Old Man has the word out."

"And his stooges aren't talking. Terrified of the Old Man. No D.A. pleas for those boys. They ran like hell and now they're chewing their own tongues," Armstrong added. "And the Blade — well. he isn't talking to anyone."

"Yeah. Rumors says, 'not even his own lawyers'. Something scared them, but nobody's talking about it. Must have been pretty damn scary though." His blood-shot eyes reflected inward, as if he were seeing something unexpected inside his own mind. "I didn't think 'The Blade' was scared of anything," he added. It was a pausing statement almost a question.

"Maybe he'll find some scary things in the federal penitentiary," Armstrong remarked.

Judge Solvay denied bail and finally, after years of banging his head into the legal wall, Armstrong had one of the Castobelli family and he was determined to make this one stick. "The Old Man's just going to have to live with the fact that the little bastard is going up for life. Isn't that tough shit?" Armstrong added.

"Rumors says 'that ain't going to happen. They're going to get the other nun'. Rumors says, 'She's never going to make it to the arraignment'. Hell, man, most of the cops on the force don't want any part of this shit. Only you and your crew and," he paused and seemed to catch his breath, "you must be nuts."

The arraignment was scheduled for a week from Wednesday and Ben knew it would be tough protecting her even with the Feds around.

"He's going to make a war of it, huh?" Armstrong didn't doubt it. The Old Man doted on the little psychopath. His lawyers had been running roadblock for Willie since the kid was in school. The little psycho even tried to burn the high school down once but some gas cans were conveniently discovered in another kid's car. After that, the high school got lucky. It was too small time for Willie. He just dropped out and now instead of trying to burn down schools, he kills people.

"He wants the other nun," Weasel's eyes twitched and looked everywhere at once, making Armstrong wondered if they could rotate three hundred and sixty degrees. He paused for a second and then looked Armstrong in the eye, an unusual gesture for the Weasel.

"You know you've always been good to me. Never screwed me over and you helped me out of a couple of jams," he stammered. He was having a hard time and it caught Armstrong off guard.

"What the hell is this? After all these years, you're not going to tell me that you love me or something?" Armstrong laughed, a deep rolling laughter that shook the table.

Harry returned the laughter rather shakily.

"No. Nothing like that," his face once again serious, the moment of brevity had passed. "I just want you to be careful. Rumors says, 'they're bringing someone in, some kinda nutcase. Someone real good'."

"What the hell does that mean, 'some nutcase'?" Ben leaned forward, his ample stomach pushing the table against Weasel.

"Rumors says, 'A real psycho.' That's all I know," Harry answered. Sweat ran from under the brim of the baseball cap and he nervously wiped his forehead, while futilely pushing the table in the opposite direction.

Neither man spoke for a minute listening as the rain intensified.

"How do I get in touch with Rumors?" Armstrong finally asked although he already knew the answer.

"I told you before. He has informants all over town, people he's in with who tell him things. Maybe he's in the Police Department or City Hall. Maybe he's like Clark Kent, you know, Superman, and works at the newspaper or one of the radio stations. How do I know? He just seems to be in on everything. I hear he likes to play with computers and supposedly hangs around the midtown fag bars and dives. Some people know who is, but not me. I just hear what's on the street and most of it is coming from Rumors. That's all I know."

Armstrong slid laboriously from the booth. "Great food," he added.

"I don't know how you can eat here. Filthy roaches everywhere. Goddamn place is rotting from the inside. It's been here forever."

"Yeah, probably so," Ben answered, his mind on what Weasel had just said. He knew they'd be coming for the nun but why with someone from the outside? "Roaches came in on the boat with Cadillac," he added offhandedly.

"Who the hell's Cadillac?" Weasel asked.

Armstrong shook his head.

The Weasel left first, slithering out of the place like the dreaded roaches were running up his legs. Ben stood at the counter, paying his bill and talking to Cecelia. She was almost as big as Ben with probably the biggest tits in the world.

"How are you today, Benjamin?" She always called him by his full name. It had something to do with her middle-eastern upbringing. He liked it.

"The same, you know, nothing much changes."

"That's not what we're hearing. Everyone's talking about the nun being murdered and that you've got the case *and* the nephew. That's not a good place to be," she said.

"I see you've got quite a crowd today, indicating the gathering outside the front door," Ben changed the topic. He didn't want to talk about the case, especially with her. Conversations outside the department could draw the wrong kind of company.

"Well, I can't seem to stop that. I've complained to the police but they can't beat them over the head, besides Manuel likes the audience," she smiled. She was wise enough to know the crowd could be annoying but it never hurt business.

Ben thought she had a great smile. It took in her whole face and most of the surrounding room. It did more to raise his spirits than an hour with Oneida Summers, the police psychologist. They made small talk, like always, and after four or five minutes he started the four-block walk back to precinct headquarters.

Her voice caught him at the door. "Benjamin, please watch yourself." He turned back toward her and like Bogie gave her a tip of his hat as he went through the door.

The Windsor skyline to the east was bright and clear but Detroit remained under thick, twisted layers of dark gray gauze. *A bad omen?* The tempo of the rain increased and Ben pulled his coat collar up, while squeezing his neck a little lower between his shoulders. A few drops of rain drizzling cold down his spine would leave him with a chill that would last the entire day. He crossed streets through the steady drizzle, his size 14 shoes slashing out a sporadic rhythm on the wet pavement.

The Weasel had enlarged Ben's problem. The schoolyard had too many unanswered questions and now this new information added to his dilemma. Old Man Castobelli had never gone outside his own organization. He had always preferred to keep a tight hand on everything. Why would the Old Man do this? To divert attention? To remove himself from something that was going to get pretty nasty? Or did something happen that he didn't want to get involved in either? *The Weasel didn't think 'The Blade' was scared of anything.*

The raindrops, dimpling the puddles between the curb and the street, made him think of Cecelia. She had large dimples in her cheeks. She seemed interested and he liked her. Maybe he'd asked her out when this Morolli thing was over.

Several minutes passed before a large man removed himself from the last booth and exited Trendy's. The single Coney dog that he'd ordered remained untouched on his plate.

CHAPTER THIRTEEN

A t 2:30 pm, Armstrong trudged up the long flight of granite steps leading to the precinct lobby and moved slowly toward the old Otis elevator and the white-haired black man standing just inside the open doors.

"Take me up to Wickes, Yanc," he said.

"How's it going Lieutenant?" he asked while closing the doors and pushing the crank to the number three.

"O.K. Yanc. How about you?"

"One more and out the door," Yancy chimed and accompanied it with a Bo Jangles foot shuffle. "That's all I can say?"

"Well you usually have more to say than that. Everyone knows you're going to miss the old place," Ben smiled.

Yancy Bates had been with the department for twenty-nine years and was close to retiring. It was going to be a serious loss since Yancy probably knew more about the dirt pouring through the city then the ubiquitous 'Rumors'.

"What I'm going to miss the most is seeing the day you get in this box and it won't go up no more," Yancy grinned while letting his eyes run the height of Armstrong's ample figure.

"Well, that'll beat the hell out of us starting upstairs and falling straight through to the basement."

"Ha, ha. You're sure right there, Lieutenant."

The elevator staggered to the third floor and the doors laboriously opened. Armstrong exited with about the same amount of dexterity. At that moment, Ben felt older than the damn ancient elevator.

"Hey, Lieutenant?" The jovial attitude had left Yancy voice and Armstrong pick up on it immediately.

"Yeah," Armstrong paused and turned back slowly toward the future retiree.

"There's a new, bad snake in town."

"I heard he's coming, Yanc."

"No, Lieutenant. He's already here," Yancy said, giving his head a knowing shake as he pushed the *Close* lever.

Captain David Wickes was working on the morning report when Armstrong flopped into the old leather chair opposite the chief's desk and looked around smiling.

"This place looks like your maid left twenty years ago and you haven't got around to replacing her yet."

"Yeah, well I must have loved her and just can't fill the void. I guess you'll probably never learn to knock," Wickes replied.

"That's what happens when you leave the door open. Matthews and Barker back yet?" Armstrong asked.

Matthews and Barker had worked with Ben Armstrong for fourteen years. They were part of a four-man homicide unit, the best the city had, probably because the validity of every other team in the department was questionable. Something that Wickes would deny to his dying breath, but Castobelli's fingers could be felt throughout every department within the DPD.

What Harry had spoken of one hour ago was still ringing in Armstrong's head. The fourth member of Armstrong's team was Mari Gomez, a recent transferee from the New York Police Department and not one who could ever be mistaken for a man.

"They're your team and I don't really have the time to watch them but you'll probably find them at the end of the hall doing nothing. They want to be just like you," he answered. "What'd you get from your meeting?" Wickes continued. He was aware of Armstrong's many informants although, he supposedly had no idea who they were.

"Castobelli wants the nun dead," Armstrong answered. "I don't doubt that. He needs the little psycho loose. Isn't much we can do about it except fill the holes the Feds leave."

The FBI had arrived in force Monday evening and in accordance with their natural tendencies, brusquely took over, placing Sister Mary Elizabeth under their protection. The homicide stayed with the DPD but the possibility of a mob contract on the nun brought in the Feds.

"Well we've had enough experience with the FBI. They got her and they figure they can take better care of her than we can," Wickes said.

"Can you get me clearance? I've got to talk to her again."

"I guess so. Anything special that I should know about? I don't want anything surprising me on this one."

"Just a couple of questions about that playground. The left front fender on Morolli's car knocked over the lamp post and the tires left thread marks in the alley. Why the rush? Everyone they thought mattered was dead."

"Your interrogations got you nowhere?" Wicks asked already knowing the answer. They had talked about it to some extent.

"Can't ask a question without his mouthpiece answering for him. Not good. I'll keep you informed if something breaks," he added laboriously lifting himself from the chair.

"You do that. I'll have you in by the time you arrive, and take one of those two down the hall with you. You're better off in pairs when you deal with the Fed's, and send the other one out to give someone a ticket or something, that way they can both be doing something for their pay," he paused as if considering another thought then let it go.

He was reaching for the phone as Armstrong went through the door.

Something had happened in that schoolyard. Something that wasn't normal even to a murder case which was never normal. And no one was talking about it. At times, the Sister, staring off into the distance with a glazed look in her eyes, acted as if she was in the early stages of Alzheimer's; at other times she looked as if she were standing at Heaven's gate. The patrolmen who arrived first, stood back. There was no need to bother her. It was obvious by her demeanor she wasn't going anywhere. When Armstrong reached the playground she was walking in circles, like something was spinning her. A slow turning top in the middle of a graveled, dusty playground with bodies at her feet and her face turned up toward heaven or whatever.

It was at that moment that Ben realized he knew her and even so it took a while to place her. It was about twenty-five years ago and hard to remember. All you can see with a nun is her face, everything else is covered up. But when she walked, he could see the limp and when she looked at him, the eyes had the same gentleness from when they first met. Back then it was because of the boy.

He was a small boy, maybe ten or eleven years old; his life was full of misery, a life of watching his mother beaten by his father until she retaliated in the most impulsive and bloody fashion possible in front of her two sons, resulting in the smaller boy spending several years in both a psychiatric rehab and a center for wayward children. The state wasn't equipped to handle it any other way. As the years passed his only friend, his only real visitor, was this nun, Sister Mary Elizabeth, his grade school teacher.

The boy was seventeen when Sergeant Ben Armstrong first met him. And death was still with him, only this time the boy was suspected of doing the killing. Maybe it's a family thing, maybe killing is genetic. Or maybe once you're a part of it, it never leaves you. Seventeen then more death, like a deadly partner, a ghastly shadow walking in your footsteps. Back then she said the angels were watching over the young boy. And last week on the playground, she told Armstrong, the angels were talking to her.

I could use a little of that myself, Ben thought.

Sergeant Gerry Matthews drove silently up Gratiot and turned east on Mack Avenue toward Indian Village. Gerry preferred to be a responder rather than the initiator in a conversation and with his partner, he rarely spoke first. Usually when they rode together it was a very quiet car.

Armstrong sat stoically in the passenger seat watching rain fill the space wiped clean moments before as Detroit technology simulated life's unresisting cycle. Each generation splattered its shit upon the windshield of life and, in an instant, God or Mother Nature or whatever you choose to believe would wipe it clean and prepare for the next deluge.

Five years earlier, Ben and Edna were driving east on I-94, north of Vernier Road. The car in front of them blew a right front tire, twisted hard to the right, buried the wheel under the fender and spun out of control. The car on his left clamped on the brakes, careened sideways, glanced off a bridge abutment, slid along the guardrail and somehow made it through. Ben went right and would have made it except the semi in the right lane slammed on the front brakes and jackknifed. The passenger side of their car went under the rear of the trailer at sixty miles per hour and compressed like it had gone through a crusher at the scrap yard.

Edna didn't make it.

And now he was thinking again, watching the old neighborhood drift through a rain shower and thinking. It was his worst enemy - thinking was. Sister Mary Elizabeth, Willie Morolli, Cecelia, Edna and the playground. Too many things going on in his head that he had no control over. They kept popping into his mind and there was no way to shut them down except through exhaustion buffered with Valium.

Oneida diagnosed him with 'Post Traumatic Stress Syndrome'. An anxiety disorder caused by what the doctors call a trauma experienced by a death or terrible injury. *Really! What Bullshit!* Hell, every cop on the force has that problem. When you put your life on the line everyday it is unavoidable. Certain thing's had to be let go. He knew he couldn't go forward or make any progress with his life if the visions of the past kept lying like fuzzy transparencies over today's snapshots. They came one after another. One vision then another and another. Then another and now if everything else wasn't enough he couldn't get that damn playground out of his head. Something happened, he was sure of it now. If anyone had popped up, if someone had inadvertently, at that moment, arrived in the alley and saw what had happened, Morolli would have simply killed them. That's exactly what he did to the first nun. Why the skid marks? Why not a nice slow ride out of the alley? He wouldn't have run like hell. It just didn't fit.

Matthews turned onto Seminole Street and the rain picked up in intensity. *Another omen?*

In earlier times, the Village had been one of Detroit's most prestigious neighborhoods. The streets were double-wide boulevards lined with stately old homes built in the early 20th century. Street side they showed two and three stories of solid brick with elegant balconies extending over wide shadowed porches. The allure of what had been was not completely lost. The area still possessed the scent of Sunday strolls with spinning parasols and bowler hats, chugging model-T's alongside rocket bicycles, little girls in gingham and boys in knickers.

The Village, like most of Detroit, had gone through years of neglect. The old houses had suffered. But the new mayor, Elaine Starker was fighting to bring Detroit back. She spearheaded a *City in Renaissance Movement* and neighborhood groups throughout the Village were joining together to make their communities good places to live. New young oak trees, planted to replace the ravaged elms, lined the boulevards and the alleys behind the old mansions were being cleaned and rejuvenated. The Village was responding nicely.

A young traffic cop working at the precinct had bought a three-story brick house in the Village. He was spending his off time fixing the house and when the feds were looking for a safe house to keep Sister Mary Elizabeth, it seemed a good choice. Needless to say, the whole situation was unacceptable to her.

The address was a corner lot, the sidewalk raised and broken by the roots of an elm, the grass mostly missing and the dirt at the corner, where the walks met, was muddy and rutted from bicycle tracks. The once white picket fence running along the side yard was broke in two places before it met the alley. Clumps of rhubarb, dark green with streaks of deep ruby red, dominated the open space between the side street and a garage in a diabolical state of needed repair. Armstrong made a mental note to let the young traffic cop know that he should hire some help. He was lagging behind the rest of the community.

Matthews drove around the corner and parked. A large black man sat in a dilapidated rocker on the front porch and appeared to be enjoying the rainy afternoon under the protection of the grandiose roof. Armstrong extracted his huge frame from the passenger seat and walked the three steps up the porch. The man had already risen and was standing between him and the door.

"Armstrong DPD here to see Sister Mary Elizabeth."

"Special Agent Filmore Gill. I got the call from Captain Wickes but she's not here. She's confessing for her monthly duty," the agent answered.

"What does that mean?" Armstrong asked as a second agent stepped through the door.

"That's what I asked", the second agent said. "I didn't think these nuns had monthlies," he laughed.

Agent Gill ignored his partner, "Seems they have to go to confession once a month whether they need it or not."

"How many took her and how long ago?" Armstrong asked.

"Two. About fifteen minutes ago."

"Thanks, I need to talk to her. I'd appreciate a call back."

"No problem."

Armstrong left Agent Gill his cell number, lumbered down the porch steps and with a noticeable effort squeezed back into the car.

"Monthly duty my ass," he wheezed.

"What's up?" Matthews questioned.

"The Feds took her to the church. Assholes. They're acting like they're guarding someone for outstanding parking tickets."

"You better take it easy on those Coney dogs or you're not going to be able to get into this car anymore or go talk to anybody," Matthews remarked.

"Get us to that church FAST," Armstrong said.

Sergeant Gerry Matthews had been there for him when Edna died. Her death had rendered Ben useless. Ben and Edna had two sons, William, 14 and Thomas 13 years old. Without Edna's sisters, Thelma and Clarisse, the kids wouldn't have had anyone.

Matthews never left Ben's side, through the hospital stay, the funeral and the long drinking bouts which Oneida diagnosed as his personal attempt at suicide. The diagnosis was right, what he really wanted was to crawl into that coffin with her and just die. Take the blame; shoulder the guilt and just die. That would have been the easy way out and at times like that, easy always helped.

Their life together had been a true partnership. Ben was big on partnerships, they both were. It was a smooth even flowing marriage, nothing flamboyant or by any means exciting. As a cop, he never wanted that. They blended perfectly. Their marriage together had been someplace secure, reassuring and comfortable. She provided that and so much more. Without her, he saw no reason to go on and in the days following her death, the boys never once crossed his mind.

With the help of Matthews, he slowly, dug himself out of the mental cave that he'd been buried in. He saw a little light and felt the extended hand of Matthews holding on and telling him that it would get easier. Not better, just easier. Oneida told him the images and sounds would fade: the twisting, tearing metal ripping through the semi-trailer as it smashed into the center abutment, the rear end crashing through their windshield and slamming through her body like a cannonball going through a newspaper. The blood – God - the blood!

But the images didn't fade. They were as sharp today as they were when they took Edna in pieces from inside of their car. And the transparencies were always there; right in front of his eyes. He blamed himself. Maybe if he'd been driving a little slower, paying closer attention, maybe she would still be here. Matthews had been a true friend and now he was telling him that he'd gone from 225 to 300 pounds in the five years that had followed and food could kill him just as fast as the alcohol.

"Wickes' going to put you behind a desk and leave my back wide open, partner, and I don't look forward to that."

"Yeah, you're right, next time I go to Trendy's I'll cut my order in half. I'll only eat four dogs," he flipped back. "Go to the church. I don't like this deal. I don't know what these Feds are thinking. They should have never left the house." Matthews turned left on Grand Boulevard and headed toward the river.

CHAPTER FOURTEEN

Originally, the Cathedral of St. Joseph the Roman, built in 1902, was an architectural attempt to duplicate the cathedrals of Milan or Florence. Initially it was reasonably successful. That was many years ago. Now it was a perfect candidate for the Mayor's new Renaissance program.

The majority of the houses, boarded up or burnt out, had become a graveyard of decrepit bungalows. The in-between lots were flattened like they had been hit by enemy mortar fire. Cement blocks, shingles and porch railings, became urban shrapnel. The roads were fractured and lined with innumerable cracks, the walkways broken and heaving upward, as if some unknown earth monster was pushing its way upwards, breaching everything above. Dirty brown piles of uncollected garbage and graying stacks of wrapped newspapers covered the sidewalks. There were no trees, no flowers and even the rare patch of grass was blatantly missing.

Sitting in the midst of this urban chaos, the cathedral stood like a misplaced relic against a broken skyline. It resembled a huge buzzard, looking confused and lost upon returning to a nest of shattered eggs.

Some serrated rays of the afternoon sun, finding their way through a rain dampened sky, cut the stained glass of the steeple tower above the balcony and glistening through the brass chimes of the ancient organ settled in staggered, colored bars across a shadowed area beneath the organ.

The shadow was more of a dark spot, an inky, dreaded, bulky lump tucked into the dark corner at the back edge of the organ and the inside wall of the balcony. It could have easily been something that had slipped off the balcony during last month's cleaning, possibly an organ shroud left unnoticed by the organist.

At precisely 4:00 pm, the lumpy spot moved, stretched the soreness that comes with total stillness, sat up, and looked out across the church. Everything with the exception of a few pews directly below was visible between the balcony rails. The commotion below coupled with the sun's sporadic, warm rays had raised the shadow.

It was time for the handmaidens' monthly duty, a confession to cleanse their ivory souls and communion to prepare them for another chaste month. Their counterparts, the saintly priests, couldn't claim with any veracity equal purity. A misunderstood touch here, a gentle pat there, maybe an occasional altar boy or, better yet, some devout parishioner, who through some deviate sociological aberration tried to get closer to God by getting next to his earthly representative.

At that moment, two priests entered the church through the side doors and dividing themselves at the main altar, genuflected, and walked solemnly down the central aisle, under the rear archway, past the balcony stairs and around the large foyer columns to the side aisles where each would entered a confessional, one to the right, the other to the left.

The voice, very feminine, echoed down the stairwell and the old priest paused on his way to the confessional. Perhaps someone was in the balcony preparing for Sunday services. He knew so little of these preparations, preferring to leave them to Mrs. Oberinsk, who coordinated the Sunday music program with Mother Superior. He thought that if there was someone there, maybe he could be of service. He went up to see.

That was only moments ago and now his hands and feet were tied around the large circular marble column. He was hugging the huge pillar like Samson before he tore down the temple of the Philistines. It had happened so quickly. His mouth was taped and there was a strong taste of blood in the back of his throat.

And now the voice was very masculine. It leaned close and held his ear. The words were moist and stunk of death. He wanted to scream, to open his mouth and lungs so loud that this demon would be destroyed by God's wrath, but he couldn't. He felt like his tongue was stuck in the back of his throat. His heart was trying to beat a way out of his chest, sweat was running down his forehead and there was a distinct smell in the room and for a moment, he thought he had lost his bowels.

Fingers were on his lower spine, searching. For a brief moment, he caught a glimpse of the weapon, black and viciously curved like a Turkish scimitar. Then it cut. The curved point pressed inward, slicing between the vertebra, crushing through the spinal cord and making him an instant quadriplegic.

"See, that didn't hurt much, did it? Just one little cut and I have graciously taken you past the point of all pain," it hissed in his ear. "Today is the most wonderful day of your life, Father, and you have me to thank. I am your truest friend, the truth giver. The real truth, the one which you have always been afraid to admit to yourself."

The priest closed his eyes and forced himself to shut off the words. He knew that somewhere deep inside of him was the strength that God had given all good men. The power to turn away from evil and the strength to handle the pain it brings. It was his moment to find that strength, to look into his own soul because, like Christ, he was upon his cross and his time had finally come.

"Isn't it amazing that they call you 'Father' when you've never had enough balls to father anything? But here I am, your validator, your honest-to-God travel agent." The voice chuckled. "Death is, after all, the gateway to heaven. That is what you teach, isn't it? It is, after all, the purest form of freedom and an enormous contradiction that a holy man like you should fight it. Today I am opening the door for you to a better world and you, dear Father should welcome it, even beg for it. You, not being allowed suicide, are condemned here, sentenced to live with the stupid, sneaky weaklings of this earth, while secretly waiting for some blessed event to intervene and allow you to meet your God where you can beg his forgiveness for trying to ream every little altar boy left in your charge."

"Our Father who art in Heaven," the words were controlled and came from deep within his throat between lips that were taped together. They came slowly, evenly spaced and with great strength.

"Aaah, I hear you," like a snake, the hissing continued. "In your last moment you call to him. But he does not answer. Listen. You cannot hear a thing. Because," the voice rasped, as black as the voice of Satan himself, "there is no real God, only pretenders, and to prove it I'm going to send you on a mission to find Him."

The knife, with a thin red line dripping across its brilliant blade, slid across the priest throat. Blood squirted from his severed jugular and splattered a brilliant red against the white column. The priest choked, his head slumped sideways and aspirated blood filled his lungs.

"Ha, ha. There, see if you can find Him, now."

Blood slid quickly down the polished column, fanning across the balcony floor and splattered the shoes of the assailant. He stood and watched it encircle his feet.

Matthews pulled around the front and parked near the side door in the no- parking/shipping zone. A dark Ford cruiser was parked across the street beneath a billboard with the center section missing. The driver sat behind the wheel with a nonchalant ease. Armstrong extricated himself from the car and paused to look skyward. The rain continued to keep the day drab and dismal. The clouds resembled a protective shield set in place to deter any celestial spirits from peering downward and witnessing some unwanted calamity about to fall upon the heads of the faithful. It struck his inner monitor, another premonition. He was big on premonitions.

"I don't like this. One's still in the car. That means there's only one man to protect her."

"It sounds normal to me. Maybe that's why they get the big money. One of them is worth about five of us," Gerry answered, "besides the one in the car looks like he needs a nap."

"I'll put it in my report. One sleeping FBI agent is worth at least five DPD offices," Armstrong answered. "Let's get in there."

Matthews opened the side door and the two Detroit detectives slipped unseen into the church. They paused for a minute to let their eyes adjust to the darkness before Armstrong motioned Matthews down the right side toward the balcony. Ben took a position beneath the high arches that led to the spacious, velvet clothed altar at the front of the church.

Pillars of stained glass, on each side of the church, ran from waist high up to the cathedral peaks, over four stories above. The Stations of the Cross, five feet high hand carved depictions of Christ's journey to the crucifixion, surrounded the outer walls and accentuated the massive glass columns they interrupted. Beneath the carvings, near the rear of the church, were four ornate walnut confessionals and above the carvings was the balcony, covering the entire width of the church. It was large enough to hold a choir of sixty, raising their lofty voices to such a din that they could raise the heavens, which it attempted every Sunday.

Matthews, appearing every bit the fervent parishioner, walked toward the confessionals.

The parishioners knelt piously and waited as the priests closed the central doors and turned on the occupied lights. Redemption was a rosary away.

Minutes later, Rocco Medici, beads of perspiration reflecting in the same light, exited the confessional. On shaky steps, he headed toward the ornate entrance door. Rather than stop and kneel in one of the outer pews to say his penance, he skirted around them and left the church.

Rocco was born twenty-three years earlier to a strict Italian family. He was raised by devoutly Catholic parents and educated in a Catholic school. His father had taught him to work hard, buy only what you can afford, pay your bills and stay out of trouble. His mother taught him, go to church every Sunday or you'll go to hell. Don't lie, don't cheat and don't steal or you'll go to hell. And don't hurt anybody - you'll go to hell for that too!

Rocco never listened. *Work hard all your life like his father had done?* Where the hell did that ever get him? His old man never made any *easy* money. He worked the assembly line for GM. Ass kicking work. Sixty cars an hour non-stop. He couldn't even take a piss unless he asked permission. What kinda fucking job was that? Bust your ass, come home so exhausted that you eat dinner and fall asleep in front of the TV, wondering all the time if you'll be able to pay your bills. Then you read in the paper how the guys who run the company are laying themselves down with fat bonuses and unbelievable stock options under some bullshit theory that it will improve their performance, while all the time it's the workers that get screwed.

Congress and the Presidency were exactly the same. The whole world runs that way. Fat - suck. Fat - suck. That's how you got somewhere in this country. Skim the fat for yourself and make everyone else suck. That's what Rocco wanted, some of the fat. He figured he knew how to get it. Rocco worked for Willie 'The Blade' Morolli and Willie hated big shot politicians as much as he hated big shot executives. He was raised in the same neighborhood as Rocco and taught the same things, especially the part about DON'T STEAL. And that's what that fool Bobby Falhone did.

Jesus Christ! Rocco thought when he first heard about it, *Stuffed in a potato sack and then sliced up like a French fry.* 'The Blade' wanted everyone to know and *everybody* did! The families, the cops, everyone from the toughest thug to the worst street pusher or pimp, they all knew that you didn't mess with 'The Blade'. He wanted everyone to be scared shitless of him and it worked!

When old man Castobelli wanted something from one of the fat cats, he sent Willie 'The Blade' to talk to them. He didn't have to send him twice. The old man always got what he wanted. Rocco had even heard Willie remark that he wanted the old man to send him to D.C. "Washington needed a nice fat .45 caliber bullet in the head. Then the country could go back to letting families take care of themselves."

Rocco was with 'The Blade' in the limo one afternoon paying a visit to some big shot in Grosse Pointe. Willie had the driver pull over next to the country club. Rich assholes with their rich bitches were everywhere. It was unbelievably cool. A Wednesday and the place was loaded.

"See them assholes," Willie said. They're working now. The goddamn place is loaded and they're all pretending to be working. That's how it works Rocco. While your old man is busting his ass, these pricks jack up the price of the cars to pay for all their good times and then they go play golf and pump their snob-nose bitches. If they didn't pay us so well, I'd kill all those mutha fuckers."

The afternoon rain had intensified, filling the bright spaces between the clouds and beating down on the shoulders of Rocco's new leather jacket and splattering the tops of his Bruno Magli shoes and soaking in around his new silk socks.

It was a prepaid bonus. Old man Castobelli had sent it to him personally. Rocco had already spent it on the new jacket, the Italian shoes and a few knits. It was easy money!

But a thought stuck in his head and he couldn't shake it.

Allspice, a pinch of cinnamon and something else. What was it? That smell? It was in the confessional.

Rocco's shoe's matched the rhythm of the old-time street-car wheels striking the gaps between the rail seams. Clack, clack, clack. But like a poor dancer learning to tap, the notes disappeared like the streetcars had, and the tempo evaded him. Something didn't fit. *Something else with the cinnamon?*

The nuns always entered the Church from the left side, the side nearest the convent. They would stay on that side and use those confessionals. Rocco had to watch the nuns come in and pick out Sister Mary Elizabeth. That was no problem. He knew her well enough. He'd spent eight years at the school before it was closed. He knew all the nuns, at least all the ones who'd been there at least five years. Most of them were nuts. They spent most of their time wondering what you were doing with your hand in your pocket. Or what you did with your girlfriend the night before? Then they wanted to smack the shit out of you.

One of the nuns had actually gotten the paddle, a one inch thick piece of maple with holes drilled all over it, held out her hand and told him that for doing some shit wrong, *he* had to hit her! Then she stood there looking infinitely pious with her hand extended waiting for him to hit her. Naturally, he didn't, because you can't hit a nun, but he should have. He should have cracked her upside her head. Then we'd see how many times she'd pull that bullshit. Damn crazy nuns!

Sister Mary Elizabeth was the second nun in the row.

Just go into the confessional and tell the priest the nun was the second one. That's all! He knew who she was. That's why the Old Man picked him. That was the easy money! The priest was going to talk to the nun. He was going to explain to her that maybe she didn't really see nothing at all. That it wasn't good for the Church to get involved in these things. Rocco did good. He did exactly like he was supposed to but something wasn't right.

Two years ago, the Rottweiler on the next block caught Fritz, Rocco's beagle. The Rottweiler ripped him up real bad. Rocco had to carry Fritz to the vet. There was blood all over.

He'd taken Fritz home after the vet was done. Took him home, put him on his bed and tried to get him to eat but Fritz wasn't hungry. Rocco figured nobody would be hungry after being chewed up by something three times as big as you. So, he went to the fridge, got a nice meatball, wrapped it in wax paper, walked over to the next block, through the alley, put the meatball over the fence and when the Rottweiler came to get it, Rocco shot it twice in the fucking head.

Pepper. Yes, pungent black pepper! Now he remembered.

The puddles formed along the cracks in the pavement, shiny black with questionable depth. At first only fractions of an inch deep but at a second glance it seemed to Rocco that he was looking into darken pits flashing ominously beneath his feet and there was something in that darkness that was feeding a sickening thought.

He knew it. He just wouldn't allow his mind to get a good hold on the thought, but it was still there, lurking. His feet increased their pace until he was almost at a run. The confessional, the one he'd just left, where he'd told the shadowy figure of the priest leaning close to the screened window, that the second nun was the one. The one he needed to talk to.

He had watched as the small priest, his head bent over and shrouded, walk down the center aisle but the shadow inside the confessional had been much larger and the smell had been unmistakable.

That confessional smelled like Fritz.
The confessional stank of fresh blood!

CHAPTER FIFTEEN

Matthews stopped ten feet from the pew where the nuns, all lined up like perfect erect dominos, were kneeling. Sister Mary Elizabeth, her head bent downward, her face hidden somewhere within the black habit, the large white bib and the austere cap perched precariously upon her head, was praying.

Today the confessional was bathed in colored ribbons as the sun cut through the heavy clouds and sent beams slicing through the leaded glass columns. It was made of walnut, naturally ripened to tones of a deep indigo. The center opening was filled with an ornately carved door, latticed on the top with hand carved walnut and screened with black gauze. The two side openings were shrouded with deep purple velvet curtains that hung from solid brass rods embedded in richly filigreed mounting brackets.

The oak flooring of the church was darkly stained except for the walkways which were worn white from the passage of the devout, and strangely speckled with irregular shaped spots.

People moved in and out of the confessional with an almost planned methodology. Right now, they were moving rather quickly and Sister Mary Elizabeth was second in line.

Matthews took a moment to survey the church. The interior was as out of sync as the exterior. The whole scene disturbed him. It was a period throwback. An ornate European monument set amid the poverty of an American ghetto. The stillness left the impression, not of a sanctuary but of a morgue. The feel of the place made him shiver. Matthews had been trained to live more by what his senses told him than what the rules dictated. He didn't know any other way and now, those senses were screaming at him. He searched for anything that didn't fit, the parishioners, the nuns, — anything.

Everything did and yet nothing did.

"Bless me Father for I have sinned."

"Yes, yes - No - no— Three Our Fathers and three Hail Mary's."

The mutterings from behind the curtain reached his ears. Moments later the curtain closest to Matthews moved slowly outward and a slick young Italian, draped in leather and silk, stepped into the aisle, paused momentarily, looked furtively around and hurried toward the front exit. He looked nervous and didn't look like a kid who would be too interested in telling anyone his sins.

Sister Mary Elizabeth, her head down in an attitude of atonement, was getting up. She paused and moved her habit to one side to facilitate an easy exit from the pew.

The young Italian didn't stop to say his penance.

She cleared the pew, her foot moved into the aisle and she reached for the velvet curtain.

The young Italian didn't genuflect. Instead he hurried under the balcony, the overhead light reflecting off his moist forehead, and he quickly went through the large exit doors.

Do young wannabee thugs sweat in a confessional? Matthews's nerves were tingling. The Italian didn't fit.

The nun's foot covered one of the dark spots on the oak floor. Like leaves on a forest path, they speckled the aisle leading to the confessional. The spot smeared and, with no help from her bad leg, she slid ever so slightly and Matthews bolted.

"Sister stop. Stop!" his scream slammed across the church like an arctic wind instantly freezing everything. He took three long strides catching the startled nun her by the right arm and dragging her toward him. She went down landing hard as Matthews crashed on top of her. The momentary stillness that followed was unpalatable. It lasted briefly, less than anything measurable, and then the confessional door exploded outward.

The flick of a red laser beam flashed across Matthew's eyes and he instinctively rolled hard against the wall. The bullet smashed into his left shoulder. The laser searched again as he rolled, reflected off his cornea and his head exploded.

The FBI agent rushed around the corner and toward the screaming melee of nuns.

ONE. *Take your time — The fucking nuns are screaming. The fat cop is still across the church, looking this way.* TWO. *There's always more time than you think. Still time for fat boy. Here comes his dumb buddy.* THREE. *Hold — steady — squeeze. Ha. Ha. Got you!*

The laser, a beam of focused light, ornamented the FBI agents' chest, and two 9mm slugs smashed into his Kevlar vest. The impact knocked him backwards. A third slug caught him just below the chin as he was falling and removed the top of his head.

Armstrong couldn't see him. The shooter was down below the top line of the pews. A laser flashed over his shoulder and Armstrong pressed his unwanted bulk into plaster and steel as two bullets tore a chunk off the column, narrowly missing his face. He dropped to his knees, waited a moment then rushed forward to the next column.

People pandemonium, screaming to pierce an ear drum, running hell bent for salvation, clawing to get past the sinner in front of you, Hail Mary's on the fly. Forget the golden rule, this was life or death. A frantic, screaming dash toward the rear of the church, a blur of parishioners crossed before Armstrong's eyes, the nuns clustered around the spot where Matthews and Sister Mary Elizabeth went down, the noise tumultuous. Then one of the nuns standing and looking toward Armstrong while pointing toward the side door. The look on her face was obvious. Gone!

Captain Wickes looked out the corner window at the cars passing beneath his third story window. Headlights glistened off puddles lining the street. The light from the digital clock on his desk read 9:05 pm. His mood was loathsome.

"The Mayor is pissed. The press is climbing up her ass. Someone has to come up with some answers. A fucking gun battle in a church. The local venerable priest sliced up like a plate of Chinese vegetables, two Federal agents murdered and one of Detroit's finest in the hospital shot to shit and lucky to be alive. My head's going out on this one and yours is going with it."

"The second FBI agent? You mean the one out front in the car?" Armstrong shook his head. He had been at the hospital with Matthews and wasn't up to speed.

"Yeah, a bullet hole in the head. Apparently he was dead before you and Gerry got there."

"I should have known. He looked too rested."

"What the hell does that mean?" Wickes asked.

"Nothing but that puts someone else in the game. If the killer's hiding in the church who took out the agent in the car."

"I don't know, with the group were dealing with, it could be any of a dozen or more but you find out and pretty damn soon or we're in the shit." Wickes paused, "How's Gerry?"

"Gerry is luckier than anyone thought. The second slug scraped his skull, actually took a little bone. Another sixteenth of an inch and his brains would have been all over the nun," Armstrong answered.

"Terrific. At least we've got a survivor." His tone changed, "We've got an eight o'clock meeting in the Mayor's office tomorrow morning. Make sure you're there," he paused again, "Where's the nun?" Wickes asked, although at this moment he wished he'd never heard of her.

"She's safe," Ben replied, "Barker and Gomez got to the church within minutes of the shooting. They've got her and I'm going to keep it that way."

"For now you mean! We don't have any idea who this bastard is. A psycho nut! It looks like he enjoyed cutting the priest. I mean, right there in a crowded church. He actually took the time to fuck with the old man. Some kind of sick bastard we've got running around."

"She's safe. And damn lucky the priest's blood got on the assailants shoes. He walked spots of blood down the stairs and along the aisle. Matthews caught it or she would have never come out of that confessional."

"The Feds are going to want her back," Wickes answered.

"That's going to be your job. You're running interference. The case belongs to us. Homicide is all over that church."

"Tell that shit to the Mayor tomorrow and see if she'll listen."

Armstrong moved slowly toward the door.

"You better lose some goddamn weight if you expect to keep chasing every asshole that screws over this town," Wickes' mood wasn't improving.

"Yeah, and if I had weighed a little less, been a little faster, I'd probably be dead," Ben countered leaving Wickes standing by himself.

Armstrong's walk to the elevator was even slower. His head was packed with questions and all his answers said this case was inside out.

CHAPTER SIXTEEN
Wednesday 2:00 am

The phone woke Armstrong from a ragged sleep interrupted by persistent dreams of squealing tires, tearing
sheet metal and thoughts of the excruciating pain. The call was
from Wickes and he personally wanted Ben to see this one, for
whatever reason. Wickes also said "Sick" and Ben didn't care
for the sound of that. Wickes was feeling the pressure. Things
were closing in on him. He already had his hands full with the
FBI pulling his chain and threatening the Mayor with interfering with a federal investigation. So when he called, waking Ben
from a sleep he'd rather not be in anyway, Ben didn't give him
a hard time.

He drove the Chrysler Freeway around Jefferson, made a
right on Woodward and within minutes slid into a spot between
two unmarked cruisers. The address was a loft near the corner
of Grand River and Woodward and the Blue and Whites were
three deep, blocking off the spectators and keeping the press
with their ubiquitous cameramen at bay.

He was having premonitions, hoping that whatever this
"Sick" was, it wasn't connected with the nun and Willie 'The
Blade'. The nun was gone. Barker and Gomez snatched an

unmarked white from the motor pool and disappeared with her before Matthews had reached the hospital. Wickes didn't have any trouble explaining the missing police car but the missing Nun had every damn newspaper in the country screaming for a headline. Two federal agents were dead and Washington wanted a head. Preferably, the killers, but Wickes' would do as a cheap substitute. The Mayor needed to give Washington some believable answers and, right now, she didn't have any. Armstrong refused to give anyone information on Sister Mary Elizabeth's whereabouts except that he had moved her to a new safe house. His argument was simple, the less people who knew where she was the safer she would be. It sounded good but it wasn't going to work much longer. Armstrong wasn't too far away from being arrested himself for kidnapping and hiding a federal witness. Wickes kept reminding him that the Mayor's patience was wearing thin.

Armstrong flashed his shield at the patrolman guarding the door and followed a forensic group laden down with their small aluminum suitcases filled with all that scientific bullshit that nobody knew anything about except them. The elevator stopped at the fourth floor. The door to the loft was a ten foot steel ensemble with three separate sliding bolts coupled with u-shaped lock brackets bent from half inch steel. Armstrong thought, *Nobody was kicking that door in, not without waking the neighborhood for five blocks around and ruining some good boots.* Whoever lived here was definitely worried about intruders.

The main room was a huge affair, at least forty by forty. A ragged black and white striped couch and matching chair, loaded with tech journals and computer magazines, were off to one side. A small television and a cheap Formica coffee table, covered with half-filled Coke cans, the scattered remains of chips and some green moldy gook that might have at one time been considered food, made up the rest of the decor. Armstrong passed without pausing. The rest of the room was a geek's dream. Six computer terminals covered the back wall. A large raid server, that would have made the DPD's systems manager jealous, filled the middle space with its myriad rows of flashing red and green lights blinking out some code known only to the nerd who designed it. A cheap pine shelf ran at a seven foot high level around the entire room filled with every data router imaginable. Finally, enough wires to fill the Pentagon dangled off the shelf, like living branches from a huge vibrating electronic tree.

Wickes stood waiting by a door near the rear of the room.

"Alright, what is it that I have to see? Where's the corpse?" Armstrong asked walking through the rubble toward what he assumed was the bedroom.

Wickes turned and walked into the room without answering. Armstrong didn't like the feel of this and lumbered behind, his apprehension growing with each step.

"That's your boy if I'm not mistaken, isn't it?" Wickes asked.

Harry Teasel hung, stripped naked, inverted from a slaughterhouse spreader. His legs were lashed to each end of the y-shaped fork. A three-inch long incision above each ankle allowed the insertion of an electrical wire that was held in place by strips of black electrician tape. The plug end was stuck into an outlet in the back of a computer power center. The power line from the CPU ran to a 25-pin plug. Weasel's throat had been sliced open on one side avoiding the jugular and the plug was inserted into the opening and secured with more electrical tape. The single wires inserted into his ankles ran from his legs up to the connector in his throat. Harry had been a living circuit breaker.

Every time the master switch on the power center was turned on, Teasel got 110 volts of lightening through his body, bubbling the blood in his veins and frying his brain at the same time. The flesh around his throat and legs was seared black. The veins and arteries in his legs, throat and chest stood out like grossly swollen purple worms. The blood around the wounds fanned out in strings of fried black lines like the creation of some warped spider. His eyeballs looked as if they were about to explode across the room like sight-guided rocket balls. Harry's mouth was duct taped shut. His unheard screams had echoed madly within the pitch-black space of his own mind. The whole place had a putrid smell, which must resemble some madman's concept of a stinking, rotting hell.

Armstrong tasted the bile roll in the back of his throat. He turned abruptly, and left the room. Wickes followed.

"His name was Harry William Teasel. You knew him as Weasel, a mob runner, and an obviously good source," Wickes said catching Ben in the outer room.

"He was harmless. He didn't deserve this," Armstrong answered. "Where's the john?" His stomach was sending him a bad message.

"That door next to the dresser," Wickes answered indicating the door at the far end of the room.

Armstrong hurried into the room, slammed the door behind him and retched into the open toilet. Several minutes passed before Ben felt well enough to come out. When he did Wickes was still talking.

"Well the look of this place tells me something else was going on." Wickes continued. He paused long enough to let Ben gather himself. It was apparent to Wickes that Armstrong was blaming himself. After all, he was good at that.

"Harry was a first rate hacker who supplied the mob with a lot of inside info. He went by a geek handle and thought nobody knew who he was," Ben said.

"Well, my guess would be that they knew exactly what he was up to. And I would venture that every tidbit he gave you they approved. Except this time, Ben. This time he must have given up something that wasn't supposed to come out. Any ideas?" Wickes asked.

"He told me that Castobelli was bringing in someone from outside the family. Someone special to get the nun. He wanted me to know. He didn't seem to think that it would matter to them. If he had, he wouldn't have told me."

"Well, it looks like he was wrong because it sure mattered to someone."

"Yeah."

Armstrong was staring across the room, watching the blinking lights, his mind on something else. It didn't fit. It was there but he couldn't put his finger on it. Someone had known about the FBI at the church and someone had also fingered Harry.

"The name Ben, what was his handle?"

Armstrong shook he head. Tears were at the corners of his eyes. His stomach was still rolling.

"Some bastard toyed with him," he said. "This took a long time doing. Some sick son-of- a-bitch did this. Someone who really enjoys this kind of killing." Ben was agonizing. Without ever admitting it to himself, he had liked the little guy and if Harry wasn't on Ben's payroll, he would still be alive. It was Ben's fault. He knew it. He was guilty by the association. He turned and walked slowly out the loft door. He had a phone call to make.

"The name Ben," Wickes asked again.

Without pausing Ben threw the name "Rumors" over his shoulder.

CHAPTER SEVENTEEN
Wednesday 11:00 am

T he woman applied the makeup very carefully blending the foundation over the edges of the white wig. She brushed the thick powder from the center of her face outward to her temples and watched the application in the mirror like a hopeful artist. Her experience with make-up was minimal but when she was finished, the effort was rewarding. She had achieved the desired effect of an older woman trying to look 20 years younger. She closed the kit, tucked it inside her purse, and smile whimsically at the middle age gentleman sitting opposite her. He hadn't spoken to her since they left Detroit.

Sergeant Andrew Barker had been in homicide for 14 years. Before that he worked a beat on Detroit's east side. It was there, because of his stellar work with the youth gangs that he had met Armstrong. A camaraderie had formed and when Armstrong had gone to homicide he brought Barker along with him. Barker lived out near the Pointe, south of Altar Rd. and east of Jefferson. He was married with two daughters and now getting close enough to retirement to consider it a possibility. But this assignment bothered him. Never in all of his years on the force was he asked to go, not only outside the boundaries of the city but completely, out of the state.

There was nothing naive about Barker. The woman sitting across from him, putting makeup on her face like she was a teenager and this was her first attempt, was the most perilous person he was ever asked to guard, the target of the Castobelli mob. Worse than that, it was motivated by the little monster Willie 'The Blade' which placed a huge target on Barker's chest and marked it with a dollar sign.

"You don't like being here, do you Sergeant?"

"Doesn't really matter that much to me ma'am."

"But it can't be dangerous here, can it? After all, nobody knows where I am," she smiled while talking.

"That's exactly why it is," he countered sullenly wondering why some people can always be so happy. *What world is she living in,* he thought?

Barker was drinking a cup of black coffee, his stiff right extended leg into the aisle way. He turned his head, ignoring her as best he could. Sister Mary Elizabeth picked up the second cup in front of her and sipped it slowly. The silence between them was thick. They were waiting on a carry-out order to be filled.

The Circle Loop Restaurant, forty miles west of Sioux Falls, South Dakota off US 90, was ending the morning rush. The coffee was always hot and a sign above the entrance announced that their biscuits and gravy, a local specialty, was world famous.

The place was filled mainly with truckers and local ranchers, some travelers completed the mix. Most of the truckers were usually in a hurry to get back on the road. They were the restaurants main business and were treated as such. A second sign, next to the cash register, announced to all customers, 'PLEASE WAIT TO BE SEATED. TRUCKERS SEATED FIRST.'

Four locals sat in the first booth inside the door, drinking coffee and listening to the local grain and feedlot prices on a small, portable radio. The radio was a little louder than normal and the waitress on one of her passes tersely commented, "Would you lower that thing, Chet? Everyone don't want to listen to that stuff."

"Would you jest hush it up, Doris? Can't hear anything with you jabbering," Chet answered. Nobody lifted his or her head and Doris continued behind the counter and into the kitchen.

In the booth next to the older couple, sat a young couple with their two small children. Their trailer was parked across the parking lot, partially blocking off the white Ford LTD Crown Victoria. The kids were unruly and neither of the parents seemed to be enjoying their breakfast.

Across the room, two drivers, dressed in matching green uniforms, sat at the cloverleaf counter eating eggs, biscuits and a large saucer of the famous gravy. Both of them smoked while they ate and flicked their ashes into one of the heavy glass ashtrays spotted around the counter. Their green baseball style caps rested on the counter on either side of the ashtray. Bold letters stating 'Sun Cartage' circled around a golden reflective logo just above each brim. The highly polished logos reflected as well as any small compact mirror, which in fact, they were. The caps were set so the golden mirrors framed the old couple on the opposite side of the room.

Two ranchers hauling some breeding stock up to Pierre were seated next to the Sun Cartage boys. They both laughed softly at Doris' statement. She would be back in a few minutes to try again. This time she would be completely ignored. It happened almost every morning. They also gave a knowing glance at each other and nodded slightly towards the old biker sitting at the very end of the counter.

"Doris better watch him instead of Chet and the guys. He doesn't look like he can pay for a cup of coffee," the first said.

"Doris watches everyone," was the quick reply.

"Yeah," he paused, "but looking like that, he must be poorer than dried shit. And wearing them sunglasses! Hell, that old and he still thinks he's cool."

"Well, Doris has given away more than one cup of free coffee," the second answered.

The sunglasses wrapped around most of his face. They were coated and one-way. His leather coat was the kind a second hand store would refuse to sell, preferring to give it away. It would be a compliment to call it ragged. The back was shredded as if some mountain lion had used it for a scratching post. The left sleeve was torn from shoulder to cuff and the right one wasn't much better. Half the collar was missing and the gloss from the leather had worn off years ago. He wore a black tankers cap pulled low over uncut gray hair that extended to his shoulders. His beard and mustache looked like they hadn't been trimmed in at least a year. The combination made his face impossible to see.

His pants weren't any better. They were split open on one side and bulged around his stuffed midriff. The black boots that finished his outfit should have been thrown away years ago. The two seats on either side of him remained empty. He gave the impression that if you got close enough, you had to smell him. You just didn't even want to look at him. The ranchers were relieved when he paid for his coffee and lumbered from the restaurant.

Doris was passing by again and the talkative one remarked loudly, "We're all glad that's gone, eh, Doris?"

"Well, I never seen him before," she paused and shook her head, "Thank God." She continued past the front counter and asked Chet to turn the radio down again. This time he ignored her.

Large rigs, Peterbilt, Kenworth, Freightliner, International and Mack, filled the parking area like huge, rumbling logs of living aluminum and steel. The two drivers from Sun Cartage walked behind an eighteen-wheeler and stopped next to a parked red Lincoln. They opened the trunk, took off their green jackets and hats and flipped them inside. A couple of casual jackets were removed and quickly slipped on, covering almost identical shoulder holsters and semi-auto 9mm pistols. The larger of the two, Jim Gracey leaned across the roof of the car, shaking his head.

"Hey, git your lousy ass off the car. Don't you know you can scratch the paint," snapped his smaller partner, Charlie Breen.

"Fuck off Charlie. It's only a fuckin' lease car. Who gives a shit? They'll rub it out when they get it back and give you another." Charlie was a regular pain in the ass when it came to his car. He even wanted a person to wipe the bottom of their shoes before they got in.

"Well I give a shit. It's mine while I got it. You lean all over it, rub the damn dust that's blowing all over this filthy place into it, and you scratch the paint. It looks like shit then." Charlie walked over and looked very intently at the spot Jim had been leaning on. "You see it isn't shiny there anymore. You dumb fuck."

Jim walked around to the front of the car. Still looking at the entrance they had just come through. The old couple was still inside. Nothing had changed since they came out. The old biker was off to one side of the parking area, apparently having a hard time getting his Harley running. It kept starting up and running for a few seconds, then quitting on him. Every time it started, he would stick it in gear and the bike would jump forward 10 or 20 feet then shut down again. Jim looked away from the old derelict and back to the front door.

"I don't like this," he said aloud. "Nobody knows from nothin'. Who the hell are these people? Nobody tells us anything. Not my kind of a job, too many threads out on this one."

"Eh, what the fuck! We're just supposed to stick with them. Nothing to do, just watch them. Find out where they end up. We tell the boss and he tells some people someplace. Chicago or Detroit, I think. No big deal and we get paid."

"Yeah Charlie", Jim countered, "but the boss says he 'don't know' either. I mean like, we're watching them but whose watching us? You see what I mean. We don't know."

"Hey man. Nobody's watching us. Who the fuck would be out here? Stinking sand hole. Nobody, period."

Jim leaned over the roof of the Lincoln again shaking his head from side to side. He didn't like it, hadn't liked it from the beginning.

Jim and Charlie met while working in Las Vegas. Jim was a bouncer at a strip joint that Charlie hung around whenever he had a little free time. Late at night when the sightseers were back in their hotel rooms and the action had slowed down to a few slots, they would end up sitting at the bar and talking about their equally diverse misfortune, with Jim doing most of the complaining. Working as a bouncer was, according to Vegas standards, the worse job on the strip. It was cheap paying and had almost no benefits except what you could work out for yourself. And that's what he did.

Once the owner realized that Jim was regularly humping a sweet little eighteen year old waitress, he wanted to dock his paycheck for screwing the girl. Jim had convinced the girl that she was supposed to take care of the bouncer. It was pretty good while it lasted but nobody was charging him for any pussy. So, Jim quit.

Charlie worked at a variety of places, usually as a pit boss, but the management of his last job found out that, while the customers were at his tables, he was spending too much time in their rooms stealing expensive little odds and ends like earrings, bracelets and watches; anything he could easily hustle on the street. They never knew that anyone had been in their room and usually never realized anything was missing until later. Most of the time, they would wonder if they even brought the trinket with them in the first place. It didn't really matter. They were back home by then and it was too late.

Jim and Charlie, for lack of any worthwhile employment, ended up together. They began working the airports and hotel lobbies as a pickpocket team. One of them would bump the mark to turn and then distract him with some inane question, while the other made the lift. They eventually pissed off some hotel owner who had the cops on his payroll and after that, every time they tried something, there happened to be a cop around. The message was clear, 'Leave town or end up in jail'. So they left.

They ended up in Chicago working for the Alliance Investigative Association. They were called private investigators and even had business cards alluding to the fact, but there wasn't any real investigating. At least, not what either of them thought it would be like when they first took the job. What they mainly did was tail people. Or they'd stake out some house or apartment and watch, sometimes for days. Their boss called it surveillance work.

But this one was different. Joe Marchione, the President of Alliance called early Tuesday morning at 1:00 am. He was in a bind and needed them immediately. It was a good paying job. Simple too, but they had to get moving.

Actually, it was the best paying job either of them had in a long time. Two hundred bucks a day each, plus gas and motel expenses, no fancy hotels and food, regular food, no expensive steaks and no booze. Mr. Marchione didn't like pissing his money away.

The car they were supposed to tail was parked behind a Days Inn, 20 miles west of Davenport, Iowa, in a town called Wilton. They had to get there ASAP. Joe would be waiting for them. He had no idea where this car was going and because of that couldn't stay on the job himself. He needed their help.

They left within a half hour and met Joe at four in the morning and it was none too soon. There were three people in the car, a woman in her early thirties and her parents and they were leaving just as Jim and Charley arrived. The job couldn't have been any easier. All they had to do was tail them, call in every night, AND make sure they didn't lose them.

Real easy. Too easy!

That's what was bothering Jim. Four hundred bucks a day plus expenses to follow a broad and her parents. Hell, you could hire two punk kids in a pickup truck for twenty bucks a day plus gas.

And what was really fucked up was the broad. They never really got to see her. Lying down on the back seat all the time. She never got up. She was there right now. The old couple would get her a carryout and she would eat in the car. Must be sick or something. Fucked up.

Jim didn't like it but maybe Charlie was right. Who the fuck's out here anyway?

The engine coughed, sputtered twice and quit again, this time right behind the Lincoln. The old guy was cussing.

"Sonofabitching effing piece of shit. Never did run worth an effin shit."

His voice had a cackle in it. Actually, he sounded just like he looked, an old worn out rooster. Finally, the old man tried to get off the big bike and the Harley, leaning hard, rolled sideways and fell on its side. The old guy stumbled backward, caught a heel, and fell flat on his ass.

Jim shook his head in disgust and turned back to his vigil but Charlie was laughing pretty damn hard and went over to help.

Jim's head hurt like hell. He could feel a lump starting to swell above his right temple. He wanted to reach up to touch it but he couldn't move. His head was butted up against Charlie's. The center seat belt of the Lincoln was wrapped tightly around both their necks. It was locked in place and drawn tight. Hands, feet and mouth were all properly duct taped, tight and closed. He had just started to come out of it when Charlie was dropped onto the seat alongside him. It had been quick, real quick

The old guy had gotten up bitchin' and tried to lift the old 'hog' from the ground. He just didn't have the strength to do it by himself. Jim had ignored him, 'Fuck the other guy', that was his motto, but Charlie went to help the old fart.

He had said, "Thanks partner," to Charlie and stepped aside.

The old guy got Charlie first and Jim never heard a thing. Now they were thrust up like pigs going to a slaughter.

The sunglasses leaned over them and the ignition clicked on long enough to lower the front windows about two inches each. He turned it back to the off position and left the keys. Then he lowered his head so that his mouth was slightly above their ears. Jim tried to twist his head and look up but his movement was limited and all he could see was the edge of those metallic one-way glasses and part of a thick gray beard. The biker held a long narrow knife in his hand and he ran the blade very slowly, like an insect crawling, across their throats, first one, then the other. Jim started to piss his pants and Charlie was near a faint.

"Go home," he said softly, the old man crackle was gone from his voice. "No second chance," he finished.

They heard the door slam and both laid perfectly still for several minutes, afraid to even breath. Outside the car, the motorcycle came to life on the first try and the two professional surveillance detectives remained motionless until the sound of its engine faded in the distance.

CHAPTER EIGHTEEN
Wednesday Afternoon

The beard, wig and ragged clothes were gone and a much younger rider sat the Harley. The bike hummed up a long gray rise of concrete. The evening sun bumped swirling shadows from the glistening silver spokes onto the rider's boots. Both sides of US 90 flowed golden, in waves of tall yellow grass, edged with fresh new shoots, turning brilliant green from the morning rainfall. To the west, a bright azure sky faded into a blanketing mass of dark cumulus clouds that covered the horizon. The rider was near the small town of Aurora, west of Mitchell, South Dakota. Hopefully the last touch point was four and one half hours away. He needed to stop and stretch. The bike was pinching inflamed nerves, sending numbness down his left leg, and creating a knot between his shoulders at the base of his neck.

Small moving spots, pheasants picking pea gravel on the side of the road, speckled the highway one half mile ahead. He squeezed the clutch and toed the shifter into third gear, allowing the chopped Fat-Boy to back off just as an older couple in a Crown Victoria sped by. The woman, her mouth a red slash of vermilion, her face flushed with rouge and pancaked with thick powder, glanced at the lone ridre on the bike, a question immediately hit her eyes and look of bewilderment on her face.

The rider looked away and eased the bike back.

There were times when he wondered what it would be like if he was the only person left on the whole damn planet. *Hmmf, that might be nice!* He thought.

YOU WOULDN'T LIKE IT, was the reply.

You're right. I probably wouldn't. Just thought it might be fun to give it a try.

A glance in the rear view mirror assured him that no one was behind him as he slid a .22 Ruger out of his right boot. At forty-five mph and seventy-five yards, the pistol laid over the throttle, held gently, very naturally, his index finger caressing the blued frame, like it had spent a lot of time there. Forty mph and fifty yards, thirty mph and twenty-five yards. There were five of them, three drab hens and two roosters. The roosters gaudily decked out in their mating colors, iridescently reflecting the sun's rays in hues of magenta, green and crimson. They stopped pecking in unison and jerkily looked up.

The vehicles that travel the highway usually press the speed limits to NASCAR acceptance and the birds had learned to ignore the noise and the swift rush of wind. The solitary motorcycle gave them a brief pause before they returned to their pecking.

Today, even the loud popping noise of the small caliber semi-automatic didn't disturb them, but the cackling of the largest rooster as he lay thrashing on the oily, carbon scented gravel, his burnished feathers misting with bright red blood next to his dead companion, sent the three hens quickly aloft and headed for the safety of the deep golden grass.

The Harley stopped slowly alongside the two roosters. Ralston lifted the dead bird and closely examined it. There was a slight predatorily pleasure in his eye. Sure, that it was dead; he tossed it into the right saddlebag. The three hens were into a long glide, getting ready to drop into the gently, shifting grass.

IT WAS RIGHT TO CALL IT 'AMBER WAVES OF GRAIN', the voice said.

Small bumps rose on his back and along his arms and with an imperceptible shake of his head he shrugged off the thought.

"They'll have a couple more cocks hanging around them by nightfall," he said aloud, then adding, "Always do".

YOUR CYNICISM NOW APPLIES HUMAN ATTRIBUTES TO THE ANIMAL WORLD.

Ralston picked up the struggling bird by its feet and stretched it out exposing its throat. He nonchalantly sunk his teeth into the bird's throat, with a quick upward motion tore its jugular vein open, and spat the feathers and blood onto the gravel. Nonchalantly he let the bird flap its life out next to his pant leg. He liked bleeding the bird and took some private form of pleasure from feeling the slowing wing beats upon his thigh. "This one will taste better than the first," he said aloud again.

YOU DIDN'T ANSWER NICHOLAS.

I didn't like the thought.

IT WASN'T MEANT FOR YOUR PLEASURE.

The pheasant's blood dripped on his boot and he inadvertently reached up and removed a small feather from the corner of his mouth. When the bird was still, he put it into the bag with the other one. He added two rounds to the Ruger's clip, slid the light semi- auto back into his boot and toeing the shifter up moved the hog back onto the highway. He wanted to say, 'what about Oscar', but he already knew the answer. Oscar never guided him. Quite the opposite, he always guided Oscar.

The Harley rolled smoothly into the exit lane and around a long circular curve. It passed over US 90 and glided past the rest station that over-looked the Missouri River and the city of Chamberlain. The white Crown Victoria was parked in the front handicapped spot, a red clip-on tag hung from the mirror. He pulled into the last parking space and killed the engine. It was seven o'clock, the sun was cooking him and he needed to rest. Sitting in the same position on the bike wore him out.

An hour later, the pheasants skinned, split and washed from the hose behind the rest rooms, were flaming on an outdoor grill. The rest stop was empty except for the biker and the old couple. They were sharing a sandwich at the other end of the parking area. Ralston kept a casual eye on them. The man was gray-haired and moved slowly with a slight limp in his right leg. There wasn't any flex to the knee. Either the joint was fused or the old *looking* guy was wearing pants with a tear away leg concealing a long gun. Ralston knew the knee was fine.

The man walked to the car and stood next to the back door, casually looking over the roof of the car and across the parking lot at the lone biker. He had watched the biker with a concerned caution ever since he entered the rest stop. Now he appeared to be talking to himself. Finally, he left the car and limped back to the white haired woman. She was sitting on the edge of the park bench, drinking a Pepsi and taking in the big country around her.

The first piece of pheasant wasn't done but he ate it anyway. It needed some salt. When he was eating the third piece, a dark head rose from the back seat of the Crown and looked his way. She had a babushka wrapped tightly around her head and an oversized pair of Audrey Hepburn sunglasses covered her eyes. He looked away without appearing to notice and concentrated on his meal. This piece had some resemblance of being cooked.

She got out of the car and, with the old man on one side and the old woman between them, moved toward the rest room. The old woman limped. A few minutes later Audrey Hepburn came out with the old woman glued to her backside like a Siamese twin.

A van was making the long climbing circle to the overlook bringing a carload of easterners and their screaming kids to see the west. The threesome immediately became fidgety, got back in their car and hastily left the rest stop, pausing just long enough for the old man to glance sideways at the loner.

The whole thing looked like a screenplay that had been poorly scripted. The group in the white Crown would drive through Chamberlain, find a small, inconspicuous motel on the edge of town, and check in as a couple. They would request a room with two large beds and sneak Audrey Hepburn in later. Either the old guy or Audrey Hepburn would go out just long enough to get a carryout. Then they would shut down for the night and leave unnoticed before sunrise.

An hour later, he discarded the pheasant's bones into the wire trash container and let his gaze drift eastward across the long prairie. The trail of nature flowed smoothly across the golden grass, abruptly ending at the stained cement parking lot.

I want this to be the last time, he thought. *If it weren't for her I wouldn't have come. I won't be going back after this one.*

He walked the lone pathway along the scenic overlook until he came to a ridge overlooking the Missouri River far below. Night was closing quickly and he knelt facing the western sun. He became very still, closed his eyes and cleared his mind. All his outward perspective faded, the awareness of an inner void became central and the emptiness that accompanied it was now tangible. It had an essence of oneness, a unity with everything in the universe. He could feel everything around himself slow down.

Tonight there were many voices. They came from all around him as if he was in the middle of a great gathering. They started out quietly, as a whisper and ultimately built into a great raucous roar. Outwardly, silence permeated the area around him but inside the shell that made the image of the man, was a great melodious euphony of voices. They were his only peace.

And they were all talking to him.

Out in the grass, a cloud of honeybees descended over the bright yellow stamens of a cluster of Black-Eyed Susan, draining the thick pollen from the lovely wild flowers before the dropping sun hid them from view. The loner, his eyes still closed, could see them clearer than if he had searched them out. He felt their direction and their vocation. He loved their necessity and thought aloud, "Life has a way of draining the sugar, doesn't it?" — a moment pause, a slight musical note and a then a voice.

A PERFECT CIRCLE. EVERYTHING IS USED.

He waited. The night darkened.

The river below was a flowing current of lost knowledge letting everything that was wild and unencumbered soak into it, washing the city and humanity from its soul.

"A man should have essence - value. All I have is emptiness. I am a hollow gourd left alongside the paddy by rice pickers. There is nothing left," he said aloud.

YOU WILL KNOW WHEN NOTHING IS LEFT. HE WILL ALLOW YOU A MOMENT OF REALIZATION.

"I see dead bodies all around me."

NICHOLAS. LISTEN.

The image of a man, kneeling on a lone promontory high above the dark, murky river faded with the arrival of nightfall.

It flickered in the approaching moonlight and like a whisper of vanishing fog rising from the prairie grass.-.disappeared.

It was after midnight when the Harley rolled back down the long incline and crossed over the dark Missouri River heading west toward a local truck stop where he had parked his vehicle that morning.

He wonder if he should have handled the Lincoln differently. He needed to head west tonight but he had added on unnecessary time. Now, he had to check the roads coming east before he left. It was going to be a long night. He hoped the Lincoln took his advice.

CHAPTER NINETEEN

It was 6:30 Wednesday evening. Wickes and Armstrong sat across from each other in the Captain's office. The day had started with a dead Harry Teasel and it hadn't improved much since then.

"You know these things can't stay secret, Ben. Hell, I knew he was your informant two years ago on the Marcus case," Wickes said.

"I thought some things were still secret. I guess I should know better by now." Ben stopped for a moment, lost in some errant thought. "He was the syndicate hack," he continued, "had been for years. He seemed to enjoy the games. Always gave me just a touch, never too much. Took a little money and had a little fun. Castobelli might have even directed it, but this is all wrong."

"Yes. You're right; too many things don't fit. And being right begs the question, "Why did they kill him and why like that?" Wickes answered. He knew that Armstrong was holding back. Ben never revealed everything. A habit that had proven a problematic more than once and Wickes was trying to get him to open up. It wasn't working and he needed more answers.

"I don't know. He got a little cash from me, passed on mostly useless info but this time it was different. This time he was concerned. He told me they were bringing in a killer." Ben answered. The usual mocking banter between the two men had ceased. "And then there's the church." Ben was worried. He figured someone had watched his meeting with Harry at Trendy's and whoever that someone was, they were a step ahead.

"How did they know? Who placed the killer in the church?" Wickes asked. It had been two days and Wicks still didn't know where the nun was.

Armstrong got up and looked out the window at the dismal streets below. The weather hadn't improved much. It was still rainy, dreary and a morbid dull gray. Plus the smoke wafting up from the sewers added a stinking mist to the entire metropolis. The whole damn city was looking like the Gotham City set from a Batman movie.

Matthews was doing fine. Gomez, Barker and the nun had reached the safe house without any problems.

"We have to keep the nun protected until she testifies. After that she'll be safe. I can't imagine Castobelli taking revenge on a nun," Armstrong ventured.

"Maybe not but the Blade might, even from prison. And at this very moment the FBI is crawling up the Mayor's ass and she doesn't care for anyone packing her."

"Yeah, they lost two agents and they're the only ones who knew the nun was at the church, besides us," he paused shaking his head. "It just doesn't make any sense."

"You heard from Barker and Gomez yet?" Wickes asked.

"No. They're not supposed to check in until they're buttoned down. Hopefully tomorrow, if everything goes well." Armstrong lied. "Then, we'll sit down with the mayor and I'll let you know where the nun is. Besides I'm going to need your help getting her back for the arraignment."

"Yeah, well that will have to do for now." He paused, "You know this weekend was my getaway but I don't know if I can afford to take the time off," Wickes commented. "It seems like every time I make plans something comes along to screw them up."

The Captain had bought a place up around Traverse City a few years ago. A 'Place away from Places', he called it. Wickes was single. He got divorced fifteen years ago and never remarried. The place was his completely. No one had ever seen it. He never invited anyone to join him when he went there. He would check in on a daily basis but otherwise kept his cell phone turned off. He left a phone number in case of an emergency but any call would lead to an answering machine. If you needed him, you had to wait for his call back.

"You should go," Ben said, "I'll let you know when they call," he left the street scene below and turned toward the door. "I've got work to do. See you Monday, if everything goes well."

Ben walked from the Captain's office without looking back, mumbling something about this case being a Reno Runaway. He walked down the hall to his office, switched on his computer, logged in and entered his password, one that he changed on a weekly basis. He opened his e-mail. One message appeared in darkened text. He clicked the message.

Need info on Lincoln plate. R.

The message had been sent earlier that day. Ben clicked on reply and typed.

Lincoln registered to Charlie Breen. Working with James Gracey for Alliance Investigative Association out of Chicago. Small time. Used for surveillance. Might be trying to upgrade their pay. Caution advised. Will keep you updated.

He read the message then deleted the words *'Caution advised'* and hit the send button. He closed his e-mail, called the airport, got the desk for American Airlines and booked an early flight. Then he drove slowly home. He had to pack an overnight bag and catch an early flight. He already knew that a few hours of sleep was impossible. The playground just wouldn't leave his head. Drive slowly, like he was doing right now. Just drive slowly out of the alley. Simple.

He'd be up all night. Tomorrow was going to be another long day.

CHAPTER TWENTY
Thursday 9:00 am

The sun rose over the eastern skyline, a brilliant golden disk that seared the clouds and burnt red into the western horizon. It was a sunrise that scorched eyes and sucked moisture from skin. Bolts of luminous yellow filtered through a forest that was emerald green and deep blue and dripping with dew. The mist rising off the river smelled of sunken logs and green algae and wet fish skin.

The sound of tires crunching gravel forced the boy to look up just as he slid a nice eleven-inch brown trout into his makeshift canvas creel. A black Ford pickup with a sleek Harley lashed to the bed and a matching black trailer had made the turn off Dark Canyon Road and was heading into the hills toward the Ryken place.

Rainsford William Rivaneau had never seen that rig and someone new heading to the Ryken's made him curious. He slipped his creel over his shoulder, disconnected his rod and dropped it into a round cardboard rod holder that he had improvised and tied to his Honda 125. Then in one singular motion, like it had been rehearsed by a Hollywood stunt coordinator, he landed on the bike's seat, slammed down the kick starter, slipped the clutch and popped a wheelie for thirty yards up the road, spitting gray rocks and mustard colored dust into the wet morning air.

He pushed the small dirt bike over the low ridge that ran parallel to Rapid Creek and came out alongside the fence bordering the back edge of the Ryken's forty-acre parcel. He cut through an opening at the end of the rear cattle fence and followed the tractor ruts that ran across a two-acre parcel of scrub pines and ended between the old barn and large sprawling white painted ranch house. Rainsford came to a skidding halt on the gravel driveway next to the Ryken's front porch just as the Ford pickup came off the hardpan and made the turn under the white arched entrance gate.

"He's here," Brad said looking out the wide front window.

A flight of swallows like an ominous shadow coursed above the roof and a light breeze swayed the yellow daylilies that lined the driveway bending them low, seemingly into a position of homage.

As Amy and Brad Ryken walked tentatively out onto the front porch together, the man jumped from the front seat of the pickup and landed softly, almost too softly, on the driveway. Even the gravel beneath his brown elk skin boots seemed cautious.

He was a man of approximately six foot, slim hipped and deep chested giving his shoulders an appearance of great width. He wore a pair of jeans, a dark blue chambray shirt and held a brown Stetson in his left hand as he walked toward them. There was a broad smile on his face and Amy thought he was rather handsome in a hard way. His hair was straight black and tinged with gray at the temples. *Mexican or Indian*, she thought, or *possibly southern Mediterranean*, but his eyes strangely, were not. When he stopped in front of them she thought, *a very light brown, almost golden.*

"Morning folks, I heard you were looking for a hand. I thought I'd come by early and get the jump on anyone else," his hand was extended and the smile almost effervescent. Both of their hands came out automatically and the stranger shook them both. They smiled back.

"Name's John Sachs and I'm needin' some work."

"Hello, Mr.Sachs, we're Amy and Brad Ryken. Nice to meet you." Brad paused wondering if he should ask the next question. It was, after all, simply role-playing and he had never been much on formalities, usually figuring they got in the way of getting business done. But this was a strange business. He'd got the call that morning. It woke him from a sound sleep, the first one he'd had since Ben had called asking to use their place as a safe house.

"Got much ranch experience, Mr. Sachs?" he asked it anyway.

"More than most I guess. I'm a pretty quick study and I don't need much in the way of accommodations," he said, quickly holding both of his hands up like an outlaw caught in the act. That smile was on his face again. "Just a bunk in the barn and a place to park my rig. Heck, you'll hardly know I'm around."

"And who's this fine young man?" he continued smiling at the young boy quietly sitting on the dirt bike next to the porch.

"I'm Rainy Rivaneau. I live just down the road. You got a cool bike there, Mister," he said excitedly, while looking at the Harley lashed to the truck bed. "Mind if I look at it?"

"Cool? Eh! What's that mean? Cool," the man asked.

"I don't know," Rainy thought for a second before he answered. "Like real and neat!"

"Well if it's someplace between real and neat I guess it'll be okay. Just don't touch anything you don't understand. I've got a few mods on it. Might blow up if you touch them," he was smiling again.

"Well then we've got a room in the barn. Nothing much but let me show you. See if it's okay," Brad continued.

"That sounds fine," Mr. Sachs answered.

Amy watched as the two men walked off toward the barn while Rainy headed toward the pickup. She was worried. *Why was this man here*, she thought? This was *'the man that no one knew'*, Armstrong's man. They had heard of him but never met him, nobody had. From what was said back in Detroit, maybe they were better off not to. But it was too late now, he was here and it was Ben who had sent him.

The men were back within fifteen minutes and Mr. Sachs, naturally, had gotten the job. A decision that was preordained.

When Ben had joined the force, Brad was Deputy Chief of Homicide and Amy was a sergeant working in the records department. Over the years, Brad and Amy and Ben and Edna had become close friends. They attended social events, shared many dinners and even spent a couple of vacations together. After Brad and Amy retired, the couples still continued to see each other once or twice a year. Ben and Edna would send their boys out to spend part of the summer in the Hills. It was an arrangement everyone was pleased with. But after Edna's death, Ben spent most of his spare time with the boys and eventually they stopped coming.

The original call came two days ago. Ben needed a favor. Three people, a nun and two detectives, for maybe one week or until the feds could provide him with something very secure. Brad and Amy had agreed. It wasn't much of a choice. They were both retired police and Catholics. How do you say "No" to a nun?

The second call came this morning. A man was going to be looking for a job. A job that Ben knew they didn't have to offer. Just provide him with a place and pretend to *everyone*, and that point was rather specific, that he was an employee. And then just leave him *alone*.

"Boy, you sure got a lotta boxes in your truck," Rainy said as the two men returned to the front of the house.

"I sometimes need things," Mr. Sachs answered.

"What kinda things?"

"You sure are the little inquisitor, aren't you?"

"Inquisitor, what's that?" Rainy asked.

"Hmm," Mr. Sachs thought for a moment, "how about a nosey guy, who's pretty tough."

"I like that," Rainy smiled. He was pleased this new Mr. John Sachs thought he was tough.

"Well?" he asked again.

"Well what?"

"What kinda things?"

"Well, I've got a lot of things to do today Rainy. First, I've got to get settled in and see what this new job has for me. Then, I've got to get some things in town. You come back tomorrow and I'll show you some of those things. All right?"

"Sure. That'll be cool."

John Sachs walked to his truck and effortlessly leaped back into the driver's seat. He drove behind the barn where the large rig disappeared from sight.

"Rainy, you had breakfast yet?" Amy asked, knowing that he hadn't.

"No ma'am. Not yet."

"Well, why don't you come on in and I'll fix you some."

"Yes ma'am and thank you." Rainy trailed Amy into the kitchen while Brad remained on the porch considering what they had gotten themselves into. *Why would Ben send this man out unless there was a real problem?*

Friday early morning

He was fifteen feet above the entrance road coming off Dark Canyon Road. He set the camera angle and the rotary adjustment; then attached the lead from the battery and locked the watertight cover. The camera activated with any motion within a fifty-foot radius and tracked whatever moved. It was 1:30 am and that was the last camera. He had two covering the house front and driveway, two sweeping the back and rear corners and one on the entrance road. The ranch had a very large, accessible area and it was the best he could do on a short notice. He wished he had several more but right now, he'd have to bank on the naiveté of his enemies. Not the best scenario.

The night was bright. The full moon appeared guarded by paladin clouds, their shadows almost tangible. Covering pines, stood like solitary sentinels alongside the dirt road, watching anything that neared the entrance. He hoped his cameras achieved the same efficiency. John Sachs leaned back against the spongy, corklike bark of the Ponderosa Pine. He was tired and a symphony of voices filled his head, softening the evening and allowing him to relax. Tonight he wasn't searching, he already knew his direction.

This wasn't a job to help just *any* nun. At one time she was the only friend he had. The one person that made him feel like he still mattered, that he had the right to want to live. She was the person who prevented him from becoming something even worse than he already was. How many had died and how many more would have died if she hadn't convinced him that everything had some value? There were times when he doubted himself but the things she had told him always gave him a measure of balance.

Ben knew who Sister Mary Elizabeth was but he had simply asked him to protect a nun. But she wasn't just "*A*" nun, she was *his* nun and it clearly wasn't her time to die. If he could help the others that would be fine but they were really on their own. Get to the nun, get her safe and stop anyone in the way. That was what he was going to do, a simple agenda. If there was something he needed to know it would come to him. It always had. A symphony was starting. He smiled broadly. They liked the boy.

Rainy was hiding behind a fallen tree that was black and rotting. Rotting trees were filled with large crawling dark worms, slimy slugs and voracious bugs with poisonous mandibles. He didn't like the bugs so he kept his head down but didn't touch the tree.

When he arrived at the ranch, he had seen Mr. Sachs take something from his truck and walk into the forest. He had followed him all over the Ryken place and watched as he climbed and put things in five different trees.

Finally Mr. Sachs stopped and was leaning against the tree trunk. He didn't move for several minutes and Rainy starting to get worried. Then Mr. Sachs got blurry and he couldn't see him anymore. Mr. Sachs just disappeared.

Rainy thought that maybe Mr. Sachs had fallen. So he rushed forward to help. When he got to the base of the tree Mr. Sachs wasn't there. Rainy instinctively expanded his search area. He still didn't find him. Mr. Sachs was gone and with that knowledge came a feeling of dread. Rainy became scared. He backed up retracing his steps and was about to run when a voice stopped him.

"So, what did you learn?" The question echoed out of the darkness, frightening him and causing him to stagger back, bumping into the rotting tree and forcing him to instantly think about bugs.

"What?" he stammered back, searching the darkness while moving away from the tree.

"Well, you must be trying to learn something, following a person around in the dark like this."

Finally, Rainy could see him, but just barely. He was close, no more than twenty feet away but Rainy had to keep blinking because his eyes weren't working very well.

"I wasn't looking to learn anything. I just came to ask you what time in the mornin' that I should come by and I saw you a goin' into the woods. I wasn't 'sneakin or anything like that." He knew that he was. He'd been following Mr. Sachs for over two hours but he just didn't know what else to say. He didn't think of it as lying but his Ma always told him, "*Making excuses was, sometime, the same as lying.*" He hoped this wasn't one of those times.

"Just I was alone. Ma doesn't get home on Friday until three in the morning, so I just came over," he added.

"That's it, then?"

"Yes sir, that's it."

"Well, what did you learn?"

Rainy paused a moment trying to think of the best answer and finally just stuck with the truth. "I saw you puttin' things in trees. I don't know what and I don't know what for."

"Well, it's a security system. Most of the ranches hereabout are having them installed. It makes their place more secure. That's one of the things I do. Very simple. Nothing fancy. But because it's for security, the Rykens wouldn't want you telling anyone they have it. Right?"

"Right!" Rainy tried to talk in the right direction. But one moment Mr. Sachs seemed to be in one place and the next moment, he was someplace else. It was hard to see and the boy got the impression the man was always moving.

"Well then, I guess we shouldn't wait until morning." A reflection stepped from the shadows and shimmered down the tractor path.

Rainy ran to catch up.

"You want a job? I'm looking for a helper," Mr. Sachs asked.

"Well sir, I don't…."

"It pays well but if you don't need the money, that's alright. I can get someone else."

"No sir. I mean, yes sir. I could sure use a job and Ma and I, we *always* need money."

"Well that's good then. You're hired."

They walked across the pasture along the tractor path and toward the back of the barn. For Rainy, the walk seemed to last for hours.

Rainy Rivaneau would never forget that night. Mr. Sachs talked most of the time, asking him questions about himself, his family, his mom, his school, where his dad was although he seemed to already know that his father had left his mom and him several years ago. They talked about all kinds of things. Sports - his favorite? And girls did he have a favorite? His noisy motorbike - who taught him to ride like that? And fishing - and would his Ma cook the nice trout he'd caught that morning?

Mr. Sachs just seemed to know.

They walked together and occasionally bumped into each other but Rainy had to keep looking up to make sure he was really there. Sometime he could see him real good and then he couldn't see him at all, like he wasn't even there.

CHAPTER
TWENTY ONE

It was 7:30 am Friday and Mari Gomez sat in a wicker chair on the right side of the front porch. The house faced south and the sun was just starting to reach for her. It carved the eastern sky with surgical slices that cut through the Ponderosa pines like ribbons of yellow dandelions and bright citrus lemons and bounced golden roses off the surface of the river. She leaned back and let the morning heat sink in.

They had arrived at 8:30 the night before. The Ryken's had three bedrooms ready and after the long ride and poor motels, it was glorious to take a hot shower and fall into a soft safe bed. She was in the first room at the top of the stairs. Sister Mary Elizabeth was in the last bedroom down the hallway. Barker took the one in the middle. The choice had been his. If anyone came up the stairs, they would have to get passed both Gomez and Barker before they reached Sister Elizabeth's room.

Since Matthews had been shot, Barker was in a vindictive mood and waiting for a chance to get back at someone. He stayed as close to the nun as possible.

The Crown was hidden in the garage and right now Gomez felt safe and relaxed. That feeling was usually enough to put an edge back on her senses. There was always an inherent danger in thinking you were safe.

A ranch hand was taking some old boards from the peak of the arched entranceway and replacing them. He was moving up and down the ladder like he had spent years in the roofing business. She watched him intently for several minutes before rising and strolling down toward the front gate. She was dressed in figure revealing slacks, a snug black, short-sleeved V-neck top and black walking shoes. The heat of the sun penetrated her clothing, running warm down her spine. He glanced at her for a moment, his brief look seemed to blend with the heat, and then looked back to his work. He was standing on a ladder and nailing some boards in place.

That's unusual she thought, *a man who doesn't look twice, especially when he should.*

She had a black nylon hip pouch on her left hip and a cup of coffee in her left hand. Her eyes moved up and down the dirt road beyond the entrance like a radar scanner. She didn't mind playing cops and robbers, actually, she rather enjoyed it. It kept the adrenaline flowing. But she didn't belong on this trip. It was a big mistake.

"Good morning, looks like a nice day," she offered.

"Yes ma'am seems to be started that way." He was an exceptional looking man in a dark European way. She would guess Mediterranean, Greek or Sicilian. She didn't like exceptional looking men. Most of them knew it and her experience had all of them seeking to gain some selfish advantage from it.

"Many hands work on the ranch?" she asked immediately knowing the question sounded foolish.

He gave her a very large knowing smile. "Not much of a ranch ma'am, just a few acres."

"You live here."

"For the summer, I do. The Rykens let me stay in the barn. Actually, it's a pretty nice setup. It's too cold in the winter though. Then I have to find a place in town. Not much to do on this place in the winter except keep the roads clear."

"You worked here long?"

"On and off. Not enough to keep me busy full time so I do some jobs for other folks in the Hills," he paused and looked directly at her. The sun reflected off his face and his eyes gave her pause. "Visiting for a while?"

"Yes," she hesitated momentarily, "just for a short time."

"Relatives?" he asked and then seemed to catch himself. "Oh, excuse me. I shouldn't be so nosey. None of my business."

"No problem. I'm Mari Gomez. Mister?" she hung the question out.

"John Sachs, Ms. Gomez. Real nice to meet you," the smile was back and now she stood close enough to see his face. She had seen it someplace before, if not the face at least the eyes. They were too pale to forget.

He looked east into the sun and reached into his shirt pocket retrieved a pair of wraparound sunglasses and put them on.

"You must have got in late last night. I didn't see anyone arrive," he said looking back at her. Actually, he'd gone to town and spotted them in the late afternoon. They had spent several hours, doubling back around town. Parking at the golf course and at Canyon Lake Park, stopping and moving every fifteen minutes, splitting up, the two women walking into the front door of a business and out the back door where the man was waiting in the car. Whitewashing everything behind them until

they were sure there was no tail. She didn't answer, preferring instead to look at the results of his handy work. He had
clamped a board across an opening and was preparing to nail
it in place.

"Nice job." She commented. "Well, have a nice day, Mr.
Sachs." She turned and started back toward the house.

He stopped her.

"Excuse me, Mari Gomez?" he said smiling.

"Yes sir," she turned and slowly flipped a pair of sunglasses
down from their resting place above her forehead to cover dark,
smoky eyes, the color of rich chocolate, and in the same inten-
tionally distracting moment moved her right hand toward the
hip pouch.

"Was that a Mrs. or a Miss? I didn't quite get it," he asked.

She relaxed and smiled back this time. "That was a Miss."

"Well, thank you, Miss Gomez," he smiled and it seemed to
fill the whole area around her and she wondered why she was
feeling good. '*Must be the morning*,' she thought. No man had
made her feel good in a long time. She'd have to watch out for
Mr. Sachs.

Mari reached the house just as Barker came out on the
porch.

"We were followed," he spat. Neither of them had felt right
since Matthews had been shot but Barker was consistently on
edge. The look on his face could ignite cold charcoal.

"What?"

"Armstrong just called. Two men in a red Lincoln, Illinois
plate, tailed us across the state. Guess he's got a backup watching
our tail. He had them detained at that restaurant in Chamberlain
yesterday. Said to keep our eyes open, they're still on the loose."

"You've got to be kidding. Has he got a sheet for us?"

"Ben says it's already in your e-mail. As soon as you hook up the computer we'll check it out."

"Damn. And I was having this nice warm and cozy feeling, almost like I was starting a vacation."

"Well you're not, unfortunately. By the way, Sister Mary Elizabeth wants to see Mount Rushmore while were here," he said.

"You've got to be kidding?"

"Nope. She's at the kitchen table right now telling Amy how it would be such a shame if she didn't bring back some pictures to show the other sisters. Shit. People all over the country want to put a bullet in her head and she wants to go sightseeing. I guess the world looks a lot different when God's on your side," Barker offered.

"Everything's different when God's on your side Don. You should seriously think about it. A little church might smooth out some of those rough spots."

"Yeah, sure. Gerry went into a church and look what it got him," he paused for a moment, looked out at the front and then continued. "Who's the cowboy?"

"Looks like a cowboy, acts like a cowboy, even talks like a cowboy but something about him says, 'No cowboy'. I just don't know what," she answered. "Kind of nice looking, too."

"Forget it. You're not on vacation," he said. "Why don't you go inside and talk to the Sister. She'll probably listen to you better than me."

"Why? Could it be that you didn't say more than ten words to her since Detroit?"

"I don't think that she likes men. I don't think that any of them do. And while you're at it, talk to her about her touristy inclinations and since we had a tail, tell her not to leave the house," Barker added.

"Whew, we're having such a bad day already. I'll talk to her and then hook up and pull the sheet. I'm kind of curious as to who's been watching my backside," she said turning toward the door.

"Everybody," Barker opined.

Gomez shook her head and left him on the porch staring out at the hired help and the bright yellow sunrise.

Friday 9:00 am

"Well, I just think it would be marvelous. After all I might not ever get this chance again."

Sister Mary Elizabeth was on her own stage. Before entering the convent, she had majored in drama in college, and years later, she was in charge of the school's drama productions. When she had an audience, at this moment Amy and Mari, she was hard to stop. It was one of her vanities. She said it was forgivable because it was a minor vanity and God would allow such small indiscretions as long as they didn't interfere with the important things; like her calling and teaching drama.

"This is one of the great national monuments," she continued. "I've seen all of Washington D.C. but I might not be here again and... well, it would be such a shame to miss it. Don't you think?"

"I really think that we .....," Mari started.

"Besides I could always dress up as the old lady. That was so much fun." When she had a point to make, she wasn't about to let anyone else get in too many objectionable words to distract her intentions.

"What old lady?" Amy asked.

The three of them were at the kitchen table, the morning sun had crested the eastern sky and the room was flooded with warm expectations. Sister Mary Elizabeth and Amy had hit it off very well and it now became evident the sister was into side trips. Mt. Rushmore was now number one on her agenda.

"Sister Mary Elizabeth has enjoyed our attempts at disguises. Actually, she's very good at it. On our ride here, Barker and she were dressed to look like police protection in disguise, while I stayed half hidden in the car. We figured if anyone was following us, they'd wait for Barker and her to go into a restaurant and when they'd come to the car to get the Sister. They'd get me instead. We didn't encounter any problems on the way, but if she ever quits the nun business, I think there's a big job waiting for her in Hollywood as a make-up artist," Mari laughed.

"That was pretty dangerous for you, wasn't it?" Amy questioned.

"It was Barker's idea, definitely not one I would have chosen myself," Mari answered.

Mari wasn't exactly sure what she'd got herself into but it wasn't a vacation, although the Sister was pushing hard that way.

"Well, we can do that and maybe we could get to see that Crazy Horse Monument while we're at it. Wouldn't that be exciting?" Sister Mary Elizabeth continued. For all that she'd been through, her spirit was unflappable, her exuberance was contagious, and Mari was beginning to think that sightseeing was a possibility.

"Let me check out the town and make sure we're clean. Then we'll talk some more about this," she said rising from her seat.

"The pickup is next to the barn; keys are hanging by the front door," Amy said.

"Thanks, gas is on the City of Detroit," Mari countered as she picked the keys off a wooden plaque spotted with yellow daffodils and shaped like a kitten.

"I'd rather charge it straight to Ben," Amy laughed thinking that maybe this wasn't too bad after all. Some nice female company and apparently no one in the world knew they were here.

Mari crisscrossed the town. The two main roads were both one-way and by dividing it into quarter sections, she covered the area rather quickly. She worked all of the shopping centers, parking lots, hotels, motels and local restaurants. She checked out every auto repair shop and gas station, even to the point of looking inside to see any car that was being worked on.

She finished at noon on the east side of town, stopped for an ice cream cone, one of her great passions, filled the tank in the Ranger and returned to the heart of town. If there was one thing she had learned during her life, it was always to double check.

The e-mail from Armstrong read:

Two men in a red 1985 Lincoln with Illinois plates.

She found nothing that even resembled that vehicle. She was pissed at Armstrong. She didn't mind someone watching their backs but they should have known about it, besides who was doing the watching. That was regular department procedure. Armstrong should have told them. Not knowing was bullshit and it made her suspicious. Armstrong was up to something. According to department gossip, he was always up to something. Right now, she'd like to kick his ass.

She found a phone booth and placed a call to New York. She knew she was going to regret the call. She was in over her head.

Then she bought a coffee and a bagel at the Town Center Deli and sat outside at one of those high-top European bistro-style tables with wire-backed chairs, the kind you can lean into and relax. She turned it so she could watch the entire street.

Across the street was the Alex Johnson Hotel and adjacent to it was a small Irish pub with outside seating. The locals were filling the seats and the street traffic was moderately busy. She liked the town. It was a little touristy but subdued. Small shops sold Indian jewelry and pottery. There were displays of Native American artifacts and art throughout the town with small mom and pop restaurants and coffee shops mixed in. The pace was slow and there was a cosmopolitan air about the town, artsy but not the least bit decadent.

She was sipping the hot coffee and thinking that she had to work on improving her diet. Coffee, ice cream, more coffee and a bagel wasn't exactly the breakfast of champions.

"Coffee's pretty good here, isn't it?" the question startled her.

"Yes it is," she answered. She'd been watching both sides of the street and hadn't seen him walk up.

"Sort of reminds me of that Caribou Coffee place at the Minneapolis Airport," he continued, a broad smile on his face. The same one he had this morning while working on the ranch entrance.

She was also sure he hadn't been in the deli when she purchased her items.

"You spend much time there, in Minneapolis?" She didn't consciously think about it but the interrogatory automatically popped out. She was more concerned with where he had come from.

"No ma'am. I shy away from big cities but I've been to the airport." He glanced at her momentarily, a casual look but at the same time rather intense, then quickly looked away and scanned the street in both directions. His sunglasses covered his eyes preventing her from getting much of a read from him but the feeling that she had seen him before was still very strong.

"You don't like the big cities?" she asked.

"Not many feelings one way or the other. Just a little too busy for me. I once heard it said that big cities fill your life with emotional bumps. Sort of like a boat bouncing over the waves in the ocean."

"And there are no waves out here?"

"I wouldn't say that. People, they get depressed. Lack of work probably the biggest problem. But out here, it's slower. Not as many bumps. You have more time to think things over. More time to get it right."

She looked directly at him, "I could get use to that," she said smiling.

"Are you enjoying our little town?" he asked, his eyes on her once again. He moved closer to her table and for a moment she thought he was going to join her but the intention obviously passed and he stepped back.

"Yes, I like it. It's very nice. No more work for you today?"

"Not much ma'am."

A young couple exited the hotel. The man was helping the woman into a horse drawn carriage. The driver, a septuagenarian dressed in a baroque style costume, remained seated and didn't make any move to help. The horse, a dapple gray, looked to be about the same age.

"We're not in much of a hurry around here. Sort of like that old horse. He looks like he's already done his life's work."

"Are you a horseman, Mr. Sachs?" she asked still bothered by her feelings about him from this morning.

"No, Mari. Not a cowboy. I never spent much time with horses."

"You look like a cowboy." This morning he was a cowboy, she thought.

"Everyone out here looks like a cowboy, especially, the easterners and the tourists. No, Mari, I'm just a hand."

"What does *just a hand mean*', John?" It was a hard question but it didn't seem to faze him.

"Well, I guess I do whatever it takes. I get the job done." He changed the subject. "You folks going to take in any of the sites while you're here?"

"Possibly, but no decisions as of yet."

"Well, let me know if you do. I'll be glad to show you around. *Sachs Guide Service* at your request," he released that smile again.

"Thank you, John. I'll keep that in mind."

"Well, I've got to move on. I got a couple of small chores to do this afternoon. Been nice talking to you, Mari."

"Feelings are mutual John," she realized that somewhere during the conversation it went from, Ms. Gomez and Mr. Sachs to Mari and John and she wondered if that was well planned or unintentional. She continued to sip her coffee and tried to digest what had just happened while she watched him walk across the street and round the corner heading west. She couldn't say he was flip-flopping and he wasn't evasive. And it wasn't so much his answers as it was his attitude and the way he put things. It was the same feeling she had earlier. He acts like a cowboy and talks exactly the way a cowboy would be expected to talk, but she had a distinct feeling that he wasn't. He says he isn't working but she suspected he was because he did leave and men usually don't leave her when they have a chance to stay. Then he says he's a working hand but her guess is that he isn't that either. He says he likes it out here because it's less complicated but Mari had more than her share of experiences with men and Mr. Sachs is much more complicated than he appears.

She stayed a while longer hoping to see the red Lincoln, allowing her thoughts to come back to Armstrong and tomorrow. At this moment, she had several dilemmas bigger than John Sachs.

Mari Gomez had inherited a job that she didn't want or like. The transfer from the NYPD to Detroit was supposed to land her in the narcotics department. She had work to do there, work for the cartel. The ladder she was climbing went a lot higher than running around South Dakota protecting a nun who was going to be dead soon anyway. And now New York, very pleased when they found out Mari was along for the ride, wanted her help. She told them that providing information was okay but she didn't kill people. She wouldn't have any part of being involved with murder. They weren't happy with her but at this moment but she didn't give a damn. They should have set the transfer up so that she was in narcotics instead of homicide.

Sister Mary Elizabeth, the nice little non-stop talking lady that she was, should have died in the confessional back in Detroit, but Matthews got in the way. And Armstrong with his hidden tail and two guys in a red Lincoln had become a pain in everyone's ass. Now she was being given instructions by some dago goombah in New York. She finished her coffee and got up to leave just as a red Lincoln turned from Main onto Sixth Street.

It isn't getting any better, she thought. *And tomorrow morning I have to make the pickup.*

Sachs reached his truck and sat inside feeling exhausted. He had almost sat down at the table with her but a voice named

Danger warned him back. The aura coming off the woman had literally knocked him backwards. Her presence was powerful, maybe even more than she was aware of. It was controlling and manipulative. That complicated essence is what made a man want to please a woman, to do anything to gain her favor. It was at her disposal and it was as if her entire being was designed around presence control. He had been literally pushed back from her.

He waited a few minutes longer trying to place things in perspective. The situation had now changed. This woman added a new dimension to the puzzle and totally changed the rules.

CHAPTER
TWENTY TWO

"Nope, never seen them folks. Two days ago, eh? Nope, can't remember 'em."

The attendant had pierced earrings in both ears and long black hair draped Indian fashion over a gaudy INXS t-shirt. His jeans hung threateningly low on skinny hips, begging the help of a belt, and a pair of old sandals covered feet that hadn't seen wash water in several days. He couldn't have been more than twenty-five years old.

"Do I still get the twenty?" he grinned.

Charlie put the pictures and the twenty back in his pocket. The sky above the hills was a dull dirty blue filled with wet clouds of mottled gray hanging just above the tree line. His mood matched the dismal skyline. It had been that way since getting loose from the seat belts and duct tape. For a day and a half, they had stopped at every gas station from Chamberlain to Rapid City, plus every little burg in-between. The Crown would have stopped for gas someplace unless they'd changed cars and that didn't seem very likely.

They'd called Marchione at Alliance immediately after getting free. Joe was really pissed and threatened to fire them on the spot with no pay, and no gas or expense money, - nada. They called back an hour later and Joe was better but they had to find the Crown Vic and its occupants ASAP. According to Joe, whoever was paying the bill was getting pretty anxious and needed some answers very soon or nobody was going to get paid.

The Super Speed Fuel at Jackson and Sheridan Lake Drive was just about it for the city. Charlie walked back to the Lincoln where Jim stood leaning against the front fender watching both ends of the street simultaneously.

"Anything?" he asked.

"No, nothing. First we're looking for a white Crown and now I'm looking at every damn motorcycle that goes down the road." He shook his head slowly. "I swear to God, Charlie, if I see that old coot, I'm going to shoot him on the spot."

"Wait a minute," the young Indian attendant was shaking his hand in a pumping motion, "wait a minute, wait a minute," he repeated, gathering an idea that had almost left his mind somewhere between his fogged out early morning sanity and his afternoon pre-evening buzz. "I'm thinking of the wrong shit. Yeah."

"What?" Charlie asked anxiously as the attendant walked back toward them.

"The chick man. The chick. Wow! I don't know how I forgot her. She came in yesterday about five o'clock in a white Ford or Mercury. You know, those cars all look the same. Had an older couple in the front seat. I tried to see who they were, to see if I could place the chick, you know! But with a chick like that, I mean, who was looking at anything else. She walked in and paid. Wow man!"

"That's it?" Charlie said.

"Yeah man. That's what you asked wasn't it. Did I see anyone, eh? Well I did! How about the twenty?"

"He just made that shit up to get the cash," Jim said.

"Hey man, I don't make up shit."

Charlie dropped his voice enough to only be heard by his partner. "Now the hider from the back seat gets out in broad daylight, walks in and pays. That make any sense to you?"

"I told you the punk's making it up," Jim said raising his voice.

"Hey, I heard that. Fuck you guys. Trying to rip me off. Fuck both you guys."

"You want me to kick your scrawny little ass, punk?" Jim fumed.

"Sure, sure tough guy, you ain't kicking anybody's ass because for your info, she came back this morning and now it's going to cost you fifty."

"She came back!" Charlie snapped.

"That's what I said, didn't I? You guys don't hear too well, do you? And I also said FIFTY?"

Jim hit the guy hard against the side of his head and caught him as he was falling. He pulled open the door of the Lincoln and shoved the attendant's head through the front window, while holding the button forward and closing the power window slowly around his throat.

"Now cut the shit and answer the question or I'm going to snap your neck like it's a pretzel," Jim hissed. He'd had enough of the smart ass and would have enjoyed popping his head off.

"Okay, man, okay." The attendant's head was twisted sideways and he was looking down the street while the window glass pushed into the side of his throat. Jim was standing inside the door next to the window with his arm around his head, slowly applying pressure to the top of his head. The young Sioux's eyes were bulging and his guts were making a strange sound, like he was going to shit his pants and his voice had developed a definite squeak. "But, it's not good shit."

"You let us decide that. Okay?" Jim gave his head a threatening twist.

"She came in right around noon eating a chocolate sprinkle cone from Angel's Ice Cream Parlor, down the street. Man, that chick's hot. I almost lost it in my pants. I'm watching her walk around inside the place and, shit man, I'm going nuts. Then she comes to the register to pay for the gas and, like man, I got to say something so I asked her if she's Lakota."

"Lakota? What's Lakota?" Jim asked.

"You're not from around here are you?"

"One more smartass remark and it'll be your last asshole. What'd she say?"

"Well, I kinda hang onto her change and she gives me this funny look and asks if I am going to stop screwing around and give her the change. I tell her that's exactly what I was thinking about, locking up and screwing around, and would she like to have a few beers. I'm ready to close up this dump and leave right then." By this time, he's squirming around and his feet are moving like he's ready to take a dump. "Hey, you mind letting me out of here? My neck is hurting like hell."

"Just finish the story or I'll slam the door with your head in it," Jim answered.

"Okay, okay," he continued, "she leans on the counter and smiles, and I'm thinking, '*Well alright. I'm in.*' then she flips open her wallet and flashes me a shield while her right hand is moving to a little pouch she has strapped to her belt. She says, "Why don't I drag you down to the jail and lock your ass up for a couple of days. And after that I'll talk to the owner of this place and instead of 'locking up' you'll be 'locked out'." Shit I don't know what to say. Hell, I thought I knew every cop in this town but she's a new one. You know they carry guns in those hip pouches, don't you?"

"And...?"

"And nothing. Shit, I give her the change and she goes out, gets in the truck and splits."

"The truck! What kind of a truck?" Charlie asked anxiously.

"A 4 by 4 red Ranger. It belongs to the Rykens off Dark Canyon Road in the Hills."

Jim opened the window, pulled the attendant out and shoved him toward the front door of the station giving him a hard kick in the ass.

"You're a lucky little punk that I don't beat your fucking ass. And you don't get the twenty either, you little prick," Jim said angrily.

He slid into the Lincoln next to Charlie who was already putting the car in gear.

"Hey, fuck both of you cheap assholes," the attendant screamed as they drove out. "And don't come back here either or I'll call the fucking cops on you."

Charlie and Jim drove east on Canyon Lake Drive until they found a phone booth where they looked up the Ryken's address. They weren't interested in going out to the Ryken place, all they needed was the location. Besides they were pissed. They were going to call Marchione and find out what was happening.

"We're tailing cops! What the hell for? I don't like this shit," Charlie said.

"I told you this was bullshit. Two hundred a day plus. Now we know why. Remember I said 'who's watching us.' Cops! What bullshit! If we're following the cops, who the hell are we working for?" Jim answered.

"Yeah. What has Marchione got us into? Cops! And that old asshole on the bike, who the hell was he? Another cop or what?"

"We've got to call Joe," Jim stated.

Joe Marchione answered his cell phone on the third ring. "Hello."

"Hello Joe, this is Jim and we've found your Crown."

"That's great! Terrific! That sure takes the heat off us."

"Yeah, that's great but there's a problem."

"What's wrong?"

"These people that we're following are cops, Joe. That's what's wrong. Why are we tailing the police all over the country? And after you answer that, tell me who the hell are we working for? I mean are we doing something illegal? Because Charlie and I aren't looking to do any time."

"Hey, take it easy. I don't know anything about who the people are. I just got the job and it paid well. I'll check it out and let you know. Relax. When are you guys coming back to town?"

"We're going to stay a couple of days. Probably be back on Tuesday."

"That's fine. I'll have your money for you by then. Now where is the Crown?" Joe asked.

It was 6:00 pm Friday when Armstrong sat down in front of his terminal. The flight had tired him and he was ready to crash. The e-mail had been sent two hours before.

Contact made.

Good spot - bad spot.

Hard to find - hard to defend.

Lincoln in town.

Dangerous woman!

Switch R/JS

He slowly typed in his reply.

Has your location been compromised? Must inform Gomez and Barker.

Woman!!!! Baa Humbug.

BA

He shut down the computer and slowly walked down the long hallway, past the duty desk and out to his cruiser. He slowly drove home, exhausted and filled with premonition. His flight had been successful but sometimes success is painful. Maybe he was ready for an easy desk job.

Friday 7:30 pm

The FireStation Brewery, located on W. Main Street in the heart of town, was an old brick firehouse complete with brass poles and a curling staircase, which had been nicely converted into a two-story walk-up brewpub. The top floor has a glass-enclosed area fully equipped with polished brass and stainless fermenters and aging vats where the entire brewing process takes place. The customers can watch as the malted barley and grains are cooked into a bubbling mash to break down the fermentable sugars. Then, in the last few minutes of the boil, the selected hops are added. The wort, as the mixture is called, is quickly cooled before introduction of the yeast culture. After a seven-day fermentation process, the wort is racked through a centrifuge into an aging vat. Ten days later, the frothy ale is dispensed into chilled mugs to eager customers.

Charlie and Jim arrived at the pub early Friday evening and found seats on the upper level. By the time Charlie was working on his third ale, the bar below had filled up. It was a good night and he felt fine. He was involved in a personal celebration. Their job was done. They had located the Crown Vic and its occupants. The fact that they were tailing cops was taking on less significance. What did it matter? Marchione was extremely happy and that meant from now on they would get better jobs. Jobs that paid good money. In a few days, they'd be getting paid and tomorrow they were thinking of going to Sturgis where the big bike rally was happening and take in the sites.

They should both be happy but Jim was being a regular pain in the ass. At this moment, he was outside looking over all the bikes and their riders, searching for the old man from Chamberlain. Jim had a stubborn streak that wasn't going to be satisfied until he found that old goat. Charlie just wanted to let it all go. He was apprehensive. There was something about the old guy, *if* he was an old guy, and that never felt right. And if they did find him and he was another cop..... well, they didn't need any problems.

"Hey Renee! How you doing? I haven't seen you in a while."

The waitress had just put a tray full of empty glasses on the counter and was punching an order into the cash register. She glanced over at the guy sitting two seats down from the order area. He was sitting with a pretty, young redhead.

"Working as usual. How are you Bill? How's the airport business treating you?" she answered.

"Pretty good. I've got no complaints. How's Rainy doing?"

Bill Sempling had gone to school with Renee and at one time, they'd been friends. They had actually dated a couple of times in high school but there was never any connection between them. Her son Rainy, a by-product of her marriage to a restaurant supply salesman from Omaha who had convinced a small town Hills girl that life with him was going to be *Easy Street*, was all she lived for anymore. The salesman didn't last long. The marriage was the classic salesman story. He didn't like the small town Hills life and dragging a wife and kid along in his business wasn't his idea of living. He deserted her and Renee wasn't ever going to be *easy* again. Asking her out now was a waste of words. She wasn't going.

She brightened up for a moment, "He's doing just fine. Thanks for asking." You didn't have to be too smart to see it was a topic close to her heart.

"I pass your place several times a week and I always see him working that stream. A natural fisherman that boy is." He shook his head grinning.

"Yeah, world class," she answered, picking up her tray, now filled with fresh drinks and turning away as she headed back toward the main floor. Bill watched her reflection in the mirror as she moved away. *'Nice looking woman,'* he thought.

The FireStation put out a yearly calendar to help spice up business during the biggest bike rally in the country. Every month would feature a picture of a new or classic motorcycle draped with one of their waitresses in a sexy pose. It was great for business and brought the bikers in like cattle. A few years back Renee was always a feature shot but in the past few years, she'd opted out. Nothing wrong, she said. She just didn't want Rainy to see his mother like that.

CHAPTER
TWENTY THREE

A young woman wearing a short mini skirt, a tight red sweater and spiked heels walked seductively up the staircase and sat at the table next to Charlie. The hemline was well above her knees. She appeared to be alone. The wait staff was overloaded and she waited for several minutes for a waitress. Charlie couldn't stop himself from staring and apparently his attention didn't offend her. After several minutes, she turned in his direction, smiled at him and adjusted her legs to her new position. The dress slid up another inch.

"You live around here?" she asked, surprising Charlie. Usually, he was the one trying to start the conversation and now this one was doing it for him.

"No, just passing through on business. I'm here with my partner."

She looked around expectantly. "Where's he at?"

"He's out front checking out the bikes. He's got a thing about them," he smiled.

"That seems to go with this crowd," she said.

Charlie couldn't help but think this was his kind of a woman. Really hot. Tight skirt, tall spiked heels, a tit-hugging sweater and long black hair. Sleazy and hot! Their conversation continued for several minutes before the waitress showed up and Charlie bought her a drink. She had relaxed and moved closer. She was enjoying his company.

Charlie was already in a state of expectation when Jim appeared, a drink in his hand, climbing the long stairway and watching Charlie with some young chick, their chairs almost touching, in what appeared to be an intimate conversation.

"Charlie, my man, what have you found here while I've been gone?" Jim asked staring directly at the woman.

"Hey Jim, meet Anna. Anna this is my business associate, Jim. Anna's visiting the area and is going to party with us a little. Ain't that right, Anna?" She met Jim's stare and smiled back.

"No smart girl would want to miss an opportunity like that with two good looking guys like you," she smiled again and slid forward on her chair forcing the skirt up another inch.

Charlie signaled the waiter for another round and Jim gave the woman an agreeable grin. A first, he figured the town was going to be a big nothing but that idea was fading fast.

Down below, the bar appeared to be filled to maximum capacity. There were a lot of bikers in town for the upcoming rally and some of the locals had joined in tonight to enjoy the atmosphere. There were even a couple of Indians at the end of the bar, which was an oddity. Four bikers sitting at a table directly below were having some drinks and occasionally looking up. One was especially attentive, having difficulty keeping his eyes off the woman.

An hour later, after Charlie had ordered several more rounds, both he and Anna were showing signs of being quite needy. Charlie was stroking her right thigh and the intensity of their breathing was becoming noticeable.

"Why don't the three of us go back to our motel and relax," Charlie asked laughingly and Jim wondered why it had taken him so long.

"I thought you would never ask," she laughed loudly, the noise caused the bikers to look up again.

A lone Indian sitting at the next table shook his head at her loud laughter, got up and hobbled slowly down the staircase and out the front door. A dark woman at the bar followed him with her eyes. He moved with a distinct limp on crooked legs and after exiting the front doors continued slowly down the crowded street. When he was next to the red Lincoln, parked three spaces from the front door, he bent over, rubbed his leg near the ankle, adjusted his frayed pant cuff, snapped a small black box inside the Lincoln's front wheel well and then, raising himself slowly continued down the street disappearing around the first corner.

Charlie, Jim and Anna clung to each other as they navigated their way down the staircase and out to the dark street. The four bikers, apparently having lost interest, never seemed to notice their departure.

Jim stopped outside the entrance and looked at two chopped Harley's. "Anna baby, do you dig bikes?"

"No," she slurred, leaning hard against him, "I never liked them, too damn noisy."

"You ever ride on one?" Jim continued. He seemed really into these bikes. Charlie just wished he'd quit with the bike shit. He had something else on his mind.

"No baby," she grabbed at his lapel and rubbed her breast against him, "let's go. I'm really starting to get horny. Let's go to your place and fuck."

"That sounds good to me," Charlie chimed in and pulled her back against him.

When they reach the Lincoln, Charlie got in the driver's side while Anna and Jim piled in through the passenger door. Charlie backed out onto Main and proceeded to drive crookedly down the street, while Jim crowded against Anna, his right hand slowly rubbing her knee. As he looked out the back window, Jim watched four Harleys come around the corner behind the Lincoln.

"Honey, I've got to ask you a real personal question," he said. The bikes were three blocks back.

"Sure lover, whatever you want," she added, giving him a small peck on the lips.

"Well, I'm just checking out them long, lovely legs of yours and I'm wondering if you've never been on a bike, how come you've got an exhaust pipe burn on your left ankle bitch?" His left arm coiled around her neck and he jerked her head against his chest and pushed the barrel of a 9mm against her cheek.

"Don't move. Don't even breathe heavy," his voice had become thick and guttural.

Charlie hollered, "What the hell you doing? What the fuck's wrong with you?"

"What the fuck's wrong with *you*? Your dick is so hard you can't see the bitch is setting us up," Jim fumed. "Isn't that right, sweetheart? Your four pals from inside the bar have been on our ass since we left the place. Check your mirror, Charlie."

Charlie looked at his rear view mirror and made a right turn at the next corner. The bikes followed. "Fuck, yeah."

"They're setting *US* up," Jim laughed and leaned his mouth next to Anna's ear. "We set people up, you dumb bitch. We do! Not you. Not four, dumb fuck bike jockeys either. Nobody sets us up."

Charlie watched the bikes behind them. "She gets us to the motel and then she gets them in the room somehow. Maybe she has to go to the john to freshen up; maybe she just makes sure the door is open before she goes to work on us; maybe they just kick the goddam door in. Then they beat the shit out of two horny businessmen, steal our money and - shit, and maybe even kill us. God, what a bitch this is."

"What do you think about that, sweetheart," Jim twisted her head back and went nose to nose with her, the gun held close to her left eye. "How many times you play this game?"

"You better not hurt me. They'll kick your ass," she answered.

Anna didn't know how else to act. Maybe she could get them to worry enough to back off, but the gun changed everything. She figured these guys weren't real salesman but she couldn't believe they had guns. No one had mentioned any artillery. They were supposed to be easy cash. They had pulled this caper more than a dozen times. Usually they didn't even have to touch the mark. They didn't want their wives or companies to find out, so they would just turn over their money. This one was a little more personal. The boys were supposed to rough these guys up a little. Someone wanted them noticed. And the pay was a lot higher. The guys and she were making a move to the big time. Now this asshole with the gun had her worried real bad.

"Look, if you just stop the car and let me go, they won't do anything," her voice had developed a tremor.

"Shut the fuck up," Jim raised the gun as if to hit her and she cowered back down.

"Maybe she's right Jim. Maybe we should just let her go," Charlie offered.

"What? There's a big ass rally starting up. We let her go and the four assholes behind us and their five thousand buddies are all after us. Just keep driving. At least right now they think their little game is still on."

"Look, asshole just let me ......" Anna thought she'd try again.

Jim slammed the barrel of the 9mm under her chin. Her teeth cut into her tongue and her head snapped back.

"Shut up! I'm not going to tell you again. Now stick out both of your hands. I'm going to show you a little trick a biker friend of yours taught me." This time she didn't argue.

Opening the glove box, he took out a roll of duct tape. He wrapped it around her hands and then around the seat belt strap and drew it tight, pulling her hands across her lap and locking them in that position. Then he tore off a strip and secured her mouth.

"Turn right at the next block. See if you can get a little more distance," he ordered. Jim had obviously taken control of this situation and Charlie, because he had no idea what to do, was glad to let him.

"I hate these bikers. First that cocksucker in Chamberlain. That bastard gave us more trouble than we needed. Now these fuckers. I mean, they think they're going to fuck over us." Jim looked in the side mirror. Charlie had them four blocks back. Then he looked at Anna. The arrogance that only a moment before filled her eyes was replaced with something closer to fear.

"Charlie, what do you think? Aren't you sick of these bastards?" Jim said.

Jim was at a level that Charlie had never seen and that had a calming effect on him. He glanced at the mirror. 'Just four guys who don't know from nothing. They ain't shit,' he thought. Then, much calmer, he says to Jim, "Yeah, yeah. Fuck these bastards." He grinned maliciously at Anna. "You want to know something bitch? The party is still on!" he let out a small laugh, "and we're still going to fuck you."

Andre the Horseman, Johnny Silver, Samson and Cool Duane rolled around the corner in a smooth wave. The Lincoln was almost four blocks ahead but that was all right. No traffic lights ahead and traffic was light. The sky had a thick cover with dark clouds rolling eastward like globs of dirty gray cotton candy. It looked like rain was coming, again. They hated the rain.

The car ahead turned into an industrial and commercial area. All the lights were off. The businesses were closed for the weekend. Their hotel must be somewhere close and in this area it wasn't going to be one of the fancier ones and that was good. Anna was sitting in the middle and the big guy in the passenger seat was all over her. Johnny didn't like it when someone mauled her. The last guy who did that, a fat ass ice-cream executive from Duluth, Johnny damn near beat to death. Now this guy up ahead was getting Johnny pissed.

The Lincoln pulled off the road into a strip mall, swung the corner and disappeared down a long, narrow alley behind the stores. The four bikers looked questioningly at each other and accelerated. The bikes, almost in unison, skidded around the corner and rushed into the alley.

The alley was narrow, dark, and damp from an afternoon shower. It smelled of mold and maggots and wet mushrooms. The edges were lined with overflowing garbage containers and the cement leading to a center drain was cracked and pitted and clogged with debris. The alley forked near the end, the left side turning off first, dividing the stores into two sections. The right side split thirty feet farther along, butting up against the back of a new row of stores.

The Lincoln was gone and Johnny Silver could feel that something had gone wrong. He turned up the throttle and pulled ahead. The four Harleys roared down the alley, the sound of their motors pounding the brick walls and rattling windows like a jet engine reverberating through a sound tunnel.

Anna twisted around as far as she could, frantically trying to tear her hands free. She bent her head forward and banged it in rapid successions against the center horn pad.

Johnny Silver spooked at the sound of the horn just as he caught site of the two men standing in the shadows at the opening of the left alley beneath a garage overhang. Before he could react, Jim shot him in the center of the face from not more than three feet. The bike cartwheeled and slammed into a doorway covered with steel grating. It bounced off the door, completely flipping and crashing to the pavement where it spun in slow circles. The rider, lying under it, was faceless except for a piece of dangling meat that resembled a nose. The second biker, Andre the Horseman, a look of astonishment on his face, took the next two slugs in the center of his chest.

Charlie, his 9mm held straight out in stiff arm fashion, rapid fired eight rounds as the last two bikers passed within six feet of him. Each was hit at least three times. The pounding engines of four big Harleys, echoing down the narrow chamber of the alley, had all but eliminated the sound of the pistol fire.

Jim and Charlie ran, leaping over bikes and bodies, back to the Lincoln. Jim, slamming into his seat, grabbed Anna by the hair and forced her head over the back seat.

"Look at that bitch. See what your four buddies just got."

The bikes were still running, their dead man throttles still turned up. Fifteen feet from the chaos, blood was flowing in wide rivulets toward the center sewer drain. The four bikers were dead where they had tumbled and Anna, behind her taped mouth, was screaming an agonizing wail that only her brain could hear.

Jim twisted her head back around and shoved it down into his lap. "Head west into the hills," he snapped at Charlie, "we've still got things to do with her."

Charlie put the car in drive and carefully inched out of the alley. Everything was clear. There was some light traffic passing by but no commotion. Nothing!

Anna was turned on her side, her head being pressed tightly against Jim's lap. She was terrified; tears were streaming down her face. Fear had locked her up and she could barely move. Her skirt had slid up to her waist exposing her silk panties.

Charlie reached over, stroked her ass, and realized he had an erection. "Yeah, we're not done yet," he says excitedly, "hell no, we're not."

The Lincoln shot out across the south end of the parking lot, turned toward Route 44, and headed in the direction of the Hills.

Mari got to the truck quickly but it wasn't quick enough. She'd lost them. Now she was circling the business district. That's how she'd been taught. Just keep making circles and eventually you'll find either the center or the edge.

It was a perfect set-up. The woman had moved on the two men. She was a pro, either a hooker or *something else*, take your pick. But a smart hooker doesn't pick up two at a time and go to their room. The situation is too hard to control. Besides this one was too good looking. She could get what she wanted from any one john; she didn't need to complicate things. By the way the four bikers left, Mari figured they were the *something else*. Mari shouldn't have gotten involved, she knew that, but she wanted to know who the guys in the Lincoln were. She was even considering approaching them herself. Maybe she could get some information, but this woman had come into the bar and gone straight to them.

She was two blocks away when she heard the crashes and what sounded like muffled gunfire. It took her several minutes but she located the alley by the sound of the running engines and drove straight into the mess. The bikes were piled up like a disposal unit at the end of a local drag track. Blood and gasoline flowed together like something natural. The four bodies had slid until they slammed into something solid. All were grotesquely broken and twisted. It looked like a scene from a Stephen King novel.

She checked the bodies, all of them were dead, then she backed off the area far enough to be out of sight and called the local police. They arrived within minutes and cordoned off the area. Her job was the nun. At least, that was how it had to appear and that was where she went. She reported to Barker while driving back to the ranch. He needed to watch the front gate. She'd talk to the locals in the morning but the girl and the two from the Lincoln were still out there, and she needed to talk to Ben. He wasn't going to give her much but she needed to know how many players were in the game. It was starting to get a bit crowded.

It was trouble. Whenever the phone rang at 2:30 am, it was trouble. Armstrong rolled over and reached for the receiver.

"Hello," he moaned. Just from his tone, the caller realized the call was not welcomed.

"Ben, it's Mari and we've got trouble here." Ben sat up, suddenly wide awake.

"What's wrong?"

"The Lincoln showed but along with it were what looked like five shooters."

"What does that mean 'looked like five shooters'"?

"The boys in the Lincoln took out four of them tonight. The fifth was a woman and they still have her. I lost them. Someone put the hit on them and it backfired. God knows what they're going to do to her. We need some backup. Two of us aren't going to be enough."

"For Christ's sakes," he paused and she could tell he was making a decision. "Well, I've been getting enough pressure, so I guess we're going to let the FBI in again but this time from another group. I can't let Detroit in. Let me see what I can do. Those guys in the Lincoln have outdone themselves. They're just small time."

"Well, small time grew up tonight. I'm going to check with the local Police tomorrow and see what they've dug up. I'll get back with you."

"Do that! You should have backup within two days. "

"Sorry about ruining your sleep. It's earlier here."

"Thanks for the reminder. That's going to make me feel a lot better."

"By the way, are you ready to tell me about who's been watching our back?"

"No. Some questions are not allowed. Good night."

"Good night, Lieutenant."

CHAPTER
TWENTY FOUR

A dark overcast sky occasionally allowed the quarter moon to flicker from behind rolling waves of clouds like a child playing peek-a-boo in the shadows. The red Lincoln slithered like a snake between trees lining the two-track in the deserted campground. The two conspirators with their captive had driven deep into the Black Hills until they found a small two-site campground that somehow had eluded the opportunistic bikers. They drove silently past a single outhouse and the empty campsites, each with a fire pit and a weathered picnic table. Charlie continued around the circle and stopped near the entrance, blocking the entrance road, and parked the car.

"This is perfect," Jim said, "it has a picnic table." He stroked Anna with his free hand and affectionately whispered, "The late night snack that we're about to enjoy has to be spread out on a table. Don't you agree, sweetheart?" His laughter sent ripples of fear through her. She mumbled behind the duct tape and Jim grabbed a corner and tore it off her mouth. The tape ripped at her lips, creating dozens of small blood spots. "You want to say something. Go ahead, honey. Talk dirty like you did back at the bar."

"Please let me go. Please. I won't tell anyone what happened. Please." Her pleads were a prayerful beseeching. A beg for mercy. A death row walker entreating her executioners for one last chance at salvation.

The whimpering incited Jim. He grabbed a handful of her hair and dragged her, stumbling and falling toward the back end of the isolated campground. Anna saw a picnic table under several tall trees and realized where he was taking her. She dug her heels hard into the moist ground. It was her only way to resist. Jim slapped a heavy blow to the side of her face knocking her backward to the ground. Her hands were still taped in front of her and she was unable to soften the fall. She landed hard on her back and twisted in pain.

"No, you're not. I'm not going there. You let me go," she demanded. "Please. I don't want to be here, please," she screamed, struggling against her bonds and further irritating Jim.

"Shut up," he hollered. Dragging her back to her feet, he punched her hard in the ribs, doubling her over in pain.

"You just don't seem to understand. Remember the bar bitch? This was something that you started. You said you wanted to go and fuck. Well, here we are and now you want to change your mind. Well that's not going to happen," his voice was a raucous bark. He had become something animal, something sub-human.

Jim's mood was beyond anything he had ever experienced. It was both deliciously foul and psychologically erotic. He killed those bastards on the motorcycles. It was the first time he ever killed anyone and the feeling of power was overwhelming. Now the prospect of making this bitch do what he wanted had him extremely excited. She was going to please him immensely. Every time she cried, he smacked her and then she'd cried again. Seeing her shake with fear gave him a hard-on. His cock felt like it was going to explode. He was going to do her good, scare the fuck out of her until the fear caused her to snap and then he was going to - hell, he hadn't figured that out yet, but he would. He was sure of it.

He pulled a lock blade knife from his pocket and flipped it open. She stared at the steel blade shining in the moonlight and he could see the tears forming again in her eyes. 'What a rush,' he thought. He didn't know why he hadn't done this years ago.

Charlie was standing next to him with a smirk on his face. "I found her," he said. "I get to go first."

"Charlie, you asshole. She found us. Go back to the car and get the tape. We're going to make sure she doesn't try to run away and miss out on all the fun," Jim said. "I'll just get her ready." He grabbed her skirt, ripped it off and threw it at Charlie. "You can have that first," he laughed.

"Sure, I'll get the tape, man, but I still get to go first." Charlie argued turning and running back toward the car.

"You wouldn't want to run away and miss out on any of the fun would you sweet-heart?" Jim said, laughing as he grabbed Anna by the throat. "See the blade?"

Anna nodded her head in the affirmative; her tear filled eyes never wavering from the tip of the blade. Jim forced her steadily backwards onto the picnic table holding the knife just inches from her eyes.

"Now don't move even the tiniest bit. We wouldn't want you to get cut, would we," he chortled. The noise coming from deep within, from someplace a man shouldn't go.

He moved his knife hand under her sweater from her waist to her breast and in one motion sliced her sweater open. Then he cut each arm free. He put the knifepoint under each bra strap and sliced them apart. Then he laid the blade against her abdomen and slowly ran it upward between her breast and under her bra.

"Careful now," he said. His voice had become lower and the words guttural, almost undistinguishable, "I'm just going to set these two beauties free," he paused and wets his lips. The knife cut slowly through the bra material and the brasserie folded open.

"Now, isn't that nice," he growled. He put the knife against her throat, freezing her and rubbed her breasts, slowly, one at a time. Jim slowly dragged the knifepoint down between her breasts, letting the point trickle down her abdomen. He slid it under her panties, flipping the blade over and with a violent jerk cut them free.

Anna was terrified. Her friends were all dead, shot to death by these two monsters and now her anger was gone, driven out by absolute panic. She had seen women pushed around before. She had seen it at rallies and bike clubs but this was totally different. She knew they were going to kill her. Fear had removed her ability to act. She couldn't move. She could barely speak. He had her hair held tightly in his left hand while his knife was running circles around her left nipple.

"I ... I ..won't tell. Honest, I won't tell."

"Oh, hah, hah, ha. I know you won't tell! And you know something, darling? You're going to do everything I tell you. Do you understand?" He pushed the point of the knife slightly below her nipple and hard enough to cause a sharp pain and draw a drop of blood.

"Yes, yes… yes. Please don't hurt me," she pleaded franticly, "please, please."

Jim backhanded her across the face, slamming her head against the picnic table.

"Shut up! I don't want to hear your whining. One more peep from you and I'm going to cut this pretty little nipple off, pop it in my mouth and eat it. And you can watch. You don't want to see that, do you?" He laughed again. The rush….the fucking rush….he couldn't believe how hard his cock was.

She shivered at the look on his face. Her head moved sideways to signify a negative answer. Tears poured from her eyes and a fear unlike anything she had ever known shook her body in violent sobs.

"Please, please…please," It was only one word. It was all she could think. She didn't even realize she was saying it. The word was rolling sporadically between sobs, "please…please,".

"Charlie," he yelled, "hurry up with the tape. Damn it."

He moved the knife to the right side and started the pattern around the right breast. "Let me show you what I've got for you sweetheart." Unbuckling his belt, he shoved his pant and shorts down around his knees. "Look what I've got for you. Meet your friend for the night," he laughed. She sobbed and turned away from his penis.

"I said 'look' goddammit," he backhanded her across the face again, smashing her face into the table. Blood was running from her nose and her lips were bruised and swollen but, thankfully, she was beyond that form of realization. Her mind was shutting down, preparing itself for a form of agony that Anna couldn't handle in any state of awareness.

"Charlie," he repeated and a roll of tape spun like a Frisbee over his shoulder, landing with a flop on the table next to Anna's leg.

"What the fuck's wrong with you, Charlie? You could have hit me asshole," Jim exclaimed. He quickly turned around and found himself looking straight into the muzzle of a short-barreled automatic.

"Your pants are down," a voice said softly.

Momentarily confused, Jim looked down. The gun flicked and dealt him a crushing blow to the side of his head. He fell backwards, stopping only when the back of his naked thighs banged into the picnic table. A second upward blow tore into his right cheek driving him toward the girl.

As Jim fell Anna kicked viciously and rolled sideways off the table. She struck the seating plank and slammed hard onto the moist ground. Jim landed on the table stunned. Blood poured from a fierce gash running from his jawbone to just below his eye.

Anna slid away as quickly as she could until her back bumped into the trunk of a large overhanging tree. The fear, which only moments before controlled her, was still deep inside. She huddled against the coarse bark, shivering, unable to distinguish reality from imagination; unable to know if her mind was working properly or if she was already dead.

The man was dark and although mostly hidden by the night shadows, appeared to be an Indian or an oriental. His hair was dark and held in place with a soft leather headband. He was wearing a dark chambray shirt and jeans. He resembled the locals that could be seen around town or at the Pow-Wows in Rapid City. His image shimmered every time the moonlight passed him, and when he moved, she wasn't able to hear him. She wiped the tears from her eyes but the image continued to flicker.

He worked quickly with the tape and wrapped it around Jim's neck. Then he slipped the tape between the boards tightening Jim's head to the table. He proceeded to secure his hands and feet, lashing them to the seating boards until Jim was spread eagle.

All the while Anna sat motionless. It was as if she had become a block of petrified wood, unable to move, a part of the visual landscape of unexpected events of which she was such a critical part. She wasn't sure if what she was seeing was reality or some wish her subconscious was providing. Maybe she was still on the table waiting for Jim's knife. Now he was there then he wasn't, flickering like a celluloid vision in some theatrical dreamscape.

The man finished what he was doing, stopped and picked up Jim's fallen knife. He walked toward her and extended the knifepoint. He nodded and she instinctively extended her bound hands. He cut her loose. She crawled to where her skirt had fallen and quickly pulled it on. Her clothes were ripped and strewn all around. She was looking for the scraps of her sweater when the chambray shirt hit her gently in the chest. She pulled it on quickly and, embarrassed by her nakedness, looked away from him toward Jim, who now appeared to be fully conscious.

"Who the hell are you?" he screamed. "This bitch was trying to rob us. Let me loose asshole! We're detectives and she has to be turned over to the police. Charlie? Charlie? Where the hell are you? Come over here and shoot this son-of-a-bitch," Jim screamed.

The dark man pulled a strip of tape off the roll and placed it tightly over Jim's mouth then he turned back to Anna.

"Are you all right?" he asked. The voice was smooth and monotone, as if nothing at all had happened. It had an immediate settling effect on her.

"Yes, I think so," she was still trembling and placed her hand across her mouth and against her throat. It came away bloody.

"You're injuries will be okay but what about what's going on in your head? Is that all right?" he asked.

"Yes, I'm okay," she answered, "but that bastard was going to cut me. He was going to kill me," she sobbed, her entire body shaking. The relief of being off the table and free was almost uncontrollable.

He turned toward the supine man and threw the knife. The point buried itself into the table between Jim's legs and vibrated moonbeams. Jim looked down at the blade and momentarily stopped struggling to free himself. Beads of perspiration appeared on his forehead, ran down his temples and finally dripped onto the table.

"This has to be finished here," he said, once again looking at her. "I don't hate this man, maybe you do. Justice is sometimes done in unusual ways. It doesn't really matter to me as long as it gets done."

The man walked over and removed the 9mm from Jim's shoulder holster, slid the clip loose and checked to make sure that a shell was chambered. Then he replaced the clip and set the gun alongside the knife.

He stopped briefly and Anna watched as the two men stared at each other. Jim struggled to speak from behind the tape. He wanted a second chance to be heard. The man looked at him stoically, bent down and whispered, "No second chances," and suddenly Jim's eyes rolled backward and he became very still.

The dark man turned back to Anna and now he looked very oriental. He was hard to focus on. One moment he appeared solid, the next she thought that she could see through him.

"I need to know who hired you and why. I need the truth." He made it sound like a request but it went deeper and she couldn't deny it.

"Alliance Investigating Association from Chicago. We always do businessmen. They're easy money. We thought this one must be some big time corporate stuff because it was bigger, a lot of money, four grand, usually it's just six or seven hundred. Everyone thought it was too much but Duane said we were moving up. Duane always handled the connections and the money." She felt herself starting to calm down as she talked.

"Anyone of your guys carrying hand guns?"

"No. No one ever carries. We were just going to rough them up a little. That's all."

"Unfortunately you weren't told everything or you might not have gotten into this. I got to the scene immediately after it happened. Two of your friends were armed, small calibers with silencers, and I think the pay was a lot higher. Probably around ten or fifteen g's. You get the marks into the hotel and let the boys in. They rough them up a little and fleece them. Then you leave the room. Your job is done but after you leave, they put a couple bullets into the marks head. You get paid a couple hundred but your pals make thousands. You weren't a partner. You were a low priced employee," he continued.

She shook her head confused. "Why wouldn't they tell me?"

"Maybe you're not in favor of killing people, which now puts you in an odd position. You'll have plenty of time to think about that later but it better be away from here. The other man is lying next to the car. He's dead. The keys are in the ignition. When you leave, take both wallets. Drive in any direction. Do not stop. Every time you cross a state line, change the license plate. The car should be good for about three days after the bodies are found. Read the papers and listen to the news. Burn the wallets and all their contents. People who knew your friends will want to know what happened to you. Disappear for a while. Don't get pulled over for speeding and don't call or talk to anyone. Make sure the car is clean when you dump it. No prints. These people have friends coming into this area who would like to finish what was started here."

He did a small walk around the picnic table and picked up the remnants of her clothing and dropped them next to her. Take all of this with you, don't leave anything behind. He looked over at the struggling Jim and back at Anna. "Do you want to do this?" he asked.

Anna looked at Jim and thought about everything that had happened in such a short amount of time. He had killed Johnny and the guys. He had stripped and beaten her. He and Charlie were going to rape and kill her. He cut her, fondled her and stuck his penis in her face. She thought about what her team would say and what they would want her to do. She might have only been a pawn but she owed them something. Their scam was blown; the two marks weren't marks at all, but some kind of gunmen. Everyone was dead and at this point and she would be also except for this guy who came out of nowhere and whom she could hardly see. She stared for a moment at Jim who was looking directly at her. *His penis isn't so hard now,* she thought.

She thought other things too. She had no idea who this dark man was. No one had mentioned another person and besides that, *Where in the hell did he come from?* And, *he keeps fading in and out and I just want to get the hell out of here.* She looked away from him into the dark night forest. *Why does anyone walk alone in the forest at night?*

"Yes," she says softly. "Yes, for me I want to do it but for my friends, I need to do it." When she looked again, the man was gone.

He opened the passenger door and lifted her purse from the floor. Inside he found a pen and some Post-it notes. He copied her id, social security, address and all the pertinent info he could find. Then he placed the purse back on the floor and closed the door. As he reached under the fender and retrieved the tracking device, he heard the first shot, followed moments later by a second. *Always two*, he thought. *Good!*

Ralston watched as Anna removed Charlie's wallet and what appeared to be loose money from his coat pocket. She threw the items on the passenger seat along with her shredded clothes, got into the Lincoln and drove slowly from the campground. At the entrance, she turned south and disappeared down the dark road.

There was certain arrogance about how she had stepped over the body instead of walking around it. Ralston liked that. You put a gun in someone's hand and they get nervous, in others, their confidence soars. *She'll show up eventually*, he thought, *and someday — he might need someone like her.*

How come some of us are so good at killing? I can do it but that woman couldn't do it. Some would rather die or at least consider the possibility before they would do the deed. I think they have peace. I think they are capable of sleeping through the night without some demon waking them.

THE DEMON IS YOUR OWN. YOU HAVE CHOSEN TO BE A WARRIOR. AND WHILE MAN WILL ALWAYS HAVE THAT NEED, THE WARRIOR WILL AWAKEN TO THE REALIZATION THAT HE DOESN'T LIKE WHAT HE HAS BECOME. THE WARRIOR OFFERS HOPE OF BETTER THINGS BUT LIVES WITHIN THE WORST OF TIMES.

Then I am the worst of mankind.

THE WORST ARE THOSE THAT KNOWINGLY DO IT FOR A PERSONAL GAIN.

In the jungle, if you go without shoes, the worm will burrow into the bottom of your foot. If you catch it before it fully imbeds, you can kill it and pull it out but if it gets completely under the skin, it will form a large feeding area. Then the wound fills with pus and larva and can cripple a man. The worm is within me.

DID YOU THINK THAT YOU WALKED AWAY UNHARMED?

I fear that I have a deep wound. I don't like what I've become. I've known this for some time.

YES, YOU HAVE!

The contract's done. They have to pay. The thought stuck in her mind and it was perfectly clear. All that leaving the area got her was *away* and she deserved more than that. She parked the Lincoln one block from her motel and walked the rest of the way. It was 3:00 am in the morning. The bars were closed and the streets quiet, at least in this part of town, but about one mile away the police were probably swarming. She was scared but it seemed as if she had been terrified the whole night.

This was new to Anna. The game with the marks was always that, just a game and some quick cash and she really felt they deserved it. They were always married and they paid because they didn't want their wives to find out. Men were like that.

She took a long shower. She needed to scrub as much of this night off her as possible. Then she used the wet towel to rub down everything in the room that she imagined she might have touched. The Shadow Man, that's how she had started thinking about him, told her to make sure the car was clean. Well it wouldn't hurt to do the motel room either. She packed her luggage and changed into a jogging suit and running shoes then she went through everything the guys had. She spent extra time in Duane's case. Finally, she found what she was looking for, the phone number to Alliance Investigating Association. She was lucky, he might have kept it on him but he fancied himself a businessman and he like to carry a briefcase. She took the case also.

She walked back to the Lincoln and drove to her rental car, which she had parked around the corner from the FireStation. She put her bags and the briefcase in the trunk and left. She drove the Lincoln to the address embossed on the motel key from Charlie's pocket and parked it in front of the room number. She had Charlie's cell phone and all of the numbers he had stored on it. She put the phone in her pocket and jogged the two miles back to her car. Then she drove south through town in search of another motel. One that was away from the area the police would be investigating.

The Shadow Man was both a miracle and a source of confusion. He knew a lot more than she did. If what he said was true and there was no reason to doubt it, then she had been worse than a low-price employee, she had been a stupid fool. She had, although inadvertently, been hired to kill Charlie and Jim but it had backfired. Johnny Silver, Cool Duane, Samson and Andre the Horseman were dead and the Shadow Man said they "have friends coming into this area who would like to finish what was started here." Meaning, they would like to kill her. But first, she was going to get paid!

CHAPTER
TWENTY FIVE
Saturday 5:30 am

Small problem.
Five-man team sent to polish Lincoln.
Four members rubbed.
Lincoln crew dismissed.
Any info, please forward quickly.
The race has started.
JS

Ralston hit the send button, opened up the survey window and sequentially switched on each camera. The third camera showed Gomez and Barker on the front porch. It was still dark, predawn, and they were drinking coffee and apparently going over what transpired last night to the Lincoln and its occupants. The Lincoln had to be on their minds. She had been there and he was interested in how much she knew. The red pickup was parked in the driveway pointing toward the front gate. Apparently, one of them was leaving.

He made one bad mistake on this job already and was determined not to let it happen again. He had underestimated the men in the Lincoln. He would pay special attention to not underestimating Mari.

He had left the bar within minutes after she entered but her eyes never stopped moving. He didn't think she could have marked him but that would be his second mistake.

The sound of a motorcycle interrupted his thoughts and moments later Rainy entered the barn. *AN EXCEPTIONAL CHILD,* a voice said.

"Good morning Rainy."

"Good morning, Mr. Sachs," he answered. "Did you find the red car?"

"Yes, Rainy but they were just leaving town. So I don't think we have to worry about them anymore. Are you ready to take over?"

The boy was good and caught on immediately but Sachs had still insisted on spending several hours teaching him the 'how to's' about operating the system. Rainy was more interested in the set-up which Ralston thought was both unusual and commendable. His constant questions were always directed at capability rather than operability.

"Yes sir."

"You remember the rules? The phone is on the counter. If anyone enters the barn, you flip to the games. Okay?"

"Yes sir."

"Good, because I've got some things to do. You're in charge now. And don't take anything apart," he added with a smile as he walked out the rear door.

Caitlin Evans followed Bill Sempling out of the terminal building at the Custer Municipal Airport. The plane was circling again. On top of being confused, Bill was upset. The plane had flown over the airport twice, the pilot apparently trying to find a good reference point to line up his landing. The airport didn't have any runway lights. He should not be trying to land at this time.

"What the hell is he coming in this early for? It's still too damn dark," Bill commented. Caitlin didn't respond. She knew nothing about airports or airplanes. Bill was the terminal manager. He had total access to the airport. They had spent Friday night together on the couch in the terminal meeting room and she hadn't gone home yet. She and Bill had been dating for several weeks. The relationship, so far, was definitely motel orientated. It was what she expected. She had watched Bill over the years utilize her parent's motel with his various love interests. Now it was simply a different motel or the terminal and she was the current interest.

Caitlin was only twenty-two. Bill was thirty-one and she knew going in this wasn't long term. Bill had the physical distinction of being hung like a small horse, something well known throughout the Hills and, because of this, he held the distinct position of being the Hills area *Little Big Man*. It kept him rather busy. She had already admitted to herself that his reputation was what had attracted her to him, so she had no hopes for anything more. In reality, why would she? Bill was one of those guys who was always looking at the sampler tray even when there was a main course right in front of them.

The plane had set down perfectly in the minimal light and was taxiing up the dark runway. Bill was just ready to start walking toward the oncoming plane when a small red pickup drove past the terminal building and alongside the runway to meet the approaching plane. Bill, with Caitlin at his side, walked off the outside porch and stopped just short of the runway entrance as the pickup stopped next to the plane.

A tall, dark-haired man stepped down from the Piper Saratoga and walked to the waiting vehicle. It was dawn and as he looked to the northeast, light was sneaking through the dark creases in the Hills. The wetness in the air was palatable, something that lingered on the tip of your tongue like salt on the edge of a margarita glass. The sky was a picture of wet, dirty grays peeled from an artist's canvas and pasted against the eastern skyline. It was bordered in short brushstrokes of muted violets and dull blues meshed with sooty white lines streaked in black. It reminded him more of the Detroit River skyline than the eastern edge of the Rockies.

He threw his large leather bag into the back and slid into the passenger seat. The driver waited silently until the door was shut before putting the transmission in gear and moving away from the runway. They drove passed the main building and the Phillips fuel station. Two people had come from inside the dark building and were standing near the entrance. It was questionable where they had come from. The airport, at this time, should have been empty.

As the small truck passed, the driver smiled, waved and continued down the road and out of the airport. Bill Sempling for lack of anything better, waved back. The vehicle drove east to 385 and slowed long enough to watch the Piper lift off the runway, bank to the right and disappear into the eastern sky.

"You said the airport was going to be empty," the man said.

"There wasn't supposed to be anyone here at this time. I checked. The terminal is open from eight until six, seven days. I have no idea what they're doing here," the driver answered.

"That's rather obvious. They're using space. Bad luck," he said. He was silent for a moment, and then added, "He gave you a rather nice smile. Didn't he? Did you make a new friend out here?" There was a strong hint of sarcasm in his voice, which veneered a deeper anger, and without looking; she knew that his face had a smirk devoid of both warmth and humor.

"I'm not in the mood, Tony. Why are you here anyway, because the guys in the Lincoln screwed up?"

"Elena, oops, excuse me! It's Mari now isn't it? I don't know anything about the amateurs in the Lincoln. I'm here because you won't do the nun. It's as simple as that. Old man Castobelli is arguing with New York. He's having a fit. He wants to know why you can't do a simple thing. And now the people in New York are getting pissed at me because my lady friend doesn't want to do what she's paid for."

"I'm not paid to kill old ladies, besides you missed her in Detroit," Mari answered.

"Yes I know," he sighed. "A miscalculation but you and I are going to fix that."

"It's not my job. I don't kill people. I came here because the Detroit Police Department has over 200 lbs. of pure coke locked in their storage vault. I was supposed to transfer into the Narcotic Department but Armstrong's group needed another team member. I got elected. More of your so-called 'Bad Luck'. All I want to do is get that stuff out of the basement and back to the real people who pay me," she said angrily.

"Well, as soon as we're done here, you're being moved into the snort squad. The top cop in the Department said it would be done. Castobelli has guaranteed it. So, all we've got to do is take care of this nun business and everything will be fine. It should be fun."

"I'm not doing anything to the nun, Tony," she snapped. "I like the old lady. She hasn't done anything to anyone. Besides, I'm Catholic. She's Catholic. You can't be anymore Catholic than being a nun. If you've got to do it, do it quick and leave me out of it."

He was laughing. "You haven't got any choice. There are too many people watching this. If you don't help, it'll be a very severe mistake."

She didn't have to ask what that meant.

For twenty-two years, Jesse Evans owned the Sunset Morning Motel, on Route 16 east of Hill City. He and his wife, Sarah, bought it two months after their last daughter, Caitlin, was born. She was their late-love child, pretty damn late according to their two older daughters. He was forty-six when she was born, way in the hell too late for any sane man to be fathering children, at least the ones he plans on actually raising.

The delivery had taken a severe toll on Sarah. She developed a heart murmur and diabetes and her general health went into a steady decline. They thought that buying the motel would allow Jesse to be close to her and in time Sarah would improve, but it didn't help. Sarah had always been his bride but she didn't look like one in that hospital bed. She withered like fresh flowers before his eyes and, when the damn doctors were done with her, she'd smelled like the fertilizer sprayed on them. It had been slow, over five years, before she finally passed away. They were five agonizing years. That was almost eighteen years ago, but it felt like yesterday for Jesse.

When are you going to get on with what you want to do, Jesse? When are you just going to quit this? Caitlin can hire a maid to help her run the place.

"Caitlin ain't doin' this work, Sarah. What'd we send her to college for? Besides we agreed we don't want her doing the rooms."

Jesse was sitting in a dilapidated high back padded rocker on the back patio. The rocker stayed on the patio until the first snow covered the seat then he shoved it into the mower shed until spring. Actually, it wasn't a real patio either, not like those in the travel brochures, those flowered and hanging pot wonders of Europe. He didn't know if anyone in the States had a patio like the Europeans. His patio was more or less just a concrete slab but it had a nice border of roses and geraniums and it gave him a place to sit and talk in the afternoon. There were some daisies and a passel of those Black-eye-Susans around the walkway and sometimes he imagined it was European.

"No, Sarah we talked about this enough. We ain't having her do this and the motel ain't bringing in enough money to hire a maid."

Jesse still changed the sheets. He wasn't giving that job to Caitlin. It wasn't something he wanted his daughter doing. He'd changed enough bed sheets in his life to match the outlay from the laundry at any major metropolitan hospital. Terrible job, the thought of it upset him. Cum stained them sheets. Jesse Evans will clean them for you - no problem. Piss all over the toilet - no problem. Jesse cleans up. Beer and piss and cum, the staples of the motel business - no problem. Jesse cleans it all.

Well you're tired, you get up too early, and you and Caitlin can't do it by yourselves. You should sell the place.

"We ain't selling. Not jest yet. We already talked about that."

If we sell it, we can give her the money. If we leave the motel to her she's going to get into a catfight with her sisters over the property and probably have it all wasted away in court.

"I don't think they'll do that," he said, but he knew she was right.

Her two sisters would descend on the place like two alley cats in a fight for tuna scraps. He didn't like thinking about it anymore but when Sarah got going on something she just wouldn't quit and he *was* tired. He wanted to lie in bed one morning. Just lay there. Maybe get up when he was too tired to stay in bed. Sit out in front with one of those fold open metal tables with his coffee and newspaper on it and look east to the sunrise; nobody bothering him for anything. He wanted to put a sign on the office door

No coffee and donuts from Jesse today.

Get your own, asshole!

What he wanted was free time for Jesse Evans, free time to talk to Sarah. They had wanted to travel. They had talked about going to Europe, maybe Italy or Spain, someplace where it was warm. Maybe even Hawaii; there were flowers all over Hawaii. But they never got the chance! Now he didn't want to do any of that. It wouldn't be right without Sarah. Caitlin tried to talk him into going someplace but she knew it was a waste of words. Jesse wasn't going much farther than his patio. When he was ready he'd just sell the place and give the money to Caitlin.

There! I told you that's the right thing to do.

"Hello anyone home?" a voice called from the front entrance.

Damn it. It was just eight in the morning and he really didn't feel like moving. The place was almost filled. Well, maybe he could fill it, then flick on the 'NO VACANCY' sign, and relax. He got up from the rocker and pulling the back door open walked past the large industrial washer and dryer and into the registration room. A smallish man in a light blue blazer with a shiny blue sport shirt dotted with ivory diamonds stood by the door. He had a hard scar that started above his right eye and slashed downward, cutting deep into his right cheek. He wore a pair of large, black wrap-around sunglasses that made an attempt to cover most of the scar. The gross effect was highlighted by a white streak coursing through his hair above the scar. He reminded Jesse of that character in the movie 'Scarface'.

If this guy would immediately standout in a crowd, his partner had to qualify as the exact opposite. The man standing at the registration desk was larger but patently normal. He was fair-haired, wore a blue suit, white shirt and a matching blue tie. His hair was cropped and he looked like Howie Long, the football player. The comparison of the two men was unusual. They didn't look like they belonged together.

"Yes sir, you gentlemen looking for a good quality room. You come to the right place," Jesse said as he walked into the registration room.

"How you doing old-timer?" The one at the desk asked. "We need two doubles, adjoining if possible and a quiet area. Preferably no kids and not facing the street."

There were four of them, two more were waiting outside.

Seem pretty picky, Jesse thought. *This time of the year, most people were happy, because of the bike rally up in Sturgis, jest to get a room.*

"Well, all I've got left is one double but I might have something open up later in the day," he answered.

"Well that won't get it," the Scarface answered. He was standing next to the brochure rack.

"Hmmm, let me see. I think Hanson's, two miles up the road should have what you're looking for. I talked to George last night and he has a convention group leaving this morning. You might want to try there," Jesse answered. Scarface was thumbing through the brochures on the Borglum Museum and the Crazy Horse Monument and seemed to ignore what Jesse had said.

"Plenty to see around here. Probably something there for everything going on in the Hills," Jesse added, referring to the brochure rack. Scarface still didn't answer.

"Well, we'll give them a try," the fair-haired one said as he opened the door. "Thanks a lot," he added. The Scarface slipped two brochures into his pocket and they left.

"No problem," Jesse answered, "Have a nice stay here in the Hills." They were already gone and Jesse thought it strange. They had two identical vehicles with Colorado plates, each of them large enough for four of them.

Well, who cares anyway, he thought as headed out the back door to the patio, *let someone else figure it out.*

CHAPTER
TWENTY SIX
Saturday

M ari arrived at the Rapid City police department at 10:30 am unannounced. She knew she was about to receive priority status. An alley full of dead people has that effect on a police department.

Usually this was a peaceful town, with the exception of bike week and the rally; it was a relatively quiet, crime free city. And even during those few hectic weeks, the police kept tight control on the crowds. She could tell that today was something pretty damn new. There was an intense look in the eyes of everyone in the office.

Dead bikers in an alley of blood – was printed across the morning addition of the newspaper. Some reporter at the local paper had the opportunity of their career and wasn't wasting it. It was one hell of a headline.

Welcome to western Transylvania would have placed a close second.

"Police Chief, please," Mari said flashing her badge to the female officer at the front desk.

"Yes, Sergeant," the woman gave her the expected confused look, "What's this about?"

"I made the call on the mess you had in the alley last night," Mari answered. The woman lifted the phone and before she had time to place it back on the cradle a large man who looked like a poster ad with a snout for the Royal Canadian mounted police came bursting from the back room. He was in his mid-fifties, round-shouldered, bald-headed with baby pink fleshy skin. He extended a large, pudgy hand as he reached her and his eyes ran over her like he was giving her a visual CAT scan. She shook his hand and he hung on a just moment too long. It was clammy and mushy and reminded her of a bucket of shucked oysters that had sat too long on the pier.

"Sergeant Mari Gomez, Detroit Police. I made the 911 last night."

"I'm Chief Ray Staff. Come on into my office," he continued. He turned to let her pass and Mari caught his reflection in the window glass as he looked over his shoulder and gave a leering smile to the female officer at the main desk. The officer shook her head and returned to her work.

"Coffee or something to drink?" he asked as he seated himself behind a huge oak desk.

"Nothing, thank you," she replied. He hadn't taken his eyes off her and his attitude was bullishly aggressive.

"I am glad you came in today. We were wondering who made the 911," he said.

"Sorry I didn't have time to stay around. I was just a few minutes behind the shooters and thought I had a chance to catch up. Unfortunately, I didn't."

"Well, let's start at the beginning. Exactly what do you know about last night, Sergeant? A Detroit Police Officer, way out of your jurisdiction and chasing murderers in my town, is quite unusual. I don't suspect that you're just here on vacation." He was large with a round, jovial Porky Pig face, not as big as Ben, but harder looking, a mean Porky Pig. He appeared serious about the 'my town' reference.

"At this moment, I'm involved in a rather high profile case and I'm not sure how much liberty I have for disclosure. I'll have my superior call you and clarify my situation. Something I personally can't do."

"Well, tell me what you can and I'll get with your boss later. How did you happen to be at the scene? I don't think that was a coincidence."

It was difficult for Mari to answer anything without divulging that she was in the area protecting a witness to a nationally prominent murder case. She decided to simply avoid answering.

"Some of the people involved last night were under surveillance and as I've already said, I can't say why. Have you found anything on the bikers or the Red Lincoln? They're something new. We didn't expect them." He really did look like Porky Pig.

"We put out an all points on the car," he answered, "even before we cleaned up the mess but nothing as of yet. As for the boys on the bikes, we're still checking. They were armed which is not unusual with some of the bike clubs, but these guns were silenced. Now my question is: 'were they after the guys in the Lincoln or was it visa-versa?' You could help me out with that one." He watched her intently with eyes that were small and black, like a ferrets.

She had a friend back in her home town whose boyfriend kept a ferret in his room, a mean little fucker that would sneak under your chair and nip the back of your ankles. She had to keep her feet up because she never knew when it was coming.

The Chief gave her the impression he would sneak up on her too.

"I'm not so sure they were bikers. A possible paid hit changes that. Is there any place around here where someone can rent a bike during the rally?" Mari asked.

"Sure, the Black Hills dealership." He picked up the phone and spun his chair toward the large window at the back of the office never taking his eyes off Mari. "Abby, call Lenny at the Harley store. See if anyone has rented any bikes recently. Yeah, let me know." He turned attentively back to Mari. She was becoming very uncomfortable

"Why do you think they were rented?" he asked. He wasn't making eye contact. His eyes were always some place on her body. His apparent focus was unsettling.

"The silenced guns you mentioned change everything. They were traveling with a woman and it appeared they were working a simple scam. She picks up the men and goes to their hotel. Her buddies show up looking real tough. They threaten to let the wives know and then help themselves to the marks money and leave. No one calls the police. It's easy money. But this was different. The guns indicate they might have intended to kill the marks but ran into the wrong people and now the killers have the woman. There's no telling what they might do to her."

"Almost everyone in the FireStation saw the two men leave with the woman. They were quite a spectacle. And I've got at least five witnesses that noticed the four bikers follow them, but I doubt anything will show up. We're trying out of state also, and we need to find that girl before it's too late," he said. A large fat tongue slipped out of his mouth and wet his over-sized lips.

Mari's instincts told her it was intentional. Something he did, apparently, for her benefit. *That girl might be better off with the other two creeps,* she thought. *This guy could feel you up with his eyes. It was like somebody was already in your pants.*

"Well, if my vacation comes to a quick end, I may need to get some federal help and at that point, you'll be notified," Mari said rising from her seat. She wanted out of the office. Her comfort level was non-existent.

"I sure in the hell better be. I don't care for something happening in this city without being informed," he exclaimed. He was excited.

"That won't happen I can assure you, but I could use some info on those stiffs that you scraped up in the alley." He might not want to be of any assistance but the mention of federal intervention would help her.

"And I'll need a number where I can reach you," he answered with his hand already extended.

She pulled a card, wrote down her cell phone number and left it on his desk. She didn't want to hand it to him, didn't want to risk another contact. Then she walked to the office door. He watched. *Like being coated with gelatin,* she thought.

"Come by this afternoon, we can catch lunch and I should be able to fill you in. Make sure your boss calls in the meantime and, as for that fed stuff, make sure I'm in the loop. Nobody likes them coming into their jurisdiction. They want to run everyone's party and this town is my party," he stated.

Sure she thought. *Except* everyone's *party is about to change, Porky.*

CHAPTER
TWENTY SEVEN

Armstrong drove through the town of Acme, Michigan, along East Grand Traverse Bay and finally along the wonderful Miracle Mile into Traverse City. '*Wonderful*' was what the local advertisers, real estate agents and town promoters wanted everyone to believe. Both sides of the road were overrun with the ubiquitous motels, hotels and poor restaurants. If you got tired of looking at those '*wonderful*' sites you could feast your eyes on the '*wonderful*' and much-demanded water parks and miniature golf courses. Like most of the beautiful watery spots of the world, the term '*wonderful*' would have aptly applied only if the development was absent. The town was quickly becoming what one local writer had dubbed a "Tourist dream and a resident nightmare". Some residents, naturally, would disagree, especially those that lined the road with overpriced boutiques in anticipation of gouging the next oblivious tourist with some unique native artifact with 'Made in China' stamped on the bottom.

Armstrong took the turn into the center of town, passing several more restaurants plus a few boutiques and knick-knack stores and parked across from City Hall. He labored up the entrance steps and stopped at the information desk. Minutes later, he was in the Land Survey Department. The Chief surveyor, a middle-aged man, was waiting. It took the Surveyor's assistant twenty minutes, but he finally found what Armstrong had driven four hours to locate. Ben got directions and one half hour later pulled off the side of a county dirt road and parked.

The property was probably the cheapest five-acre parcel in the county, consisting of burnt over scrub and something that would have to be called uncultivated farmland. Two to five inches of brown-oily water covered most of the area, filling everything between the clump grass and the road's edge. The burned area provided access to the local power corridor that ran straight through the middle of the plot. A local access power line ran from an auxiliary pole to the back edge of the property where a small copse of trees stood. He knew exactly what he was looking for and had no doubt that was where it would be. He slipped his feet into a pair of oversize rubber boots and, looking as out of place as a Hippo in a flower garden, trudged forward through the brown, stinking muck.

The phone rang five times before it was picked up.

"Hello, Alliance Investigating Association," a man's voice answered.

"This is Rapid City calling Mr. Marchione. Is he in?"

"Who wants him?" Joe answered. He didn't know what to make of it. Regular phones were off limits.

"I want the money and I want it within two hours."

"Who the hell is this? And what money are you talking about?"

"Is this Mr. Marchione?"

"Yes, who are you?"

"This is Anna Klemm. I worked with Duane. You remember the job in Rapid City. Unfortunately, you also hired the two guys who were supposed to….how should I say it over the phone?"

"Hey, don't say a goddamn thing. And I don't know what the hell you're talking about," Joe snapped

"Listen to me Marchione, listen real good 'cause I'm only going to say it one time then I'm getting the hell off this phone. Duane and three of my friends are dead. The other two goons, let me see what their names were," she looked at the names on the two Chicago licenses in her hand, "Charles Breen and James Gracey, killed them. I'm the only one left alive and I want the goddamn money you promised."

"Listen lady I don't know what the fuck you're …."

"Shut the fuck up," she screamed into the mouthpiece, "or tonight your ass is going to be in the Chicago jail." The blood was pounding in her head and she felt it thickening and turning into a red slurry. She could feel her temples throbbing and a nervous headache was blackening the space behind her eyes but she had made up her mind to do it and there was no turning back now. "Are you listening?"

"Yeah, I hear you."

"Every dime of the money is to be wired to the Western Union Office in Rapid City. I'm giving you two hours or I'm calling the cops. Wire it to ANNA KLEMM. You got that?"

"I can't do that. It isn't enough time."

"Listen asshole. In two hours you can't get anybody to me. You can't fly one of your fucking no-brain asshole friends out here and nobody can drive to Rapid City from anywhere in two hours. And two fucking hours is all you got. If I don't have the cashier's check in my hand in two hours, I'm calling the cops and your ass is going down. The name is Anna K..L..E..M..M."

She slammed the phone down and fell back against the door of the phone booth. She was shaking and scared. They had her name now but they probably knew that anyway. If she got the money in the allotted time - GREAT. If they didn't send it, she would call the cops and make Marchione pay. What did the Shadow Man tell her – "run like hell." Well, that might turn out to be good advice but it would have to wait for two more hours. Right now the money was a much better idea.

Saturday 2:00 pm

Alliance Investigating Association was located in an industrial complex in a western Chicago suburb populated with small machine shops, startup businesses, computer service centers and one cad training company that gave crash courses in Catia and Unigraphics guaranteed to prepare you for a job making sixty thousand a year in six weeks. Joe Marchione had even thought about taking some computer classes. It wasn't a bad idea. Get a little training and change your occupation, besides they had some good-looking women that worked there. All you had to do when you completed the class was find the job. Not that it was impossible, but the job was always an entry-level position and the pay was closer to twenty-five a year including overtime. That was two years ago. Joe had sloughed it off. Not only wasn't there enough money but it was too damn dull. Until now, that is. Right now, dull was looking damn good.

All the units in the complex had an office entrance in the front of the building and a large overhead automatic door in the back, usually used for receiving. Joe used the building as a garage to park his Buick and the company's surveillance van. The van contained expensive wiretap and photo equipment and he didn't like parking it outside. It was old but he couldn't risk losing that equipment.

Joe put the phone down. He had some bad days since opening this business. After all, running an investigative association that provided special procedures for the proper price could be quite lucrative. But some clients had a tendency to be very demanding and became greatly stressed if their demands were not met. Today was probably the worst. What would forever be known as his *Day of Days*.

Charlie and Jim were a couple of screw-ups. He knew that when he hired them. And because of that, their use was dedicated strictly to stationary surveillance. Lately, they were getting bored. It was normal. Everyone who did surveillance work eventually came to that conclusion and then you had to get them re-interested in the work again.

When Detroit called, he thought he'd throw them a bone. He liked to do that with his people. It made them think they were growing into the job and becoming more professional. It was all bullshit, but it worked. It was an easy job and it paid well. There wasn't much they could screw up. Just stay out of the way and call in the location two or three times a day. The key words were "stay out of the way". In other words, don't get caught.

Unfortunately, they got caught. And even then, it would have worked out if they hadn't called in. When Jim mentioned that they were tailing the police, the red flags went up. Even Joe hadn't known that. Now if a cop winds up dead in South Dakota, Jim Gracey and Charlie Breen could point to Joe Marchione who could point to Detroit and then to New York. Detroit told Joe to fix the problem. Simply put, get rid of Jim and Charlie.

Joe couldn't believe it when he found out that Duane and his group was in Sturgis for the bike rally. It looked like everything would work out perfectly. The client in Detroit was very happy. Hell, Joe had people already there, waiting to do the job. If it had worked out, Joe's status as a go-to man would have increased ten-fold. Detroit even agreed to pay for it. Joe should have gotten away with it. Duane should have handled it easily, but apparently, Charlie and Jim got lucky. It had to be pure and simple luck because it sure in hell wasn't talent.

Earlier that morning, he had checked the Rapid City paper on the web. Duane's group was dead. Unfortunately, it didn't work out and .. well, he could easily see who was next on the list. Everything could be traced right back to Alliance. What a mess!

Now the broad in Duane's group survived and wants the money. Hell, no one even knew where Charlie and Jim were. The cops could have them already. But that still didn't matter because she's threatening to go to the cops. So, he made the call and Detroit reluctantly sent the money. They weren't happy with the situation. Charlie and Jim were still alive and some crazy, pissed off broad was now in the mix. Joe knows what that means. He fucked up and he's holding the bag, except the bag is going to contain his head if he stays around too long.

The *Day of Days*. It's the day that everyone in this type of business has to plan for. Joe went to the rear closet and removed a large brown naugahyde suitcase and a matching toiletry bag. He carried them through the garage entrance and put them inside the van. Unfortunately, because of the equipment, he was going to take the van. He had a plan and he was going to stick to it. The Buick was newer which was another reason it should stay. It looked better that way. If he were running, the police would expect him to take the best vehicle, not an old van. This way they might suspect foul play. They would probably think that one of his unnamed clients got rid of him and it wouldn't be long before they stopped looking. That would suit him just fine.

He emptied the top two drawers from the filing cabinet, stuffed the contents in a cardboard box and threw it in the back of the van. He removed the false backing from the front drawer of his desk and took out an Indiana driver's license with a very good picture of himself issued to a Robert Marks. He also had a VISA, a Social Security card, an AAA auto insurance card and an Indiana vehicle registration for the van all made out to Robert Marks. Joe Marchione of Chicago, Illinois had sold the van on a duplicate registration to Robert Marks of Indianapolis, Indiana. The van was legally registered with two different owners and licensed in two different states. The legal one depended on which plate was attached to the rear bumper. Joe replaced his ID with the Marks credentials. The Marchione stuff from his wallet, he cut into small pieces and dumped into a plastic bag that would be discarded along the interstate in a rest area dumpster. From the bottom drawer, he opened his cash box and removed five thousand dollars, which went into his inside jacket pocket. Beneath the box was an Indiana license plate. Joe went into the garage and changed plates. The Illinois plate was added to the bag.

He estimated they would be here within an hour. No use wasting time. Get the job done when it needs doing. That was what he was taught. Roberts Marks learned a long time ago, when you deal with people like Detroit, it was best to have your escape route planned before your first job. There was a small bank on the western edge of Pensacola Florida. It had a nice little savings account owned by Robert Marks. Somewhere along the panhandle, Marks Investigative Services would be starting business within the next year. Maybe by then, people would have given up on Joe Marchione.

Robert Marks splashed gasoline on the desk and the storage cabinet. Then he made a sweep through the rest of the office. He flipped a match over his shoulder, shut the door behind him, jumped into the van, and headed out the exit, onto the freeway and into the southbound lane. Joe Marchione no longer existed.

Her phone was vibrating and there was only one person she'd given the number to locally.

"Sergeant Gomez? Chief Ray Staff here. Thought you'd like to know we found the Lincoln. It's parked right in front of their motel room."

"Any signs of the perps?"

"No, not yet. I just got here."

"Mind if I come by?" she asked.

"Come right ahead," he answered.

She got the name of the motel and went for the pickup. Barker and she had decided the Crown could still pose a problem as long as the two men in the Lincoln were around. He wouldn't leave Sister Mary Elizabeth and someone should find out as much as possible about these guys. Personally, Mari was worried because Tony said that he didn't know about them. And Armstrong didn't know, either. Someone was lying.

It took her twenty-five minutes to get to the motel. The Chief was in the process of hooking the car to tow it back to the station. He watched her as she slowly walked toward him. This time she slowed it down on purpose. *Let him look,* she thought. *Like wearing a dress made of cellophane.*

"Everything appears to be normal here," he said, "luggage, clothing, toiletries, nothing out of place. We came in fast and there is no way out the back. They weren't here. The manager said he saw them leave yesterday afternoon and never saw them come back but the car has been here all morning."

"Any sign of a struggle?"

"Nothing. Looks like they went out for a while and haven't returned. The car is a problem. I don't know what the hell it's doing here."

"You've got a couple of killers hanging around and I think they're enjoying trying to confuse us," Mari answered. "They should be running like hell, instead they drop their car right where you'll find it and they don't even go into the room for their things."

"Yeah, what the hell is that supposed to tell us?"

"It tells me that someone's fucking with the police," she turned toward him as she said it.

He glanced downward, a shade of pink rising from his size twenty collar. When he thought he was controlling the situation, he stared a hole through her but when she opened it up and cussed like a man, he flushed and got excited. She liked that. Men were such assholes. They loved swearing in front of women. It was their way of bringing a woman down to their gutter. But if a woman threw it back at them, then she controlled the situation and the word, and then the assholes became little boys once again.

Rapid City Regional Airport was about nine miles from town and most of the flights arrived from Minneapolis or Denver. Families and college kids were arriving daily to visit Mount Rushmore and Custer State Park. They came to hike and camp in the Hills, or just party and dance around the Needles. No one caught his attention.

While he was watching this end, Ben and the FBI were monitoring every flight coming in from Chicago, New York and Detroit. Nothing looked unusual. Ralston couldn't put it down. It didn't make sense. Hadn't the two in the Lincoln made the call? Were they going to wait until morning? Maybe they decided to do a little partying for being successful at finding the nun after they had already lost her. A celebration! Let Detroit stew a little before they clued the old man. That's a possibility that made sense. If it was reported they screwed up, Castobelli might have put a contract on them. Or could it be that they had never told of the first mishap? But that didn't seem to fit. They must have called and reported that they had found the Crown. Then Detroit decided to have them removed. Maybe that was the plan from the beginning. The only way to insure that Willie 'The Blade' Morolli didn't stand trial was to kill everyone involved. Maybe that was why they went through Alliance instead of using their own people. But Ralston knew that none of these people were the 'someone special,' who Ben said was after the nun.

The town seemed clean and the way he thought, *that didn't fit!*

His phone rang and it was Armstrong. Their conversations were always deplete of names.

"What do you have?"

"Our sister has to be back to town on Wednesday day for the appointment. We're sending a private plane to get her early. That's one, now two. Barker and Mari checked in and your Lincoln is back in town. They found it at the motel where the two drivers were staying."

"Christ! She's after the money."

"Who's after what money? Do you have a problem there?" Ben sounded exasperated.

'Maybe? Look, I've got to go. What've you got on airports?"

"Nothing yet. Everything's silent there. Must be local. I'm still checking. Watch your back. And who's 'She'?"

"Later," Ralston hung up and raced to the exit.

CHAPTER
TWENTY EIGHT

The Mail Boxes Etc., which housed the Western Union office, is located at the end of a row of small business outlets on the west side of the shopping center on Jackson Blvd. On the left side of the store is a Blimpie's Sub Shop, a Hallmark Card outlet, a drug store and a continuance of chain stores; all part of the new American landscape that goes on forever.

Anna had driven through the parking lot and, ignoring the patterned yellow-lined parking protocol, pulled up next to the side of the brick building and parked. She was hoping for an easy in and out. That was almost two hours ago. She walked back up to the desk.

"Anything yet?" she ask the dark haired woman behind the Western Union counter.

"Nothing yet, honey. I'll notify you the moment I receive it."

"Thank you, again," she said. She returned to the chair she had been sitting in for the past hour and a picked up the local paper. The dead bikers' story was all over the front page. Nice headline and a great story, she thought. Apparently, according to the papers investigative reporter, two rival gangs had been having problems for years and brought their problems into the city. It also noted that this was the first occurrence of this type since the Sturgis rally had become a nationally significant event.

It was 3:45 pm, fifteen minutes to go. She was getting nervous. The building was air-conditioned but her clothes were starting to stick. The sun was baking the asphalt, cooking up some nice carbon monoxide toxins and giving off that wonderful vibrating heat reflective illusion that looked like one end of the lot was a pool of steaming water. She thought she'd drive through it on her way out with the check.

A man walked past the front of the building and picked a copy of the paper from the rack outside. He was dressed in a flashy, cheap looking suit. His eyes were covered in wrap around glasses and he had a streak of silver hair above his right eye. He glanced at her momentarily, stuck the paper under his arm and walked on. She waited.

It came exactly on time. The agent endorsed it and passed it over the counter to her eager hands.

Pay to the order of ……….. ANNA KLEMM.

She had it and could hardly believe it. Amazed and pissed would be a better way to define her feelings, a cashier's check for twenty thousand dollars.

Shit! Duane had set her up also. At least two of them had been armed. Were they all in on it? Had they taken out people before? She felt stupid. She thought that she was making a living putting the squeeze on some asshole salesmen that cheated on their wives. She always felt they deserved to get the shit scared out of them. They deserved to feel the pocket pinch. Right! Now it turns out the *Shadow Man* was right. It was a big *hit*. Twenty grand! And what did the big guy say? "You don't set us up. We set you up." Those guys weren't businessmen, at least, not the kind of businessmen she was thinking about.

The questions were bouncing through her head like balloons hitting the ceiling on New Year's Eve. If someone paid them twenty thousand to kill the guys in the Lincoln, what would they pay to kill her? And who the hell was the Shadow Man? How did he appear in the middle of the forest in the middle of the night? He wasn't a camper. He was armed and he seemed to know the big guy. At least he said something to him that made it appear that way. Was he a backup to make sure the boys in the Lincoln really ended up in the shit can? It was starting to look that way. But if that was true why did he let her go? The more she thought about it the more twisted it became.

"She's moving," Max said. He backed the Mercury out and drove toward the end of the parking lot.

"Did she get it?" Silky spoke into the microphone built into the wraparound glasses.

"Has it in her right hand. She's coming out now."

His phone started vibrating as he watched her leave the building and walk to her car. He pushed the small tab on the collar of his t-shirt.

"Mr. Sachs?"

"Yes Rainy."

"There's a car and it's driving back and forth, - three times already!"

"What kind of a car and can you tell how many people are in it?"

"A big black car. Two men in it and one has binoculars," Rainy answered.

"Very good. Stay where you are. Somebody might leave the house in the next few minutes. That'll be okay. Keep watching the camera and call if anything else unusual happens. Keep it up, you're doing terrific."

The kid called on everything. He never missed a trick. He'd already called on the mailman and a UPS delivery truck. Ralston couldn't have done better with a professional organization. The kid was a one-man surveillance team.

A man appeared from behind the Mail Boxes Etc. building and walked quickly toward the woman's car.

Anna put the key into the ignition and paused long enough to look at the check again. She smiled and let herself sink back into the seat. Finally something right for her. This was going to make her life a bit easier. Up until this point, it had never been easy. Her mother had been married five times and Anna had always been a spectator in their house, a bystander who was pushed to the side in favor of her mother's current love interest. And although there was always someone new, coming or going, Anna considered her mother a single mom. They had always been, more or less, alone. Men came in and out of their lives, but no one ever stayed long enough to make an impression. The men, if they worked at all, were poorly employed. Most were heavy drinkers and to some degree abusive. Her mother told her on more than one occasion that, "being used was just part of being a woman and she had to get used to it." As a child, she recalled solitude being a place of safety. A place where screams were absent and threats unheard. At fifteen she had enough; she left home and never went back.

During the following frozen January, she was found in a deserted tenement on the south side of Chicago, suffering from exposure and near death. She was rushed to emergency. After recovering, she refused to give any information and, like so many other children, was registered as homeless. For Anna, juvenile detention was better than going back with her mother and her steady string of losers. She finished high school at the homeless center in west Chicago. They presented her a diploma with simply `Anna' written in and told her that she could fill in the last name whenever she felt it was appropriate.

At eighteen, she went to L.A., selected the name 'Klemm' from a movie marquee, and tried some bit acting while starting a career in waitressing anywhere that paid enough to cover the rent. Four years later left her standing in exactly the same spot. She went back to school and six years later got her degree in Drama and Psychology. Drama because she wanted to pursue career in acting and the psych because, like most young women, she wanted to find out what made men tick. Long before she graduated she realized that all the psych degrees in the world were not going to answer that question.

Anna was engaged twice and both flopped before the altar appeared in front of her. She figured most men were polygamist and trying to convert one was a waste of her time. She'd tried enough.

She looked over the steering wheel for that imaginary puddle at the end of the long lot. She wanted to drive through it. It had taken on a symbolism. A vision of wet heat, a wall to wash her clean, to sterilizer her and allow a different person to emerge on the other side, a new Anna Klemm.

Just as it all seemed to becoming together, a noise to her left distracted her. Her head exploded and smashed into the passenger seat, banging her cheek into the steering wheel on the way. The vision of the puddle was replaced by a big gob of numb mud sitting in the middle of her brain. There was blood in her mouth and her eyes gave her a hazy impression that the dashboard was tilted on its side. She shook her head trying to fix the picture. She vaguely felt the check stripped from her hand.

"Move over sweets, we're going for a drive," the words were all mixed up, like the cubes on a scrabble board that was floating on water. The door opened and she felt someone grab her legs and flip her over into the passenger seat. She could hear herself moaning. It was a sad moan gurgling in her throat. She was aware of the vibration of the engine as it turned over and started.

Anna's head was forced against the door, her arms underneath, hands palms down on the seat, her back was arched and both of her feet were dangling above her head. She could see his face just beyond her boots. He was the man who picked up the newspaper. The bastards did get someone here on time.

"These people have friends coming into this area who would like to finish what was started here." That's what he had told her and here they were, in less than two hours. Son-of-a-bitch. She was snake bit. Her stomach was rolling and she felt like she was about to upchuck all over the bastard. For the second straight day she tasted blood in her mouth and she wasn't in the mood to take another ride with another son-of-a-bitch. The thought cleared her head and forced her to react.

"I'm not going anyplace with you asshole," she screamed and lashed out with both feet catching the man in the face. He was propelled back against the open door, his hands going to his face. All she could think was, *He's wide open.* She pushed herself up on her hands and pumped her legs like she was working out on a leg press machine, kicking him repeatedly in the head and the upper body.

The door flew open and he fell from the car. Anna landed in the driver's seat and without thinking how she did it, was speeding across the parking lot cutting between parked vehicles and driving hard through that imaginary puddle of shimmering water.

Ralston watched as the girl's car did a one hundred eighty degree turn and spun from besides the building, knocking over two trash containers and leaving the man sprawling on the ground. The thought that she seemed to wreak havoc wherever she went crossed his mind. She was supposed to be gone but he instinctively knew why she hadn't left town. She had never intended to go anywhere and now it would be very easy for her to end up dead. A large black Mercury pulled out from a line of parked cars. It raced across several crowded lanes to the fallen man who hobbled to his feet and was holding the side of his face. He swayed to the car with a disoriented swagger and some-how managed to avoid a wildly swinging door as he fell into the passenger front seat.

She drove out of the lot careened across Jackson Blvd passed Sheridan Lake Road and turned onto Mt. Rushmore Road. It was Friday afternoon and the traffic was getting heavy. She was forced to swerve between slower moving vehicles.

Anna checked the rear view mirror. The Mercury was about three blocks back and closing the distance. She accelerated and hung a hard right onto a side street and was racing through a neighborhood of small bungalows with almost nonexistent front yards, kids were out, there were bikes and skateboards, some kids were playing a game of driveway basketball, and a soccer ball rolled out into the street, a block ahead. She squealed her tires, made another side street turn and cut back toward the main drag with the Mercury a half block behind. A motorcycle appeared suddenly from a cross street and turned between her and the Mercury. The large black car screeched up on the bike's rear fender and blew the horn. Anna slowed at the corner of Mt. Rushmore Road. She took a moment to look back. The biker had stopped in the middle of the street. Anna cut hard back down another street and left them to argue it out.

Max was trying to get around the bike but cars were parked on both sides of the street. The asshole biker was stuck between them and it looked like his bike just quit. The bike pulled up about five feet and stopped again. The girl was turning ahead and Max laid on the horn. The biker turned slowly around on his seat and gave them the finger.

Silky leaned out of the passenger window and screamed, "Move it asshole or we'll kick your fucking ass." Max backed up several feet and turned out to get around the bike. The biker moved forward and again blocked off the opening. He stopped again. Max cut hard and squeezed between the bike and a parked car. It was amazing that he didn't tear the side mirrors off both cars. He managed to get the car up alongside the bike and Silky leaned out the window, a gun in his hand.

"You fucking asshole, get the fuck out of the way."

"Hey, you guys cops or something?" The gun didn't seem to faze him at all.

Silky thought he must be stoned. "Yeah we're fucking cops. Now get out of the fucking road or I'll stick your ass in fuckin' jail where you belong, asshole," he screamed.

"Okay, okay. Take it easy for a minute. The bike keeps stalling on me. I'll have to push it."

"Then push the fuckin' thing!" Silky hollered.

The old biker got off the Harley, struggling to hold it upright, and pushed it to the side of the street.

"Fuckin' asshole," Silky screamed out the window, "you ain't strong enough to push a ten speed racer."

Max squealed the tires taking off, Silky looked back, and as they reached the end of the street, the biker gave them the finger again.

"Fuck. I should have hit that bitch a little harder and put her out completely. And I should have gotten out and busted that old punks face in," he said.

Max was looking both ways down the street at once. The girl was gone.

"Well, it sure in the hell would have saved us some trouble," Max answered. "Check in and tell Tony that we got the money but the broad slipped us. Tell him that we're gonna see if we can find her."

"Yeah, the old man will be happy but Tony wanted the girl. He's gonna be pissed," Silky steamed.

"Well, that's not a fun thought," Max answered.

Ralston opened his cell phone and hit the preprogrammed button for Armstrong.

"Yes." Ben answered.

"I need a credit card check ASAP on Anna Klemm, two mm's. LA County, California. Do the same for Gracey and Breen. She has both of them. And give me locations on the last times used. I'm looking for a motel, someplace in the area. Gas station, car rental, etcetera."

"Is she the one who wants the money?" Ben asked.

"Yeah, the woman with the bike shooters. She was supposed to leave but she didn't. She put the squeeze on the old man without knowing it."

"Well, that's not a good thing to do. That could get her dead."

"That's in the works and I've got to find her quick or she will be."

"How many?"

"Two that I've seen, probably at least double that. I also need a check on 839 HGS Colorado plate. Black Mercury- probably a rental."

"Give me a few. They're probably chasing the same trail for the girl." Ben responded.

"That's what worries me. They've had a head start and, while you're at it call Gomez and Barker. It's time to fill them in on Gracey and Breen. They also have another black car casing the front entrance to the Ryken place. They might want to see who it is."

"Will do. By the way, you might have bigger problems. Call me as soon as you're clear. Oh yeah, I don't want to forget. The FBI should be at the ranch on Sunday. They're out of Dallas. I thought you'd like that."

Ralston hung up and rode back into town.

"What in the hell is my goddamn problem?" Anna berated herself. "This is the second time in two days that I'm getting knocked around." The thought, stuck in her head, was that her whole life had gone exactly like the last five minutes. She was shaking again. Maybe she should have just gotten out of town last night. She surely would have been far enough away by now.

Actually, the call to Alliance was good but then she should have left town! Draw them this way then go another, it was just that the whole damn idea of running stuck in her throat. She was tired of running from everyone.

When she had left home, her mother had been going with some slime ball named Eddie Martin. Squirrelly Eddie Martin! Eddie was five years younger than her mother and was always hitting on Anna. He would tell Anna that he was really in love with her but she was too young and he would get in trouble if anyone found out. But if she could keep it quiet, they could have some real good times. If he hadn't been so afraid of jail, Anna probably would have been in a bad spot with Eddie.

While Eddie was having the *mother/daughter fantasy*, Anna was having the *leave home and make it on your own* dream. Neither worked out well. What she should have done was taken a baseball bat to Eddie's head, stayed home, and tried to help her mother live a dream of her own. She shook her head. This was a great thought to have fourteen years later! It had taken some years but she had finally realized that running never helped anything and today running was something Anna Klemm just didn't do well.

She drove all the way through town and then swung back. She'd seen it in some Hollywood movie. Go right back to where you started; they'll never look there. She parked in a used car lot across from the small shopping center. When it got dark, she'd go back to her motel and get her things. She was moving uptown. Then maybe she would take a little time to cruise the other motels. Maybe she could find that Mercury.

The phone was ringing.

"Mr. Sachs?"

"Yes, Rainy."

The white car just drove out. I think they went after the black car. I don't see it anymore."

"Good. You keep watching and remember the rules. Okay?"

"OK."

Tony slipped from the rear passenger door and rolled into the ditch on the opposite side of the road. He crawled down the ditch for about two hundred yards, and then crossed over to the ranch side. He waited for a couple of minutes until the white Crown drove past before he moved deeper into the forest. He worked slowly, repeatedly stopping and scanning the area with a high-powered spotting scope. He knew what he was looking for and it took an hour before he finally found the first one. He worked his way on his belly parallel to the ranch perimeter, fifty yards deep into the forest, then he turned ninety degrees and came up beneath the tree with the camera. He checked the pointing angle and without disturbing the camera approximated the azimuth. From his position at the tree base and with the help of the spotting scope and a compass, he drew a small topographical map of the property marking the location of the house, the barn, the outbuildings and any significant landscape data. From this spot, he located another camera that appeared to scan the front of the house. With a pair of draftsman dividers, he estimated the distance between the two cameras and swept a few additional arcs. He quickly located two additional cameras. Now the path to the ranch was as clear as a walk down Broadway.

He retraced his path to the main road and crawled down the ditch to the original drop off point. Then he stood and jogged off toward the west. One half mile further, he ran into a small group of pines where the Mercury was parked. He was smiling to himself, pleased it had gone so well. Broadway was comfortable and fun, just like this would be.

CHAPTER
TWENTY NINE

There is an old Kodak Photo booth on the edge of the Bakken Park parking lot. Some creative person with an entrepreneurial vision had converted it into a drive-thru Expresso/ Cappucino shop. Right now, it was enjoying an evening rush and seemed to be doing great. *With something like that,* she thought, *6:00 am until 5:00 pm, and I could make a nice living. All I needed was that twenty-thousand bucks.*

Anna was entertaining herself by watching the flow of traffic through the coffee shop and waiting for dusk to fall. She didn't know what else to do but figured leaving town was still her best option. But now all she had was a rental car and the police would be after it within a couple of days. *I should have kept the Lincoln. I should have just run.*

An old biker, who looked similar to the one that cut off the Mercury, pulled up to the drive-thru window. He leaned forward, ordered from the young girl inside and then casually looked around while waiting. Finally, the girl pushed two large hot cups on a tray through the sliding window. He paid, set the tray on top of the tank and rode carefully away.

Several minutes passed. Business was brisk and she was day-dreaming of her own coffee shop, with donuts and fresh bagels delivered daily. Add some country collectables, scented candles and chocolate treats. Maybe a small magazine rack, with Vogue, Elle, Redbook, and some romance novels that she loved. And iced coffee in the summer. Why not? It sounded great and she would be fine.

"I hope you like Mocha Supreme. It's pretty good."

The voice shocked her and she jumped. He was stand-ing alongside her door, the coffee tray with the two cups held casually in his left hand. A glance in the mirror showed a large bike parked directly behind her car. He must have killed the engine and coasted up, she hadn't heard a thing. A car was parked in front of her. She couldn't move without crashing into something.

"Hell of a way to try to pick up a girl. Coffee in a used car lot. Why don't you just move the hog and I'll be leaving?"

"Not too good an idea, but you're not doing so well in the idea department any way. You've got hit men running all over town trying to bring you down and you don't seem able to leave. Obviously, you want to hang around until you're dead." He wasn't even looking at her, choosing instead to look over the car roof to the street.

"Who are you?" She didn't know this guy and wasn't in the mood to listen. She had a headache, probably the result of being smashed in the jaw and she wasn't thinking too sharp. Her hand slid over and flipped the clasp on her purse.

"You've still got the guns from last night. That's good! But even with two guns, you can't seem to take care of yourself. You let that jerk in the shopping center use your head for a punching bag." He still hadn't looked down.

"You! You're the guy from last night?" She was startled and blurted it out.

"Some guy I should know about?"

"I don't believe you. You don't look like he did."

"Then I'll just go my way and let you deal with the new guys in the black Merc but if you're planning on going back to your motel when it gets dark, well that's another bad move. The best I've got on them is they rented that Mercury in Denver, all phony ID's. I haven't had time to find where they're staying but I do know where they are right now."

"Where?" she answered for lack of anything intelligent to say.

"The Super 8 Motel on Mt. Rushmore Road, Room 28."

"That's .."

"Yeah, I know. That's your room. Hell of a coincidence, isn't it? Look, right now you're easy and pretty damn lucky. You're using the credit card of a dead man after I told you to burn it. If the locals check it and find it is being used by the girlfriend of the dead alley boys, well, I wouldn't bet on you making it through the next encounter. So, either I can move the bike and you can go on your way or ....," he paused for a moment, "well do you like Mocha Supreme or White Chocolate Ice Storm?"

She didn't have to think too long. She had obviously been stupid or else he wouldn't be standing next to her.

"I'll try the Mocha Supreme. The other one sounds too complicated."

"First good idea," he said, while he walked around and got in the passenger seat. He handed her one of the hot containers and took a good look at her. For a girl that had just been in another fight, except for the bruise growing over her left eye, she seemed unruffled.

She took the coffee and stared back. "You look different than last night. Larger," she said, never moving her eyes from his face.

"How's your eye?" He reached over and touched her lightly above her cheek.

"It's alright." She pulled her head back, drawing away from the contact. "I never saw him coming."

"It's going to be quite a shiner. You seeing okay, nothing double?"

"Yes, I'm fine."

"You seem to have your problems with men, don't you? Every time I see you someone is knocking you around." He smiled at her. "Maybe you just naturally provoke them?"

He had black wavy hair, a strong jaw line, weird colored eyes and a big wide smile.

"I haven't met a good one in a long time," she answered.

"We're going to leave the car right here. The dealer will find it Monday and report it to the police," he answered.

"I need the car."

"The car is hot. You rented it from Avis at the Airport. The police are already looking for it. Like I said, you've been lucky."

She was flabbergasted that he knew about her room and the car. "What else do you know about me?"

"Not much, mostly preliminary stuff. We're just starting to fill it in. Anna Klemm. Not your real name. Graduated from college in L.A. Apparently going to school didn't do you any good. Changed jobs a lot. Not much on working for anybody. Got to hanging around the Venice Beach bunch. Hooked up with your biker friends. Nothing much good from then on." He paused a moment looking at her hard this time, like he was trying to read her.

"Now you want the hard stuff?" he questioned.

His eyes were looking through her and she felt transparent.

"Yes," she almost stuttered it out.

"Anna Morkosnov from Chicago. Ran away at fifteen. Street thief. Stole anything you could trade for drugs. You were a dealer for kids. You even pimped some of the young girls but never got picked up for turning tricks yourself. You must be the first or else you got lucky. Somehow you stayed out of any big trouble. Ended in juvenile for petty larceny. Released at eighteen. Supposedly disappeared but the only people who really disappear are the ones the government helps disappear. They know where everyone else is, even Jimmy Hoffa, they just aren't telling."

"I didn't turn any tricks," she said quietly.

"You never went back home and, in case you don't know it, your mother's still alive." He paused for a moment. His face looked strained as if he was thinking far away. Then he added, "She's in a state funded assisted living complex on the south side. I can get you the name if you're interested. Should I go on?"

Her voice dropped so that he could hardly hear the question. "Who the hell are you?"

"Finish the coffee. It's time to leave," he said while getting out of the car.

She opened her door and stood up next to the car. "Why should I go with you? Why should I trust you? I'm still not sure if you're the same guy. You don't look the same. You're bigger and a hell of a lot more talkative."

"You don't have to. You can leave anytime you want, but for your own good if you're going to leave, then leave. Don't show up tomorrow. It's not a good town to be in right now." He climbed onto the bike and started the engine. "I'm done talking. What will it be?"

She followed somewhat reluctantly. She didn't like being without a vehicle but in her current situation, it was probably the best thing to do. He had helped her twice, him or his partner. He sure didn't look the same as last night. There must be two of them, she thought. Without their aid, she would have been dead last night.

She stopped long enough to get her bag from the trunk then slipped onto the back seat and pushed her feet against the pegs. A moment later, the bike rolled out of the car lot.

The sun was dropping quickly behind the western hills and the heavy shadows of the day had become skinny stick-like images wandering across the intersections. He drove over the shadows, through town and parked the bike on the east side 6th Street north of St. Joseph Street across from the Alex Johnson Hotel. He quickly replaced his leather vest with a sport coat from his right saddlebag and his sunglasses with a pair of square wire framed clear lenses. His boots were dropped into the opposite side bag and a pair of Italian Ferragamo loafers took their place. A newspaper was tucked under his arm and Anna had to run to catch up. He had changed and the change was dramatic. Now he appeared smaller, a businessman, very eastern and proper. A broker from New York or a college professor from Boston. Either would have fit.

He walked across the street and into the wide lobby of the Alex Johnson Hotel. The elderly man behind the check-in counter looked up as they passed.

"Good evening Mr. Wellston. Fine day isn't it?" asked the concierge.

"Good day to you Leonard. And how are you?" He said with a slightly British accent.

"Just fine and thank you for asking. Are you enjoying your stay?" Leonard had been with the hotel for more than forty years, always appropriately discreet but the young woman with the bruise over her left eye did seem to catch his attention, although only momentarily.

"A very cosmopolitan oasis in the middle of the wild west, Leonard. Extremely proper."

"Well, thank you sir," Leonard answered as the couple walked to the elevators. Leonard was pleased.

The elevator stopped at the third floor. The three-room suite was at the far end of the hall. The windows looked out over the east side of town. The bike was clearly visible as were Main Street and a large portion of the business area. She sat on the edge of the sofa facing him.

"How long have you been here, Mr. Wellston?" she asked a slight smile finally finding the corners of her mouth.

"Name's Earl Wellston and I haven't stayed here, but this is where you should stay until we can get you on a plane to somewhere."

"How did they find me so quick?" she asked.

"You used a charge card. They can find you immediately."

"How can they do that?"

"Almost anyone can find you through the use of a charge card. It doesn't have to be a legal organization. Any good hacker can have your location within minutes.

"I didn't use mine. I used one from those guys last night.

"Worse yet. When they find the bodies, they're going to want to know who was in the new motel room you rented. You'll draw them like young girls to a rich old man."

She thought about that for a moment and seemed to accept his logic.

"Well, they have my money," she commented.

"And you want to just charge in there where they are waiting for you with loaded guns. Hell, haven't you been beat up enough in the last couple of days? You want to go for it again?"

"They have my money," she repeated.

"Say it again if you like repeating yourself. You keep that up and you'll be very dead, very soon. You want to live, you'd better start listening."

She stopped talking. Of course, he was right. At least as far as the game she was playing. It was much better to listen or at least appear to listen. She had originally thought all she was going to do was get the money and leave town. Simple, but nothing was that simple, especially when it came to money.

"What do I do?"

"First of all you stay here tonight. Call downstairs and order something to eat. I'll take care of it with Leonard. We want them to think that you've left town. That way they'll finish up what they're doing here before they look for you."

"Look for ME!" she snapped. "What the hell for? They've got the money."

"I'm starting to have a problem with you and I don't like having problems that I know I'm going to feel bad about later," he appeared frustrated. She liked that.

"Your thinking can get you killed," he continued. "They don't really care about the money. What they care about is you wandering around knowing enough to implicate them. They're not going to let anyone who can do that stay alive. The money is just an added incentive. They're not done with you until you're done."

"Done! Like forever?"

"Most likely."

"Damn it! I had it and the SOB ripped it right out of my hands." Her mind felt like brown mud, thick, slow and dirty with an occasional streak of clear water. She tried to grasp at that. "Well, he has to return it to someone. It's endorsed and it's live money. He won't tear it up."

"That's true."

"Then I'll just have to find the freak with the streak and get it back."

"Hell, you don't know how to quit, do you?"

She was excited and her eyes had a distinct way of shining. Blazing might be a better word. And now she was up and pacing.

"You're right! I'm not going to quit. They agreed to pay and even though I didn't know what the contract was, I was on the team. And the job got done. And they owe the money! I'm the only one left. So they owe it to me."

Ralston felt like laughing. He had to appreciate her. She must have already got past last night because today she was fearless. She cared little about the danger or being in a life threatening situation. She had something she needed to do and that was where she focused. But she was annoying him because her thinking leaned away from the smart side of the scale and he didn't have any more time for her problems. He had helped her twice and that was enough.

"Listen, the truth is they were probably going to kill all of you anyway. I can assure you they never intended to pay a small group of thugs."

At that, she turned and stormed across the room until she was almost touching him.

"Is that what we were, thugs?" she demanded. The corners of her eyes were moist. "They were my friends."

"I'd say that's a good word. It more or less catches the whole idea and I'm getting tired of telling you. You should pick your friends better. Now, you either get smart or you're going to get dead."

She stood very close and their eyes locked together. His eyes were light and streaked with lines of ivory and they drifted around her face. She could tell that his mood had changed. She started to feel uncomfortable. His smile had disappeared.

"You know I owe you a lot," she said her voice dropping at least one octave until it had a throaty vibration.

"I know," he answered and stepped back from her. "And if I had let those two have you last night, I wouldn't be wasting my time with this conversation. You can either do as I say or I can take you across town and dump you in the back seat of a black Mercury. What do you prefer?" He turned away and moved across the room. *What the hell was that* Ralston thought? *Thankfulness?*

His image was flickering again, like it had last night. Anna could see him and then he blanked out. It was like something was throwing a switch on and off in her brain. He was there, and then he wasn't. Flickering like a celluloid vision in some theatrical sci-fi movie. She backed away and blinked her eyes in an effort to adjust the picture she was getting.

"What do you want me to do?" she asked.

He flipped the key on the dresser. "Call the airport. Book a morning flight out of town. Use a different name. Put it on my hotel account. Leonard will okay it. Then call a cab and get there.

It'd be best if you were gone early. Forget the damn money. It'll only get you killed."

He turned and quickly left the room closing the door behind him. He stormed down the hall to the elevators, frustrated at her insistence and her attitude. Voices started laughing in his head.

WELL, WELL. WHAT DO YOU THINK, TIGRESS, AMAZON, WARRIOR QUEEN OR SIMPLY A FOOLISH WOMAN?

They continue laughing and by the time he reached the street his mood had changed and he couldn't help but laugh himself.

The small municipal airport was closed at night, and for the most part, like so many small airports throughout the country, it was left unattended. During the day aircraft would come and go at will. The location of the office door combination was noted in any Airport Directory Manual and if someone needed fuel, a number was posted on the board near the front door. Bill Sempling, the terminal manager, would usually be out within a half an hour. For ten years, the County Council had been discussing the cost of installing runway lighting and probably would continue for another ten. For Bill, it was fine. He wouldn't have cared for the responsibility of a night crew, besides he was single and he liked to keep his evenings open. He also liked the availability of the conference room. It was Saturday evening and Caitlin was going to stop by.

Dusk was settling over the Hills and gray lines, drawn like sinister fingers reaching downward from thickening clouds limited visibility. There was nothing on the radar for fifty miles and Bill was shutting down when a black Mercury pulled up and parked outside. Three men got out and walked toward the office.

Caitlin didn't see the fire until she turned off 385 and was near the entrance. Later, she remembered reading that a fire contained within a building doubled in size every minute. It didn't take a whiz kid, which she wasn't, to figure that a fire started in a ten by ten interior room could take down a 2000 square foot building in about five minutes. That was about how big the terminal was at the airport. The building was about half gone when she first saw the dancing red and orange fingers licking at the roofline.

She called 911 and waited. Three minutes later, what was left resembled the high school homecoming bonfire minus the drunken revelers.

Bill's truck was outside but it never occurred to her that he might have been in the building. Besides why would he be? The building was long and narrow with several exits and nowhere to get trapped inside. She was still looking around and expecting him to show up when the police and the firemen arrived ten minutes later. By then, the flames were licking up what was left of the roof and all the firemen could really do was focused on wetting down the fuel tanks.

It wasn't until later when she saw EMS carrying Bill's body out on a stretcher that she remembered the Mercury. She'd seen it turning off the airport entrance road onto 385. It had driven slowly passed her and the driver looked very similar to the dark-haired man that had been on the early morning arrival.

It was all in the report she gave to the police.

The call from Chief Ray Staff came at seven o'clock. He wanted to speak to Sergeant Gomez.

"This is Chief Ray Staff."

"Yes, Chief? Something new come to your attention?" Her tone was patronizing. She obviously held him in low esteem. Most women did. He didn't like that but her attitude was about to change.

"Did something just come to my attention? Yes, yes! Something rather unusual."

"And what might that be Chief?"

"We had a fire over at the Airport in Custer. It took down the terminal building. Some pretty intense hot spots. Looks like it was deliberate. The Terminal Manager died in the blaze and it's evident that he was murdered but I'll wait for the coroner's report on that. We've also got a witness that saw a vehicle with a dark-haired man leaving the airport while the building was going up in smoke."

"Well, this isn't Norway. There's probably plenty of dark-haired men running around," she answered.

"On top of that the same witness saw the same man arrive this morning and drive away with a woman in a red pick-up," he paused for a moment waiting for a reaction and when he got none, he continued. "I think you should come in and talk to me."

"How late are you in the office?" She didn't seem the least bit concerned and that confused him. The way he figured she should be.

"I'm on the other side of the Hills, right now. I won't be back in the office tonight but this is serious and I think it would be better if you stopped by my place this evening. I'll be home within an hour."

"That sounds cozy. What will your wife think?" she asked.

"I don't have one. I live alone." She could almost see him sweating on the other end of the phone.

"That's a possibility, if you can bring the report with you. I might be able to help you out on this one."

"I have it in my hand right now."

"Good. We can probably solve this problem ourselves."

"I hope so," he answered.

"I'll be there around eight." She got directions and hung up. "Fat bastard," she said to herself.

CHAPTER THIRTY

The Sheriff's house was on five acres, off a dirt road, surrounded by huge growths of large pines oozing black pitch and suggestive shadows. It couldn't be seen from the road and if Mari had failed to see the wooden address pointer, she would have driven past the entrance. The drive to the house was narrow with untrimmed pine branches reaching out far enough to scrape the side of any vehicle. In the center of a large group of pines was the small ranch house with a detached garage and a pole barn, both located behind the main house. She parked the pickup off to the side of the driveway and walked to the front door.

He opened the door and stepped aside allowing her barely enough space to get by. He was still dressed in his uniform and had a .357 Smith and Wesson strapped around his more than ample waist. She squeezed past making sure that she didn't touch him.

"Would you like something to drink?" he asked as he moved to the counter that divided the kitchen from the living room. The kitchen was large and simply flowed into the living area. There was a bottle of Jack Daniels and a two-liter plastic of

Coke sitting on the counter next to a bucket of ice and two glasses. It looked like he planned on her drinking with him.

"No thanks," she answered and watched while he dumped a double in a glass and splashed it. "What's this all about?" The question challenged him. She needed to know what he knew.

"We're you the woman at the airport?" he asked flipping the report on the table in front of her.

"Why would you ask that?" she answered.

"Because the woman in the red pick-up at the airport had dark hair and because every time a dead body shows up lately, you seem to be around."

"If I'm not mistaken, wasn't the woman with the two shooters dark-haired? Why aren't you looking for them?"

"Well the witness said the pick-up was a red Ford Ranger extended cab, newer model with a bed cover. Just like the one owned by the Rykens."

"That doesn't mean they haven't picked up on us and rented a red truck. That would be pretty smart of them. And your witness could have made a mistake on the model. Maybe it was a Chevy. Witnesses have made mistakes before. It changes everything."

"The attendant at Custer Airport didn't die immediately. He was a big strong guy. He was fried up pretty damn bad. But he still had a little left in him. He said "the same guy," and then something about a private flight that morning. The other witness corroborated that fact. Those things add up," he paused a moment and looked her over. "I figure that was the Ryken's red pickup. The one parked outside."

"Are you accusing me?" she showed a startled look. He paid no attention to it.

"The witness is very credible. A Hill's girl. You know, they grow up with trucks." He looked her up and down real slow and she got that same feeling she'd had in his office that morning. "I want to know what's going on and what you were doing at the airport. So yeah, I think it was you. And I thought before I carried this any further maybe you and I should talk about this. I could arrest you right now, take you to jail and hold you on charges of arson and murder. Or else I could just let you leave, disappear and let the feds try to find you. What do you think of that?"

"I think that's a very good idea," she had a strong feeling where he was going with this. "But why would you want to do that if you thought you caught a killer?"

"First of all, I don't like your boss, this Armstrong character. He thinks he can take over my whole town. He sends in Detroit Police, talks about sending in the FBI, and has something happening at the Ryken place up in the hills that I'm not privy to. Shooters from all over the fucking country coming in. Detectives that aren't really detectives and maybe even a cop that isn't a cop," he paused and then added, "You know being a police officer runs a lot deeper than most people think. Sometimes you have to make decisions. They might not be exactly legal but in the long run they're for the best. And besides you have to take care of your friends and you and I are about to become good friends."

"How do you figure that?"

"Well you're either going to jail tonight or we're going to spend some quality time together tonight." He paused, a very confident look spreading across his face, "would you like that drink now?"

She turned and her right hand moved across her hips to her hip pouch. She stopped when she heard the distinctive cocking of a Smith's hammer.

"I wouldn't do that Gomez."

Mari turned and faced Chief Staff. He held the revolver pointed at her chest.

"I wouldn't want to blow a hole through one of those lovely tits but I'm real close to it. Just unsnap the gun pouch and put it on the table."

"Why do you want to do this?" she asked.

To him she finally appeared concerned. "Why not? You're leaving town, one way or another. So just do as I say and put the gun down."

She unsnapped the gun pouch and set it on the table. "Now what?"

"I already told you. You see the fire job wasn't good enough. Office furniture ninety percent gone. Outside structure a total loss. The fire truck drenched everything. It soaked everything that was left around the desk but you know something, I'm looking for the flight logbook and it's gone. Now, I'm thinking those guys from the FireStation got out of town on a plane. I think your partner put them on a plane and didn't want to leave anyone around who knew about it. So, he kills a guy and burns down the terminal, trying to make it look like an accident and then he steals the logbook, probably thinking that it would be forgotten in the blaze. You see, he's the one I want. You're just frosting on the cake."

"I'm just some frosting for you? That's a different thought."

"Bill Sempling wasn't a friend of mine. In fact, he was a damn pain in the ass. He screwed up more marriages than a divorce court. He was always banging someone else's old lady.

Maybe he was completely innocent or maybe he was involved in something illegal that I should know about it. Either way you are going to tell me. You tell me here and then you can disappear or you can get your ass down to the jail. Either way, I'm still going to pick up your partner at the Ryken's. It's up to you. You see, nobody lands in my town and takes over. This is my place! Now, I can help cover your pretty ass for a while but you have to want to be friends first. You see, I only help my friends."

"Cops are the same everywhere. They've got ass on the brain," she commented.

He laughed, "That the truest thing I've heard in a long time." He put the gun down on the table alongside her pouch, "Well, what are we doing?"

"What do I get out of this?"

"You get to leave. Take the truck and disappear. They'll call and ask where you're at and I'll play dumb. I'll give you twenty-four hours then I'll go get your partner. Hell in twenty-four hours you can be in Costa Rica."

She walked slowly to the front door and looked out into the yard at the truck.

"You can run if you want. I'm not going to shoot you. But we'll get you before you get out of the Hills."

The right corner of the truck bed cover was unsnapped and flapping lightly with every errant breeze. The soft rain, which was falling when she arrived, had turned hard. She looked outside a moment longer; thinking how much better off he'd be if he were only a little dumber.

"Oh, I'm not running," she answered as she turned toward him and slowly undid the buttons on her blouse. She slipped it off her shoulders and seductively dropped it over the back of a Lazy-Boy recliner. She wore one of those black Victoria Secret, gather-um all up and push-um all out, lace brassieres. Ray really liked that.

She stopped right in front of him and as he reached out to touch her, she gently took his hands in hers, "Easy," she said, "you'll have your chance. But first, can I be excused to use the ladies room for a moment. I'll leave the door partially open and I'll be out in one minute." She could see he was close to losing control and thought if she just walked back and forth in front of him he'd probably cum in his pants.

"Sure," he stammered, "but hurry up."

"Only a minute. It'll be worth it," she smiled and walked provocatively down the short hallway until she found the bathroom. She closed the door halfway. Then she spread the curtains over the tub, unlatched the window and pushed it upward one inch to be sure it would move. From her hip pocket she pulled, a small mag-lite, twisted the shaft to turn it on, placed it in the corner of the open window, and closed the curtains. The high intensity light sent a laser like beam into the night forest and created a pathway to the open window. She flushed the toilet then took a minute to wash her hands before she walked back down the hall.

He was waiting anxiously as she walked to where the bedroom was and looked inside. The bed was a large four-poster. She liked it. She really didn't know why but she'd always liked sturdy, old fashion things. Apparently, they symbolized something lasting and dependable, something she never had as a child. She walked into the room and stood next to the bed. Ray Staff followed but she stopped him at the door.

"Stay there for a moment. Let me get these off first." She stood ten feet from him and slowly unsnapped the top of her slacks and slid them down. She did it gracefully with an effortless elegance that held him frozen. He didn't think he'd ever seen a woman as sexy as she was. She stepped out of her slacks, folded and put them on the end of the bed, and then she removed her arms from her bra straps, unsnapped the fastener and laid it on her slacks. She stood before him in her panties.

"Are you ready, Chief," she laughed.

"You … bet," his mouth was dry and he could hardly get the words out.

"But first maybe you could tell me why you haven't asked me about my partner, the man who was at the airport with me?" she asked.

"You mean the other detective?"

That's better; she thought looking past him into the living area. Things just got a lot better.

"No," she said, "I mean the man who is standing behind you with your gun pointed at your head."

Ray was naked, tied hand and foot to a high back oak kitchen chair. The chair was lashed between the heavy oak dresser and the bedroom door. There was dried blood on Ray's face and his left eye was badly swollen.

The man was big, six two or three and very well-muscled. He had black wavy hair and a slight hook to his nose. *Italian* snapped through Rays' mind. He looked like he worked with weights. He was hard with layered muscles. He put Ray down easily. Sergeant Gomez and the man were on the bed together and there wasn't anything, even in his own sick mind, Ray couldn't imagine that the man, her partner, hadn't done to her.

She had tried to put her clothes back on but the man stopped her. He wanted her in the bed but she refused. She said that she just wanted to leave but the big guy was insistent. He pushed her around some and forced her onto the bed. She seemed afraid of him and finally she gave in.

The performance had been going on according to the bed-side clock for just over two hours. Ray couldn't believe himself but he was actually timing it. Possibly, he was amazed at the man's prowess or maybe, realizing it was more of a death knoll, he was subconsciously counting the remaining moments of his life. She would actually turn toward Ray so he could get the best view and then she'd smile at him. He had an erection which he tried to will down but it wasn't happening. He couldn't believe he could be both erotically stimulated and terrified simultaneously, but he was.

The man paid him no attention at all, which was adding to Ray's shakes. The woman, throughout the sexual display was putting on a continuously show, acknowledging the fact that he was there, less than six feet away, a captive in a freak sex show. But the man, intent on what he was doing didn't recognize Ray's existence.

"How thick do you think your fat is?" Ray couldn't answer, his handkerchief had been stuffed down his throat and his neck-tie wrapped and tied across his mouth. "Hey babe, what's this cop's name?"

"Just call him Chief. He loves that. Makes him feel real important," Mari hollered from the bathroom. She wanted to get the hell out of there. Tony was in a vicious mood. The Sheriff had been ogling her since the moment they met. Well she had given him an eyeful. Tony wouldn't take 'No' for an answer. As it went on, she actually found herself enjoying tormenting the bastard. *You wanted to look before*, she thought, *well, look now.*

"So Chief, how deep does your fat go? I mean if I cut you open, how deep do I have to cut before I get to anything important. He held the knife blade between his thumb and forefinger allowing almost an inch and one-half to protrude and punctured the point into Ray's side. Ray shook violently and tried to scream. The gag choked him and he started to gasp within and almost swallowed his tongue.

"See, look at the tip," he almost requested the attention, holding the knife in front of Ray's eyes, "almost no blood just a little dripping, clear oily stuff, like grease. See I was right. Look, I'll do it again. The knife punctured another hole and then another. He continued until he had at least fifteen small puncture wounds across the policeman's stomach.

Ray retched behind the gag and swallowed his own vomit.

Every word drifts upward. Above the ceiling of the room in which it is spoken, above the building in which it is uttered, above the noisy streets and the silent mountains, above the wind swept plains, silent meadows and turbulent oceans and above the din of the world that suppresses it; upward it flows until it becomes part of the hum beneath the clouds and it is there that it is heard by God and by all who have received His gift of "The Listening".

Tonight, the wind whistled through the tall, heavy pines and the thick dark firs. Tonight the branches, at the tops of the Aspen, bent with an angry noise. Between the highest trees tops and just below the wet dampness of the evening clouds where the wind passed unfettered, there was a slight whistling and within the whistle a hard, deep howl existed, almost as a soft hum, and even deeper within the hum there was a tumult that only a rare few could hear. Ralston heard the words.

Almost on its own accord, the bike rolled off to the side of the road. He usually felt it before he heard them but tonight they were exposed and very clear. It was a bad night and someone else was dying. It was the second time within the last few hours. The first had been quick, hot and very terrifying but this was calculated, torturous and pleasurably demonic. This was madness! He was here!

"Just call him Chief. He loves that. It makes him feel real important." Ralston had heard that voice before. In the background, the screams that followed were muffled but the voice was clear and familiar. The rain had intensified and something was causing a disturbance. He drove the bike under a large quaking aspen and listened as the sheets of water formed a wall of wetness between him and the darkening roadway. He felt as if he was there. As if, beyond the noise was a presence that equaled his own It was something he had never felt before, something that was interfering in a unique way. In his mind, he could see the scene, as if he were looking through the eyes of one of the participants.

Passing vehicles began turning on their lights and within minutes, the Hills had passed another day; but the night was dealing this place a package of terrifying death. He felt it in his bones, heard it in his mind, and knew it wasn't far from where he now sat with water dripping from his clothes and running in his eyes like unwanted tears. Someplace very close a man was dying. In the rain, wet and confused, he asked the question. The same question he'd asked himself so many times years ago in Vietnam.

Who is my enemy? Tonight the answer was more clear than ever before but equally confusing.

It was *Redemption, "CAIN, THINE ENEMY."*

He wanted more but the voices became unusually selective. He stayed there, next to the road and listened. They were allowing this man to die. Evil was confronting evil and the outcome, either way was acceptable.

CAIN!

Mari walked into the kitchen and flopped into a chair. Don Barker was at the table playing Euchre with Sister Elizabeth and the Rykens. Sister Elizabeth and he made a great team. The Rykens couldn't buy a game.

"What did the Sheriff want?" Barker asked.

"It seems they had a fire at the airport over in Custer. The night shift manager died in the blaze. Somehow he thinks those guys in the Lincoln got a plane ride out of town but not before they burned down the airport and killed the guy."

"What do you think?" Barker asked.

"I think the Sheriff's a little loosely wrapped. If they wanted to leave town they could be in Costa Rica by now. They didn't have to leave their car and all their clothing and jump a plane and burn down the damn airport. Something else happened there."

"Well, we know who the two shooters are and who the bikers were but we haven't been able to nail down who the girl is yet. Ben is still digging for that," Barker added.

"Maybe tomorrow will bring us something," Mari said.

"Well, we've got to keep a lid on this for three more days. Then I'm going to catch a hop back to Detroit with the Sister," he smirked at her.

"Wait a second, what does that mean? Who's driving the damn car back?" she asked.

"I'm the senior officer so you'll probably pull the job of getting the Crown back to Detroit. I wish I could help you out on this one Mari, but when duty calls and all that stuff," he was laughing and dealing at the same time.

"If it comes down to that, tell Ben I'm on vacation for a couple of weeks," she grinned back.

"It'll be my pleasure," Barker answered.

She walked to the front door and looked out at the falling rain. It was the second time tonight she had made a similar walk. The rain had eased off to a light drizzle but the moon was missing and the sky a dead black with a promise of more storms to come. The horizon was covered with blankets of thick dark gray clouds and she could see thunderstorms over the western Hills. A motorcycle picked its way slowly through the slippery ruts in the dirt road leading to the front gate.

"What do you know about this Sachs guy that works for you?" she asked over her shoulder.

Brad and Amy looked at each and simultaneously shrugged.

"Not much," Brad answered. "He does odds and ends for us. I'm getting too old to be climbing on top of barns, so I let him do that kind of stuff. He works around for a lot of people."

"You don't mind him staying in the barn?"

"He doesn't bother anyone and it's nice for Amy and me to have someone else around."

"I guess so," she answered and walked out onto the porch, leaving the four of them to their game.

"Pretty nice place," she commented entering the rear door as Ralston closed the survey window, "for a stable, that is."

She was in her early thirty's with the pitch black hair of a Spanish beauty queen. She had the classical Mediterranean profile accented with good cheekbones and full rounded lips. Her eyes were best described as a rich chocolate with dark brows and long thick lashes. She reminded him of a girl he had known in Rio, dusky and very Brazilian. But she possessed a hardness in her face that he could only assume came from years of being in a hard place. Flesh chiseled into bone. Lips that had a hard time turning upward and a look that could melt ice. She stared straight at him. The look was unsettling. He remembered that afternoon in town and the feeling she had left him with. There was a hum starting in his head and he opened up to the voices.

"Not many folks get to live in a stable. That's mostly for TV westerns," he answered.

"Maybe that's what you are, a TV show all by yourself." She glanced around the barn, "Computers in the barn, phone line, hmm, and a modem up and running. You seem to have most everything. Kind of high tech for just a hand." she added.

"Well, yeah. This new stuff keeps me in touch. Not much to do in cowboy country."

"I'll bet there is if you know where to look," she said as she moved over to the stall where the bike leaned on its stand. It was dry. He had already wiped it down. She looked directly at him as she flipped a leg over and sat on the bike. Those chocolate eyes forced him to return the look.

"You know you have to stop doing that," he couldn't help but grin.

"What's that John?"

"Well you look at a guy with that intensity and he's forced to look right back and before he knows it, you're sitting on his bike with a gun in your hand. That's pretty unfair."

"I'm a police officer, Mr. Sachs."

"One second I'm John. Then you pull a gun out and I'm Mr. Sachs and you're a police officer. Our relationship is quickly deteriorating. I hope you're not going to shoot. I'd just hate that." He was surprised that she knew he was involved.

"You've been following us John. That first afternoon in the park, an old man, like an Indian and then the same guy in the bar Friday night, younger and with a limp, but still the same guy. The eyes are a giveaway to anyone who really looks. You should get yourself a pair of contacts. Try a different color. Something a little more common."

"Actually, I tried them once but the damn things are so itchy. I kept blinking all the time and I wanted to scratch them out. But you're right and obviously, I couldn't fool a real police officer. I apologize but I didn't have much time at the park. I should have gone for the hippie with shades routine. But there aren't many of them out here and most of the bikers aren't taking strolls around the park."

She slid off the bike, sort of slow and silky, and he was starting to think that maybe he shouldn't be watching this woman at all.

"How long you been working for Armstrong and why didn't he tell us you were following us? Why all the secrecy?" she asked.

"I don't know any Armstrong, Mari," he answered. "I work for the Rykens most of the time and do odd jobs. The Chief of Police, Ray Staff, got a hold of me a few days ago. He said some folks were going to be staying at the Rykens. He told me to disguise myself and follow them. Hell, he even knew the car you were driving and when you would be coming to town. He must have been in contact with someone who knew you were coming here. Maybe your boss or someone, I don't know. I just hung around outside of town until I caught site of that Crown Victoria you've got in the garage and I followed you in. It wasn't hard." It was a half wild stab but when she spoke, he was sure of the voice. He was also sure who, the words *Just call him Chief,* referenced.

"Why in the hell would he do something like that?" Mari asked.

"Hell, I don't know except he sounded pissed. As far as he's concerned, this is his town. You ask anyone. Nobody crosses Ray Staff. He just wanted to know what was happening here at the Ryken's place. Since I work here he got a hold of me."

"You really want me to believe that you don't work for Ben Armstrong," she probed.

"Mari, or police lady with a gun, whoever you are, I'm telling you that I don't know anyone named Armstrong." He reached over and put his cell phone on the table alongside the computer. "Here's my cell phone. I'll give you the Chief's number. You call and ask him. Tell him you got your gun out and ask who the hell I am working for." He stopped for a moment. "Hell that might be a mistake." He smiled and shook his head, "maybe he'd like for you to shoot me since you already caught on to me following you folks."

"I'm not going to shoot you and I'm not calling the Chief either," she answered. "You can tell him anything you want but if you don't stop following me, maybe I will shoot you."

She holstered her pistol and walked slowly back toward the double door. She could feel his eyes on her. All men are the same, she thought. She stopped at the door and turned toward him.

"Were you following me tonight?" she asked her hand still next to the pouch.

"Well I thought about it. In fact, I was already out there but the Chief called and told me that he had it covered for the night and I could let it go. There was too damn much rain, anyway. I had to get off the road. I stopped at a roadhouse and had me a coffee until it slowed down enough to keep the bike on the road. You can get killed trying to ride in the rain," he smiled again.

She shook her head, dismissing him as Ray Staff's country stooge. There was something about him that she couldn't quite figure, but he definitely wasn't Armstrong's man.

"That was a smart decision," she said. "Good night, John Sachs," she added as she left the barn.

Anna slipped easily passed Leonard, through the lobby and into Paddy O'Shannon's Pub. She took a seat at the bar and ordered a Guinness with a burger and some fries. When it arrived, she asked the barmaid to call her a cab. Thirty minutes later, she was back in her rental and staked out across the street from her motel. The black Mercury wasn't anywhere around.

She had to assume this Earl Wellston was right and that the Freak with the Streak had been to her room. Her location had been easy enough for him to find, so why not the silver streaked one? He could still be in her room waiting and he still had her check. He was probably lying on the bed waiting for her to put the key in the lock. Wellston hadn't been wrong yet and he knew a lot more about everything that had happened so far than she did. He also knew more about her than she felt comfortable with. Actually, she thought she was doing alright. She had the guns next to her that belong to the men who tried to kill her. She also had their wallets and credit cards. Across the street were possibly two more men who were now trying to kill her and whoever else was looking for her, and apparently there seemed to be plenty of them. So why was she trying to figure out how to break into that room and get her money back?

Anna decided the room was off limits simply because it made more sense to break in on someone who wasn't waiting for you than someone who was. She needed to find Streaky's room and wait for him. She'd have a better chance that way. Anna drove around for another three hours checking the parking lots of every motel, hotel and bed and breakfast in Rapid City. She even checked the travel guides at the local airport and did it categorically. Nothing, at least no black Mercury.

At four in the morning, she went back to the Alex Johnson, took a shower and washed the clothes she had on in the bathroom sink. She hung them over the shower bar to dry and crashed in the king size bed. She felt like she could sleep for a week.

CHAPTER
THIRTY ONE
Early Sunday

The phone call interrupted another thin sleep.

"Hey Ben, it's Matt."

"Matt, why the hell are you calling me at this time?"

"Hey it's 5:30, time to get up and besides I got some answers for you."

Matt Delwar was in the Division of Information and Statistics. He'd graduated from the University of Michigan with a degree in Statistical Analysis and somehow found himself a job in law enforcement. He had a reputation for being relentless, which was an understatement. When everyone else had gone as far as they could go, Matt proved that he could always go a bit further.

"You guys really screwed up on this one," Matt chided.

"Wow. I can't wait to hear," Ben grumbled. He felt like he had just laid down and any chance for sleep had disappeared with the ring from the phone.

"Yeah, I know you love it when I tell you how the cops screwed up but this one is even better. This is a screw up within a screw up, inside an even bigger fuck up. I love it. What a fucking mess!"

"Okay, Matt get on with the damn thing."

He rolled over, sat up on the edge of the bed and thought about walking down the hall and starting the coffee pot but he was sure his eyelids were stuck together. He was probably still asleep and he'd trip over something and break his damn neck.

"Well, everything was okay in New York. Well, it wasn't really okay. They fudged the shit around until it looked like chocolate and that made it acceptable, at least by police standards," he laughed.

"Matt, I've got to get the coffee on, but you just keep talking and I'll listen."

"Well, she was a good cop. Worked hard at what they gave her. She worked a beat on the east side. She apparently liked being on the street but she had some problems on a couple of occasions. She couldn't handle the street hoods. So, they put her inside and she didn't like that at all. She raised a lot of hell. Eventually they gave her another chance but it continued to happen. This went on for over two years."

Armstrong couldn't remember if he put the coffee into the basket the night before so he had to open the damn thing and check. Hmmm, no coffee!

"You still there?"

"Yeah, I need one of those coffee pots that has its own water line, grinds the beans by itself and starts at the right time, which is different every morning."

"Yeah, well I don't know if they make that yet but Hudson's will gladly put you on their list as 'first to receive' if they ever do. Anyway, her problems continued and they pulled her again. She just couldn't handle the street."

"I don't understand that. We've never had any problems like that. Actually it's just the opposite, she can handle anything," Armstrong added.

"Exactly! That's the rub. So she puts in for a transfer and they promote her to detective!"

"What?" He hit the switch and heard the damn thing gurgle. It sounded like a frog. "Wait a second Matt. Let's go back. Why couldn't she handle the street? I haven't got that straight yet."

"Ah ha. Now you're catching on! Here's the big screw up. Because the records are straight and there is nothing mentioned anywhere else, just a simple transfer request for a detective to move to a different city. Nothing too damn unusual. It's says she has family in Detroit. You ever met any of her family?" Matt asked.

"No, I haven't. The situation never came up. I've got enough to worry about with my own family."

"Correct! We're all in the same boat."

"You been up all night working on this?" Ben questioned.

"Yeah."

"I thought so." The pot was half full and he pulled it out and poured a cup. The coffee kept dripping through onto the table. He shoved the pot back in place. The new pot should stop dripping when you remove it from under the spout. It shouldn't continue to drip all over the damn counter. "Why couldn't she handle the job, Matt? Answer that, okay?"

"Well, like I said, nothing is in the records, so I called New York and talked to some of the guys there and it's kinda unusual because she didn't have any real friends in the department. Nobody has heard from her since she moved to Detroit seven months ago. And just to answer your question, she was too small."

"Too small. What the hell does that mean?"

"That's what it means, Ben. Mari Gomez transferred from NY because she kept getting roughed up on the streets because she was too small. The guy I talked to, a Sergeant Pietrangelo, said she was about five two and stocky. Small to be a cop but you know all about the EEOC."

"Gomez is about five eight and nobody calls her stocky."

"That's right and this Pietrangelo says she looks Mexican."

"What does that mean Matt? It's too early for this shit. So just keep it clear."

"Well I remembered, you know Willy Clemens, he's a patrolman from the second. He always hangs around The Red Wings Café, a real sports jock. You know who I mean. *There aren't enough women in the world for me*, Willy. I heard him once say, *"If he was the only man on Earth, he would repopulate the world in twenty years."* Well anyway," he paused for a moment, "you know I did a little calculating on that and in the city of Detroit alone, when you eliminate the women that are too old and too young, and I mean legally too young, well Willy would have to have sex with one hundred and fifty thousand women a year. That's twelve thousand five hundred women a month. Hell, I'm not sure we even have that many women in Detroit. Anyway, I told him that and you know what he said?"

"I can't wait to hear." Armstrong was now starting to hear more clearly. The buzz from the bed bugs was receding with every sip of coffee.

"He said he's up for it."

"Where's this going, Matt?"

"Anyway, a couple of months ago I'm at the bar with Willy, who's a big soccer fan. He was watching the Brazilian team and their fans celebrating after winning a round in the World Cup and Willy, who's got Gomez on the brain, says, 'she looks like one of those great looking Brazilian chicks'."

"Okay, so what?"

"So what? Are you awake yet Ben?"

"Almost. So what?"

"So what? For the last two years, the Cartel has been dumping coke into this city like we're a designated landfill and so I start thinking, maybe not Brazilian, but how about Colombian? A short Mexican leaves New York and a tall Colombian shows up in Detroit. We don't have a Colombian working in the department, do we?"

Armstrong's eyes snapped open. "Get me a picture, Matt. And be quick about it."

"Sunday morning, but I'll do what I can."

Sunday 9:30 am

Their house wasn't much bigger than a barn stall, but unlike most barns, the house was built on a slab and slabs were always cold. They were forced to wear thick socks and heavy moccasin slippers at all times, even in the summer. It was so cold and damp that it reminded her of a fruit cellar and Renee knew about fruit cellars. When she was a child living on a small dairy farm in western Minnesota, her father dug a fruit cellar into the side of a hill behind the house. He shored it up with 6 by 6 timbers and framed a thick door for an entrance. Shelves were constructed of rough sawn pine that he drove into the hard-packed earth wall and then supported with 4 by 4's. Her mother filled them with everything they could spare from their summer harvest. It maintained close to a 37degree temperature throughout the year. During the heat of summer, she and her brothers would hide from their parents and play inside. Now, she felt like she was living in a fruit cellar. It didn't bother Renee as much as it would have another woman who had grown up in a different environment but sometime she would find herself becoming physically ill thinking about raising Rainy there.

The house was cedar shake sided and painted a sickly light green. Renee could handle almost anything, but the green paint was nauseating. And the constant repairs were depressing. Last winter the bathroom pipes froze to a trickle and she had cut all the plaster free from behind the tub so she could pack insulation around the ice-encrusted pipes. No one told her about fiberglass and it took almost two weeks before she stopped itching. The pipes warmed up but she never replaced the drywall. Now the pipes were part of the inside of the house and rarely got cold enough to freeze. If they tried to, she would attack them with a hairdryer.

There were two small bedrooms, one on each side of the torn up bath, plus a ten by ten living room and a small kitchen, which finished off the floor plan. Stuck onto the front of the small eyesore was a mudroom separating the front door from the kitchen. In the winter, it served as a coat and boot room. A California condo it wasn't, but a move right now was financially impossible.

The house was situated on a small patch of pea gravel twenty feet off the creek, which was its only redeeming feature, especially if you were a young boy who loved to fish. Renee knew that Rainy would raise all hell if he had to leave the creek but she had dreams of a bigger, better place, someplace closer to the school and with adequate insulation. She knew the only way a better place would come true is when she could make one hundred a night in tips for a solid year. So far, she had never made more the two hundred bucks a week.

"The man for the plumbing is coming this week. Maybe we can finally get the sink fixed. You're going to have to be here when he comes," Renee said.

"Sure Ma. What time?"

"Early Wednesday and let's hope he doesn't charge too much?"

"I can help. Mr. Sachs said he is going to pay me," Rainy offered.

"What are you doing over at the Rykens?" she asked. She was concerned. She had never met this new Mr. Sachs but she had complete faith in Brad and Amy Ryken. She knew they would never put Rainy in a bad situation.

"I'm helping Mr. Sachs. He works for the Rykens, I told you that. I'm helping him in the barn. He's got a computer in there and he's showing me how to use it."

"Well that's good. You need to know how to use a computer today if you want to find a good job," she paused. "What do you know about this Mr. Sachs?"

"He's a real nice guy but he's too old for you," he laughed.

"How do you know that?"

He was standing by her bedroom door flipping a ball. *It was a shame* she thought, *every boy should have someone to play catch with.*

"He has gray hair by his ears."

"Well that's a pretty good sign. I don't think I'm ready for gray hair yet but maybe I should check," she laughed back.

"He has a lot of cool stuff, though."

"Like what?"

"Well he has a lot of stuff in his truck, like computers and electrical stuff. But I don't think he likes the word 'cool'. Every time I say it, he asks me what it means."

"What *cool* means?" she questioned.

"Yeah, and then I have to tell him what I mean. He says that when I talk to the angels try not to say *cool* because they'll ask me what I'm talking about."

"Talking to the angels?"

"Yeah, Mr. Sachs talks to angels."

"That's what he told you?" she asked.

"Yeah, but I told him that I don't talk to any angels and he said that it was my fault if I didn't but if I tried real hard, I could do it too."

Now, she was wondering about Mr. Sachs.

"He says they're all around and they like talking to people but most people are too busy with their own stuff to think about it," Rainy said.

"He's probably right about that. Most people are too busy to even talk to each other," she reflected.

"Well I don't think it works because I tried it and it didn't work for me."

"You tried what, Rain?"

"Tried to talk to the angels," he added.

"You did? Now I'm gonna be worrying about you. I go to work and you hang around here trying to talk with the angels."

"No Ma. I tried," he answered, exasperation in his voice and she felt bad for a moment that she had teased him but then she laughed. "But nobody answered," he continued, "so I figured ain't nobody listening anyway."

He left the room shaking his head and still flipping the ball. Later she would try to squeeze in some time to play catch with him.

Barker returned from the living room. He had just got off the phone with Armstrong. Ben informed him that two men fitting the description of Charles Breen and James

Gracey had been seen arriving at O'Hare. The video camera at the airport confirmed their arrival. The police hadn't picked them up yet but they had an APB out on them. They apparently left the car and simply ran. Finding them once they got to Chicago would be more difficult, but they were the main suspects in the multiple murders in South Dakota and the state wanted them back.

Ben wanted to let Barker and Gomez know so they could stop worrying about the two gunmen in the red Lincoln. Everyone was in the kitchen, and as large as the kitchen was, it suddenly seemed smaller. Sister Mary Elizabeth and Amy Ryken were bumping into each other like bowling pins in the middle of a strike but if Amy resented someone taking over her kitchen, she certainly wasn't showing it.

"I haven't been able to do this for years. I use to help my mother, God rest her soul. But since joining the order and accepting Our Lord Jesus, other duties have held priority. Besides, Mrs.Tischet, a wonderful German lady, runs the kitchen and she is very tough about letting anyone through that door. We, the Sisters, always joke that it's easier to get into Heaven than to invade Mary Tischet's kitchen."

Amy was thinking that Mrs. Tischet would have probably made one hell of a cop since she could keep an entire convent of nuns out of her kitchen and Amy was fearful of restraining one. Their collaborated effort to produce some form of a breakfast dissipated quickly and Amy finally got out of the way. It was immediately clear to everyone that if the Sister ever possessed any culinary skills, she lost them somewhere between her mother's kitchen and the convent. The oatmeal turned out runny, the eggs hard, the bacon over cooked to the point where it crumbled when touched and the toast was too dark. But nobody complained.

The fact that Breen and Gracey were gone brightened everyone's spirits and got Sister Mary Elizabeth back on track. The main excuse she had been given as to why they couldn't venture away from the ranch house was Gracey and Breen. Now she did not see any reason to prevent a trip to Mount Rushmore. The breakfast table became a forum on Mount Rushmore and all the complaints quickly dwindled. Amy and Brad finally agreed that they could make a quick drive that afternoon, catch the evening show and be back by ten-thirty. Brad even assured Barker and Gomez that he knew a sufficient number of back roads to allow them to get there undetected.

Mari wasn't paying attention. Her mind was still focusing on John Sachs. His attitude disturbed her. It was as if he was not only hiding something but he was laughing at her, too. The first impression she had of him, on the morning after they arrived, was that he wasn't what he appeared. That hadn't changed; in fact, he gave off the same vibes no matter how she approached him. After last night in the barn, she was ready to dismiss him as the sheriff's underling, but then something stopped that. If Chief Ray Staff had known they were coming into town, then it could have only come from one of two sources, either Armstrong or Barker and she automatically eliminated Barker. Armstrong hadn't been upfront with them from the beginning. He didn't trust them and it was possible that he had contacted the local police. That would account for her chance meeting with Sachs in town and the fact he was following them, but if Sachs wasn't working for the Chief, then that only left Ben Armstrong. There were stories that floated around within the Detroit Police Department that Armstrong worked with someone outside the department. No one ever met the guy and most members of the DPD thought it was all rumor, smoke and mirrors. But it was a quick way to explain why there were never any *'loose ends'* on Armstrong's cases. All the potential *'loose ends'* ended up dead.

And that thought alone, that one simple idea, made going back to Detroit a really bad idea. Mari found it hard to believe the guy in the barn, this pseudo cowboy, could be that man, but at the same time tickling the back of her brain was the fact that even the gun didn't faze him. It was as if it presented no threat to him at all. He had actually laughed at her. She couldn't get the guy out of her head.

She had a phone call to make.

It was 9 am Sunday morning and the sun lit the treetops up like main street lampposts, while the low ground still clung onto last night's dew. Caitlin Evans was returning from the police department in Rapid City. The road twisted nicely through the hills and her Chevy convertible handled the curves very well. She was enjoying the ride. It made her feel like a race car driver.

Lieutenant Harman needed some final details on the airport fire last night and asked her to come in early. Chief Staff took Saturdays off and the Lieutenant handled the Department on that day. He was interested in the logbook. Apparently, it was missing. She thought that if it was in the fire and it was missing then it must have burned but Lieutenant Harmon thought differently. He thought someone took it.

The questioning left her feeling very uncomfortable. She and Bill had spent Thursday night on the couch in the airport office. They had done that several times in the past few weeks. It was where most of their dates ended. The Lieutenant was a very attractive man and admitting that she and Bill spent their nights at the airport, embarrassed her.

Now, Bill Sempling was dead. The idea of him dying in the fire was so excruciating that she preferred to simply eliminate it from her mind. It was the way she always handled things. If something bothered her, she just forgot about it. After a while, it became easy. If someone bothered her, she just forgot them, like they no longer existed. It worked. Now she was just going to forget about Bill.

It was a nice morning and the drive back was exhilarating. It would help. Maybe this was better. All Bill wanted was to screw her. He was a jerk anyway. It would be easy to forget him. Caitlin pulled up through the motel driveway marked 'ENTRANCE' and drove around the back of the building just as a large sedan pulled up to the front lobby door. She parked next to the storage shed and went in the back door. Jesse was watching a rerun of last night's ballgame on TV as the customer entered the lobby.

"Good morning. Nice place you've got here," the customer stated. "I've been up and down this road and it's the best I've seen."

"Yeah, that's why we're always filled," Jesse answered without looking up.

"Hey, I see you've got donuts."

"Help yourself," Jesse answered.

"Thank you. Maybe I will before I leave." He paused looking around the lobby. "I need a room," he continued.

"Well as you can see from the sign, I'm filled up."

Caitlin stuck her head around the corner. "Hey dad, I'm home."

"All right, Cait. I'll be back in a minute."

"Your daughter?" the tall man asked.

"Yeah, just her and me," Jesse offered, not turning around.

"That's great! I'll hold off on that donut and I guess I won't need a room," he said. "I'll use you're place." He went back to the door and flipped the lock up.

"What are you doing?" Jesse demanded.

Then the man turned the OPEN sign around, exposing the word CLOSED to the outside.

"You've just closed for the day," the man answered.

"Hey get out of here. You can't come in here and do that," Jesse yelled pushing himself up from his seat. Caitlin heard the commotion and came around the corner again. She stepped behind the counter.

"What's going on here?" she said and then taking a better look at the customer added, "Hey, you're the guy from the airport."

The stranger snapped a hand across the counter, grabbed her hair and gave it a savage twist, wrenching her neck and dragging her toward the floor. He slammed her down on her back and dropped a knee across her chest and shot the rising old man twice through the forehead. As she tried to scream, he shoved the smoking silencer into her mouth.

"Don't move. Be very still," he said, then added, "It's hot, isn't it?"

She didn't know what to do and nodded her head in the affirmative.

"Just hold it. Don't try to spit it out. It might go off."

From the corner of her eye she could see the body of her father lying in a puddle of blood and still twitching. She closed her eyes and tried to forget what she saw. She knew she could make it go away.

"Good," he said. "I want you to hold it like that. Just think of it as practice."

CHAPTER
THIRTY TWO

Ralston watched the Crown travel under the arched gate and drive out toward the main road. It was 4:30 pm and the sun, hot, yellow and ringed with red hydrogen fire, was reaching downward searching for the mountaintops to the west.

The evening show in the amphitheater started at 9:00 pm. They had plenty of time to do some sightseeing along the way, a trip to touristy Keystone and maybe a drive through Custer State Park.

He was deeply troubled and had been since last night. He wasn't able to put a finger on it. The woman was disruptive to his thought processes. She was surely the voice he had heard. He was so sure of it that he had taken a chance. The Chief of Police was dead. He didn't doubt that. She was there and that made her a contradiction, a contradiction with a deadly partner. She could be a lot of things: a mole within the department; part of Castobelli's organized syndicate; maybe a drug connection for some outside group? A lot of possibilities but definitely not a cop.

Ralston was also sure that she wasn't a killer. The way she handled the gun last night in the barn assured him of that. It wasn't a killing tool to her; rather it was something she used as a scare tactic. Pull it out and people run. He had watched her hand. It wasn't relaxed. She had squeezed the pistol until her knuckles were white.

As long as she was away from her mysterious partner, he didn't think the nun was in any danger but the man was here now and he would be looking for the right time to attack and it wouldn't be anything as detached as sniper attack. He knew what had been done to Harry Teasel and the priest in his own church and Ralston had listened to the cries of the Sheriff. This killer enjoyed the pain he inflicted during the killing. He liked talking to his victims while they were dying.

His mind had been going double-time and the noises in his head were starting to become raucous again. They were talking to him, their intensity was growing, and they were all speaking at the same time. It was as if they were arguing for space. This was different than it had been in the past. One voice had always become definitive and the rest would fade. Now he could barely hear.

Rainy was in the barn. He was playing some songs on a small portable radio. The music was loud and commingled. Ralston could hear voices within the tunes. He needed solitude and walked away from the barn along the fencerow next to what had been a chicken or hog pen before you reached the back pasture. The alfalfa was getting thick. He walked through the heavy grasses that crowded the fence. When he was at least one hundred and fifty yards from the barn, the music became distant.

There were times when everything came through sharp and clear, like having a conversation in a private room, with every word clearly enunciated and the background noise completely silent. Today, it seemed like a hundred voices were screaming at him at the same time and the background was like New York City during rush hour.

He had to go after them. The man whose voice he'd heard last night was close. He leaned against the fence and listened as the noises grew. They had been loud before but never to this extent. The fence posts were made of angle iron with slotted tabs bent outward to loop the fence wire over. Right now, his thoughts were like the tabs on that post; they bent outward, away from everything and then just stopped and went nowhere. The voices were like a virus scratching at his sanity and the confusion became a plague in his mind. Previous disruptions had always been focused, in planned unison. Now they were screaming from every direction within his head and he.......CRACK!

The pointed-soft-point bullet exploded against the edge of the angle iron, where it shattered into several pieces. From such a great distance, the reticulated crosshairs had centered on Ralston's head but the high magnification failed to define the thin iron fence post. The lead tip bullet split and part of it slid along his skull. Several smaller pieces splattered across the side of his face and one piece pierced a round hole through the tip of his ear. The largest remaining piece deflected downward and passed through his left arm where it met the muscular part of the shoulder.

Rainy looked hard at the screen. Had something moved? Then he heard the shot and saw a man standing behind the broken fence in the opposite pasture carrying what looked like a rifle. The man laid the rifle over the top of the fence post, sited through the long scope and fired again. Then he turned and walked through the woods in the direction of the main road.

Ralston's head exploded in pain, as if he'd been hit with sledgehammer, and the voices suddenly stopped. He fell into the high grass growing between the fence poles and rolled down into a slight depression in the ground. Instinct forced him to look through the grass in the direction of the shot. He saw the shooter stand and aim again. Ralston knew there wasn't much to shoot at and the shot was over four hundred yards, but it was coming again. He rolled just as the second bullet stuck alongside his head, then he twitched and flopped his left arm. He had seen the same movement many times in Vietnam when an unconscious wounded man took a second killing shot. It was a twitch of death. He lay perfectly still but the ploy was wasted.

"Mr. Sachs, Mr. Sachs," the boy was running toward him.

"Get down," he hollered but the boy kept coming and in a moment, he was there. Ralston reached up and pulled Rainy down alongside him. "He's still out there. You could get killed".

"No, no," the boy's intensity was beyond his own, "I saw him leave. He was over there," and he pointed to where Ralston had seen the sniper.

The blood was running from the hole in his left shoulder and he could see the wetness dripping from his cheek onto the blades of dry grass beneath him. The left side of his face had no feeling and there was some blurriness in his left eye. He grabbed the fence and pulled himself up. He was nauseous and dizzy and everything was spinning. The boy leaned against him and they stumbled along together back to the barn.

"Check the cameras again," Ralston said. He must have spotted them; he must have known they were there. The wound in his shoulder was bleeding profusely. He could stop it but he needed ome medical assistance.

"There's nothing there," Rainy answered as he sequenced through the cameras. "You need a doctor, Mr. Sachs. I'll call my ma. She'll get a doctor."

Ralston pulled a handkerchief from his pocket and rolled one end until it was the diameter of his small finger. He stuffed the cotton cylinder into the bullet hole, pulled his belt off, strapped it around his arm covering the wound and lashed it down tight. The effort wore him out and he was starting to get groggy. He picked up the cell phone and dialed. It rang twice.

The attendant at the registration counter answered, "Alex Johnson Hotel?"

"Room 324," Ralston requested hoping that she stuck to her original plan and ignored his instructions to leave town. If he had her figured correctly, she didn't listen to anyone.

The phone rang several times before she answered.

"Hello?" It was a question within a question. She didn't know why she answered. *Who would call?* And it couldn't possibly be any good. It couldn't be Wellston. He had told her to get on a plane and get the hell out of town.

"A black case in the dresser drawer. I," the weakness had taken over "I...the...cas" then the floor rushed up and rubbed dirt into the untended wounds in his face.

"Hello who is this?" She didn't really hear what was being said, something about a black case in a dresser.

A young voice came on the phone. "Mr. Sachs has been shot. He's hurt real bad. He needs help. He needs a doctor."

"Mr. Sachs. Who's Mr. Sachs?" but the young voice kept saying the same things. "Mr. Sachs is hurt". ...... and "Mr. Sachs has been shot."

Anna drove under the arched entrance and a small boy was running from the barn franticly waving his arms. Moments later, she was running with him, the black case under her arm.

While he instructed, Anna put four nicely spaced sutures in his left shoulder and gave him a shot of some narcotic, which the little black bag was adequately supplied with. She unwittingly had to admit, she had prior experience with administering injections and he didn't question her competence.

She still wasn't sure why she came. They had more or less parted company at the hotel and it would have been easy to leave it at that. But she felt she owed him something or maybe it was the desperation in the boy's voice. The wound to his shoulder didn't bother Sachs, as Rainy called him, half as much as the three-inch long gash on the side of his head. Anna tied off the last stitch, giving it an extra tug that made him winch before she turned her attention to his head.

"From the way you're looking, you're not too good at taking care of yourself, are you?" she asked.

He didn't answer.

"Your face looks a little shrapnelled and you got a hole in your ear. It looks like you got smart with some biker and he pulled your earring out. You're going to have a hard time living that one down with the boys at the bar on Saturday night."

"Maybe I'll just take you with me and you can kick the shit out of everyone that gives me a hard time," he finally replied.

"Nah. I'll just let them have a go at you. I'd enjoy watching that," she was obviously enjoying the current role reversal.

"Are you done yet?" he questioned.

"A couple more little pieces and we'll have all of the lead out of your cheek." She said while removing two more small pieces of the shattered bullet from his face. "There, that should do it and I think this head wound should breathe a bit, so it can dry out. The hole in your ear will heal itself. Do you happen to have a skull cap with you?"

"Now why would I have one of those?" he asked.

"I just thought I'd ask. After all, you've got enough outfits back in that hotel room to have your own vaudeville production."

"See anything you like?"

"Granny dresses and babushkas are not quite my style."

"Rainy?" Sachs asked looking toward the boy.

"Yes sir, Mr. Sachs," the boy had been sitting quietly alongside Anna watching her repair skills with the interest of a surgical intern. Ralston found the boys reserve to be very interesting. The shooting, the blood and the danger hadn't dampened his intensity or interest. It was the same as how, without any prior knowledge, he approached the computers or his fearless wandering through the forest at night. And there wasn't any false concept here, like this was a cops and robbers show on television. Rainy realized the danger was real and he could be hurt, yet, there was no indication that he wanted to withdraw. As Anna finished up, Ralston listened to the quiet laughter going on in his head. Someone else agreed and found it amazing that he had found two of a kind without looking for either.

"There's a black knit cap in one of those boxes next to my bunk. Could you see if you can find it?"

Rainy was back within a minute with the cap and Ralston carefully pulled it over the wound on his head covering both the gauze bandage and the injured ear at the same time.

"Thank you, Rainy. Now I want you to go home and I want you to stay there. Do you understand?" Ralston said.

He knew what Rainy's reaction was going to be but this situation had reached a final level. He had brought the boy into this game and knew he couldn't watch both Sister Mary Elizabeth and the boy at the same time.

"No sir! I can help, Mr. Sachs. I already did."

"You certainly did and I appreciate it, but you've already seen things a young boy shouldn't and I'm sorry for that. Now it has become very dangerous and I've got some things to do, and I need to know you're safe. So I want you to go home now." He said it sternly and this time the boy didn't argue.

"Yes sir." Rainy answered dejectedly moving toward the open barn door. "Does that mean, I'm fired," he asked. The thought of paying the plumber went through his head.

"No Rainy. You did a great job. It just means there's nothing left for you to do right now and I would rather have you someplace safe."

The boy left reluctantly without another comment and moments later the engine of the small bike kicked to life then faded away in the direction of his house. Anna gave Wellston/Sachs a sideways glance, got up, and moved toward the door. She caught a last glimpse of the small bike as it disappeared into the trees that edged the back pasture.

"Pretty special kid," she said over her shoulder.

"That's what I was thinking," Ralston answered.

CHAPTER
THIRTY THREE

They passed through Keystone driving on route 244 heading up to Mount Rushmore. Ralston was feeling better. The Darvocet backed up with two 750mg Hydrocodone, had kicked in. He was on the phone with someone named Ben who was apparently talking on a couple of other phones at the same time. The two of them had been talking since Anna left the ranch. Their conversation was intense. It went on for twenty minutes before he finally hung up and leaned back in the seat.

She was driving a black Ford F250 that had been parked in the barn. It wasn't a normal F250. This truck had some unique custom features. The phone he was talking on dropped out of a custom front door panel and the 9mm Beretta with a short silencer lying on his lap had been hidden behind the center section of the passenger seat. Center sections of seats usually don't come apart, at least to her knowledge, but this one did. The center console had some sort of a tracking device attached. Right now, a red light was rapidly beeping on an overlay map of the Mount Rushmore parking lot.

Although there were a hundred questions she wanted to ask, Anna remained silent but her nature wouldn't allow her to remain that way for too long.

"I think I should have a name to call you that agrees with what other people call you," she said after what she thought was an appropriate delay. "Any suggestions?"

"John will do," he answered.

"Not Earl but John. Okay. Today you're a John. I think I've heard that before."

He didn't answer.

"I noticed some strange scars on your back, John. Where did you get them?"

"When I was a kid."

"When you were a kid?" she shook her head and disregarded his answer. Once again, she questioned herself as to why she was even helping this guy except that he had helped her. Maybe she was just paying back a favor. Maybe it was something else. She knew nothing about him and every time she met him, he was someone else. Even his name changed on a daily basis.

"You know how kids are," he continued.

"No I don't. I never had a chance to be a kid and besides those scars don't look like something you get falling off a bike."

"What if it was a motorbike?" he said offhandedly.

"What happened? Some four-year old kid shoot you off your tricycle?"

"Something like that. Are you done with the questions?"

"People like shooting at you, don't they?"

"Seems like it, but then you're not too popular yourself, are you?"

She had started to realize since it only took Marchione two hours to get those thugs to Rapid City to kill her that this situation was bigger than she originally thought. She and Duane and Company were simply add-ons, an after-thought at best. But Mr. Wellston/Sachs was something out of a James Bond movie or the ringmaster beneath Barnum and Bailey's big top. Take your pick.

He was sitting next to her looking exactly like something everyone tried their best to avoid on a vacation: a tourist. The knit cap was now covered with a NY Yankees baseball cap. He wore a multi-colored Hawaiian shirt and a pair of checkered shorts. The left side of his face looked like he had done battle with a razor and lost. Anna had placed three small Band-Aids over the wounds in his cheek, which added to his haphazard image. The outfit was finished off with white-rimmed oversized sunglasses. Then he added the obvious camera slung around his neck and a handful of site seeing brochures, proclaiming the verifiable authenticity of every local wax museum, houses with sideways gravity and strange animal farms where the donkeys have three front legs and the rabbits have real antlers. Everyone who saw him coming would get out of his way. He was apparently ready for an evening out and Anna had made up her mind, she wasn't going to miss a minute of it.

It was 8:30 pm on Sunday evening and the parking lot was almost filled. The array of license plates displayed a colorful geography lesson of almost every state in the union. At opposite ends of the parking lot were two identical black Mercury Marquis with Colorado plates, something that didn't get past Ralston's scrutiny.

"I have to go in there and I don't want you involved. There are a lot of cops in there and…"

"Is the freak with the streak in there?" Anna asked.

"I hope so, more importantly, a female police officer remembers you from the FireStation and she's definitely in there. If she spots you, she'll do whatever she can to get you. But besides that, I need you near the entrance on the outside where you're not noticed. So stay out of the way. If anyone breaks to leave and gets through, I want to know which way they are going."

"But nobody's going to recognize you, are they?" she had a large grin on her face.

"Look, I really don't have time for this," he was trying to stay serious but he had to admit he must look ridiculous to her and a grin was sneaking into the corners of his mouth. The ridiculousness of the disguise was perfect. It allowed him to enter unfettered and provided him with a large degree of freedom. He would be left alone. If approached and questioned, his very appearance provided an excuse to be inane and naive. Stupid or ignorant responses to questions could be easily accepted where with a normal suspect they would be considered misleading.

"Okay, okay." She stifled her smile, "besides there's something else."

"I know, I know. Hell, this is crazy. I'm starting to understand how you think. It's the money. What does that say about me?" he questioned.

"You're smartening up. You might even make it through this mess," she answered and allowed the smile complete access to her face.

"I'll keep it in mind," he said slipping out the door and closing it behind him.

The weather was pleasantly warm. The heat of the day had subsided and the scent of fresh pine boughs and mountain wildflowers and damp stones nestled along the edge of fast flowing streams permeated the hills. Soft classical music drifted through the air currents like invisible waves flowing through a warm summer evening. In less than 30 minutes, the lights would be lit and a video program of the four enshrined Presidents and the life of Gutzon Borglum, the sculpture of the mountain, would begin.

The walk up the steps to the entrance area seemed long enough to wear out the aging Sister and the retired Rykens, but it was Mari and Barker that had to race to keep up. Sister Mary Elizabeth didn't want to miss anything and, even with her cane, found it rather easy to stay ahead of everyone.

The crowd was heavy and the amphitheater seating was quickly filling up. The park rangers, employees of the National Park Service, were busy giving assistance to the incoming visitors. A ranger standing near the Avenue of Flags leading down to the amphitheater was cordially talking to Sister Mary Elizabeth.

"The best places to sit are on the left side, the furthest from the restrooms," he told her. "You'll be disturbed less and when the program is over, take the President's Trail beneath the sculpture to the exit. It also affords the most dramatic view of the monument."

He was a pleasant man with an unusual scar across his right eye that ran up into his hairline. He was wearing a hat and she couldn't see beyond that. The Sister wondered what tragedy the poor man must have endured to receive that wound. He was probably in the army and, although she really wanted to know, she felt it would probably embarrass the ranger by asking. She let it go and said a short silent prayer for the man.

A rather comical looking man with oversized sunglasses, in spite of the lack of sunlight, and a large camera draped around his neck seated himself in the last row. With a huge grin on his face, his appearance drew a brief glance from everyone who passed and no one chose to sit next to him. Sister Mary Elizabeth said another prayer.

Barker was nervous. He didn't like being out in the open. The story of the two shooters being seen in Chicago hadn't caused him to relax, simply because he didn't believe it. Two killers from Chicago don't travel to South Dakota, kill four men, leave their car and jump a plane back to The Windy City when they know everyone in law enforcement was looking for them. Hell, why didn't they get off the plane with a big sign announcing their arrival? And all of that belies the question, "If they were spotted, why weren't they picked up?" They weren't. They were just *seen*. What bullshit! As the program was ending, Barker's cell phone started vibrating.

"Don, its Ben." Armstrong was checking in.

"What's up?"

"You're in a bad spot."

"I'm in a bad spot? Where am I Ben?" Barker asked, seemingly perplexed. Armstrong's tail had to be close.

"You're at Mount Rushmore."

"How in the hell do you know that, your tracer still on our ass?" Barker was about as pissed at Armstrong's evasiveness as was Gomez.

"You're goddam right and be thankful that he is. I call to tell you that Gracey and Breen are accounted for and you think it's all right to go goddam sightseeing? Why didn't you just keep your ass nailed down like you should have? Now you've got even more trouble. The monument is being staked out by local police. The FBI that I promised are finally there, four of them. Two black Mercurys are in the parking lot and a minimum of two hit men are also on the grounds. Be prepared for more. You have to leave the area immediately. Let the police take care of it."

"Well, give us something on them. I need something to look out for!" Barker's nervousness was intensifying.

"Here's what I've got – a tall white male Caucasian approximately 30 years old – 220lbs with blond hair and a military style crew cut and a white male Caucasian approximately 45 years old - 180lbs with dark hair, medium height and a large scar across his forehead. He has a streak of white hair above his right eye. That's all. And one more thing, are you listening?"

"Yeah. What the hell do you think I'm doing?"

"Don't trust anyone. And I mean ANYONE. Not even your partner. Something came up and I'm still checking on it but something isn't right. Remember what I just told you. Now get out of there!"

Mari had to get everyone moving toward the exit. Barker was nervous. She had never seen him this upset and any form of delay on her part could make him suspicious. Without wanting to be, she found herself in the middle of this mess again.

Tony could still take the nun but with the police covering the area, it wasn't smart. Tony was very cautious. Most likely, he would leave and select another time. Neither of the two descriptions given by Armstrong fit Tony and that was causing her some concern. Why were other people involved and why wasn't she told? She stood up and slowly looked around.

Four park rangers were standing together at the left rear of the amphitheater waiting for the program to end. One was talking to the others. He was obviously in charge because the others were intently listening. A comical looking tourist with a camera was the only person seated near them.

Silky said the plan was going to be simple. They had studied the target pictures and spotted the group as soon as they arrived. It would be easy. Dressed as rangers they'd sideline the path and pick up the targets as they walked past. Then they would turn behind and follow them along the path. At the least inconspicuous spot, they'd shoot them all in the back of the head. Max and Silky would hit the nun. Jack and Ziggy would put a couple of rounds into the Mexican broad and the tall old cop. And make sure they're headshots; they might be wearing body armor. Pretty simple. Silky even talked to the nun and told her where to go when the program ended.

Easy hits. That's what the big shots in New York like to tell everyone. When you're young and you have to make your bones, they give you an easy hit. But there is no such thing as an easy hit. There are a few guys, even some broads, who can just knock someone off without a second thought but those fuckers are screwed up. For everyone else, when you kill someone, it ain't easy. Most guys shit their pants doing it. Play the hard ass, yeah! That's how they act but then they go home and clean their shorts.

After the nun and cops go down, kill the old couple too. That was what the Old Man wanted. Get rid of the whole group and Willie Morolli would walk. And when everyone starts screaming and running, just walk away. Get behind some cover, dump the ranger uniforms and then mix in with the rushing people and disappear.

That was the plan. Nothing elaborate. None of that complicated shit, you see from Hollywood. Nobody jumping on a fucking bungee cord, no high-speed chase in a Lamborghini with some fancy broad decked out in an Armani gown and Cartier diamonds, and no James Bond high tech shit. Just walk up and shoot them. Then leave. Simple.

The older cop had just answered his cell phone and now the female cop, the good-looking spic, was looking around. Her eyes passed over Max and Silky and seemed to pause for a moment.

"Did she look at us?" Max asked.

"I don't know. She might have," Jack said.

"It sure looked like it to me," Ziggy commented.

"She's not looking now," Max stared at the policewoman.

"She doesn't have to. She made us. We should split," Ziggy said nervously.

"Relax, there's no way for her to know we're here," Silky answered. "She's just looking around. Everyone does that at a place like this. There's a lot to see. I'm doing it myself. Besides she's a cop and that's what they do."

Silky tried to calm them down. Their nervousness was normal. First, you think you see things that aren't really happening and then you want to call it off. It happens almost every time. His phone started ringing.

"Hello."

"This place is loaded with cops. Let it go. We'll get her another way," Tony said and then hung up.

Tony was out there somewhere. He liked to be by himself. He was a fucking loner who didn't trust anyone. Silky didn't like that.

"He wants us to call it off. He says the place is crawling with cops," Silky said.

"That's alright with me," Ziggy answered. "There are too damn many people here, anyway. I don't like it. Besides, I know she spotted us."

"I don't like it either," Jack added. "If he wants us gone, I'm gone," he turned and walked toward the entrance.

"Hey, where in the hell are you going?" Silky called after him but Jack ignored him and kept on moving.

"Jack didn't like this from the beginning," Ziggy continued. "And he's right. I'm going with him. Let's get out of here."

"What's with you guys? Piss on Tony. The Old Man wants the nun taken care of. Let's just take care of her."

"Maybe we should do what Tony says, Silk. Let's go," Max finally chimed in. He always stuck with Silky but the female cop had looked right at them.

"The hell with you guys and the hell with Tony, too. The old man wants the job done and I'm going to finish it right now," Silky angrily added.

The Rykens had visited Mt. Rushmore several times and were convinced the trail under the monument to the exit at the east end of the parking lot would be the safest way out. If anyone was following them, most likely they would guard the main entrance and wait for them there. The consensus was instantaneous and unanimous. They gathered and quickly moved out of the amphitheater beneath the monument and along The Presidents Trail.

Sister Mary Elizabeth bought a couple of disposable cameras at the souvenir shop and was now upset because she didn't have time to take any pictures. She was walking alongside Amy and Brad. They had rushed her out of the program with a crazy story of paid hit men being at the Monument. The whole scenario from the beginning had been ridiculous. There wasn't anything to be worried about since they left Detroit and there surely hadn't been any problems here. But, as usual, her police escort was extremely wary and she was forced to go along with their wishes for a quick exit.

From where they were walking, they could look straight up and see the noses of Washington and Jefferson and she wanted some pictures to take back. Sergeants Barker and Gomez were nervous and seemed truly concerned that her constant picture taking was hampering the pace. She couldn't understand their nervousness. Park rangers were stationed along the walkway. The one that she had talked to before, the one with the scar, was behind them. Even the funny looking tourist was walking behind them, taking pictures.

DEATH FOLLOWS. A voice murmured.

"Did you say something?" Sister Mary Elizabeth asked Amy. The comical looking tourist paused and looked directly at the nun. She returned the look staring straight back at him. For a brief moment, time stood still and Sister Mary Elizabeth remembered the motorcycle rider four days ago.

"No, why?" Amy answered.

"I thought I heard you say something."

She heard it, Ralston thought. *She can hear them.* Amazed he looked away.

The night sky was filled with fireflies, moths, mosquitoes and flying things that only Batman knew about. The lights anchored in granite beneath the monument brilliantly reflected off their translucent veined wings and provided a moonscape of glowing targets.

High above, nighthawks circled the mammoth heads and like members of a great ordained orchestra plummeting in perfect unison. Their wings created a staccato rumble as they braked to slow their powerful decent and then, as if hand fed by some unknown being, gently snatched a glowing terrestrial from the night sky.

The hunters on the ground had found their targets and were moving with the same sureness. The group of five was slowly walking, the nun very intent on taking pictures. Two park rangers were following behind and paying special attention to keeping the crowd moving toward the exit. The tourist, dressed in a Hawaiian shirt and carrying a large camera was in between but off to one side of the group. He raised his camera to get a picture and slowly moved closer to the nun.

There were two of them left to do the job. Ziggy had followed Jack out. Now, Silky and Max had to be faster and utilize the element of surprise. Put all of them down quickly and finish them on the ground. They could do it.

A very reluctant Max, walking slightly behind Silky, was mentally preparing himself to make the move. He visualized the shot, his finger slowly tightening across the face of the trigger. He was going to get the two cops. They would kill the older couple last. He sped up and moved closer to the group. A short barrel at ten feet was easy to miss.

Silky's hand slipped into his pocket and wrapped around the handle of a semi-automatic pistol. He was going to take the nun. She was twenty feet in front of him. She had stopped and was pointing her camera upward for a picture.

Silky wanted the gun next to her head when he shot. The Old Man wanted her dead and that's how it was going down. Then later he'd figure out how to take care of Ziggy, Jack and that asshole Tony. That son-of-a-bitch thought that he was running this job…well, we'll see about that.

The nun stopped again.

Silky removed the gun from his pocket and let it casually hang by his side. She raised her camera just as Silky raised his gun. His arm was no more than one foot from her head. At that moment, the stupid looking tourist quickly cut between them bumping Silky's arm up and paralyzing him with a numbing elbow strike in the side.

"GUN!"

The unspoken word slammed into the minds of everyone within twenty yards. Silky felt a sharp pain. He hesitated, and furtively looked around. The targets turned and moved. Their guns were drawn. For Silky it was surreal. The police had turned too fast and his own moves were slow as molasses. It was a slow motion setup. His hand went to his side. Pain ran deep into his chest and his ribs hurt. Something felt broken.

Barker reached out for the nun but she collided with the tourist and they crashed against the railing, breaking it at the base. The two of them fell over the edge and rolled down toward the next walkway. A burst of gunfire broke the sound of the night, shattering the concert music and sending the nighthawks straight up into the protection of the high dark sky. Silky forgot who his target was. He tried a shot at the female cop and missed. Max was five feet behind Silky and firing as fast as he could pull the trigger. Amy Ryken went down.

Barker felt the burn of a bullet tear through his side. He got off two shots at the larger of the two rangers and saw a 9mm bullet take the man's left shoulder. The ranger flinched from the bullet's impact and kicked off another shot that grazed Brad Ryken's left calf as he dropped to cover his wounded wife. Then Barker followed the nun through the opening in the shattered railing. Mari dove for the foliage, bullets flying all around her. She turned looking for a target. She spotted the ranger with the scar on his forehead and fired twice at the man. She hit nothing. He turned and shot in her direction then staggered up the footpath and disappeared around the corner.

For twenty or thirty seconds, it sounded like the OK Corral and then - nothing. The silence was hurtful to Mari's ears. The confusion that started with Armstrong's phone call had now doubled. Who the hell were these guys? They tried to kill her and the Rykens. She thought Tony was simply going to take out the nun.

Amy Ryken was down and bleeding from a wound high in her back. Barker had been hit in the left side and Brad Ryken in the left calf. Sister Mary Elizabeth was standing in the middle of the lower walkway looking completely confused. Two FBI agents had quickly moved in and were standing on each side of her and two more were moving toward the entrance. And the tourist who had come out of nowhere? He was gone.

The steps leading into the monument were packed with a mass of frantic people trying to push their way beyond the entrance area. Some rangers were rushing up from the parking lot toward the area where the shots came from.

Silky hobbled through the concession area trying to keep up with Max who was cutting through the crowd, like a scythe going through a field of wheat. Max charged into the parking lot bowling over anyone in his way, and within several moments, he became one of the waves of terrified tourists running as fast as possible to get away from the melee. He was hit in the left shoulder and could feel the warm blood running inside his jacket. He had to get someplace where he could look at the wound.

Silky, like a caged lion that broke out of his prison and having no knowledge of the surroundings, simply ran, trying to get as far away as fast as he could.

Robert Harkens from Volga, South Dakota, a young, new park ranger was running between parked cars straight at a man with a silver streak of hair over his eye, who like everyone else was running away.

Silky didn't wait to see if this boyish looking ranger was coming for him. When he got to within ten feet, he raised the gun and pointed it at the approaching ranger. As he squeezed the trigger, a shadow crossed in front of him. The image of a young NVA regular rushing straight at him, flashed before his eyes. His mind tried to place the soldier in his rightful place, Ho Chi Minh, Da Nang? He had seen many of them before but this one had a bullet hole in his forehead. His eyes were turned backward so all Silky could see were the whites and his face was missing. It made him pause and for a moment, he imagined a horrid face, decomposed and filled with crawling creatures. A quick flash of death and then it was gone. He fired twice.

Robert Harkens was slammed sideways into a parked car. Stunned by the impact, he fell, just as two loud gunshots echoed past his head.

Silky was winded but no longer felt tired. He sagged against the car. His hands were wet and red. The ground beneath him was moist and inviting. He felt a warm wetness on his shirt and saw a splash of red on the car window beside him. His knees hit the cement, tearing holes in his silk trousers and he pitched forward to the cement, no more than ten feet from the semi-conscious body of Ranger Harkens. Air gurgled out the opening in his throat. Bubbles of blood burst into a fine red spray and fogged the air before his eyes. His last thought, in that brief moment before total darkness, was that he just saw the devil.

CHAPTER
THIRTY FOUR

Anna turned the truck in his direction and slowed down as he jumped on the running board, opened the door and slid into the seat next to her. She glanced at him as she drove past several police cars blocking the entrance to the Mount Rushmore parking lot. Even behind the large glasses, she noticed his grimace.

"Are you all right?" she questioned.

"I'm fine."

"And your shoulder?"

"I can't feel a thing," he smirked.

"You might convince your mind that you don't feel any pain but your body still knows when it's been shot," she quipped. "How's the head?"

"I still have the headache but it seems to be clearing up," he answered, while he stared out the window. The look on his face was reminiscent of when he first sat next to her in the car dealership lot. There was a small smile and his eyes were vacant, like he was seeing without actually using them.

After a minute, she reached over and nudged his knee. "Hey, are you still with me?" she asked.

"Sorry," he said. "Follow this road, there's a turnoff about a half mile up. Turn left and you'll find a parking lot. The big guy is coming that way."

"The big one, the guy who was driving the Merc?" Anna questioned.

"That's who."

"How do you know?"

"I just do. Believe me."

"Can I help?" she asked.

"How nice can you walk?" He smiled. She liked his smile.

"Well, if you're talking about men, or any man, I can make him follow."

Max slipped his gun inside his short jacket and slowed to a walk. Visitors were milling around in the parking lot looking back toward the entrance. Most were nervously aware of the inordinate amount of police cars.

The keys, damn it! Max was digging in his pocket for the keys when he realized more police cars were coming into the parking lot. There were police everywhere. Two cop cars now covered each entrance. Getting out wasn't going to be easy. He continued to maneuver his way back toward the car, trying to look as normal as possible. His shoulder hurt like hell and sweat was beading up all over his body. He shook it off. He had to keep moving.

They had been setup. Tony warned them off. Ziggy and Jack had been smart enough to leave but he had stupidly stayed with Silky. The thought caused him to remember Silky. He stopped long enough and surveyed the area behind him. Silky had disappeared.

In front of him, a police car was parked next to the Mercury. Two cops were looking inside the car. Dammit, they even had the car pegged. It was surrounded like a goddamn merry-go-around. How in the hell did anyone know? He didn't have time to think about that now. He'd worry about that later. Max turned away from the pressure and headed toward the eastern side of the parking area. He was going to have to go it on foot until he could find a vehicle. He left the parking area, got into the trees and started to jog. He headed east until he passed a nature trail and then continued another quarter of a mile until he crossed an access road into a remote parking area.

The area was heavily wooded and smelled of pinesap and decaying wood, with traces of engine oil and wet rust. It backed up to the eastern side of the monument and contained at least a dozen older vehicles most likely belonging to employees who worked the park. Most were probably leaking junks and he needed something that could run and run fast. The shed at one side of the lot looked dark and unattended. If they were all working, then it should be easy.

He was breathing hard, slightly dizzy and needed to stop and rest. He leaned against a tree to catch his breath. Moments later, the interior lights of a vehicle on the far side of the lot clicked on and he heard a woman's voice off to his left.

"Harry hurry it up, will ya? I'm getting hungry." She was coming back from the shed area. He pressed himself into the shadow of the tree and remained motionless. She passed within twenty feet of the tree without seeing him. He couldn't help but watch the way she moved when she walked. *How does a woman move like that?*

He followed her across the parking area making sure he stayed deep enough into the trees to not be seen. There was something about her. Something familiar but he couldn't place it. He stayed out of sight and cautiously moved between the vehicles until he was within twenty yards of a black F250 pickup.

The owner, obviously Harry, wore a baseball cap and a Hawaiian shirt and was standing next to an open door fidgeting with a large expensive looking camera. The woman stood next to the truck, leaning against the door. She looked disinterested and, again, he got the feeling that he had seen her before. His shoulder was starting to burn and everything inside his jacket was soaked. Nausea filled his throat.

Harry was wearing a ridiculous pair of sunglasses. He really looked stupid. So stupid, Max thought, he was perfect. Max realized he saw the man at the amphitheater, an obvious escapee from Disneyland, a geek who was dressed like he belonged on a Hawaiian cruise ship and was anticipating the afternoon circle jerk. He was no more than thirty feet away doing something with a camera. The woman paused next to the passenger door and bent over to clean some dirt off her boots. Then she stepped onto the running boards and turned sideways to stretch. Max watched her profile highlighted by the interior lights. She looked real good. She got into the truck and sat behind the wheel. The geek paid no attention to her and continued to fumble around with a camera.

Max had to move. He was getting weaker. He retraced his steps back up the path so it looked like he was coming back from the monument. He took a deep breath, steadied himself and walked into the circle of light coming from the truck's interior.

"How you folks doing tonight?" he asked walking toward the geek.

"Terrific! Great place, this monument. Been wanting to see it for years. First time out here. How about you?" The geek never looked up.

"Yeah, me too. What'd you do, make a wrong turn? The main parking lot is over that way," Max said moving closer and pointing toward the main entrance.

"Been there. Done that. But I got a great view of the monument from here. Figure I might as well get some night pics while the lights are still on and I got the chance." He moved behind the truck and focused the camera for a shot between the trees. "Just a great view. This is going to be photo-mag quality." The woman hadn't moved.

"Your wife doesn't seem too interested," Max said looking at the woman. She was sitting behind the wheel leaning back on the headrest with her eyes shut. He could see the slow rise of her breast and imagined he could feel her breath.

"She will be when I sell these pics to 'The USA Traveler,' and the check shows up in the mail. Hmmm, I think I've got just the right light from this spot."

"Nice truck you have here," Max turned back to the geek.

"Yeah, it's a custom rig." He moved a little farther away. "I've got a lot of specialized equipment in her. Lottsa bread there, man."

"Look man, I'd like to stay and talk but I'm in a hurry and I really need to borrow your truck," Max said, pointing a 9mm at the tourist's chest.

The man turned with his camera and looked at Max. He didn't appear to be scared or the least bit surprised. He looked down at his camera again, dialed a knob and looked back up.

"Do you mind if I take your picture?" he asked. The camera contained a silenced six shot .22-caliber semi-auto pistol mounted behind the lens opening with an electronic pulse switch rigged to the shutter button.

Max was baffled. The geek apparently didn't hear what he said. Max looked over at the woman. She hadn't moved and he thought for a moment about taking her with him. In that moment, the geek had moved closer and Max noticed what looked like blood spots on the geek's shirt.

Ralston stopped, his interest in Max pushed to the edge of his awareness. The sensation was so intense, he instinctively wanted to look around but *Caution* warned that feeling aside. *TO LOOK IS TO WARN. TO KNOW IS ENOUGH.*

The camera was pointed toward Max's chest but when *Caution* spoke danger was not just near, it was imminent and required immediate attention. Ralston had given name to the voice years ago in the forest of Vietnam. *Caution* was a specific voice, one that vibrated deep inside his consciousness whenever death came near and in those days, *Caution* never left his head. That afternoon at the ranch, *Caution* was there but other voices were screaming and Ralston could barely hear him over the raucous din. Now he was the lone voice.

HE'S HERE.

The words were like drops of pure water and there was no mistaking their clarity or meaning. He was a long distance away but Ralston could feel the pressure on his finger and feel the pleasure of expectation. Words were counting down in his head.

FIVE, FOUR, THREE, TWO.

The man with the pistol, confused by the lack of reaction from the dumb tourist, still hadn't moved as Ralston reacted instantly to the warning. Spinning rearward Ralston dove toward the rear of the truck just as the explosion split the night's silence. It was precisely the same noise he had heard earlier in the day.

In a panic, Anna rolled across the seat, pulled the passenger handle and landed in the grass on the opposite side of the truck. She tried to get up to run but Ralston reached for her and covered her with his body. She tried to speak but he clasped his hand over her mouth. She understood and became still. They lay like that for several minutes and Ralston continued to hold her until the night got quiet again and he felt both the shooter and *Caution* leave.

She was quiet. She hadn't spoken in several miles. The big guy was dead. At the ranch, Ralston had been the target but tonight, there was no doubt, the man lying alongside the truck was the target. The bullet had entered Max's head above the right ear, mushroomed and left a donut size exit hole. He fell against the truck's rear quarter and dropped like a cement bag in a sand pit.

"You're very quiet. What's bothering you?" he asked, anticipating her questions.

She needed to have him open up. Without really trying, they had inadvertently teamed up and she needed to know exactly what she was involved in.

"Why are all these people dying? I seem to be a part of this but I have no idea what it's really about. My four friends are dead, then two more in the forest that same night and tonight, ... how many tonight?"

"Two more," he answered.

They were quiet for another ten minutes. The Hills were dark, traffic was light and shadows covered the road. A couple of mule deer moved across the road at the edge of the lights.

At that moment, she envied their ability to disappear into the night forest and find a safe spot. She drove cautiously, wondering where she could find a safe spot.

"I have to tell you something," she said finally. She had thought about it and now she needed to say it, "the guy in the woods, at the campground. I never killed him. I couldn't do it. I left him there, alive."

"I know," he answered.

"You know? How?" she asked startled by his response.

"I went back and double-checked. It's a habit of mine."

"And?"

"They're not the kind of people you turn over to the police, Anna. They are the enemy. It's not any different than a war between two nations. You become a nation unto yourself. Each nation, each soldier, sets their own rules. Your rules become your creed. I don't take any prisoners. Eliminate all of them. Never give them a second chance. That's my creed. If you don't do that, if you turn them over to the police," he continued, "then a lawyer gets them out on some technicality and they simply rearm themselves and come back looking for you. The next time they might end up holding all the cards and you'll be dead. Right now, they have your name. If you want to survive then Anna Klemm is going to cease to exist. So, while you're sitting there feeling sorry for that guy, think up a new name for yourself." A hardness had come into his voice that indicated there was no room for discussion on the topic.

"I'm not feeling sorry for the guy. I just couldn't do that. I tried. I thought I could. He had just killed my friends, but I still couldn't. I'm sorry."

"Nothing to be sorry about. Actually I'm glad," he quietly answered.

She silently drove on. The road twisted through a tunnel of sixty-foot tall conifers. They stood like solemn sentries guarding the pathway. Several more minutes passed before she spoke again.

"How did you happen to show up that night?"

He waited several moments before answering, as if he was considering what she could be entrusted with.

"I followed you from the bar. Unfortunately, I didn't get there in time for your friends. I'm not sure I would have done anything if I had."

"Well, you got there in time for me," she said. He was a hard man to talk to. He was either stern and adamant or else he was smiling and making light of things. She wanted to know things but wasn't sure how to ask. The man was enigmatic. She felt something but she wasn't sure what. Over the past few days, every time she was in danger, he had been there to save her. And she still had no idea who he was.

"Do you have a personal name; something a friend can call you?"

"A friend?" Even in the dark of the truck cab, she could feel the smile on his face turn into something akin to a puzzled grin.

"Yes. When someone provides me with a first-class hotel room and carte-blanche for dinner, which I used extensively - no strings attached - plus not to mention saving my life, they're my friend," she laughed, but still she said it with complete sincerity.

He waited for a minute, perhaps considering the consequences. Maybe, she thought, he was just thinking of another fictitious identity. Maybe he didn't really want a friend. Maybe he didn't have any.

"Name's Ralston," he said finally. He said it in a way that made her believe it was true.

"Just Ralston," she asked?

"That's all," he answered.

She repeated it. "Ralston. I like that."

They drove back to the ranch and she watched as he removed the cameras from the trees surrounding the ranch. Then they went into the barn and Ralston turned on the computer. He entered his password, became system administrator, reset his ID protocol to the proper address and restarted the computer to access his e-mail account. Next, he selected his options and reset his e-mail account to the correct number. He had one email from Ben. The contents didn't surprise him but it did complicate matters. He printed out a copy, folded the paper and put it in his hip pocket. Then Anna helped him clear all his equipment and belongings from the barn.

He rode the motorcycle as she followed in the truck. Five miles down the road he pulled off alongside a dark gurgling river and killed the lights. He slid back in the truck next to her. The black truck, like so many of his outfits back at the hotel, seemed to absorb the essence of the man that owned it. It settled into the night and was close to invisible. The windows were down and the balmy night air, filled with the scent of mountain flowers, pine sap and damp rocks half covered with green moss and resting stoneflies, absorbed them.

It wasn't his way but she deserved something and, although he had helped her several times, he owed her something. So, he told her the story of the nun and the men who wanted her dead. He included the unfortunate Jim Gracey and Charlie Breen and tried to explain why some people felt their continued existence interfered with bigger and more important plans. He explained how, if Duane and Company had succeeded, their turn would have come quickly. And eventually Anna Klemm would have died too. He took his time. It seemed like it was important to him that she fully understood it. Not simply from a legal standpoint, that didn't matter to him, but from an ethical and moral viewpoint. And even with that, she realized that his moral view was different than anyone she had ever met. Something else guided Ralston's morality. There was a spirituality attached to his feelings and when she reflected on it later, realized he was deeply religious.

She listened quietly to it all, amazed how something so simple had become so intricate, deadly and significant to this man. She was amazed at her own persistence in chasing twenty thousand dollars when her life was threatened by mobsters and, at the same time, totally engaged by Ralston's simplistic understanding of life. The one thing he did not explain was where he fit into this whole scheme. He just seemed to appear in the middle. He wasn't a cop, that was apparent the night in the forest, and he made no mention of who employed him.

"So, how did you get involved?"

"I was asked to help," he replied.

"I assume you mean the nun?" she asked.

"The total situation but yes, I came because of the nun. People kill each other all the time but it takes a different kind of person to kill priests and nuns."

"And you eliminate those kinds of people?"

"This kind of killing hits closer to your life than thugs shooting each other," he answered. He turned and looked out the window into the ebony night. She could tell he was done with the topic.

"Are you married?" she asked.

"No, never have been."

"Why? Too fast, too busy or just no time for anyone?"

"No. Not any of those. I'm just too screwed up. Most women see what's wrong with a guy and want to fix him. I'm not fixable. I have too many problems that I wouldn't wish on any relationship. And besides that, I always take time to weigh the possibilities and every time an opportunity arose, the possibilities were on the negative. I usually just left."

"You ran out on them?" she laughed. "You're one of those guys who leave them standing at the altar."

"No. No. I don't look at it like that. They might have never known it, but I did them a huge favor."

"How do you rationalize that? You did some girl a favor by walking out on your relationship."

"My mother always said you can't change a cockroach into a butterfly. I'm just not fixable," he had that smile again and she liked it.

"Well, maybe they shouldn't try to fix you. Maybe they should just leave you the way you are," she grinned back at him.

"No, they were right. I need fixing but I'm like an old broken down car and there aren't any parts left to make it run right. This car is beyond repair. The manufacturer can't even have a recall because the model is extinct."

"You know I think you're fixable. But it would be a major undertaking because you're also full of shit… big time."

"Big time?" he remarked.

"Big time," she leaned across the armrest and kissed him on the cheek

"Thanks for showing up every time I needed it," she said.

He wrote a note, took a roll of money from his pocket, counted off five hundred dollars, and gave her both.

"Take this," he said handing it to her. She reluctantly took it.

"This is yours too," he added and gave her the check for twenty thousand.

"How'd you get this?" She asked incredulously. She had witnessed the death of the big guy first hand. Now it seemed obvious that the second man he mentioned was the Streak.

"When the time was right, he gave it up. Don't worry about it. Just cash it a long way from wherever you decide to live," Ralston answered. "You're going to take this truck and leave here tonight," he continued. "When you get someplace where you feel safe, change your name and ship the truck to the man on that note. There's no rush. Actually, a little time in between would be better. Call him first and he'll approve the freight charges through the shipper."

"And what are you going to be doing?" she asked.

"Well, first of all I'm not going to have to worry about you because you'll be a long way from here. Then, I'm not going to worry about Sister Mary Elizabeth because the police and the FBI have her safe. I only have to worry about the killers that probably think I'm dead and right now, they're probably worried about each other."

"Couldn't you use a little help?" she was puzzled by her own reaction. She had her check. That was why she had stayed in this town. She should be thrilled but now, she didn't want to leave him, especially, if he was in danger.

"No, Anna. I'm better doing what I need to do alone. I need you gone. And this time, I need to know that you're really gone. I need a friend's promise."

Anna drove south on US16. She would cash the check in Denver and from there ... well she wasn't positive, but it sure wouldn't be LA. She thought maybe she'd check to see which city was ranked the safest to live in last year and move there. Maybe a trip to Chicago was in order and maybe, in time, she would forget about the last few days. And maybe sometime in the distant future, she might even forget about this man called 'Ralston'.

CHAPTER
THIRTY FIVE

Mount Rushmore was closed. The State Police, under orders from the Governor, had shut it down. Two people were dead and three were wounded. Tomorrow it would be a worldwide headline. Reporters swarm faster than starving locust.

Now the assumed threat to Sister Mary Elizabeth became menacingly obvious. When Matthews was shot in the church, he had gotten in between the killer and his target, now the killers were targeting the police along with the nun. The attempted assassination involved a plot to kill the nun, her protection and apparently everyone in her company and it wasn't over. The FBI were setting up at the ranch and taking charge of her protection. Their orders were to personally accompany the sister back to Detroit.

The police were still investigating what happened. Two men had escaped into the parking area where one was found dead. The other was found approximately one mile away in an employee parking area. He had been shot through the head. As of now, the police had no clues as to who killed them.

The reporters were questioning the truthfulness of the police reports. The FBI was reported at the scene and that didn't help the image of the local authorities, at all.

Lieutenant Santee Harman had taken over for Chief Ray Staff. The Chief had not been located yet. The belief was he must have gone fishing in the Hills and probably wouldn't be back until Monday morning. Without being able to locate him, the Lieutenant had more than his share of problems.

Caitlin Evans, the only witness from the airport burning, and her father had been found murdered at their motel earlier that morning. It was the type of murder that could paralyze an entire state. The father had been shot but Caitlin had been raped and tortured. She had more than fifty small knife wounds on her body. There were no suspects to these killings either.

Rapid City, a city known for lack of crime and tight families, and all surrounding areas were close to a panic. Ten people had been killed in the last two days and that was assuming the fire at the airport was accidental, which most law enforcement involved in the situation doubted.

It was 1:30 am and they had been at the Rapid City Regional Hospital for the past three hours. After an hour of surgery, Amy Ryken was stable. Fortunately, the bullet had passed under the clavicle. It hit nothing vital, just meat and, although it had gone entirely through her body, it was still classified as a flesh wound.

The slug Barker took in the side tore out a hunk of meat large enough to choke a small dog. He had just come out of surgery and was going to spend the rest of his life with a dent in his side. He was fortunate it wasn't two inches to the right or his situation would have been more serious. He was staying at the hospital until Wednesday morning when a private jet would transport Sister Mary Elizabeth back to Detroit for the arraignment. Barker was going with her.

The slug to Brad's leg was a little deeper than originally thought. He needed surgery and several stitches to repair the wound. It would be fine but it was going to be a few weeks before he'd be out dancing.

Brad Ryken was furious. As far as he was concerned, it was Ben's fault for bringing this situation to his home. Friendship was one thing but not when it created life-threatening situations. Ben thought no one would know the nun's location and there would be no danger but he was wrong on that one, dead wrong. Amy was fortunate to be alive and Brad was staying at the hospital with her. She wouldn't be released for several days and, by then, they'd all be gone; something that Brad couldn't wait to have happen. The only concession he would allow himself in Ben's defense was his efforts once the danger was known. It was Ben who called and gave them warning. And it was Ben who had the FBI and local police virtually falling from the sky to save their asses. And someone literally cleaned up the mess before it escaped from Mt. Rushmore.

This wasn't unusual when Armstrong was on a case. There were never any loose ends. Ben was never implicated but as everyone on the force was well aware of, the opposition always died off at an amazingly fast pace. And as Brad knew very well, *'the man that no one knew'* was around. Too bad he couldn't have tidied up before they started shooting at Amy. There was talk about the tourist but as of yet no one had a lead on him.

Sister Mary Elizabeth was locked in a solitary cell in the Rapid City Police Department. She had finally agreed to the confinement. Two men dead at Rushmore plus the shooting of Amy, Brad and Don Barker had left her in a state of shock.

Two State troopers were stationed inside the cellblock and, beyond the outer door, two more sat like guard dogs. The lobby had two local police officers at the front desk and two homicide detectives from the state capital in Pierre, sitting on different sides of the room deeply engrossed in the local newspaper. All the outside doors were locked and barred. To get in a person would have to come through the front. And a police car, with two more police officers sitting in it, was parked in front of the building. Everything looked regular and nothing was out of the norm until someone entered the lobby. Even then, unless you were a local, you wouldn't realize the lobby had four men in it instead of the usual one.

Mari was in the hospital waiting room. She had just left Don who was in recovery and heavily sedated. The original plan had been not to draw any attention, keep a low profile and leave the local police out of it. Right now, it seemed that every law enforcement officer in South Dakota was in or around the jail. She dialed Armstrong's number, took a deep breath and changed faces one more time. Finally, he picked up. She knew he was awake. He had been on the phone with Captain Walksfar of the state police and Lieutenant Harman for the last two hours. She didn't even wait for his 'Hello'.

"Ben, what's going on? You're on the phone with everybody except me. We're supposed to be a team. What the hell is happening?" she complained.

"You've been with Don and Sister Mary Elizabeth and I had to bring the locals up to speed on this mess," he answered. "Besides people shooting at you, how are you doing?"

"I'm confused. We're all shot up and I still have no idea who the enemy is."

"The enemy, Sergeant, is anyone who tries to interfere with you protecting the witness. You know that," Ben stated.

"There wasn't supposed to be anyone, Ben. This was going to be an easy ride out to South Dakota and back. 'Just keep the nun moving and no one would be the wiser,' that's what you told us. But everybody in the whole damn country seems to know where the hell we are."

"Unfortunately you picked up a tail right out of Chicago. It wasn't supposed to go that way. But I've kept you informed, Mari. I called you the moment I found out about the gunmen at Rushmore. And nobody knows where you are at. The National News is reporting a shooting at a national monument. There has been no mention of Sister Mary Elizabeth."

"Great! But who the hell told you. It wasn't the State Police or Lieutenant Harman, because I've talked to them and you informed both of them. The two shooters in the red Lincoln have shown up dead. Some campers near Hill City found their bodies in a ravine next to a small campground and the police shutoff that area. The point is the info about them being spotted in Chicago was bullshit. And that came from you!"

"We had an APB out on them and they were reported as being seen there. It must have been a mistake."

"That's bullshit, Lieutenant. They were killed and my guess is that it was the same night and no one has a clue. And then two more gunmen escaped the attack at Rushmore and got clear into the parking area. None of the Park Rangers or the State Police saw either of them. They're dead also. They were both from New York. You have their names by now. The one with his throat sliced was Silano Pratza and the one with a high power rifle bullet through his brain was Maximillen Freidich. Both on loan, probably, from the Albriati Family to old man Castobelli. The fact is that someone else is running around out here and I believe you know who it is."

"I don't know what that means, Sergeant, and I don't like the inference but for now I'll attribute it to you being distraught and upset. It isn't everyday people try to kill you. As for now, it's apparent they have at least one more operative there and he killed his own people before they got caught and talked. That's typical for the people were dealing with. You just need to get control of yourself. "

"Ben, I want to know."

"I wish I could help you on this Mari but I can't. Sister Mary Elizabeth is going to be held under heavy protection by the state and local police. No one is going to be able to get near her. We're setting up a dummy safe house at the ranch. We want it to look like she's still there. The FBI is in control of the situation now, but I want you to be there. My belief is that this SOB is crazy enough to try again. He shot Gerry and Don and tried to get you also. I want this bastard before he decides it's too tough and leaves the area."

"Ben, how do you know someone won't kill your boy instead?"

Ben had received a memo from Matt Delwar along with a picture of the real Mari Gomez. It was like comparing a Bull Terrier to a sleek Wolfhound. He didn't know what to expect from her but he needed her around and he needed to keep her worried.

"Mari, have you ever met a ghost?"

"A what?" she asked.

"A ghost. You know. Now you see it – now you don't. A ghost. Have you ever stood face to face with a ghost? It's a simple question. Have you?"

"You're shitting me, aren't you?"

"Have you ever met one, Mari, a real one?" Ben persisted.

"No... I guess...no I haven't." She didn't understand the question.

"Well you don't want to start now. So just let it go." He hung up. Ben didn't want to go any further with her. His whole objective was to keep her pissed. She had to be pissed, maybe so pissed that she would bring the killer to them.

Monday 3:00 am

Mari drove the Crown west on Kansas City Street. Everyone she had gone to Mount Rushmore with was staying at the hospital with the exception of Sister Mary Elizabeth. Everything had gone wrong and she realized how lucky that made her. If it had gone as planned, a plan that was completely different from what she had been told, she would be dead. She was alive and her instincts were telling her that she had been set up. A dark storm was moving in from the western hills. The clouds were like mountains of sheep's wool, dipped in tar and thrown into the darkest part of a lightless cave. She could feel the blackness creeping in and the chill that preceded it ran down her spine like ice water slicing down a mountainside during an early spring melt. It reminded her of Tony.

It had been planned as a wholesale hit. A total kill. Everyone was a target. Nobody was supposed to come out of it, including her. Tony had lied to her. He was still out there and if he was in any way connected, and it was impossible to believe he wasn't, then he expected her to be dead right now along with the rest of them. She wondered if he had been in the parking lot making a body count as they carried out the stretchers.

Lieutenant Harman said the witness from the airport had been raped. The bastard raped her before he killed her. Right now, she believed Armstrong was right. He needed to get Tony before he decided to leave. It was late enough to avoid a phone call and besides she needed some time to think this through. Maybe she shouldn't make any call. Maybe she should just keep driving. The FBI wouldn't miss her and nobody at the hospital would even question her whereabouts until late tomorrow. She could be in Mexico by then. That sounded pretty good right now.

She had gone to Rushmore believing that Tony was going to kill the nun. It was supposed to be for business. All it would have taken was a simple long-range shot but Tony didn't want that. That wasn't why he did these things. Tony killed for pleasure. He really enjoyed it. He could have taken care of the nun days ago. That was the plan and it was so smooth that it backfilled its own holes.

Her story would have been accepted without question. *Barker and she did the best they could but they never saw it coming. It wasn't expected and it surprised the hell out of them.* Then they'd find Chief Staff dead and blame it on the hired guns from Rushmore. Even the two shooters from the alley who were thought to be in Chicago would end up being victims of the killers at Rushmore. Add the guy and the girl at the local airport, and you can close the file. All the victims and their executioners were accounted for.

It was a pretty neat package except someone else was here. The two from Chicago were dead before Tony arrived. And the two who thought they had escaped at Rushmore well, who got them? Something scratched at the back of her mind and that something was Armstrong's man, the man who tailed them from Chamberlain. It couldn't be the guy in the barn. He was dead by the time the Rushmore incident happened. Or maybe he wasn't. Maybe Tony had lied about that, too. She was no longer positive about anything. She found herself in a situation where she could trust no one but herself. And now, Armstrong was talking about ghosts and she felt like running.

When Mari got back to the ranch, she had some investigating to do. What she had told Armstrong was, in reality, at least her reality, the real truth. She didn't know who the enemy was!

The FBI agent who was blocking the entrance to the arched driveway recognized her and let her enter. Two more agents were inside the house. One was ransacking the refrigerator when she walked in. He looked up, surprised, and then continued his search. The second one was working on surveillance equipment in the living room. He ignored her.

She walked upstairs without speaking to anyone and went into her room. It was 4:15 am and she was exhausted. She undressed; dropped her clothes on the floor and fell into the bed. Tomorrow she would decide if there was a way out of this or if she should take a long ride and not return. Amazingly, the stress didn't keep her awake. Within five minutes, she was asleep.

A nightmare, something she rarely had, snapped Mari out of a deep sleep and forced her upright in the bed. She looked furtively around the room. She was fully awake and the feeling of what she'd seen or thought she had seen was insidious. Something had moved in the room. It had been at the foot of her bed watching her sleep. She was as sure of it. She didn't believe in ghosts but she just had a vision of one standing over her and the thought was terrifying.

She glanced at the clock on the nightstand. It read 5:15 am. She had only been in bed for one hour. She picked up her pistol, turned on the bedside lamp and slid out of bed. She checked the room and closet. She dropped to the floor, pushed her clothes and shoes aside and checked beneath the bed. She found nothing and finally sat on the bed feeling quite foolish. The doorway to the upstairs hallway remained locked, as she had left it.

Except for herself, the room was empty, but when the fear of the supernatural crawls up your spine, your stomach starts to roll and your nerve endings tingle. That was what she was experiencing now. It was an eerie feeling to awaken that way and she attributed the feeling to Lieutenant Ben Armstrong. Ben had asked her, *'Have you ever met a ghost?'* And the way he said it disturbed her. He didn't ask if she had *seen* a ghost. A lot of people think they have seen ghosts. They believe that what they've seen were visions of supernatural images, simple manifestations that were either real or imagined, but they were almost always just visual interpretations. What Ben asked her was if she had *met* a ghost. There was a huge difference between *seeing* and *meeting*. And now she was having nightmares.

She stretched out on the bed and knew that it was decision time. She had known it driving back last night. She had a few of these definitive moments in her life and usually, at those moments, she knew that if she made the wrong choice she was going to die. This was one of those moments. It wasn't about the nun anymore or the job she was expected to carry out. It was about staying alive when nobody wanted you that way.

Elena Soora came to New York from Columbia.

She worked her way up through the cartel by being tough and doing exactly what she was told. And doing what she was told came naturally for a poor tin hut Columbian. It didn't take long for the right people to recognize that she was capable and efficient. That, coupled with the way she looked, made it easy to want her around. Besides that, she was smart enough to strategically put her sex where it was appreciated the most. Fuck the right guy and you move up. Fuck the wrong guy and the line of wrong guys grows longer.

She came to New York with the knack for handling the logistics problems of large drug deliveries for the cartel. The timing, preparations, handling, deliveries and the payoff had to be perfect. Then she would make sure the deposits were placed in the right accounts and washed into other multiple accounts, until they finally ended up in one of several Cayman Island banks *as* the deposits of legitimate tax paying mainland businesses. Elena didn't make any mistakes. When problems of that nature started to occur in Detroit, it was decided that she was the person to fix the problems, except this time they needed her on the inside.

A NYPD patrolwoman had requested a transfer and was a perfect fit. Their connections within the department held the transfer up for three weeks, while the family got the new Mari up to speed. Actually the real Mari Gomez did leave New York, but she never got as far as Detroit. A little offshore in the Atlantic was far enough.

The real Mari Gomez emigrated to the U.S.A. from Mexico. Her parents were dead and she had no known relatives. She joined the police department as a cadet and worked for six years on a street beat. Now she was fish food. Cut open, filled with steel balls, the size of marbles, sewn up, anchored hand and foot with cement blocks and then sunk five miles offshore. She'd never come up. The fish eat everything. It was the syndicates contribution to perfect recycling.

Elena Soora had picked up the airline ticket booked in the name of Mari Gomez and flown to Detroit. The only problem with the plan was because of a minor error, she was transferred into homicide instead of narcotics where the New York people wanted her. She ended up on a four-man homicide squad working for Lieutenant Ben Armstrong. The New York organization was disappointed and was in the process of remedying the situation when they found out that she was in the car with the nun and heading west. Then, they couldn't have been happier.

It was 9:00 am Monday morning and the phone had become a curse put upon Armstrong by some devil. It was Wickes.

The Captain was forced to work Sunday just to catch up on the Rushmore fiasco. A police department is not a Monday through Friday operation. It is a 24/7 job. In fact, more hard stuff goes down on weekends than during the week. If you give people extra time they use it to get into trouble. Wickes wanted to see him. It was no surprise to Ben. He had been waiting for his call.

Mari awoke at 9:30 am and instinctively patted the sheets along her right side, searching for her gun. When her hand found nothing but bedcovers, she quickly sat up. She relaxed when she saw it next to her cell phone on the nightstand. She had to let the cobwebs clear. Her mind needed a moment to put things in place. Sometimes when a person first awakens they're disoriented. It takes a moment to realize where they are at and what they're doing. She looked back at the gun and was immediately puzzled by its placement. She didn't recall setting it there. In fact, she had been so nervous last night that she definitely remembered keeping it on the bed next to her.

She rolled over towards the door, swung her feet over the bed and froze with her feet dangling above the floor. Across the room, her clothes were neatly folded and hung over the oak slats on the quilt rack. Her shoes, which she had kicked off as she entered the room last night, were set side-by-side and placed beneath the rack. But the most startling thing was that her thong was missing. She was naked from the waist down.

She sat up in the middle of the bed and rummaged the bedcovers. Then she checked the floor alongside and under the bed. It wasn't there. It was gone! Quickly, she got dressed and went downstairs. Sister Mary Elizabeth was sitting in the kitchen having a cup of coffee, as if it was something she had done for years.

"What are you doing here? I thought you were at the jail?" Mari asked, startled at the site of the nun.

"They brought me back here last night. Agent Granson says the FBI is in charge of my protection now," Sister Mary Elizabeth answered.

Mari shook her head in an effort to clear the cobwebs and walked into the living room where Granson was sitting on a large sofa wearing a headset and looking out across the front lawn

"I thought that she was being kept under tight security in Rapid City," she said

"The FBI is now in charge of the Sister. The orders came straight from Washington. Even the President wants this project properly completed. After what happened with your people yesterday, no one is very comfortable. We set up a diversion at the jail," he continued. "If the same people want to make another attempt, they'll have to figure out how to penetrate the jail. Hell, that will take at least two days of planning. By then we'll be gone." He appeared cocky and self-assured. The 'your people' tone in his voice made it obvious. He didn't want her around.

"What can I do to help?"

"Why don't you make breakfast?" he answered sarcastically.

"What's the matter?" she snapped back. "Momma never showed you where the kitchen was?" she threw the words back at him.

"Why don't you just stay out of the way, then? We'll take care of this," he continued without looking at her.

"Good luck," she answered and walked out onto the front porch.

Mari crossed the front yard and slowly walked the open space between the driveway and the barn. The sky was overcast and a light drizzle had started. It looked like another day of heavy rain was approaching. Puddles were already forming in the gravel driveway and the raindrops striking her arms gave her an ominous chill. She walked behind the barn and slid the wide double doors open and cautiously moved inside. It was empty. All of John Sachs belongings were gone. If John Sachs was dead then the question of who emptied the barn played across her mind. She needed to talk to Tony. Unanswered questions were stacking up in her head like old shoes in a closet and no one was willing to supply the answers.

She dialed his number and waited, trying to anticipate what he would say. He didn't answer. That puzzled her. He was there. She knew that but there were several reasons why he might not answer. The worst being that he had cut her out. Meaning since she didn't want to help with the nun, New York's drug connection inside the Detroit Police Department was no longer viable and she was expendable. She tried the call again, her frustration building with every ring. He didn't answer.

She spent the next several minutes searching the barn for anything that would give her a clue as to what might have happened to John Sachs. She found nothing. Her phone started ringing and a sense of relief engulfed her.

"Where the hell have you been?" she asked anxiously.

There was a delayed pause on the other end.

The word CAIN echoed through Ralston's head for the second time in just as many days.

"That's good," he answered. "You're expecting someone else. That means you haven't talk to him yet."

"Who is this?" Mari questioned.

"Good morning, Elena. Apparently, having your partner try to kill you didn't disturb you enough to keep you awake. You slept well. That's admirable. I didn't disturb you, did I?"

"Who are you? Were you in my room?"

"I have been following you since your arrival and you're quite interesting for a police officer. I wanted to talk to you before you made any foolish phone calls because today you have a new set of rules to live by."

"Who is this? Are you Armstrong's man?" she repeated.

"Elena, listen! You're still alive. Your partner tried to kill you. As of last night, you're all alone in this mess. The chances of you surviving are growing smaller by the minute. Are you listening?"

"Yes," she tried to settle down. She was right about last night. Someone had been in her room.

"I could have killed you last night and I could have killed you at Mount Rushmore. Right now, I need you, so I'm going to make a deal with you."

"I don't make deals," she answered.

"Today you do. I have your missing piece of lingerie. It's an interesting piece of silk, isn't it? But it doesn't really accomplish anything except provoke the opposite gender. That is unless, I place it with the dead police officer that you left in the trunk of his cruiser. The DNA on this thong will match what was on his bed and it will put you at the scene and then in prison for life. And even if you didn't personally kill the officer, you were an accessory to the madman that did," he paused to let her think about what he had said. "I've been to the morgue. Did you see what he did to that girl?" he questioned.

She didn't answer. The thought of the raped girl and what Lieutenant Harman told her last night was still in her head.

"You should go. You should see what your friend is capable of," he paused for a moment. "Are you listening now, Elena?"

"Yes," whoever he was, he seemed to know everything.

"You have a phone call to make and it must be a very convincing phone call. Everyone thinks the sister is at the jail, even him. You're going to tell him that she is there with you, that the FBI has switched plans. You have to convince him. I suspect that he is ready to believe she is there with you, so it should be easy. He'll like that. You already know that you're on his list. Maybe he'll take you off."

"What do I get from your deal?" She finally asked.

"Elena, breath in and slowly let the air out," his voice commanded her. Without willfully considering it, she took a deep breath.

"Did you do it?"

"Yes."

"Good. That's what you get," he paused for a second time, letting the implications sink in. "I won't call again," he continued. "You won't be given a second chance." The phone went dead.

She stood in the center of the barn, staring at the phone in her hand and feeling more scared than she had been ever in her life. She knew she just had a conversation with Armstrong's ghost.

CHAPTER
THIRTY SIX

Finally, after an entire week of rain, the weather in Detroit cleared. The sun sliced warm, yellow rays between the Renaissance Center Towers and the air had a warm, moist feel. Unfortunately, it was just for one day. The morning weather report had said another bad storm was brewing out west and moving this way. *How damn appropriate*, Ben thought. He didn't need the weatherman to tell him that.

He knew what the Chief wanted and he took his time driving down Woodward formulating his responses. Since Matthews went to the hospital, Ben was forced to do his own driving. It seemed like it was getting, if not better, at least a little more tolerable. He still didn't like it and thought he probably never would. Consequently, he was walking more, usually back and forth to Trendy's for lunch. He was even planning a little time at the gym. It had a track on the upper floor. Just walking at first, but he had to start somewhere.

The walk to the elevators was shorter than usual. When you're going someplace you really don't want to go, you always get there too fast. And to top it off, Yancy wasn't working today, so there wasn't anyone to take his mind off the third floor interrogation on the ride up.

Today Armstrong didn't sit down. He just stood inside the doorway. It was going to be short anyway. No sense wasting time sitting down and then having to expend the effort to immediately get back up. *Hell*, he thought, Matthews *was right*. When you start thinking like that, you're ready for the big one at weight loss clinic.

Wickes was in a foul mood today. That was obvious from the phone call and Armstrong wasn't much better. They weren't going to be in each other's company too long. Wickes wanted some answers, but he wasn't going to get any.

"Good Morning Chief. What besides the normal bullshit is so pressing that I had to leave my flower garden to come and see you?" Ben asked, leaning on the door jam.

"You know what the problem is. Up to now, I've had a hard time keeping them off our back but that's not working anymore. Somebody leaked to the newspapers and the damn conflict between the DPD and the FBI was on the six o'clock news. Everyone in the country wants to know who's watching the sacred nun. Washington wants her back now. They feel that she'd be safer here under maximum security."

"Then why in the hell were they holding her in a safe house. That's simply bullshit!"

"They believed she was well protected," Wickes countered.

"Yeah, and if the Old Man found out, he would have sent in twenty or thirty guns, whatever it would take. He would have killed a dozen agents to get to her. And you know the lockup wouldn't keep them out either. Somehow, they would get her. A little bribe and maybe a little poison in her coffee. Hell, the only way to keep her safe is not letting anyone know where she is, — period. Keep her moving, keep her isolated and that's what we've done."

"She's been gone since Monday night, the Mayor's in deep shit and your job's on the line. That's seven days. Starker's going to have both of our asses and if you don't let the FBI in, you'll find your own ass in the lockup."

"That's all right too. Just do it. See where it gets any of you. I've had it with this bullshit case anyway. I have to run a murder case, that's on the National board, according to the rules of some punk in Washington. Piss on them."

"Ben, you know that attitude won't work. You know who we're dealing with."

"No, I don't. I know someone leaked information that the nun was going to the church last Monday. They were waiting for her and Matthews was shot. The old priest was brutalized before he was murdered and two FBI agents were killed. Have we got the person who leaked the information? How many people knew about that? Where are the people responsible for those killings? In this city, whenever the mob is involved, no one is ever caught. Well, I've got one of them now and that little bastard is going up forever."

Wickes didn't answer. He just sat at his desk shaking his head.

"It'll work for two more days," Ben added, "that's all I know. Besides, they're blowing smoke. They know if they don't know where she's at, then nobody else knows either. She's safer this way. Hell, they already lost two men. The FBI doesn't want to risk a higher number then that. When she shows up Wednesday for the arraignment, safe and unharmed, they'll step in, take all the credit and as long as we shut up, nobody will bother us. It'll be another job well done but no brownie points and no extra bonus. My best friend and partner is in the hospital and lucky to be alive, no thanks to the Feds. The whole DPD gets another list of demerits in Washington's book but we saved their asses and that's okay." Ben was starting to get pissed.

"Well, you haven't let me in on one thing that's happening." Wickes flopped back in his chair. He appeared completely worn out.

"No need for anyone to know. We got her out and everything's fine. They're on vacation."

"I called you in because I thought we could talk about it. There are four dead men out in Rapid City and two murder suspects running loose," Wickes commented.

"There are murderers running loose in this town also. Those two won't last too long. They're both amateurs. They'll make a mistake and Chicago will have them. Amateurs always do. Then we'll find out who hired them."

"You've been bullshitting me Ben. I've called Chicago. They didn't know anything about Gracey and Breen arriving at the airport. So, I called Rapid City and talked to a Lieutenant Harman. They found the two of them yesterday. They've been dead a couple of days. They were getting a little puffy. The bugs and worms were starting to do their thing. Rapid City doesn't have a clue as to who killed them. Harman also told me your group got shot up a little and two hoods from New York were wasted. Nobody knows who got them either. The National news is talking about the fracas at Mount Rushmore but none of the papers mention that it is really about our missing Sister. The reporters are sniffing this one out. Hell, even the Police Chief is missing and they think he's probably dead too. And the FBI is already there. You haven't told me anything."

"I don't trust the group that's in this town. So, I pulled them from Dallas," Ben countered.

"You don't trust anyone in this town, do you?" Wickes asked.

"After what's happened, why should I?" The two men glared at each other for a long moment.

"Maybe because it doesn't sound like your team is on much of a vacation. It's more like a war," Wickes answered. He stopped for a moment, and then added. "I think you've got your man out there."

"Yeah, I've heard that story before." Ben commented.

"How many people has he killed? How many is he still killing? How do you live with that?"

"It's the only way the nun lives. It's the only way that the law wins. They're justifiable."

"Justifiable murders?" Wicked questioned.

"You just let the Old Man and New York know, anyone they send out there is coming home in a body bag. Tell them that Armstrong didn't send his man out there, tell them I sent a ghost and he's damn well pissed off." He turned to leave. "I'll be home if your FBI want me, otherwise I'll give them the nun Wednesday at the arraignment." He stopped and then added, "tell them to send enough men this time."

"Get the hell out of here," Wickes answered.

The elevator door closed but the conversation with Wickes had opened old questions that had plagued him since the week before he had put that young boy on the bus twenty years ago. The boy had a gift then, a magical gift. A gift of never being seen, if he didn't wish it? Armstrong's investigation had turned up some unusual questions. He had pulled in most of the gang leaders and some of their best boys. Although none of them would admit that since the disappearance of the older brother, everyone was on the lookout for the kid. It was apparent that after his beating, which Armstrong discovered came from the same boy that was burned to death, they could never find him.

How does a boy leave school every day without anyone seeing him? Armstrong had interviewed the school principal and most of the teachers. None of them ever gave Nick DiCicci a ride home. No one helped him.

Then Vietnam. Whatever was going on in Detroit magnified exponentially in Vietnam. What left Detroit was a young boy who could hide very well, what came back from Asia was a man who could disappear.

And now the nun had changed Armstrong's perception on the entire situation. Magical was one thing, but now his thinking had shifted. Ralston's help wasn't magical it was more than that, much deeper. The situation created with the nun had convinced Armstrong, it was spiritual.

He slowly walked to the parking lot. Everything that he did lately seemed slow. It made him wonder if he was saving himself up and was going to live longer or he didn't have enough energy left, making it a sign of a much closer ending. He almost thought *fatal ending* but all endings are pretty damn fatal. He had to think about that.

Wickes was getting nervous. He knew that the FBI didn't operate the field with different degrees of separation. The same people in Washington were still directing the divisions in Detroit and Dallas. And no matter how much bullshit Ben gave him, Wickes knew he was being left out on this one.

Ben slid behind the wheel of his car, reached into his coat pocket, removed the tape recorder and pushed the stop button. Then he dialed a number on his cell phone, let out a deep exhausted breath, sunk as deeply as he could into the seat and waited. On the third ring, a woman answered. "Hello?"

"This side is closed. The police in Rapid City haven't given him anything. Everything came from Gomez." he said.

"I'm sorry to hear that," the woman said quietly.

"Well, you let me know when you want it done."

"No, the Feds will do it," the Mayor paused a moment, "and Ben.."

"Yeah?"

"Thanks. I know this is not your kind of police work. But thanks."

"Yeah," he said again.

There was a momentary, strained pause and then both phones went dead.

Mari's phone was ringing again.

"You haven't called. I feel like you've forgotten me," Tony said.

"They tried to kill me at Mt Rushmore," she was still angry. The fact that she had survived had been more luck than instinct.

"That's not true. They knew not to. It must have been a mistake, darling. The excitement of the hunt. How many of them are dead?" he asked.

"Some of the police were wounded but two of your people are dead. Your boys botched it. Do you have anymore who are going to try and kill me?"

"Why would I kill you darling?"

"Because you've made sure everyone who knew you were here is dead. The guy at the airport, then the head cop and you didn't kill him to help me. You killed him because a witness saw us together at the airport. Then you got the witness. They found her yesterday."

"I did you a favor. She saw you at the airport. Now, nobody knows you were there. You should be happy."

"They said, 'she'd been raped.' Is that true?"

"Well, I do try to live for each moment," he laughed. "She prayed to me. Down on her knees, she prayed and I gave her communion. She wasn't much good anyway. It was better for her," he laughed.

It made her shutter.

"Only pigs rape woman."

"Watch your mouth, Elena. I don't like that," his voice dropped an octave.

She was mad and his implied threat didn't affect her.

"Where I come from, if a man rapes a woman, her family kills the pig."

"Ah, yes! But nobody had to rape you did they, darling? Because you did the whole cartel for free."

"Don't say that to me! You raped the girl and then killed her. That makes you a pig."

"Elena!" He screamed into the mouthpiece and she froze. "Do you want me to include you with the nun?"

The threat was no longer implied. It was out in the open now and she felt the full force of it. He had tried to have her killed and his goons failed. She knew that she had to include herself in that list of people that knew he was here. He would kill her before he was done. When Tony left South Dakota, everyone involved with the nun would be dead. He would leave the way he came. *ALONE.*

"No," she muttered. No one had ever escaped him when he decided to mark them and just the thought of him chasing her, caused her to unravel. She tried to hang on and not show any fear of him, but she knew he could sense it.

"Where is the nun?" His voice took on a deadly tone. He was pressing her. She could visualize his face and she shuddered. Being afraid was something that was familiar to her. Growing up homeless amongst the cartel, if you didn't have fear, you didn't live long. But Tony evoked a different kind of fear. Tony killed for pleasure and his victims suffered pain and humiliation before they died.

Elena looked out the window. She felt the sweat oozing off her forehead and running down the back of her neck. She could see two FBI agents patrolling the perimeter of the field where it ran up to the forest.

"You can't come here," she answered, "there are FBI all over this place."

"Where is she?" he asked and she knew he wasn't listening to her warning. "She's there Elena. Do you think I'm a fool? The feds want the little mafia boy. They want to lock him up forever and break the Old Man's heart. They're not going to leave her in the hands of a small town hick police force. The setup downtown is for me but I know where she is and you're going to help me."

"She's here in the room next to mine," she answered. She didn't know what else to tell him. He already knew where Sister Mary Elizabeth was. They hadn't fooled him at all. Quite the contrary, he had them all figured out.

"Good! Tonight I will come for her. We will kill her together. I will be her God and you will see how she prays to me. She'll worship the devil before she dies. You'll enjoy it. I'll show you how."

She didn't answer. She seemed frozen with the phone clutched to her ear.

"Elena? Are you listening?"

"Yes," the word stuck in her throat before she gagged it out.

"She had an orgasm as she died."

"That's a lie. It's not possible." She said it quietly, realizing just how crazy he was.

"Well at least I did, darling. It was a real rush. I loved it. It was wonderful."

CHAPTER
THIRTY SEVEN

R enee was sitting at the kitchen table reading the Monday morning paper. The story was both unbelievable and terrifying. Rainy had been spending a lot of time at the ranch lately. She shuddered to think what might have happened if he had gone to Mt. Rushmore with them. The police had been involved. People were shot, including both Brad and Amy Ryken. Two people were killed. There was no mention of Mr. Sachs.

Rainy was standing alongside her, fixated on the large center picture. It showed Amy Ryken being loaded into the ambulance.

"Mrs. Ryken's been shot Ma."

"I know, Rain. But it says she's going to be fine. The doctors operated last night and everything's okay."

Renee didn't know anything about Mr. Sachs being shot earlier the same day. John Sachs had gotten a pledge of friendship from Rainy and it was their secret.

"Can we go to the hospital? Can we see her?" Rainy asked.

Renee could tell how serious he was. Amy Ryken treated Rainy like he was her grandchild and Renee, who spent so much time at work, was grateful that Amy was always there for him.

"Sure. Let me call and see if they're allowing visitors," she answered

It took over a half hour but Renee finally reached Brad Ryken. He said that Amy was fine but she wasn't seeing any visitors. At that moment, he was in the room with Amy. He put her on the phone.

She talked to both Renee and Rainy and told him that she would be home in a couple of days. She would call when she got home and they could come visit.

The call satisfied Rainy, but he still seemed upset.

"You working late tonight, Ma?"

"Yes, I am and I have an idea what you're thinking young man. You stay away from the Ryken place today. Brad Ryken said that it still might not be safe over there. He said some FBI people are still there. You stay away. You understand? That's an order."

"Yeah, I understand," he answered. "But I sure would like to see some of those FBI guys. And Mr. Sachs has a lot of cool stuff in the barn and I was just wondering."

"I'm very serious about this, Rain. I don't want to be worrying about you when I'm at work. We got a deal?"

"Yeah. We got a deal. I won't go over to the Rykens."

"Good, that's why I love you. You're the best son a Ma could have."

"Okay, okay, I'm not going over there."

His days, when he wasn't in school, were spent on the river. Other kids didn't live nearby and his Ma constantly reminded him to stay around the house. The river was at his door step, not much more than twenty yards away. It was his constant companion.

When his Ma was home, when she wasn't working, they would take walks together. She always held his hand. It was all right when he was younger but now that he had grown up and actually had a job, he thought it was silly. But he would still let her do it, as long as nobody saw.

In the summer, they would sit and dangle their feet into the cool running water or just walk along the edge splashing small, cool waves on warm, sun-drenched rocks. At that time of the year, the river smelled of new moss, green plants, fresh fish and hatches of Caddis and Stoneflies. She had taught him to look at these things and to understand that everything, no matter how small, was there for a reason. There were no useless things in the world, she explained.

Her teachings caused him to pay special attention to the little things, especially the hatches and when they occurred. He had taken books from the library and became very proficient at understanding the life cycle of the fish that inhabited the river and the things they ate.

In the winter, ice crystals formed rings of sparkling diamonds along the river's edge and snow piled up like miniature mountains on the frozen boulders in midstream. Then the air snapped a special freshness into their chests and their breath would exhale like hot steam. They would always have a contest to see who could blow the warm steam the furthest. He always won.

What she seemed to enjoy the most was telling him river stories. Scary stories meant to keep him home when she wasn't around. During the day, she told him, the river breathes life like a stream of plasma feeding everything it touches and brilliant beams of sunlight bounce like the words of God off every ripple. But at night, when the half moon was shrouded in a dark purple cape and the crater of Copernicus peered from behind the cover of a black sky, like a ghastly one-eyed assassin, the tempo changed and the smell that filled the air was one of dread. Then the water's surface turned opaque and what lay beneath always warned of something fearful. If a person was foolish enough to walk in the river at night, they were always looking behind, fearful that something was catching up. At moments like that, even the most avid fisherman responded to some unwanted internal warning and became more cautious.

Tuesday 1:30 am

A light rain was falling, dimpling the river surface and producing a slight hissing sound in the surrounding forest. It could be heard for over a half mile. Rainy moved slowly upstream, occasionally looking over his shoulder. His Ma was right. The water, gurgling against the rocks, perfectly imitated the sound of approaching footsteps. With each step, he carefully felt the gravel bottom before placing his full weight on the foot. His pace was timed to blend the sound of the water rolling against his waders with the rush of the current. He was sure the Old Brown trout knew the ripples that every rock in the river made and the additional vibrations caused by Rainy, even standing absolutely still, might cause him to shy away.

When Rainy reached his destination, he paused for several minutes and allowed this new sound to mix with the river's flow. He stood close to the river's edge in the twisted shadow of a water-stunted Aspen tree. The deep hole beneath the ancient willow was just across stream. The Old Brown was lurking below; his nose pointed upstream waiting for any tender morsel the river might wash his way.

Rainy's cast was extremely smooth for such a young boy. The line curled overhead and the number 14 Black Stone Fly nymph dropped toward the shimmering dark surface. With an almost imperceptible motion, the rod tip rose slightly to set the nymph softly upon the water a split second before the line, like a thread of silk, fell effortlessly behind. The nymph drew the large browns attention to the concentric rippling vibrations. Rainy mended the line to remove any drag and let it quickly sweep beneath an overhanging willow branch. The nymph drifted as a natural, perfectly in tune with the current.

The boy, hidden in the darkness, froze in a statuesque position and waited for the anticipated strike. He'd seen the picture on the cover of an Orvis catalog and had become the perfect mimic. The large brown that lived beneath the willow was in his thoughts but so were the events of yesterday and as hard as he tried, he couldn't forget them and concentrate solely on the fish.

First, Mr. Sachs had been shot and now Mr. and Mrs. Ryken were in the hospital. He couldn't understand that. He knew there had been men sneaking around the property. At first, he thought they were bill collectors or maybe those guys from the court who serve papers to people.

It happened a lot of times at his house and his ma and he would slip out the back door to go for a walk in the woods. Once, they just went into Ma's bedroom. She gave Rainy a book and told him to read for a while. They sat on the edge of the bed and eventually the man left. But nobody was trying to hurt them.

He thought it was the same at the ranch. That was until Mr. Sachs was shot. He had wondered why Mr. Sachs would set up all those cameras to see if a bill collector was coming.

He was trying to figure some things out, but he was still confused. The job had been fun. He'd sit by the computer all day and kept a check on the cameras. He left a game running in the background in case someone came into the barn, but that wasn't really a problem because he could see anyone who was coming. And he called Mr. Sachs several times a day on the cell phone that he'd been given. He still had the phone. He liked having it. He liked working with the computer but he didn't like the Ryken's being in the hospital. That bothered him.

Tonight his Ma was at work. She wouldn't be home until 3 am and he couldn't sleep so he was fishing. His job with Mr. Sachs was done. He still had to get paid but that would probably be tomorrow.

A loud splash caused only his eyes to move. It happened all the time. A fish would leap and the young fisherman would respond with a flick of the rod in the same direction, a roll cast to search for the concentric ring and a fly to deftly find its center.

But this time, at one-thirty in the morning, as his wrist started the roll cast the word, *STOP,* loudly flashed through his mind as if someone on the bank hollered it at him.

Rainy held back, and a moment later a man emerged from the blackness of the adjoining woods and stepped noisily into the creek. He was no more than ten feet from the fishing boy and walked the river bottom like someone unaccustomed to it. He continued awkwardly through the river until he reached to the opposite bank. Then he climbed out and disappeared into the trees. He was heading toward the Ryken ranch.

The boy, with every nerve fiber in his body screaming, remained frozen, unable to move and, in that moment, so rare for such an innocent, the insight of what he had been doing struck him.

He had walked across the pasture that late night with Mr. Sachs and from those few minutes in the moonlit pasture, he had learned something. Maybe it was something he wouldn't understand for years but it was there, deep inside. The cameras were not put in the trees for bill collectors or court process servers. They were not put there even for the men who had shot Mr. and Mrs. Ryken. The cameras were in the trees because of this man, who had just crossed the river, sinister and hidden, during the darkest part of the night. Mr. Sachs was waiting for this man.

The man was gone now. The sounds from his boots faded into the surrounding night and Rainy was not at the computer. He was not there to see the man coming toward the ranch. He wasn't there to do his job.

He stumbled from the river dragging his fly rod behind him. The Stone Fly sprung free from the river and wrapped around a thick branch. Rainy felt it grab and gave it a sharp tug. The leader snapped and then he was running. He crashed through the heavy growth bordering the river's edge and began racing between the larger trees of the forest. He held his left arm across his face to prevent branches from slapping and stinging his face. It was a half-mile to his house. The young boy, alone in the middle of the night, weighed down with wet stream waders and refusing to drop his old ragged fishing pole, fearless of any ominous threat produced by the dark river, ran with complete abandon.

Ralston answered the phone. It was 1:50 am.

"Mr. Sachs, Mr. Sachs" the voice was two octaves higher than normal, very excited and out of breath. "He's here! He's here Mr. Sachs."

"Easy Rainy. Who's here?"

"The man. He just crossed the river about a half mile upstream. He's going to the Rykens."

"Rainy where are you?"

"I'm home now."

"Did he see you?"

"No sir. But he was real close and he kept going toward Mr. and Mrs. Rykens place."

"You stay right there and leave the phone on. Do you understand?"

"Yes sir!"

Tuesday 3:45 am

The rain continued to fall over the Hills and soak the Ryken Ranch. The road leading to the ranch, two hundred and fifty yards up a tree lined, hard-packed two track, was over-flowing with water filled potholes. The closest neighbor was three-quarters of a mile away. In the middle of a rain drenched night, the small ranch house, nestled on the front of three cleared acres and surrounded by tall pines, aspen and hard-woods, appeared as isolated as the original log cabin built by the first settlers years ago.

In 1923, most of the log cabin was torn down and the new ranch house was built around the remaining structure. The framework was the original rough hand hewed timbers. The trim was mahogany and the floors were made of red oak.

Amy and Brad Ryken had bought the place and spent three years refurbishing the main systems of the house, replacing the roof and updating the heating, cooling and septic systems. It was a labor of love and the results were extremely gratifying. The exterior had been completely renovated and had the look of a contemporary ranch. The inside was still a work in process.

One of the main problems was the floor. After many long years, the floors were showing signs of a hard occupation. The oak flooring nails, originally set at sequentially opposed angles, had worn around their thick shafts, enlarging the entry holes and now at the slightest pressure, creaks would reverberate across the grain and along the long support beams.

Tonight an almost eerie pattering, created by the rain, tapped the roof and gutters and helped wash the sounds from the floors and blanket the unwanted noises of the forest outside.

Strange, he thought, how nobody really notices those sounds during the day but late at night, when the shadows from the forest crept close to curtained windows and poked spiny fingers of darkness into even the most remote closet, the noises would leap out of the floor and scratch fear up your spine.

Ralston stood in the lower hallway pressed hard against the wall in the darkest part of the blackest shadow. The hair of his arm stood up and was the only indication that being there was a bit tense. Everyone was asleep, except for the FBI agent in the living room and he was almost asleep. His headset kept bobbing forward as he fought off the fatigue that came with being awake for over twenty-four continuous hours.

A large silky gray cat with a white diamond on his chest sat crouched in the doorway across the hall, staring into the dark spot on the opposite wall. You could never fool a cat, he thought. No matter how silent you were the cat always knew you were there. He heard it said once that a cat was the only creature alive that could actually see ghosts. He believed that.

A voice said, *TWO CATS.*

His face was blackened with camo-paint and as he turned slowly to his left, he saw the second cat, a calico, watching him from the end of the long hallway. It was staring straight into his eyes.

At the entrance to the foyer, he went up the stairs quickly, his feet spread to the wall and the banister where the floor was more restrained. The rain helped dampen any noise.

The first bedroom was on the right. He quietly unlocked the door. He slid silently inside and stood next to the bed. With the night vision glasses, he could see her clearly. She wore nothing but a thong and the room was filled with her essence. She had an earthy aroma, jasmine and sweet hyacinth mixed with a musky dark loam. The same force, that he had experience during their encounter in town was prevalent within the room. It was as close to irresistible as anything he'd ever experienced. She seemed so vulnerable, so exposed, but this wasn't the truth. The voices in his head told him that she wasn't as she appeared. She was a Venus flytrap, a female Mantis - an illusion. He reached over slowly with his right hand and held it above her thigh. The heat coming of her was like a sauna and it encompassed everything in the room. He silently left and moved down the hall to the next bedroom.

CHAPTER
THIRTY EIGHT

Ziggy spent the entire day on Monday learning the timetable. Tony gave him the approach line. It crossed the camera area three times, but when he stayed fifty to sixty yards into the trees there was enough fallen timber that, if he belly crawled, he could get through without being detected.

Tonight, there were two guards outside. One was near the front gate and he seemed to keep the entrance always within range. The second maintained a constant walk around the perimeter sometimes coming within ten yards of the hidden Ziggy.

Ziggy and Jack were in position. They had been waiting for over an hour. Tony was ready for the approach.

FBI Agents Carlsberg and Hartfield, dressed in military olive drab ponchos, were patrolling ten yards deep into the tree line that encircled the ranch. Both were finding it difficult to see anything much farther than their own extended hands. Agent Granson was on the communication hookup in the main living room. Crow was asleep, no doubt dreaming of the 4:00 am rotation, which was quickly approaching. At that time the FBI agents would switch. They did it every four hours.

The alarm on Granson's watch gave off a series of small beeps and his head snapped up. He had fallen asleep. It was 4.00 am. He flipped the switch on the control panel just as he heard a door open down the hall. Moments later, Agent Crow entered the room. He was dressed for a rainy night.

"Okay, it's time," Granson said into his microphone. "Hartfield?" he asked.

"Okay, I'm ready," Hartfield answered.

"Carlsberg, you ready?"

"A-OK, out here."

He flipped the switch back down and turned to Crow. "Anytime you're ready. Remember, only one man out in the open at any time," he said. Crow opened the front door without saying a word, apparently four hours sleep left him too groggy to speak. He moved out across the yard to make the switch with Carlsberg.

The rotation was simple. Crow would move out across the yard to meet with Carlsberg who was on perimeter watch. Carlsberg would then move to the road entrance and take over the guard spot from Hartfield, who would come back to the house and spend four hours on the communication board and Granson would get some sleep.

It was a black rain-drenched night. The sky showed no moon or stars. Dark clouds covered everything and sucked light upward like a deep black hole. Crow sleepily walked across the cleared area and into the forest fifty yards behind the barn. He wore a poncho, the hood of which was pulled over a bill cap. He kept his head low to prevent the rain from hitting his glasses. It also helped him see the fallen timber and natural debris he had to step over. Crow reached Carlsberg, and Granson watched as they briefly spoke. Crow then walked deeper into the forest and disappeared from Granson's sight before Carlsberg left the forest edge and walked toward the road entrance. It was approximately one hundred yards from the main gate.

Ziggy watched the two FBI agents stop and spend a moment talking, and then the one who had been patrolling the edge of the forest walked out to the pasture's edge and toward the front road. The other walked into the forest. It was at precisely the same spot every four hours. It was stupid. Tony had said the agent would walk right to him and it was working out exactly as planned.

Agent Crow stopped thirty yards inside the forest. His glasses were wet. He pulled a handkerchief from his pocket and removed his glasses. He held the glasses close to his chest to prevent more water from falling on them, while he started to dry the lens. Lightning split the night sky and a large crack of thunder made the ground seem to shake.

Something thick and slippery dripped from the front of his cap and splattered his lens. The shadows pushed close and he felt a tightness. Even the trees pressed him. The pressure squeezed against his heart and his head hurt. He thought about his parents. He hadn't seen them in years. Maybe he should ... something was wrong. His face felt thick and something ran down his cheek. He reached to touch it. His hand came back covered with red. He fell forward into the thick ferns.

Ziggy quickly removed Crow's poncho and put it on. He thought for a moment about getting the agent's bill cap but the bullet had entered the back of his head and exited his right eye. The cap was pretty nasty.

Perimeter guard duty was the toughest and Carlsberg was happy to be done with that watch. It was four-hours of walking through the forest in the middle of the night. Thankfully, he wouldn't have to worry about it for another twelve hours. The entrance position was much easier. He could lean on a tree and rest. Actually, he might find a good spot and sit down.

One hundred yards away, Carlsberg finally was reaching the large oak that guarded the corner junction of the two dirt roads. When he got within twenty-five yards, he could see the fiery glow coming from Hartfield's cigarette. Hartfield was standing beneath the oak. He had a good spot. He was almost invisible.

Tony and Jack waited patiently as the FBI agent came toward them. He was still twenty-five yards down the road, splashing through the puddles and ruts that covered the road. Hartfield's body was now lying behind the large oak tree. He had been shot and his throat cut. Tony was wearing Hartfield's poncho. In another minute Jack would be getting one.

Carlsberg reached the 'Y' in the road and walked toward Hartfield's position. Moments later, Hartfield, twenty yards back from the entrance road, stepped from behind a heavy rain drenched oak and signaled the house with a thumbs-up. Granson flipped a switch on his control panel.

"Come on home," he said as Hartfield moved out to the road, becoming the open man, and began walking toward the house. Jack remained behind the tree waiting for the hapless Carlsberg.

Granson watched as Hartfield walked slowly toward the house. He was taking his time. The rain had intensified and he kept his head low with his hands pressed deep into the pockets of his poncho. Granson removed his headset and set it on the coffee table. He was exhausted and four hours in the rack sounded great. He leaned back in his chair and closed his eyes as Hartfield walked onto the porch and opened the front door. He turned as he entered, closed the door and shook the rain from his shoulders.

"All clear out there?" Granson asked.

"Actually, no. There are people all over the damn place," Tony answered.

Granson opened his eyes slowly at the sound of the strange voice. Instinctively, he knew it was already too late. The man was standing directly in front of him with a silenced semi-automatic pistol pointed at his face. Maybe he could find a way out of this. Maybe there was time to talk.

There wasn't!

The man shot him in both shoulders, the small caliber silenced Beretta gave off a sound similar to gas escaping from a helium balloon. Psfft! Psfft! Granson fell backward over the table and crashed against the window ledge. Tony stepped over the table and shot him in the right kneecap. Then he bent down and pick up the agents handgun.

Granson looked around furtively, a small, "help" came from his lips.

"There's nobody left to help you," the man said. "Hurts real bad don't it? Well I'm going to take that all away in a little while," he chuckled.

He grabbed Granson by the shoulder and gave it a hard squeeze while rolling him onto his stomach. Granson made a feeble attempt to lash out with his foot. Tony smashed him in the side of the face with his gun hand, then pressed the muzzle of the pistol against the back of Granson's left leg and blew that kneecap completely out.

"There, you can't kick anymore," Tony said nonchalantly.

Tony opened the front door, stepped onto the porch and waved Ziggy and Jack in before he started up the stairwell.

"Elena, get out here. Where are you?" he demanded banging on the wall as he ran up to the second level.

He pushed open the first door and she was sitting on the edge of the bed. She was already dressed. Her slacks were wrinkled and the blouse was put on hastily. She held her gun in her right hand.

"There you are darling. You don't look too happy to see me. Well, that will change. Now go take your little gun and bring me the nun." She stood up and he followed her down the hall to the last room. She hesitantly knocked on the door.

"You don't have to knock, darling. This isn't Avon calling. Just barge right in," he said and slammed the door open. The bed was empty. The bathroom door was open. A brief look inside revealed the bathroom was empty, also.

"Where is she?" Tony asked.

"I don't know," Elena answered. "Did she go downstairs?"

"What do you mean, 'Did she go downstairs?'" His voice had dropped into that low menacing tone that always happened a moment before he exploded. He charged from the bedroom and quickly checked every room on the upper level. Then he went downstairs going through the entire house. Elena followed him, tentatively, looking quite confused.

"Where the hell is she?" he asked the house. He grabbed Elena and slammed her against the living room wall. "She was here, wasn't she?" he demanded.

She could feel the anger building in him.

"Yes. Yes, she went to bed. I walked her to the bedroom myself. Then I came back downstairs." Her voice was cracking. She looked at Agent Granson. He was lying on the braided throw rug that filled the center of the room. He had tried to crawl while Tony was upstairs. It was useless. Blood covered the rug and a large portion of the wooden floor. There was a constant moan exiting from deep within his throat.

"One of them was always down here. They would have seen her, unless they had fallen asleep," she added.

Jack had come into the house and was standing near the front door.

"Get Ziggy and search outside. Check the garage and the barn," Tony ordered. "The nun's not here. She might have slipped out on us," and looking straight at Elena, he added, "but someone had to help her."

Jack turned and hurried back outside.

Tony walked back over to where Granson was still struggling, grabbed him by the shoulder and rolled him onto his back.

"You've got one chance to live a little longer. I want to know what you did with the nun." Tony's gun was pointed at Granson's forehead. "Where is the fucking nun?" he demanded.

"Fuck you," Granson slurred back.

Tony let out a little laugh and shot him through the forehead.

Tuesday 4:15 am

Rainy led the old woman carefully along the narrow deer run. She wore a long dark rain coat that Mr. Sachs had given her when they met at the opening of the rear cattle fence. She really needed it now because the rain was coming down fast.

"She's a Catholic nun Rainy and you must be careful and get her to your house. Don't let anyone know she's there. Be careful. Do you remember the man in the river?"

"Yes sir. The one I saw tonight?"" he answered. But he was still wondering what was a Catholic nun?

"He must not see her. If someone is at your house stay in the woods and wait for me."

That was fifteen minutes ago. Apparently, this old woman, this Catholic nun liked to talk because she hadn't stopped since Mr. Sachs left. It continued to rain hard and the branches kept grabbing at her new coat, but she didn't mind. In fact, she acted as if, sneaking through the woods in the middle of the night was perfectly normal.

They were holding hands just like he would with his mother except he was leading and she was following and talking. But he didn't know much of what she was talking about.

"All of a sudden I'm outside. Isn't that strange? I'm in bed then I'm outside. How did that happen? Do you know how something like that can happen, Rainy?" She asked the young boy who was leading her through the rain drenched night.

"No, ma'am. I don't know nothin' about that stuff but I think Mr. Sachs does. He knows everything."

"Well to know everything, like your Mr. Sachs, you must have a lot of help and a lot of friends."

"I don't know if Mr. Sachs has a lot of friends. Cause I never seen any of them."

"Oh yes, Rainy! He has a lot of friends," the Catholic nun said.

"He told me he talks to angels."

"Well, did he now? Hmmm," she paused briefly, then continued. "Have you ever seen a fox, Rainy? Foxes are magical. And if they don't want you to see them, you never will."

"No, Ma'am. I ain't never seen one of them."

"I think that very soon you will get to see your first fox, Rainy."

Earlier, Rainy was sitting at the kitchen table watching the phone. It had taken a while before it rang. Mr. Sachs had told him where to wait and Rainy left immediately. He was already soaked and a little more rain wasn't going to get him any wetter. His Ma wasn't home yet but she would be real soon, and when she saw him, she was going to be really pissed. 'Stay around the house', were her orders. Wasn't much of that happening tonight."

They were just coming off the slope above the river when Renee, pulled up in front of the house. The site of her son leading an elderly woman in a long black raincoat out of the forest in the middle of the night caught her totally off guard and left her speechless.

CHAPTER
THIRTY NINE
Tuesday 4:30am

Z iggy rolled the body over and proceeded to go through the dead agent's pockets. He found one hundred and forty-five dollars in a money clip and put it in his own pocket. *No need to let the cops have it.* He thought. Then he went through the agent's wallet and found pictures of a young woman and two small children. They were standing on the porch of a tudor house, all smiling at the camera. The youngest child, a dark-haired boy held a small puppy pressed against a Yankees shirt. The older child, a blond daughter around thirteen, was a spitting image of the woman. *A man shouldn't be in this business if he has kids* he thought. Ziggy didn't. No kids, no wife, no parents and nobody to miss him when he was gone.

He found nothing else he wanted, replaced the wallet and helped himself to the agent's .357 revolver and a small hide-away that was strapped to the inside of his left ankle. He could see Tony moving toward the front porch. He was a dark shadow masked in the falling rain. He kept his head low and walked at a relaxed pace. *Boy, is that asshole in the house in for a big fuckin' surprise,*

Ziggy thought. All he had to do now was wait for Tony to finish what he had planned. He planned to stay outside until Tony was done. He didn't want to see the nun get wasted.

The rain seemed to be slowing a little. The water poured from the branches of the tall pines at a softer pace and the rivulets running across the dirt road had stopped and became puddles sprinkled with concentric water spots. In an hour, they should be out of here. He would be glad for that. There were too many dead people on this job.

Ziggy heard an owl shriek off to his left and he turned to face the noise. It was piercing and sounded like a child screaming. It was an unnerving screech that raked his backbone like a steel rasp shaving steel. He didn't like the woods. He never liked going hunting or any of that shit. Why in the hell should anyone want to kill a deer when nothing beat a good hunk of prime beef? He was getting rattled, his eyes were flipping back and forth, and he couldn't focus. He watched Tony go inside and the owl screeched again. This time it was a lot closer. Ziggy snapped around. A wet branch slapped at his face and he pushed it aside. It was too damn dark. The woods were bad enough in the day, but at night, they were damn creepy. He didn't want to be out here any longer. It would start getting light in about an hour. He couldn't wait. He looked toward the house again.

The owl screeched for a third time and it sounded like it was right above his head. He looked directly up and something moved to his right. His eyes caught a flash of gray. Something had moved between the trees, something like a large dog or a wolf. He started moving backwards toward the road. He could smell his own sweat through the rain. A wolf? A wolf was bad sign. *Mai andare dove il lupo caga.* That's what his father always told him. *Never go where the wolf shits.* If you go where the wolf shits, you're in a bad spot. Right now, that was how he felt.

What in the hell was Tony doing?

Another sound to his left and he turned quickly. Something was out there. It was too damn dark to see anything but shadows, but tonight even the shadows seemed to have shadows. He pulled out his gun. He had the silenced 9mm in his right hand and the agents .357 in the other. Piss on waiting for Tony's signal.

He started moving in the direction of the house. He needed to get out of the woods. The owl sounded again, this time it was right behind him.

Tony turned toward Elena. She could see the small blood vessels in his eyes and an unusual wetness that cause them to shine. The smirk at the corners of his mouth that appeared when he shot Agent Granson had disappeared and was replaced with a look of extreme anger. The nun was gone and whatever monstrous plans he had devised went out the door with her. He felt cheated.

Lieutenant Harman said that he had raped and tortured the girl, repeatedly cutting small pieces of flesh from her breast. The very thought of what he would have done to the old nun rolled her stomach. He had tortured the priest and what he had done to Harry Teasel was beyond comprehension.

Now, she realized he was completely mad and in a killing rage. At this moment, it was impossible to imagine what he would do.

"Did you help her, darling?" the question was threatening.

"I told you. She was in the bedroom. She was sleeping. I don't know how she got out." Elena didn't know but she had a suspicion and, at this moment, she was relieved that the nun was gone.

"Yes, yes," he started that condescending attitude that happened just before he erupted. "See, so you must have helped her. There wasn't anyone else." He said moving closer to her.

"I didn't do anything. She's an old woman. She couldn't climb out the window. It's a fifteen-foot drop. Maybe the FBI moved her after I went to bed," she was grasping, at anything that made any sense, anything to redirect him.

"Well, I already know that she would have had to walk down the stairs and I don't think they helped her. But at this point, it's impossible to question them, isn't it? You see I think you helped her. Who else could it be?" He was three feet in front of her intently watching her reaction, his eyeballs distended, glaring, burning death holes through her.

His gun was now pointed at her abdomen. How appropriate she thought. He wouldn't just shoot her in the heart to kill her. He would put one through her stomach, so he could keep her alive and toy with her. She still had her gun in her hand. She looked down at it and then very carefully, put it in her hip pouch. It wasn't worth the risk. He would easily kill her.

"I don't know, except something strange has been going on." Elena found herself an answer.

"What's strange? What does that mean?"

"The hired man, what happened to him?" Elena asked.

"He's dead."

"Where?"

"Along the fencerow, behind the barn. That's where he fell,"

"Has anyone found the body?" she asked.

"How in the hell would I know?"

"That's my point. I don't think he's dead. The barn is empty. All of his stuff is gone. If he is dead, how did that happen?" She had bought herself some time.

At that moment, Jack barged through the front door. "I can't find anything. She's not outside. I searched the garage and the barn, too. Where's Ziggy?"

"I told *you* to find Ziggy," Tony barked.

"I looked but I didn't find him. I even called to him. I thought maybe he came in here to get the hell out of the rain."

"He's not here. Find him and then walk the fencerow behind the barn. Look for a body and hurry up. And I want the car brought up. One of you, go back out to the road and bring the car here."

His hand snapped out and he grabbed Elena by the throat and slammed her against the wall. He pushed up against her and she could feel his excited hardness. His breath filled her nostrils and his sexuality that she once found attractive now became something to dread. He was keyed up by the prospect of another death. He wanted something else to kill.

"Let's hope you get lucky, darling. Let's hope they don't find him."

Jack walked along the fencerow, the high wet grass slapping his pants. He found nothing. Then he retraced Ziggy's path into the woods until he found the other agent's dead body. Ziggy had done his job but now he was gone. He might not have gotten the agent as fast as he should have. No, that wasn't true. The agent was shot in the back of the head. It was quick. Hell, Ziggy was probably at the house by now.

Now, Tony didn't want to touch the FBI's cars. So he had to walk in the rain and bring their car back. Ziggy was going to catch some hell for this.

It took more than fifteen minutes and was so dark, he almost walked right past the car. Then he drove the black Mercury back toward the ranch. He went slowly. The road was filled with water ruts and potholes and, besides he didn't want to be around Tony right now.

Fifteen minutes later and Jack was sitting on the couch. He was trembling and Tony knew being wet was the least of his problems. The Mercury was right where he had left it, the engine still running and the lights reflected off a body suspended under the arch and tied spread eagle across the entrance. He couldn't drive the car under the arched entrance without hitting the body. So, he left the car and ran back to the house. Now he was shaking like a nude virgin in a shower full of NFL players.

Tony turned off all the lights in the house. He stood near the front window and looked out at Ziggy's body silhouetted by the car's headlights. It hung inverted and reminded him of the computer geek back in Detroit. He somehow found that humorous. Was someone sending him a message?

"Go get the car and bring it here. We're leaving this place," Tony ordered.

"Hey, I can't get through the damn gate. He's hanging right there and I ain't touching him. Besides, whoever killed him is probably still out there," Jack replied.

Tony grabbed the front of Jack's poncho pulled him off the couch and shoved him toward the door.

"Get the fucking car," his voice dropped. It became soft and menacing, "and bring it up next to the porch." He pushed the muzzle of his pistol under Jack's chin. "Now!" he said.

Without saying another word, Jack left the house and walked across the porch. He stood for a moment looking at the body grotesquely hanging from the archway. He had no intention of walking across the front lawn, down the gravel drive, under the arch to the car. He would be a free target. But if he didn't do something quick, Tony would probably shoot him in the back. The guy was a full-blown wacko. He walked over to where the FBI had parked their Blazers and looked inside the first one. The keys were in the ignition. He slid inside, started the engine, pulled the shifter into drive and slammed on the accelerator. The car raced across the front lawn, through the flowerbeds and smashed through the third section of split rail fencing. Any moment Jack expected to hear gunfire. He pulled a hard left and slid next to the Mercury and dropped down on the front seat. *There'* he thought, momentarily relieved, *'you want the Merc, I'll get you the fuckin' Merc.'*

From inside the house, Tony watched the Blazer blow through the fence and pull up next to the Merc. The lights from both cars were still on and, beneath the sound of the rain, Tony could hear their motors running. The wet exhaust curled into the expectant night and hung above the cars forming spirals like deadly snow cones

Jack knew it would be stupid to go back. Tony had threatened to kill him. He sent him outside when the person who killed Ziggy was still out here. The guy didn't just kill Ziggy and run. He wanted some more and Tony had sent Jack out as bait. Maybe Tony thought the guy would show himself or maybe he just used Jack as a target. Either way too many people were dead: Silky, Max and now Ziggy. Jack knew if he stayed, he was going to end up the same way. This whole job was screwed up because Tony wanted to get the nun alive. Jack made his decision earlier when he walked out on the porch. If Tony got out of this alive then Jack would have a problem. If Tony didn't make it, at least he would still be alive.

He removed the keys from the Blazer's ignition put them in his pocket, opened the door and ran to the Mercury. He jumped inside and locked the doors. He backed up to get the Merc far enough away from the entrance and Ziggy's hanging body to allow a turn toward the broken section of fence. If Tony was going to try to kill him, he was only going to have a few seconds at best.

He put the car in drive and slowly started in the direction of the broken fence. He then cut the wheel hard to the left and slammed down on the accelerator. The car slid sideways and careened down the dirt road. Jack made a hard slide onto the entrance road and skidded through the turn, the tires pounding the ruts and splashing dirty water everywhere. He waiting for the sound of the bullets but nothing came. He looked back long enough to see the house disappear from view.

Piss on Tony and piss on New York. He was headed south and, right now, L.A. sounded damn good. He got away from Tony and if Tony wanted to follow, he would have to find the keys for the other Blazer or get the white Crown from the garage. That would take too much time, especially with Ziggy's killer waiting somewhere. He leaned back in the seat and, for the first time in days, actually started to relax.

Ralston watched the car come. It would have to brake when it reached the entrance to Dark Canyon Road. The crosshairs were fixed on the left side on the windshield. It was one hundred yards away and closing fast. When the Merc was fifty yards from Dark Canyon Road, it slowed down. Ralston's finger tightened on the trigger. The image in the scope finally took shape and he could see the man's face through the glass. At moments like this, he could hear the wind rattling through the bamboo, the hard rain bouncing off the hood of the military jeep and feel the driver racing with an unknown fury, a fury that releases itself from some hidden prison and disrupts sane thought. Then, at that moment, something darkly red fills his mind and that always looks like NVA soldiers.

The rifle kicked and the car skidded sideways, caught the edge of a rut and spun across the wet, muddy road before slamming into a large pine tree. The windshield shattered and the driver, without his seat belt on and with a hole in his forehead, was propelled across the dash and into the waiting trees. The Mercury, its hood buckled and the radiator blown apart, filled the night sky with a hissing vapor that sounded like a thousand angry snakes.

Silence again and then the word *Cain*, once more, bouncing around inside his head.

CHAPTER FORTY

"**W**e need a car." Tony said. He rolled Granson's body over and went through his pockets until he found a set of car keys.

"This whole thing has ricocheted on you," Elena commented. She couldn't help but say it. At this point, for some reason she really didn't care. Maybe it was because his failure made him appear less powerful.

"Yeah? How in the hell do you figure that?" The anger had left his voice. There was a change in him that she hadn't seen before. Whenever Tony got angry he had to take it out on someone or something. He never just let it go. This was something different.

"You surrounded them without their knowing it. You cut them off and killed them one at a time. Now, we're trapped. Maybe we're even surrounded and someone is killing us off one at a time."

"We're not trapped. Jack just got out."

"I wouldn't bet on that. He's probably dead already. Armstrong told me that they sent in a ghost. Someone you'll never see."

"What kind of bullshit is that? We're leaving here and then I'll find out where they have her. I'm not done with this thing, yet," Tony answered.

"Well, I am. I would just like to get the hell out of here. Let's forget the nun. You'll never find her now."

"I'll find her and you're going to help me. I can't believe these son-of-a-bitches have been watching us all the time. Shit." His frustration was cut short by a low rumbling sound out front, a car engine. They both cautiously moved to the front window. The Mercury was back. It was at the junction of the exit road and the ranch driveway. One headlight was out and the other was skewed in a useless downward angle. The radiator billowed small clouds of steam into the night sky.

The return of the car, that Jack had left in a few minutes ago, held them both motionless. It just sat there for several minutes. No one got out of it. Tony now looked confused as more minutes passed.

A noise distracted her. It came from the kitchen, a small tapping sound, like a bird pecking the window. Tony heard it too. They looked at each other and he started in that direction. Elena reached in her pocket to make sure she still had the keys for the Crown. They were there. She wanted to get as far away from Tony as possible. She remembered what the ghost has said to her over the phone. *"Did you see what he did to that girl? You should see what your friend is capable of."* At this point, she didn't want any part of Armstrong's ghost either.

Tony reached the hallway entrance just as the Merc's gas tank exploded, sending a stream of fire thirty feet into the air and lighting the inside of the house like the space shuttle leaving Cape Canaveral.

Then she saw him, like a specter in a horror movie, pressed against the wall at the top of the staircase. It was only for a brief moment but he was in the house. Armstrong was right. He must be a ghost. She was looking that way at the moment of the explosion or she would have never seen him. Their eyes met and then it was pitch black again and he was gone.

She had a decision to make and, in that moment, she made it. She stood behind Tony and slowly backed up toward the front door. She knew the man at the top of the stairs was watching her but that was a chance she had to take. He told her *to breathe in and slowly let the air out.* That's what she would get out of the deal. Well, right now, that would be good enough for her.

Tony sensed her movement and turned.

"Where in the hell do you think you're going? You think you're going to run like Jack? Would you like to be in that car right now? Huh, because that's probably where Jack is darling. You were right. He didn't make it."

A second explosion lit the night sky, and they recoiled. The roof of the car flew twenty feet into the air, the doors exploded off their hinges and crashed in to the trees lining the road. Brightness illuminated the room for a second time.

Suddenly, she was startled and the look on her face caused Tony to freeze. He lowered his right gun hand and slowly reached his left hand over to the wall switch and flipped it up. The living room lit up.

"He's behind me isn't he, darling?"

"Yes," she answered.

Then he turned to face whatever Elena saw. John Sachs stood directly behind him with a gun pointed at Tony's head. The men faced each other, both with shocked looks upon their faces. The word *CAIN* repeated itself in Ralston's head. It was *Danger* and now the message was clear.

Tony was the first to recover from the shock.

"Little brother, it's been a long time," he slowly raised his gun until it was pointed at Ralston's head. "What do we do now?" he asked.

Caution was back but Ralston ignored him, completely tuned him out. He was facing his brother, Anthony, and the questions accompanying the confrontation were countless. Was his family destined to kill one another? Was someone in each generation selected to kill another? Wife to husband - brother to brother. Tony was a killer, but weren't they both? He had agonized over the fact that being on the side of right, his perceptual right was interpretative and he was as evil as his opponent. And didn't Tony believe himself equally right? Even a madman, and he had met many, saw good, a perverted justification, in the outcome of their acts. Cleansing the world of evil is what evil does. Even God's biblical acts of purification, like the great flood, reeked of evil. The death of thousands to further a cause is still an act of heinous death. Didn't Hitler believe he was right, that his cause was just? And if Hitler had won, wouldn't it have been so? Doesn't history award the flag of righteousness to the final victor? For who writes the Book of History but the victor? The defeated watch silently from beyond the veil of death and no one hears their wail. Unless ... unless death wasn't bad after all. Unless death was a welcome end .. a reward. The final relief.

When this was over, when it was sorted out, the victors will tell the story and the dead will be gone and soon forgotten. He wasn't sure if he wanted to be a part of that scenario. Sister Mary Elizabeth didn't deserve to die and neither had the priest, but in the end we will all die. Did Tony deserve to die?

Brothers, Elena thought, *my God they're brothers.* She stepped back and moved closer to the door.

Caution was gone but *Wisdom* had taken his place and his warning was more insistent.

HE IS NO LONGER PART OF YOU. THIS TIE HAS BEEN SEVERED. EVIL AND DEATH ARE HIS SOUL MATES. HE SHALL SPEND ETERNITY IN THE DEEPEST PIT OF THE GREAT ABYSS.

Ralston watched as the muzzle moved slightly, indicative of pressure on the trigger. His arm jerked to his left and hit the side of Anthony's gun hand as he dove to his right. The gun exploded and the bullet missed his head by inches. He was rolling before he hit the floor. A second shot missed, then a third. Tony was spraying bullets in his direction. He paused long enough to take positive aim and as he pulled the trigger, the image before him broke apart like a starburst, forcing him to turn his head aside. The movement allowed him to catch a glimpse of Elena from the corner of his eye.

"Where do you think you're going bitch?" Tony turned and fired. The bullet hit her low on the left side of her abdomen. It knocked her sideways and she crashed into a chair. He slowed down and took his time.

"I've had enough of your shit. It's time for you to die."

The shadows between the corner and the kitchen door gathered into a shape and Ralston appeared as a spear point that dove into Tony's side. The gun went off and the bullet burst the picture window, leaving it with shattered chards of splintered and hanging glass.

Tony smashed into the upright column and hung there a second. Another gunshot ripped the night and a bullet from Elena's gun went through Tony's right shoulder. The shock caused him to drop the pistol. It fell to the floor with a deadly meaningful thud. It sounded like a death knell.

Elena fired again but he was already moving and the bullet hit him in the right tricep as he crashed through what remained of the picture window. The hanging glass exploded outward and Tony rolled across the porch. He came quickly to his feet. There was a large bloody 'X' cut into his forehead.

Somewhere deep in his mind Ralston could hear *Redemption* talking.

SO THE LORD PUT A MARK ON CAIN.

Tony's clothes were slashed and blood was running from numerous wounds. He had Granson's gun in his left hand. Ralston stood inside the broken window facing him. Tony raised the gun and started firing at Ralston. They were twenty feet apart, Tony was wounded, badly bleeding and trying to shoot left-handed. Every shot missed easily, somehow nudged away.

Elena clawed herself up from behind the chair. She rested her arm across the armrest and fired again. The bullet hit Tony high in the chest and he went down again and rolled across the front lawn. Elena tried to stand, slumped over the chair and vomited. Ralston caught her as she fell.

Outside the Blazer started. Ralston held the woman and watched the Blazer zigzag through the break in the fence, down the ranch road and past the burning Mercury.

He carried Elena to the couch and laid her down. She was leaking blood from her left hip. He pulled the top of her slacks down several inches. The bullet had hit above her hip and went out her back. Two inches to the right and it would have missed completely. It wasn't life threatening. He went into the kitchen and was back in a few moments with two compresses. Then he pulled Granson's belt off his dead body and lashed the compresses tightly against both sides of the wound.

"This is going to play hell with your tan line but it probably won't kill you. Do you want me to fix it?"

A small grimace caught the corner of her lips and she muttered, "Yes, if you can."

"I have to go and get some things. I'll be back in a ten minutes. Don't move or it will make the bleeding worse. And don't worry about him. He has been hit three times. He won't be back. His own survival will be all that matters right now."

He left and Elena lay still, afraid to move but still clutching her gun. The Ghost, because that's how she thought of him, was back in five. He had what looked like a medical bag. Something all the old-time country doctors carried in Hollywood movies, the bag that could cure anything.

An hour later, she sat on the couch and sipped a cup of tea. She felt it flood the back of her teeth and run down her throat. It filled her stomach with warmth. *God,* she thought, *that feels good. Being alive feels good.*

He had given her a hard stick to put between her teeth because he had no anesthetic. She had to endure the stitches. She managed. He stitched both sides of the wound and gave her a shot of an antibiotic. Then he gave her two bottles containing another antibiotic in pill form and an anti-inflammatory. He seemed to have made up his mind. She was going to be allowed to breathe in and out for a while longer.

He took the car keys from her and went outside. A few minutes later, he pulled the Crown up to the front of the porch and parked it. Then he went into the kitchen and filled a bag with groceries. He came back and sat opposite her. The rain had stopped and night had gone. It was 7:30 am and the Ryken Ranch was filled with dead people. He would have to let Armstrong know where they were. It would save the clean-up squad some time.

"Why did you switch sides?" he asked as if he needed to know.

"I didn't want this," she answered. It was her truth and at that moment, she was incapable of anything else. "I manage drug money. I wash it clean for the cartel. I got stuck in Detroit, and strangely, I think I was a better cop than crook. I met Tony in New York," she continued. "I knew he was different but I never envisioned him as a madman."

"Did you help him kill the Police Chief?" Ralston asked.

"I was there. I didn't kill him but I didn't care. He was a dirty cop and he tried to use me. I don't like being used. When I heard about the girl, the witness, I was shocked. I didn't think Tony was capable of that. I was wrong. He told me he did it."

"You saved my life. I pay those favors back," Ralston stated.

She wasn't sure of that, but in that moment she wasn't about to argue the point.

"He is your brother?" she asked, still not sure if she had heard it correctly. He looked away and didn't answer.

"You're from Columbia, aren't you?" he questioned

"Yes, that's my home."

"Well, go home Elena Soora. Get in that car and run. They'll be looking for you. If they find you, you will go to prison for murder. You deceived Armstrong and he won't rest until you're behind bars. The FBI has dead men all over the country. They would probably prefer to kill you than arrest you. There's some food, there's a car. You know where Mexico is and don't stop until you're in South America."

"I...," she tried to say something. Maybe to thank him, but he wouldn't listen to anything else.

He stopped her. "You're wasting time. You don't have much left. Goodbye."

She knew he was done talking. She stood up, picked up the bag of groceries and wobbled out the front door. He didn't help her. She started the car and pressed herself into the seat. She tried to find a comfortable spot. There wasn't any. She looked back one last time. He was standing there, behind the broken picture window, watching her. She couldn't imagine what he was thinking. All she really knew was at that moment she was still alive and it was because of him. He had thanked her but she never thanked him. She raised her hand to wave, but stopped. It was a foolish, senseless gesture and she had a long road ahead.

CHAPTER
FORTY ONE
Wednesday 6:00 am

Renee received the phone call at 6:00 am, exactly when Rainy told her it would come. The man identified himself and gave instructions. She didn't know why she was doing this except that her son had asked it. That coupled with the fact that she had a Catholic nun hidden in her house for the last day made her think that a great responsibility accompanying the request.

They appeared together walking from the forest at 4:15 am in the morning. Renee had finished her shift at the FireStation and the boss paid her an extra hour and a half to stay and help with the cleanup and morning prep. If she had come home earlier to an empty house, she would have been hysterical.

They were both drenched to the bone. She took them inside and grabbed a stack of towels and blankets. While Sister Mary Elizabeth took a warm shower, Rainy told his Ma what he knew, which wasn't very much, except it appeared, he had been much more involved in the events at the Rykens then she could have ever imagined.

He told her about monitoring the system for intruders and watching the front road. Then he told her about Mr. Sachs being shot the same day that Mr. and Mrs. Ryken had been shot. Renee could have exploded. But at that point, it wouldn't have accomplished anything. Instead, she waited and spent the rest of the night sitting at the kitchen table and drinking coffee with a wonderful elderly nun. She found out a lot more. Not the entire story, she doubted if anyone except Mr. Sachs knew that, but in the end, she suppressed her anger and was amazed at the resiliency of her son.

Rainy said the call would come at 6:00 am Wednesday and that was now. She left a note on the front door for the plumber. They piled into the old pickup and drove out of the Hills, through Rapid City and southeast to Rapid City Regional Airport.

She drove past the terminal, the parking lots, short and long term, and along the service drive to a locked and guarded gate at the farthest point on the airport property. Two Rapid City police cars blocked the entrance and four men dressed in dark suits stood just inside the gate. When she approached, they opened the gate and let her enter. They locked the gate behind her and one of the men directed her to the end of a private runway. She drove to where another group of men waited. One of the men approached the truck and asked them to wait.

She felt like they were in the middle of a spy novel. Two men stood on either side of the truck. Rainy sat by the passenger door and kept looking from the men outside to his mother. All she could do was hunch her shoulders in an expression of 'I don't know'.

After ten minutes, a Lear jet dropped out of the eastern sky, looped the airfield, lowered its landing gear, slid down the runway and taxied up to where they were parked. A very heavy man, dressed in a rumpled brown suit, slowly lumbered down the steps and walked to the pickup. He opened the door on Rainy's side and everyone got out.

"Good morning Sister Mary Elizabeth. It's nice to see you again. And it's a pleasure to meet you Miss Rivaneau and of course, you're Rainy. The Rykens have told me a lot about you. I'm Lieutenant Ben Armstrong from the Detroit Police Department and I'm very sorry for all the inconvenience you've been put through."

"Is Mr. Sachs here?" Rainy asked expectantly.

"Mr. Sachs? I'm sorry Rainy but I don't know a Mr. Sachs," the Lieutenant answered.

An ambulance pulled up behind the truck. The attendants waited while a wheelchair was taken from the jet and Sergeant Don Barker made himself comfortable. He was wheeled past the pickup truck en route to a seat on the Lear.

"It sure in the hell took you long enough Ben. We're talking about a raise after this one," Barker commented on his way to the plane.

"And you damn well deserve it, Sergeant. But you'll have to discuss that with the new Chief of Police," Armstrong answered.

The FBI had arrested Wickes that morning. His cottage up north turned out to be a six by six-insulated shack with a very nice telephone answering system. All incoming calls were dumped on the answering machine. Wickes could call the same number, check his messages and relay the call directly through to the police station in Detroit. The monitoring system in the Detroit Police Department would show the call coming from Traverse City, Michigan, when in fact, Wickes was calling from

Grand Cayman Island where he owned a half million dollar condominium on the ocean.

He also possessed a Cayman Island bank account with a balance of over one million dollars. It turned out that too many years of too little pay had finally gotten to the Chief. People who did a lot less than he did ended up with a lot more money. He thought he deserved a good retirement, not a simple two-room log cabin up north. He wanted a warm beach with some palm trees and money in the bank. He had it until Willie Morolli fucked up and gave Ben Armstrong the scent. Once Armstrong got on someone's trail — well, you had to kill that dog before it bit off your ass.

"Excuse me, Lieutenant," Armstrong turned back towards the young woman, "but Rainy has been very concerned about Mr. Sachs. I think he formed a friendship with the man while he was working at the Ranch and for the last two days, he's been very worried. Rainy said that he'd been shot, too," Renee said.

The large Lieutenant reached out and gently took hold of her elbow and led her a few feet away. He grabbed his more than ample pants, pulled them up a couple of inches and tucked in the rumpled edges of his white shirt. Then he smoothed down the front of his jacket.

"These clothes aren't designed for sitting on airplanes, you know," he said to no one in particular. He stood for a moment looking west toward the hills. "Lovely sight, them Hills, isn't it?" he finally said.

"Yes it is, Lieutenant." She waited. It was apparent that he had something to say and he wanted to get it out right.

"Miss Rivaneau this has been a tough one," he said as he turned back to face her. "When people will go so far as to murder a priest and a nun, well, we do everything we can to stop them and put them away. That's what I do. That's what the Federal authorities do. I hope you can understand that. I also hope you will respect that."

"Yes, but ..."

"The Detroit Police Department, the FBI and the Federal Government of the United States disavow the existence of any Mr. Sachs. He does not exist. He never did." He watched her eyes. It wasn't a hard stare but a knowing, maybe even a pleading stare. "Thank you and your son, once again, for your assistance in this matter," he said.

He held the look a moment longer and then he turned away, took the Sister by the hand and led her up the steps into the jet.

Renee and Rainy stood together and watched the jet raced down the runway and as it lifted into the sky, they reached over and held each other's hand.

Rainy thought it was alright.

Anna pulled the Ford over and slid into the passenger seat as he got in.

"Well, are you done?" she asked.

"As done as this can get it. But I have a feeling that it'll raise its ugly head again."

He put the truck in drive and drove down Woodward toward the Ren-Cen.

"I'm glad you showed up. I didn't want to replace this truck and go searching all over the country for you," Ralston said.

"Would you have searched all over for me?"

"I meant to find the truck."

"I don't think so. I think you would have searched just to find me."

"My God are all women the same?" he raised his eyes and looked upward for some wishful blessing, which he didn't get. This one was definitely different.

She just smiled at him. A very provocative smile that could easily have taken his mind off any business.

"Do you like Italian food?" He didn't wait for her to answer. "Of course you do. Everyone likes Italian food."

"Sounds great! Where are we going?" She snuggled up against him. It seemed like the natural thing to do.

"Well, we're meeting an old friend for dinner at one of my favorite restaurants but we have to leave the country to do it"

"That's interesting. We're going to leave the country to go to dinner. Not many places that you can do that."

"You're absolutely right." He pulled off Woodward and went down the entrance to the US-Canadian tunnel.

"What's this?" she asked.

"The tunnel goes under the Detroit River to Windsor Ontario."

"That's great! I've heard about it but I've never been here. Then where?" She seemed excited.

"Erie Street. Little Italy and the best Italian food in North America."

"Yummy, now I'm really hungry. To think I get all of this for just returning your truck."

They exited the tunnel, turned south on Goyeau Street and then east on Erie. They drove for about a mile in silence. The moisture from the river filled the air and gave freshness to the evening. He parked and they strolled arm in arm past dozens of ristorantes. It was a warm, balmy evening and she was just enjoying the walk with him.

When this started, when Ben had called, Ralston had decided that this was the last time, but things changed. When Anthony had driven out of the Ryken place, Ralston realized the frailty of that logic. The voices told him that this was not done and although he repeatedly tried to push the thought aside, he knew there would be more.

Wisdom was with him tonight.

THERE WAS A GIFT GIVEN.

A GIFT AT THE CREATION.

A GIFT SO PRECIOUS IT WAS ONLY GIVEN ONCE.

A GIFT FOR ALL MANKIND TO KNOW.

A GIFT OF FREE CHOICE.

BEWARE YOUR CHOICE DOESN'T ALTER YOUR ETERNITY.

BEWARE YOUR CHOICE DOESN'T MAKE YOU A CHILD OF SATAN.

At times like this, he felt a strong need for tranquility. He needed a place to go, a citadel, a refuge. In the orient, the Japanese tended their small gardens because they understood the need and the relationship between nature and true peace. The human brain associates with the beauty of nature. The fragrances of the flowers seep into your soul and there is a blending of man and God. That is the way it was intended, a way of peaceful co-mingling. He needed that now. There were too many dead people around him. They followed his trail and haunted his every hour.

The woman next to him made him feel comfortable. An aroma of fresh flowers followed her. She was young, maybe too young for him, but something in her nature, in her very essence, made him relax and that was good. Tonight, *Caution* was gone but *Wisdom* was close and he seemed to like her. Maybe this time he could win.

"Which one is your favorite," she acted as if that information was the most important secret in the world. He really enjoyed her company. They were passing an Italian import store. A worker was sitting outside on a milk crate; a large, dirty white apron encircled his ample girth. He held a glass of vino in his hand and he gave them a mild salute as they passed.

"They're all good. You don't survive on this street if you're not, but we're going in here." He had her elbow and guided her into the restaurant. Brantino's could have been on any side street in Naples, or Florence for that matter, but it fit just as well where it was. The walls were decorated, 'Old Italy'. Not fancy but somehow just right. In the back was a stage where 'Ole Sole Mio' could be heard on almost any night, usually with the owner playing the guitar and accompanied by the regular guitarist.

Off to the right at a four top table sat a very large couple. He led her toward the table. The man stood up. He was huge and dressed in a brown, wrinkled suit. The woman was Arabic and almost as big in size. Her breasts were so large they rested on the edge of the table. Anna thought that was probably a relief for her and although she was better off seated, she stood anyway. The men took a long moment to hug each other and Ralston introduced her.

"Anna this is Ben Armstrong. Ben, Anna Russell."

"Pleasure to meet you Miss Russell," Armstrong answered. "This is Cecelia Bhatti. Cecelia, Anna and ......ahh…"

Ralston paused, looked Anna in the eye and said, "Richard Houseman, but Rich will be fine."

Cecelia extended her hand to both of them, "My pleasure to meet both of you, Anna, Richard," she said. She had a large encompassing smile that had the magical ability to relax everybody within blocks.

"Well, it's been a long time and drinks are in order," Ben continued.

Richard Houseman looked at Anna. He tilted his head for a moment and a funny half smile appeared on his face as if he was listening to something.

"What would you like Anna?" he asked.

"Why don't you choose for both of us ... Richard," she grinned mischievously.

Epilogue

Renee checked the oven, the biscuits had brown up nicely. She removed them and placed the tray on the kitchen table. She was tired and worn out. She didn't get home until four in the morning and three hours sleep just didn't get it done, anymore.

"But he said that he'd pay me Ma."

"Yes, I know. But the Rykens will have lots for you to do now, especially with all the repairs going on at their place, and you did get to learn a lot about computers."

"Yeah, but I was for sure that he was..." he let the words trail off, walked slowly out the front door and flopped down on the stoop.

The morning was bright and the sun warmed his face. If he stood on his tiptoes, he could just see where the river made the bend, flowing dark blue, and frothed with tiny snow cone caps as it rolled over the small rock dam. It flattened out there and his thoughts changed to another big brown trout that owned that stretch of water. He had hooked him twice but never got him close enough before his leader stretched to its limit and broke. If he went with a heavier tippet, the old brown would see it and never give it a second glance. Rainy reached over, pick his rod off the front wall, and rolled it in his hand. The tip ferrule needed to be fixed. The braiding was broken and it had to be rewound and glued.

She watched him, not knowing what to say to such a fine young boy. Not knowing everything that happened at the Ryken's place but knowing that he deserved so much more than she could ever give him. She was pulled back from her thoughts by the ringing phone.

"Hello?" she answered.

"Mrs. Rivaneau?"

"Yes."

"Good, I glad I caught you home. This is Lieutenant Harman, Rapid City Police Department. The reason I'm calling is that … well ma'am I heard you might be looking for a job and I've got an opening here at the police station. A receptionist job. Pays pretty darn good, with daytime hours and no night work. I do understand that you have a young son and you might just like this kind of a position. That is, if you're interested."

"Absolutely, I… ahh.. ahh.. should I come down now? It'll take me about twenty-five minutes."

"Heck no ma'am. This is Sunday. You just enjoy the day. How about coming in for an interview tomorrow morning sometime, say about 10 o'clock?" the Lieutenant offered.

"You're sure? I mean about the job. Really?"

"Yes ma'am. State job. Good benefits. You come on in and we'll talk about it. See you tomorrow."

"Yes Sir — I mean Lieutenant. Tomorrow, thank you and… and…goodbye."

"Goodbye ma'am." He hung up the receiver.

She couldn't believe it. She'd been waitressing since high school. Usually two jobs on four-hour shifts. Good jobs were hard to come by and now she'd been offered a job at a state facility. A job that probably had a pension. A job where she could be home with her son. She couldn't believe it.

"Hey Ma, car's coming. I don't know who," he hollered from where he was sitting, still rolling the rod in his hand. He was thinking that he needed some strong thread and some airplane cement.

The car pulled to the end of the drive and parked. A young man about thirty years old and dressed in a dark business suit stepped from the Ford Bronco. He removed a large box from the back seat and walked to the porch where Renee and Rainy now stood.

"Mrs. Renee Rivaneau and Rainsford William Rivaneau?" he asked.

"Miss will be fine and you are?" You never knew who might be walking up to your front door. She had been taught never to be too friendly. He looked fine but after what her son had been through.

"I'm Ronald Becker, Miss Rivaneau. I'm sorry to disturb you on a Sunday morning but I was told it might be the only time that I could catch the two of you together," he said as he handed her a business card. "I'm with Thurston, Meier and Holbrook. We're a legal firm in town."

"Yes," she didn't know what else to say. She was confused by his presence. "What's this about?"

"Well, first, I've been instructed to give this to Rainsford," he handed the large box to Rainy whose eyes were stuck on the circular rod case tied to the top of the box.

"This is for me?" he asked.

"Yes sir. Go ahead and open it. I'm pretty interested myself."

Renee thought that he was a nice looking young man with a broad smile.

"Are you an attorney, Mr. Becker?" she asked.

He glanced at her rather shyly. *She's a fine looking woman*, he thought and tried not to look her directly in the eye, worried that she might see the thought.

"Yes, Miss Rivaneau. I just started with the firm six months ago. There's a lot to learn but it's going fine."

They both redirected their attention to the young boy as he slid the Orvis Trident rod from its maroon-colored tube and, delicately with hands that feared that a slight mishap would break one of the sections, slipped it together.

"Hold it Ma," he, carefully like it was made from solid gold, handed the assembled rod with gold anodized hardware, a burled maple seat and black titanium carbide guides to Renee, "but don't drop it," he cautioned and then went after the box.

"My firm has been retained to oversee Rainsford's educational trust," Ron Becker continued.

"An educational trust? I don't understand. What is that?" Her hair was a mess. She brushed a curl back from her face with her right hand. The sun left light shadows across her face, highlighting her high cheekbones and chiseled nose, gifts from her French ancestors. Her left hand held a fishing rod and for some undefined reason, she felt foolish.

"Well, the way it works is that an unknown donor has placed a sum of money, in this case a very large sum, into a secured investment stipulated to be used solely for the education of one, Rainsford William Rivaneau.

"Who would do something like that?" she asked.

"I am not allowed to divulge that information but I can say that it is or will be, when Rainsford is ready for college, large enough to provide him with an excellent education at almost any university of his choosing. It's rather nice and very adequate."

She didn't know what to say and simply sat down in the exact same spot that Rainy had flopped minutes before.

"Someone gave that to him?" she stammered, her eyes filling with tears.

"Yes, ma'am. I would think someone really likes your son. You must be very proud of him. I was also instructed to set up an appointment with you so that we can go over the details. Maybe sometime next week?"

"I am and yes, yes," she muttered. Her tears, openly shed, made him turn away, fearful that he might embarrass her.

"What else have you got there," he asked Rainy. The boy was so engrossed he had missed the entire conversation concerning his educational trust. He had retrieved a jackknife from his pocket and was cutting the tape around the box.

There was an Abel reel, a pair of breathable waders, a Brodin net, and a Rio Bravo vest, the pockets filled with everything that could possibly be stuffed into them. The boy in a state of hyper amazement, a term only a young boy could create, filtered through them. Each pocket contained some wonder that he had only seen at the stores in town or one of the fishing catalogs stored under his bed. Fly boxes jammed with nymphs, dries and streamers. Forceps, ceramic nippers, leaders and tippets, Zingers galore.

A Christmas like they'd never had and right in the middle of July. A boy, ecstatically happy and a mother with a new job, a hopeful future and the promise of a better life for her son. Tears uncontrollably streamed down her cheeks.

Rainy was pulling things from the multiple pockets and handing them to Mr. Becker who helped line everything in an orderly fashion on the steps, only to be reviewed later and a countless times in the days to come.

"Have you fished many of the rivers in the Hills, Rainsford?" Ronald Becker asked.

"No sir. Ma won't let me go wandering around by myself. I only fish this one. Down there is my favorite spot," he said pointing to the rock dam at the rivers bend. He paused, startled as a red fox walked from the woods, stood upon the rock dam and drank from the river.

"Well, I'm kind of a fly fishing enthusiast myself and, if your Ma doesn't mind, I can pick you up sometime and maybe we can go and try some of my secret spots. I know a spot where the Rainbows fight each other to get at your fly."

Rainy turned back.

"Did you hear that Ma? Could I go with Mr. Becker?" They both looked at the woman, dabbing the tears from her eyes with the hem of her shirt.

"Yes, that would be fine," she answered. "Thank you Mr. Becker."

"Ron will be just fine, ma'am," he smiled.

She smiled back. It was a lovely, lifted smile. One that she hadn't been capable of giving to another person in years. Today, it came easy and felt right.

"And, Thank YOU, Mr. John Sachs," she said. She said it under her breath where she thought only she could hear it but she meant it more than anything she had ever said in her life. And somewhere, many miles away a man tilted his head, looked upward, heard every word and smiled.

The End.